Also by Helen McCabe

(published in the Linford Large Print Series by F.A. Thorpe 1995-6)

One rainy afternoon in 1987, while convalescing in Sidmouth, I opened a book at the portrait of Mary Willcocks, alias Princess Caraboo. She has haunted me ever since.

The strange tale of the servant girl's masquerade and progress into fashionable society of 1817 is documented, but how Mary learned to be an Eastern princess has always been a mystery—as is her love story...

TWO FOR A LIE is a quest to discover the truth, not only about Mary's dream of greatness, but whether the fabulous dream I had a week after reading her history could really be true. At least it provided some pieces in the jigsaw.

The years since I found Mary in 1987 have been as painful as her progress from servant to princess, while her unexplained and frequent disappearances were strangely analogous with the twists and turns in the progress of my own manuscript towards publication.

But Mary, elusive and quicksilver as ever, won in the end and finally allowed me to tell her story.

Helen McCabe

HELEN McCABE

TWO FOR A LIE

1995

Published by Peacock Publishing
17 Wordsworth Avenue
Worcester WR3 8DN

© Copyright Helen McCabe 1995

Cover design © Angela O'Riordan 1995
Back cover photograph © Jerry Mullaney 1995

ISBN 0-9525404-0-1

British Library cataloguing-in-print data
has been applied for

Typeset in New Century 10/12pt by Scriptmate Editions
Manufacture coordinated in UK by Book-in-Hand Ltd
20 Shepherds Hill, London N6 5AH

A rose-leaf on the page of fame,
That blooms, then fades to cheat no more,
And is what nothing was before?
Say, what is love? Whate'er it be,
It centres, Mary, still with thee.

John Clare

ACKNOWLEDGEMENTS

I offer my special thanks to my mother, who did so much towards the preparation of this novel. Also I would like to thank the following people and institutions for their help in my research and for their support and kindness:

Jackie Beaman, (who typed the manuscript); Bristol Reference Library; The British Library; Mr R. Butler; Rev. Fr. A. Box SCJ; Rev. B. Carne, former Vicar of Almondsbury; His Grace, the Roman Catholic Archbishop of Birmingham, Maurice Couve de Murville; Mr Ian Crudginton; the late Mr Francis Doherty MA, former Senior Lecturer in English, Keele University; Mr Kevin Down BA, Lecturer in Mediaeval History, Birmingham University Extramural Department; Mr D. Dryhurst; Mr P. Durkin; Rev. B. Habberton; Mrs Dawn Hamilton, (representing Mr R Moon); Miss Elizabeth Harrison; Mr Haste, Birmingham Reference Library; Rev. David Hewlett, Ida and Roy Hewlett; Mr Michael Hodgetts, Director of Harvington Hall, Worcs.; Iain B. Love; Mrs Beryl Percival and Mr Eric Percival, formerly Hereford & Worcester County Library; the Staff of Droitwich Library; Mrs Louise Rumford; Sidmouth Library, Devon; Mrs Jenny Watts; Mrs Dee Wyatt.

Book One

CHAPTER 1

The girl bent her head against the wind. There was determination in the way she fought to hold down her skirts, impatience in how she thrust back her troublesome apron. Her plain cloak billowed and she pulled its thinness about her repeatedly to protect herself from that merciless sou'wester, which drove in over the coast, moaned low across Dartmoor, twisting the trees into eerie monsters crouching in the fields.

She paused for breath under the wind-whipped hedgerow. Six miles still and it would be an unfair race to Witherage with the rain; she had been through too many potholes on the cursed road already. Behind her lay Brushford—and another lost situation. Her father would beat her for it. And all for a shilling, thought Mary miserably as she stared at feet covered with mud.

If she had been a lady she would have worn pattens with wooden soles raised off the ground by metal rings to defeat the foul weather. Instead she could see the pathetic pink where she had painted her poor old clogs to go to Exeter at the New Year. She brightened up remembering herself and Milly Cater pranked up in Christmas finery riding the high road like quality.

Mary put a hand to her mouth with the remembrance of idiot Walter Megs. He drove the farm carthorse with no eyes on the reins only on the girls beside him. They had drunk a merry toast to the horse and his right ear and Mary had been forced to peck his vacant face while a giggling Milly held the kissing-bush above her and the simple labourer. 'Well,' she said to herself, starting off again, 'I shall not suffer your sly pinching any more, Walter!' She would never go back to the Moons at Brushford, should she starve for it! She stood on tiptoe to look over the gate with five bars. Two hundred moorish acres stretched soggily to Witherage. Should she take the short cut? Mary knew the tracks but was sensible of the dangers on such a wild night. The road was a steady climb upwards where the sheep, a myriad dusty white sought the banks for protection against the weather.

'You are not such woolly fools, are you?' she said and the animals lifted curious heads as she passed. The stench of damp wool was all around her. Mary Willcocks had smelled it all her life, when all she truly wanted was the scent of starched linen, rosewater and lavender. She rubbed the wind's wetness from her face with a grubby hand. 'This is a dirty night for a girl to be out,' she told herself as she had done fifty times in the last two hours. Her feet slithered on, slipping into craters. She paused, considering an impossible stretch of flood.

'It would be something if that son of a Scots shepherd, Tom Telford would come down to Witherage Village and build us a fine high road like he is doing everywhere else in England!' But there was no one to hear her wit but the wind. She knew Devon folk had not the gold, so they had to put up with it. It was my lady and my lord who rode in the coaches, not serving wenches and labourers. And Witherage was not on the road to fashionable Bath or Brighton. Mary's father had told her there were many worse things poor folk had to bear in Christian England than being drowned in mud on the king's highway. He was not up to his ankles in mire, thought Mary, but tucked in 'The Angel's' kitchen supping ale.

She swung her bundle to and fro though the sight of it made her gloomier than ever. If she had been a young lady instead of in service, she would have carried a smart 'indispensable' from which she would draw a fine cambric handkerchief with pride. Instead, Mary mopped her dripping nose with the plain stuff of her sleeve; she could not stop to ferret in her bundle for a decent piece of sheet. She tried to imagine the Misses Emma and Jemima Birt behaving so. It was impossible. They were finely dressed—but ugly. Mary did not think herself a beauty but, when she placed a rose in her curls and pinched her cheeks to redden them, she was better looking than they.

She had envied the squire's daughters many times from where she sat with the other village girls and old men beside the altar. She would have given her servant's world for a spencer like Miss Jemima wore, nipped in to show off a tiny waist. Their lady mother wore a pelisse, fresh from the capital, open down the front and lined with velvet. Its sleeves were puffed and sumptuous—Mary plodded on against the wind, dreaming of a dress of quality like the one she had seen in the draper's window next to the cathedral. If Farmer Moon had paid her one shilling instead of ten pence—she would have saved—but that was impossible too. Sighing, she closed her eyes for a moment and caught her clog on a stone, turning her ankle.

Mary sat on the side of the road rubbing to ease it, when she heard hooves approaching. Scrambling up, she sprang for the hedge. Who knew what a lone rider might do to an unaccompanied girl? There were men about, black papists with nothing on their minds but rape and murder.

The flying hooves were sending clods of mud spattering and water splashing. There was no escape; the filth hit Mary, spotting her face like some foul disease, besmirching her dress. She thought she had passed unnoticed but, to her horror, he was reining in the horse to a slithering halt.

Recognising the rider should have reassured Mary; it did the opposite! The man dismounting was Humphrey Moon! She looked away as the farmer's son strode towards her, Sweetbriar skittering behind him. When he was before her, she stared at his great riding boots.

'Look up at me, Mary!' She did not obey until he had her by the shoulder. 'Are you running away?' How many times had she trembled at his rough voice?

'I am not. I was turned off by your father. No Moon has a hold on me now!' His fingers were hurting her shoulders, so she wriggled away from his grasp.

'Turned off? What have you been up to, Mary?' She hated the mock in his tone.

'That is my business.'

He caught her again then. 'You are insolent for a servant, Mary Willcocks.'

'I am not your servant!' She was glad to say it; she preferred Walter Megs any day. He was an idiot but there was not the harm within him that she felt when Humphrey Moon was close to her. He was a dangerous young man.

'But you are my father's.'

'No more, Mr Moon!' She turned with the bob she had been trained to make. He caught her again. 'Let me go,' she said.

Her heart beat fast; her palms were wet, not only with Witherage damp, but the fear he might carry on more as he had done on Brushford Farm, when his mother heard Mary Willcocks screaming in the corn mill and had come to rescue her maid from the arms of her son.

'We are not in Brushford now, Mary.' Humphrey was well shaped with arms strong for heaving straw bales, or for wrestling in the courtyard of 'The Angel'. Mary was no Betty Bly, whose liaison with Humphrey Moon was the talk of Witherage Village.

'I know that—and I wish you would ride on to where you are bound.'

'You have spirit, Mary. Are you not afraid of me?'

He laughed, but there was no mirth. The sound reverberated in the hollow of the lane; was tossed by the wind emptily into the air. Mary swallowed. She should not be. Wasn't Humphrey Moon a good Protestant like herself? Did he not sit and listen to the minister each Sunday? He would never sin so; forcing himself on an unwilling girl, who had lived in his house for nigh three years, who had helped bring his weakly little brother George into the world. The safe picture of Mrs Moon and George was fading; Humphrey had his hand in hers; his body was holding the wind off her; his horse's warm breath and sides were steaming like her cheeks.

'Did you know, Mary, I have always desired you?' His other hand was grasping a stray curl, his eyes searching her face for a sign of acquiescence.

'I am sorry for that—' she retorted to cover her trembling.

'Why "sorry"? You have no need.' She drew herself away from his protection into the wind so she could not hear his soft words. Humphrey Moon had a way with him which made a girl's heart bound. He was a single man, with an overbearing power, which spelled ruin to any defenceless woman. She could have lain with him before in whichever way she chose. But she had no desire to feel this farmer's son on top of her. She had seen too much of him when he was garrulous with ale. In those drunken fits he had shown his true colour. Humphrey Moon was not the gentleman she craved in those nights troubled by dreams. He would never hold her tenderly, whisper sweet words, protect her from harm. Mary frowned, thinking a cross look might dissuade him; once or twice she had done so on the farm, stuck out her tongue and run for the house.

She knew he was behind her, marking every one of her small steps with those huge riding boots. She must brave it out. She stopped.

'Why are you following me? Why don't you ride off, Humphrey?'

'And leave pretty Mary wandering the roads at twilight?'

She saw nothing familiar in his expression. Instead of mock, there was a tautness in the skin—his lips were set and stiff; beneath the fashionable cravat, the Adam's apple, mark of a man, was huge in the powerful throat. She was afraid.

'I am not wandering—only going home to my father!'

'Away—from me!' The voice was low and husky.

'I cannot think that causes you worry, Mr Moon.' From her knowledge of Humphrey, Betty Bly was full of him.

'You think so.' Both girl and man were still, the wind whipping about her cloak, licking at her stuff gown, blowing Mary's hair about her face.

'Let me go on,' she said—and the words were near pleading.

'Get up with me,' he said, touching the stirrup.

'No—thank you. I will walk.' She preferred the Devon mud holes to pressing the back of the farmer's son, leg against leg.

'And if I say—you will not?' His fair hair blew back under the hat.

'You can make me do nothing,' said Mary, turning.

'Ah, Mary, that is where you are so wrong,' he said, pulling her towards him until she was close to his body. She put two hands against his chest to push him away, but he caught them in his hard fingers, pulled them up to his mouth and kissed them. Mary's cheeks flared with anger—and fear.

'One kiss —and I will free you.'

'No kiss,' she said, drawing back her head, feeling the old bonnet slip down, its ribbons catching her throat.

'Oh, Mary, Mary,' he said, bringing his hard lips nearer. It was a dusky nightmare. She felt his tongue and set her teeth against it, but Humphrey forced her mouth open, splitting her lips against his own. The kiss was suffocating in its seriousness.

'No kiss!' She struggled at its probing. She was almost off her feet. Humphrey Moon was tall and bringing her up as his desire increased. 'Let me breathe, damn you,' she spluttered. He released his grip; she was fighting to be free from his arms, beating at his chest with her hands. 'Let me be! You said *one* kiss—'

'But, Mary,' his face was close, 'it was so sweet that I want more!'

'Damn you,' she groaned.

'Mary! Such words from a maid! Why if Minister Strong could hear you, he would cry damnation on your soul.'

'You pig, Humphrey Moon, leave me be!'

'And this!' he said, holding her fast, 'is a sweet-faced girl who swears like a soldier!' He kissed her neck, dragging her and the reins of the patient horse to the edge of the ditch. 'You like it, Mary, you always have. You are hot—like me. You need a man,' he whispered.

'Do you dare—' she struggled on, 'I will cry to the parish what you have done.'

'I have done nothing—yet,' he said, dropping the reins and pressing her against a misshapen tree. His hand was pushing back her cloak, his eyes flicking over her shape. 'Would you not rather be warm, Mary, on a cold spring evening? If you say yes, we need not be in the ditch; I will have you behind me close and soon in a place where you and I—' Mary closed her eyes as he touched the top of her breasts. No one would hear her scream! Should she go with him? He was cuddling against her, thinking she had changed her mind. He had one breast free as she struggled to push him off her; the knots of the tree scoring her back.

'No, no—' she screamed, staring up at the sky streaked with the last rays of the sinking sun. The wind whipped the scream away as Humphrey put down his head. She felt the wet grass and her knees were giving way with his weight.

'Don't shriek so,' he said thickly... It was then relief washed over her like the wet wind. Another horse was galloping their way.

'Listen, Humphrey, a horse!' she cried, scoring at the back of his greatcoat with frantic nails. 'Do you hear? Someone is coming! Get off!' She caught the side of his head with her hand, pushing his great heaviness aside. 'Help!' she shouted, terrified the rider would pass leaving them together.

She had been heard. She could see nothing; but Humphrey was retreating, remembering where he was. His face was red and ugly from being cheated.

'You tried to rape me!' Mary screamed, pulling her skirts down. 'You would do anything, would you not?' Mary pursed her bruised lips while the tears rolled down her cheeks. 'I hope you burn—' She dared not look at the traveller who came to her aid in a flurry of cloak and spurs.

'You dog, Moon! Get up!' Mary opened her eyes at that imperious tone, clenched her hands to her breast as she drowned in the misery and shame of it all before her saviour, young Mr Jem Farr, Squire Birt's ward. She had heard nothing but gentleness in that voice before; now there was steel.

'Have you not enough with Betty Bly?' Humphrey rolled out of the ditch at Jem's last words while Mary tried to rise, gathering her sopping skirts, but her legs were weak. Jem Farr extended a gloved hand and pulled her up. She stood beside him, shivering. 'Here!' He unfastened his voluminous cloak. When it was round her slim shoulders, she staggered a little under its heaviness and he steadied her. 'Moon!' Humphrey turned his back, thrusting his shirt into the tight breeches. Jem caught his shoulder, spinning him round. 'Turn when I speak to you!' Humphrey growled like one of the savage Brushford hounds.

'If you had not interfered—' Mary trembled, knowing what he would have done. The men faced each other now.

'Would you have raped her, Moon?'

'She was willing!' lied Humphrey.

'I was not!' gasped Mary. She appealed to Jem. 'He is lying, sir, you know I would not!'

'I know!' said Jem. There was contempt in his eyes for the farmer's son. 'We have done some poor work in our time, but this—' he gestured Mary, 'is something I cannot stomach!'

'Then get you gone!' said Humphrey. Mary gasped at his rudeness. Jem frowned. Whether his guardian, Squire Birt wished master and servant to be equals, companions all, in keeping with the fashion, Moon had gone too far this time.

'Stop up your coarse tongue,' ordered Jem in a cold voice that made Mary tremble more. 'Why, Moon, I will teach you manners. I would not leave any maid with you. Mary needs defending.'

'Oh, thank you, sir,' said Mary. She could have flung her arms about his neck, soaked his riding cloak in tears, but she did not dare. Jem Farr often came to Brushford Farm calling for Humphrey Moon. Though the village spoke of his wildness, Mary thought much of him. Now, his dark Spanish eyes were full of contempt for Humphrey; then, she had seen those eyes, soft over a litter of puppies, bright with laughter at forbidden jokes which made her fly through the garden into the house. The men's tempers were rising still.

'Apologise!' snarled Jem. There was one thing he hated—rough treatment of women, even when they were willing. He had often thought it had something to do with the way his noble father had maligned his mother. The feeling he had for helplessness was more than pure gallantry.

'To her, my lord!' Humphrey retorted. 'My father's housemaid?'

'To Mary—and to me!' Jem's dark features were crimson.

'To you, old fellow!' said Humphrey, extending the hand which had tormented Mary. 'Put down your fists. You know I could beat you as easily as I did last week at "The Angel"!'

'To her, Moon!' Mary blushed as a throb arose from deep within her. She had always dreamed of such a gentleman to fight for her. Humphrey shook his head—and Jem caught his cheek with the heavy riding glove. She gasped at Humphrey's expression.

'You've asked for it, Jem,' said the farmer's son, swinging back. Jem sidestepped cleverly and Humphrey was sprawling. Mary stifled the cry on her lips as Jem was after him. She watched him let Humphrey rise, looking just like a hound taught a lesson by his master. Jem put up his fists again and the wind screamed its applause in the trees above.

The blustery evening was darkening on the hot heads. Then Humphrey made his final rush at Jem. It was like the angry bull on his father's farm. Jem had taken some punishment for his cravat was awry and there was blood on his lip. He stood his ground as Humphrey flayed out wildly with his fists and, with the last neatly placed blow, sent Moon to his knees again.

Mary huddled in the cloak, tired and dizzy. If Humphrey won—? But there was no chance of it. Jem was a fine fighter with nimble hand and foot. Compared with Humphrey he was all agile grace. Mary had seen men fight before. It was expected of them as women were expected to watch. Not ladies, of course, but girls in service. All she could think of as they tired was how she would get to Witherage before real night came on. She could not sleep outside in this foul weather.

Humphrey had had enough. Jem was pushing him towards her.

'Well, Moon!'

'I am sorry,' he muttered and she shivered at that murderous look.

The farmer's son twisted from Jem's grasp and the wind whirled away the muttered curse.

'On your horse!' shouted Jem, but Humphrey had no strength to pull himself into the saddle. Jem walked unsteadily towards him. 'Come on, man, you deserved it. I'll push you up!'

'Get away, Farr!' Mary had seen the look many times. It was pure malice. Jem took no notice and pushed him generously. He was rewarded by a kick from Humphrey's boot, which sent him toppling back.

'Oh, Mr Farr!' cried Mary, struggling with his cloak in the wind. 'Let me help you!' But he was up, looking in the direction of Sweetbriar's flying hooves.

'He will get over it, Mary Willcocks—in the arms of Betty Bly. Humphrey will not suffer long!' His breath came short.

'Your face, sir,' said Mary, wondering.

'It will not kill me, Mary. I have had worse knocks —and from Humphrey Moon!' He touched his swelling cheekbone gingerly—and winced.

'It needs bathing!' she said.

'Ministering to me?' he murmured and she blushed. Jem Farr had grown into a striking man. She was remembering him as the dark boy who smiled at her from his seat in church, squashed between the squire and his lady in the pew reserved for the gentry.

'You cared for me, sir!' she said, stooping to her bundle for the piece of sheeting. She found it on the top; wetted it in the ditch and brought the soaking cloth to him.

'Hold on, Mary, it is ditch water!'

'I have bathed my face in it often, sir, and it has done me no harm.'

'It has not!' he agreed as she touched his cheek gently, washing away the congealed blood he had spilled for her sake. She was glad it was too dark for him to see her cheeks go red under his searching gaze. He put up her hand and took the cloth from her. She slipped her arm out of his coat. 'No, put it back on!' he ordered. She did not understand.

'But I must be on my way.' Jem was walking along the road now, calling his horse.

'Where the devil are you?' He disappeared into the darkness to reappear leading the animal. Mary took the reins as he brushed the mud from his Cossacks. Mary thought no breeches could suit a man better. They were as wild as he. He looked into her face and the white moon was tossing in the sky. 'Let's walk apace,' he said. 'Why aren't you safe in bed at Brushford, Mary?'

'I was turned off, sir.'

'For what?'

16

'A shilling. I asked Mr Moon if he could raise my wages by twopence.'

Jem Farr stopped to look in her face.

'Why, Mary, what is England coming to when a girl is sacked because she asks for her rights—and twopence?'

'I know nothing about England, sir, except we—love her?' He laughed out loud at her quaintness.

'So do we all, Mary.'

'You are making fun of me, Mr Farr.'

'Oh, Mary, I am not. It is your innocence. So Moon got rid of you. Well, he must take you back!'

'No, Mr Farr, I'll not return to Brushford.' Her voice was high.

'So you are finished with service.' How could he not know that she would be sickened at the sight of Humphrey? Were men so dull that they could not understand a girl's true feelings? Yet Jem Farr was a gentleman, not of the common kind.

'I do not know,' answered Mary in a low voice. 'My father will scarcely be pleased.' They were coming into the shadows where Witherage Barrow cut off the rising moon from their sight. In that still darkness Mary realised the wind had ceased; she could hear the jingle of Star's bit and the creak of her rider's shoe leather.

'I am bound for "The Angel", Mary. Will you ride with me? It would be safer.' He was no Humphrey to refuse. The thought of sitting behind him brought hot blood to her cheeks.

'Thank you, Mr Farr. I would be honoured.' She wondered if the answer was graceful enough. What would the Misses Birt have spoken under such an offer? 'But first, you must take your coat. It is too heavy on my shoulders for me to spring into the saddle.' He helped her take it off. Surprisingly, Mary found the air as warm as in the Brushford byre. She looked down at her dress and stiffened. Humphrey had ripped her bodice when he had sought her breasts. And Jem was looking too.

'You will take cold, Mary.' He was smiling. 'Cover yourself against the wind.'

'I cannot,' she said. 'I have no pin!' Instead, she pulled her dress across with her hand.

'You cannot ride like that.' There was a man's experience in his voice. Suddenly she dreaded where he learned it. Jem put a ringed hand to his throat and unfastened the diamond pin from his cravat. 'Come here, Mary.' She felt a weakness run through her limbs as he drew the dress together and secured it with the costly jewel.

'Oh, Mr Farr, I cannot!' Her dark eyes were bright as he bent to place his foot in the stirrup. Even in the black night his spurs glinted. He was in the saddle, looking down.

'Cannot what? Come up, Mary. I want nothing in return. It is just a little present for a girl at the mercy of men. Up with you.' He leaned down, extending his hand. She grasped its warmth, fire starting within her belly. Legs wide and haunches taut, Mary Willcocks clung to his strong waist as he urged on the spunky mare. 'On, my lass, to Witherage,' he shouted and Star responded running out from beneath the barrow. Jem's body hid hers from the renewed freshness of the wind. Mary did not heed the heavy spots of rain as the spirited mare carried them down off the high ground towards Witherage village.

That ride was better than any dream. In the air was a hint of summer; the narrow track between the banks was lush with grasses and columbine. As the mare swerved on her mad way, Jem's spur brushed the banks, picking up the twining tendrils. In her dizziness, Mary saw the white sheep whirl as they cropped on silently. She could think of nothing but love as she and her saviour gentleman hurtled on under the sky where the night clouds drowned the stars with their black tossing.

He came to a halt above the village. The air seemed full of owls' cries as he jumped from the saddle and handed her down like a great lady. She slipped into his arms as graceful as any princess of the realm. His was all the scent of the gentleman; soap, leather, tobacco and perfumed linen. He kept her one hand in his; put the other inside his jacket, brought it out and pressed something into her fingers:

'One silver shilling, ma'am!' It was kindly mocking.

'But I have not earned it, Mr Farr.' She liked to hear him laugh.

'I think you have, Mary.' He swung up on to the mare once more. 'Now home to your father and bed. God be with you.' He gave Star her giddy head and mare and rider headed off in the direction of the nearest cottages.

Hand tight over her shilling, Mary watched him until he was out of sight.

She put a hand in her bosom and removed Jem's jewel to a secret place within her underthings. If her father discovered it he would beat her more fiercely, even accuse her of thieving.

Just to know it was there beneath her heart gave Mary satisfaction. The shilling followed; King George's mad old head warmed by her breasts. She stooped to her bundle, picked it up and made her way down the track towards the chimney smoke.

She had heard that English cottages were the prettiest in Europe. Why, Farmer Moon had spoken with contempt of those folks abroad, their homes in ruins, their women ravished by Boney's guard. It was said when foreigners landed on English soil they were dazed by the beauty around them.

Mary was not sure if she agreed with the fancies of her Christian brothers and sisters fleeing from Boney. She had never found much comfort in Witherage Village. Her father was a cobbler and Mary remembered many days when there was neither bread nor meat in the house. The Willcocks family was poor, no doubt about it; even the uncouth labourer slaving over his furnace in the Northern Counties, ate cheese, meat and ale when he came home. She was sure there would be no food in the house. Her mother was in Crediton minding sick Aunt Jenny. Mary suddenly thought what a mercy it would be if the old woman died, then sternly rebuked her own sinfulness. If the minister had heard her—! The idea made her face more pale under the mud splashes. It was good to be poor, he said. There were places in the kingdom for such as the Willcocks. It was the getting there which was painful.

Her heart beat faster and the bile was in her throat as she slipped in the sturdy gate, which hung unfastened. She hoped her father was out at 'The Angel', but she was unlucky.

He was hunched by the fire. She could tell his mood in the set of his shoulders. There was much of him in her though. She would have owned it to no one but herself. When such a blackness came over her, she put the woolly sheep to flight and tugged at the cow's udders unmercifully until the milk spurted madly over the side of the bucket.

'Father?' she said, dreading the answer. He stared. She had loved him when she was a helpless little thing to be tossed into the rafters, screaming with joy. Now she loved him as a dutiful daughter should who kept the Fourth Commandment. It was a hard task honouring Matty Willcocks with his slack jaw and face, red with broken veins come from too much ale.

'Mary?' He frowned. She knew he was forcing his sodden brain to tell him why she was in Witherage rather than Brushford. 'What brings you here in the dark?' She avoided the question.

'Have you a candle, father? The firelight is not strong enough for me to see to the tea.'

'Tea, is it?' He was on his feet. 'And talk of candles. Come here, daughter.' She stood where she was. 'Have you given up that fine situation with Farmer Moon of Brushford? Have you, Mary, after I walked ten weary miles and crawled on my empty belly to that fat yeoman who takes the bread from poor folk's mouths? I crawled, girl, for you! Or—' he towered over her, 'could it be worse? Is it a lad got in your stupid head?'

'No, father, where's the candle?' If she could light the room his ugly shadow would shrink to nothing. He caught her arm and she cried out as he bruised the skin. She hated rough men whose every blow was for a woman. Those sons of Adam were all the same—then she remembered Jem.

'Take that for your candle. It will light your brain.' It was a crushing blow, one such before had caused her skull to be sore for a month. She thought her head cracked open. She crouched against the wall knowing he would take no explanation. 'Now make the tea, before I strap you!' She moaned. Soon his rude anger would die and he would be human not beast. Gauging her moment, she fled to the kitchen, out of the door and pushed her head under the spout of the pump. She hardly had strength to clank the cold water up from the spring until its very freshness brought her to sense again. She staggered back into the kitchen, her hair plastered to her head. Mary found the candles and placed one in an earthenware holder. She carried it through into the living room, protecting the weak flame as it guttered in the draught. Her father was buttoning his gaiters. He did not speak but pushed her aside as he flung out of the door on his way to 'The Angel'.

She toppled into her seat by the fire. Later she rose, taking the looking glass from the dresser. Hers was a frightful face; curls drying hard on the crown, so she twisted them about her forehead to simulate the newest fashion of 1809. At least she could dream! Turning back to her chair she closed her eyes re-living the day which had begun so ill, but had ended with Mary Willcocks getting a taste of the lady she desperately wished to be.

Jem sprawled in the inn kitchen like the labourers on the Birt estate. Clara, the innkeeper's daughter watched him while she turned the spit to baste the meat. She was hoping she might catch a flash from that melancholy eye, but Mr Jem Farr was in a right bad humour, probably from sparring. She could see he had taken some knocks as his fine cheek was coloured and he was too languid to rise.

'Good evening, sir,' said Jawn, the ratcatcher, placing his skin cap and leather bag before him on the table.

'A pint, Miss Pussy—and mutton.' Clara nodded, seeing to the meat, motioning Betty to bring the ale. Jem Farr was rousing himself to politeness. 'Beg your pardon, sir, but you've been catching one more rat than me today!' The customers roared. The Brushford shepherd nudged the carter who swore at him for tipping his ale. Jem touched his cheek, feeling the hurt but taking the jokes in good part. This was why he came to 'The Angel'—to forget the trials of a gentleman's life.

'I seen Master Moon next door,' joined in the blacksmith. 'He be a pretty sight as well, but it ain't stopping his progress!' Jawn rubbed his hands as Clara set the trencher of steaming mutton before him.

'Thanks, pretty Puss.' He set to with a will. Jem was realising his own hunger.

'Miss Clara, bring me some of your best.'

'To eat in here, sir?' She hoped she could go on feasting her eyes.

'Why not?' said Jem. 'Why village men and masters are friends all!' They grinned happily. His mood was lifting when the door crashed open to reveal Matt Willcocks.

'What's up with you, Matt?' asked the blacksmith. 'Have you lost your wages and found a half pence?'

'I need a pint,' he thundered, taking no notice of the joke. Betty set a quart pot before him.

'Here's two, Matt,' she said.

'Well, here's a woman can keep a job,' said Willcocks, catching her round the waist.

'Get off, Matt, ye'll have Mr Moon round in a minute!' said Betty, twisting away.

'And I'll be right glad to see him,' swore Matt. 'The Moons and me have a bone or two to pick.' Jawn put down the piece of mutton. The kitchen was quiet now except for the crackling fire and the hissing kettle.

'Has Farmer Moon committed some evil on you?' asked Clara, eager for gossip.

'Ay, he and his damned son—' There was a general gasp and heads turned to the far room where Humphrey sat, 'Have ridded themselves of that heedless girl of mine.'

'Mary is sacked?' said Betty Bly.

'Ay and I shall have satisfaction.' Matt had swallowed the quart and his face was flushed. Clara could see Jem Farr drumming the heel of his riding boot on the floor. If Mary Willcocks was back from Brushford, there must be much reason.

'Why, Willcocks—' They turned to see the squire's ward twisting his whip in his hand, 'I advise you to keep your distance from young Moon. He is in a mad mood this evening. I am sorry to hear of your Mary's plight but I warn you that it will be a worse one if her father is beaten.' Matt stared into Jem's foreign eyes. He liked the gentleman fair enough; there was no harm in him and he bore no grudge against the squire. He touched the greasy hair above his brow in a respectful gesture.

'Begging your pardon, young sir, do not interfere between any man's daughter and her employer. We have enough rich masters without overbearing yeoman, who value their fifty soggy acres above the folks who break their backs for them—'

'Hush, Matt!' warned the blacksmith. It was a dangerous track to be on. 'You are speaking to Mr Farr, remember.'

'You may hunt with Moon, sir—aye—or fight with him—' Jem's face flushed, 'but there is no enjoyment in getting no wage to live on.' There was a frightened rumble of assent in the kitchen. Jem shrugged.

'Then continue with your grievance, Willcocks, but I suggest you ask your Mary for the story.' Clara blinked at the words. Mr Farr and Mary Willcocks must be safe in each other's confidence. She had heard from Milly Cater how the young gentleman was received daily at Moon's. She knew there was some mystery in the air.

Matt Willcocks thrust out his jaw at these words.

'And what do you know, Mr Farr, about my Mary?'

'Nothing, except she has spirit — and beauty.' Clara almost scalded herself on the kettle. Jawn chewed on his mutton and the blacksmith choked on his ale.

'I'll have no man, gentleman or not, speak so about my Mary.'

'Why, Willcocks, I meant it as a compliment!'

'Damn your foreign compliments. Your father knew how to compliment a woman!' Jem was up on his feet. Clara screamed and her father, scenting trouble, was in from tending the barrels.

'What goes on here?'

'Why, father, Matt has insulted Mr Farr!' shrieked Clara.

'You fool,' said William, grabbing one of his most quarrelsome customers. 'Out with you!' Taking Matt by the jacket he thrust him out of the door, leaving him to batter on it with his fists. 'Come, Mr Farr,' he said, turning to the young man, 'Come to another room. Can we make up the bed for you? You seem unwell.'

'Yes, stay, sir,' wheedled Clara, 'and I will bring the best to you; a bite of goose breast, some fowl, or ham? A pie? I picked the fruit myself! Or egg and potatoes? Father, you got a trout from the lake, didn't you?' Jem laughed.

'No, Miss Pussy, bring me a little meat and one of your sweet puddings. I'll take your offer, Bill, of a bed tonight.' He yawned and stretched as if there was no trouble in his heart, but, as the landlord's daughter led him upstairs, he wondered if he would ever be free from the japes of even the commonest man about his birth and breeding.

Matt stumbled away from 'The Angel', making for his cottage with resentment boiling within. Fine, Mr Farr might be, but a bastard for all that and disowned by his father, sent to Squire Birt's to be bred up as an Englishman. What right had the son of a black Spanish whore to tell a Willcocks what he should do with his own daughter? The more

Matt turned it over in his mind, the more he burned. What had Jem Farr to do with his daughter? She had given him no explanation as to her sudden return yet that young dog sprawling at the inn knew it all. By the time Matt threw open the cottage door, he was like a mad man.

'What ails you, father?' Mary jumped up from the chair by the fire, terrified by her father's grim face. She wished her mother was there to defend her.

'What ails me? I have been thrown like a dog from the door of the inn on account of my daughter!'

'Me, father?'

'Aye—you good-for-nothing jade!'

'Father!'

'Yes, Mary, it is jades who are talked of in "The Angel", not Christian girls!'

'"The Angel"?'

'What do you know of fine Mr Farr?' He spat the words out. Mary trembled. 'You colour, girl!' He caught and shook her. 'What have you been up to?'

'Nothing, father!'

'Then why did you leave the Moons? Were you turned out for some indiscretion?' The tone was nasty.

'No, father—I wish my mother was here to listen to such questioning. I left the Moons because—that skinflint farmer would not raise my wages!' He stopped shaking her, staring in astonisnment.

'Raise your wages? A chit of a girl like you. You fancy your chances!' He spat on the ground. 'I'll beat you for it!'

'For what, father? Asking for my rights?'

'Less of your lip, girl. For making me a laughing stock. For consorting with fine gentlemen—I will teach you to mix with your own kind!' He was taking the strap from behind the door.

'You promised Mother you would beat me no more!' cried Mary.

'You promised me you would be obedient. It is the same tale, always. Will you learn nothing? You are wild and by God, I'll tickle those intriguing fancies from your body!' He was lashing the strap wildly. There was no good calling for aid. The neighbours stopped up their ears and talked of the hullabaloo tomorrow. The first lash made a great weal across her buttocks. After six, he threw down the leather and Mary fled crying to her dingy upstairs room...

Jem sat staring at the bedroom wall thinking of his mother. He had an ideal picture of her which he held in his heart. She was bending over his pillow, her long hair upon his brow as she kissed him. Equally well, he remembered the drawling voice of my lord, his father.

'Leave the boy alone. You will smother him with kisses.' It was a voice he had learned to hate, but he had been taught that he must love Robert Castel, who had brought his mother to that loveless London house from a Paris, seething with revolution. But he had not married her, just got her with child and kept her as his whore. So Jem had grown into the knowledge he was the bastard son of one of the richest and most powerful aristocrats in England. My lord had no other living son and had supported Jem. Therefore, he sent the boy from his mother to Birt Park to be educated as an English gentleman. He saw her only once thereafter. She was dead by his tenth birthday and Jem was alone in the world, burdened with the name of bastard and French lineage.

Squire Birt had spread the rumour Jem's mother was Spanish to avoid hostility towards a boy who represented Boney to his peers. None knew the secret of his mother's birth because Robert Castel had kept her almost a prisoner in the gloomy London house.

Jem had spent his youth under a shadow and now it seemed he must come into the light. A week ago his guardian had received a terse letter from my lord, his father informing him that Jem was to return to London town in haste. There was a letter for Jem too. He had it by heart. Lady Birt saw it as a signal he was to be legitimated at last, but Jem loathed the thought of marriage for gain... In a melancholy mood, he brought up his arms and pulled off the ruffled shirt, he was about to remove his mud stained Cossacks when he heard the light step.

'Sir?' It was Clara, bearing the food. When she set down the tray, he could see why they called her Pussy. She had green eyes and a cunning look. Those eyes were appraising. 'Shall I pull off your boots, sir?' He ached for comfort. She knelt at his feet and he put his boot between her skirts. Miss Pussy Clara smiled as she heaved the military leather off, threw it away and across the floor, bent and caressed his feet...

The lark wheeled high above the barrow where the Bronze Age folk lay sleeping unmindful of her song. A cock, who had escaped both shutting-up and the fox, thrust back his comb and squawked a challenge to her; but she did not hear; she was piercing the clouds already.

Mary listened with relief from where she lay beneath the window. Her night had been filled with dreams and pain. When the sun's rays fell across the counterpane, she was touching the bruises on her arm where Matt Willcocks's hard fingers had pinched her skin. Then her hand slipped quietly down to the weals the strap had made, her face a rueful grimace. 'If only I could rest for one more hour,' thought Mary, 'or better still join the strange old folk buried up yonder in the barrow.

They are free to listen to the lark for ever.' Yet she had to be up and doing in a grey world bereft of dreams.

She pressed her cheek to the pillow and sighed. No fine goose down this as ladies loved to sleep on, only Jack Straw's prickle. The day was here again with its monotonous regularity. 'Is there nothing else in this life,' she thought again, 'but being born, breeding and, after, put in the cart to lie under the yew?' It was a dark fancy for a girl barely eighteen as she dragged herself off the bed and kneeled to pray.

'Oh, Lord, let my sinful thoughts go away. Make me a good servant!' Yet her head was never free from fancies; when she was milking or wooding; when she saw Squire Birt's chaise or ladies and gentlemen hunting. 'Oh, Lord, why did you make me a dreamer? To be beaten by my father and laughed at by the village. Amen.' She got up stiffly, pulled on her drawers and single petticoat, homespun stockings and clumsy clogs, over her head the black dress and chequered apron. She hated the cotton cap but on it went too. Clad in the ugliness of servant's attire, Mary remembered the marvellous dress she had seen in Exeter, made up with the highest of waists in white satin to adorn some ugly daughter of the gentry.

Mary's cheeks flamed as she imagined herself wearing it. Her father would have beaten her again if he had known her sinful thoughts. 'I'll have a gown just like that,' Mary muttered, her spirits returning, 'and a black boy to pull on my silk stockings and a maid to fit my satin slippers!' That was an evil thought too because Mr Wilberforce had decreed that there be no more black servants and the terrible traffic in human souls must cease. As it had. And she should be glad about it.

Mary opened the window and stared across the village roofs. She must leave Witherage again and find a new situation. She had to eat, but this time she would get a place which paid a fair price for the work she did. Her father had not beaten her for asking for a shilling; it was the idea of it when a man could only earn four and one extra shilling and sixpence for each of his family. It was not that cobbling had fallen off—it was that better folks would not pay. Matt Willcocks still rankled since that cold winter of 1795 when he could not nor would not forget the sufferings the poor endured and the riots that followed when there were no provisions for the labourers.

Mary remembered the coarse brown wheatmeal loaves she had eaten as a child. Now she and Mrs Moon made bread with fine barley floor. Across the moors lay the sea which had been life to them all since Lord Nelson's wondrous victory at Copenhagen which had opened up the Baltic letting the corn travel in freely again.

'God bless you, Lord Nelson!' said Mary reverently and shut the window with a snap. 'But, Lord, there is war still and who knows what will come of it all with Boney on our backs. Maybe my shilling will only be worth a bad six pence if the Frenchies get to Devon!'

She took the coin from the dresser, stared at the pin remembering gallant Mr Farr. She would never sell it, never. She would bore a hole in his shilling with a bradawl and wear it round her neck for ever. Just to look at the presents gave her courage. She had worshipped that fine young man all those three years he came to the Moons. He had always treated her as a lady and she loved him for it. She laid down the coin beside her love's pin. She would call him that for ever too in her imagination—not really—only in dreams...

At seven, she was bringing back a sixpenny loaf from the bakers. The smell of it was making the juice come in her mouth and she hurried on faster, longing to taste its sweetness. Then she stopped dead.

Outside "The Angel" stood a horse held by the ostler. It was Sweetbriar. She fled then up the street in case Humphrey Moon came out. At the corner, she peeped round. He was emerging with Betty Bly; his arm round her shoulder and lifting her mouth to be kissed.

Then another horse came clattering round. It was Jem's! Mary waited until the tall figure appeared. To her horror, Miss Pussy was on his arm. Clasping the bread to her like a hot little baby, Mary hurried on to her cottage, fresh tears starting in her eyes.

As the two men swept up the street which was thick with chimney smoke from the villagers' fires, Jem thought of Mary Willcocks. As he passed the garden gate of her common father who had insulted him, he murmured under his breath:

'Goodbye, Mary. May you find some village lad who will be kinder to you than Humphrey Moon!' The cottages were thinning out now like spring cabbages with weeding. Jem thrust sleepy Witherage from his thoughts. The letter from his father was upmost in his mind. He must be done with Devon life and take himself to London and Lord Castel.

Humphrey reined in Sweetbriar on the ridge with a wild halloo. His shout was enough to wake the strange old folk sleeping in their earthy barrows. He watched Jem Farr bringing Star up beside him. They had made up their differences at breakfast over the rest of the goose. Humphrey pointed to his swelled black eye as Jem reached him.

'How will you pay me for this pretty sight, Jem, lad?'

'Why, Moon, what should I do but—' Jem grinned mischievously, '—take you to London with me!' He dashed off in front. 'That is—' he shouted, 'if you promise not to force young maids against their will!' Humphrey gave a delighted whoop and spurred Sweetbriar on in chase of Mr gentleman Farr...

Below in smoky Witherage, Mary staggered about the cottage garden, thinning out the carrots, concealing the sweetest in her apron, ready for the long walk ahead. Going in, she scrawled a clumsy message leaving it on the ledge of the corner cupboard. At least, when her mother returned, she would know Mary was gone to make a new life for herself.

She felt no sorrow on leaving such a cruel father. Jem's pin, his shilling and what was left of her wages after being turned off, were all concealed next to her bosom. The rest of her belongings she tied up in a large bundle, on the top of which she placed the carrots, a heavy slice of bread and a piece of strong cheese.

As the church bell tolled the hour, a passing carter picked up the girl, who flagged him down outside Witherage village and the two of them jolted off along the Exeter road.

CHAPTER 2

The stout man shook his head making the tassels on his velvet skull cap shiver like the oat grasses growing tall in the park outside. He sifted through the papers on his desk, looked at the latter for the hundredth time and sighed loudly. Then, pushing the heavy paperweight, adorned with the Birt arms, upon the pile, he stood up and began to pace to and fro along the Turkish carpet one of his military ancestors had brought from the Levant.

'It it an estate matter, husband?' Mrs Birt was small and dark, different from her bluff fair partner, who thrust his hands into the pockets of his tailcoat. This was a familiar gesture when Harry Birt was anxious.

'I wish it was—with all my heart!' He groaned, a frown creasing his forehead to add more lines to the ones put there by the loss of one hearty son in a foreign war and the death of a baby daughter.

'Ah,' said Mrs Birt, 'it is the letter then?'

'It is!' he said gloomily. 'Damn Castel! Why does he send for Jem now?'

'Come, Mr Birt,' she said, pausing to stare at her pattern, then to thrust her needle into a Christmas rose worked on the back of Jemima's glove. 'You wish Jem well, do you not?' Her husband nodded, staring out of the great window all the while. 'Then you must let him go—to claim his birthright.'

'Damn that man!' repeated the squire. 'He thinks he can right all wrongs by the chink of money!'

'And he can, Mr Birt.' Alice was a realist. She had lived too long in London town to be otherwise. If one had the means, then one was fortunate. 'He has the wherewithal!'

Squire Birt spluttered and mopped his nose with a fine-edged handkerchief. He peered from the window.

'Here he comes, wife. Riding like the devil.' He threw up the sash and hollered into the early morning air. 'Out early, lad!'

'James has not been in this night!' She let the information slip easily from her tongue.

'Well, Mrs Birt,' Harry turned from the window, 'Is he not a young man with an appetite to match?'

'He must be more serious—if he is to make this match!' The frown was back again. Birt did not like the business of aristocrats—breeding for gain. It was all very well for horses in the stable but not between men and women. He had married for love, he told himself, as the slight figure of his wife pleased him bending over her frame.

He had met Alice Knowles in the last week before he returned to Devon after a painful season in London. Harry hated the place with its emptiness. It was said to be the greatest capital in Europe; he thought it the most false and longed for Western air and women. He still hardly believed he would have met such a woman as Alice in that frivolous market, Vauxhall. His cousin, Francis had insisted he dress fancily but Harry had resisted all attempts to go as a painted cad. Instead, he clad himself in Devon hunting colours, took whip and hound to roister through the gardens scattering ladies and gentleman before him, like foxes. As Francis tried to hurry him away, the two men were confronted by Alice Knowles and her lady aunt. Harry had never seen a fairer vixen. About Alice's neck was a cunning brown head and foxy fur; her dress was russet, slashed with golden threads like a country apple and she had glossy hair the colour of Birt hazel nuts.

He was lost from that hour, and his last week in London extended to another month and more. In all that time, he could find no fault with Alice. Within a year, they were wed. Lady Knowles had invited some fine kin to the marriage, including her second cousin, Robert Castel. That was the time, Harry Birt set eyes on the man, who changed his life.

Castel was an army commander then in an aristocratic regiment. He was also a notorious womaniser. Harry could not remember once when Robert was free of society women throwing themselves at him. When peace was made with America, France, and Spain, Castel found life unbelievably dull and took himself off to Europe where he journeyed for six years. He returned from a France threatening revolution with a girl five years his junior, who had been a favourite with the young French queen and betrothed to a marquis, yet Castel stole her away and brought her to London on the pretence of marriage. That marriage never came—all that did was the only living son born to the unscrupulous Robert. By then he was tiring of the French girl, whom he kept almost captive in the London house. He told Lady Knowles that he feared for her safety now England was at war with France in that year of 1793. His lady cousin, always a forthright woman, made it her business to visit Robert several times and took pity on the pretty whore and her six year old son. She rounded on Robert reminding him of duty and the family honour; called him cruel and cold. Six months after, the Birts received a letter from the courageous old lady requesting their help in fostering Master James Farr, who was suffering much in London and should be brought up as an English gentleman breathing in good Devon air. In that letter was the sly intimation that as yet there was no chance he would even come into the highest society although his sire was one of the most illustrious aristocrats (and awful rogues) in England; but in the future who could tell.

Within a month, the tiny Frenchman was outside on his own moorland pony, clattering around the stable courtyard; in six, riding to hunt and within a year, a proper Englishman. To Harry Birt fell the sad task of telling the ten year old with the darkest eyes even seen in Birt, that his mother was dead and four years after, Harry's own son, William was to die like a true Devonian, fighting under Nelson's flag at Copenhagen. Ever since Jem Farr, bastard of Lord Castel, became Harry's dearest and son of his soul, reared with Emma and Jemima, who still mourned a kind sailor brother and a baby sister, Anne who followed William to Heaven in the year of the Peace of Amiens. Nothing had ever come for Jem from Lord Castel, but a large sum of money yearly. There were no kind queries about his offspring, no Saint's Day presents, no personal word. It was only through Lady Beatrice Knowles came news of Robert, his father...

'Harry, your brain will burst from your head, if you dream so!' Alice's voice made Squire Birt start from his reverie.

'I am sorry, wife, but it is pure injustice!' He shook the letter violently as if he wished to tear the Castel arms from the paper. 'We have taught the lad to revere an unnatural father, who cares not a fig for him, who requests—nay, orders—him to St. James! Who will wed him to some heiress solely for gain!' Harry thundered on.

'Calm yourself, Mr Birt, or you will have a fit. An apoplexy will not do Jem any good. Think of it from his point of view!'

'And what is that?' Jem Farr hurried through the doors, laughter in his voice. Squire Birt turned guiltily. He would not have Jem think they spoke of him critically.

'Why, Jem, you have come up quickly!' Squire Birt's puzzled eyes rested on the bruised cheek. 'Had you a good night?' He looked at his wife. Just as Jem was about to answer, she rose and said:

'A good night? I think not, Mr Birt. Who did this, Jem?'

'Humphrey Moon.' Mrs Birt looked at her husband indignantly. 'It was in sport. We were sparring on the Witherage road!'

'The lad is not a child that he be questioned so, wife! Did you win, Jem? Did you sidestep as I always showed you?' Mrs Birt shook her head, hardly believing her husband's misplaced interest in Jem's brawl with Humphrey Moon when so much else was at stake.

'I won!' replied Jem, 'and Humphrey is still smarting. I blacked his eye.' The squire guffawed.

'What was the quarrel, Jem?' The young man became suddenly serious.

'Twas nothing, sir.'

'Just proving your mettle, eh?' Jem nodded, but Mrs Birt was quick to notice the change in his face.

'Pray tell us, Jem.' He looked at the woman who had been kindness itself for the last seventeen years.

'Humphrey Moon was attempting some of his usual mischief. I intervened.'

'On behalf of a young woman?' Squire Birt had caught his wife's interest and was intent on knowing too.

'Aye, Mary Willcocks.' Mrs Birt looked thoughtful. 'She has been turned off from Moons.'

'I know that girl,' said Harry Birt, wrinkling his forehead again. 'She often comes to see Flora Jessup. I have seen her in the kitchen. Why, Jem, I found her in the library one day and she fled when she saw me like a quick bird.'

'Mary is not of the village kind. She has spirit and life.'

'You would see her taken back then, Jem?' asked Squire Birt. It was a good thing to have a healthy interest in peasant affairs when one was a landowner.

'I would but—she says she will not go!'

'Not go!' repeated Mrs Birt, amazed. 'What ails the girl? Where is she now?'

'Home with her father,' said Jem, quietly, thinking of Matt Willcocks's insults.

'Willcocks has always had trouble with the girl, Harry,' said Mrs Birt. 'Why when I visited the dame school some years ago she was in disgrace!'

'Was she?' asked Jem, laughing, thinking of her quick wit and lively step. There was one other picture of Mary too in his mind; the pretty oval face surrounded by blowing curls as she stared into his eyes when he gave her a paltry shilling coin. He turned to Mrs Birt.

'I do not like the cobbler. She will find no comfort with him.'

'Why, Jem, you are turning philanthropist like Mr Cobbett in "The Register"!'

'I hope I am when the lives of the poor are miserable!' he retorted.

'Not in this village, young sir.' Squire Birt's face was red.

'They have shelter and food, but—hardly justice.' His foster parents stared at the words.

'Justice?' asked Mrs Birt.

'The girl asked tor two pence more and Moon turned her off for it, on to the road into a night like the last. Is that justice?' Jem turned on his heel. Mrs Birt rushed from her embroidery.

'Come, Jem, you are tired and out of sorts. I will send to Willcocks and see what can be done for the girl.' He stopped gratefully.

'Thank you, ma'am.' He turned to the squire. 'I have been thinking, sir, that I must make for London by the end of the week.' Squire Birt coughed and walked over to the window.

'He will miss you, Jem,' said Mrs Birt softly. Jem strode across the great room and put his arm about the older man's shoulders.

'Must you go, lad?' Harry's voice was thick.

'I think I must. I will never forget what you precious people have done for me.' Mrs Birt took out her handkerchief. 'I will return.'

'And bring your lady wife to see us?' Jem nodded. He could not imagine himself with a bride at Birt.

'God bless you, lad,' said Harry, charging from the room as if Boney himself had landed. Mrs Birt gathered up her needlework ready to follow him.

'I have directed your packing to be done—my son,' she said, hurrying after him.

Jem felt suddenly alone. He was now where he had always been. Belonging to no one and with a way to make in the world. Birt had been a wondrous home. When he had first seen its portico and gracious steps, come to understand where he was, he had counted himself lucky. They had been good years albeit troubled by rude fellows, whom he had thrashed because they called him a bastard. Jem knew he had the fighting spirit in him, because when his blood was up, no country boy could match him. As for the girls in Devon—he loved them—from Jemima and Emma, his adopted sisters to Miss Pussy and—Mary Willcocks. He hoped with all his heart Mrs Birt could do something for her. There was fire in his blood when he met a pretty woman, yet he was not like Humphrey Moon; he dampened his desire lest he hurt a sex he admired greatly. Jem always saw the mother he had lost in women's smiling faces.

The young man seated himself where he could look over the park. He took the letter from his embroidered waistcoat and stared at it again. Could his father have changed towards him? Perhaps he did regret his treatment of Jem's mother? Would he make him his heir? It was a dizzy thought that he might own a home far statelier than Birt; a castle in the south and two great houses in London. It seemed impossible. Yet Lady Knowles had much hope he would be made legitimate Lord Castel and a bastard no longer. She had told Mrs Birt in her last letter that Robert Castel was very sick of a disease caught from the profligate life he lived; that he had lost faith in doctors and feared he was near the end. Such news should have dismayed his son, instead it brought no commotion to his heart. When he thought of that unknown aristocratic sire, he was devoid of feeling. He wanted to care about his father—but it was a hard task for a boy deserted fourteen years, who remembered his sad young mother denied a marriage which would have legitimated him. Jem stared at the seal bearing the Castel arms, which should have been his own.

'My lord, you have much to answer for,' he whispered, 'but you *are* my father.' He sighed as he unfolded the parchment. The tone of the letter was imperious. Jem could see there was no use in defying it:

> The Duchess of Barton has a daughter. Miss Celia has a quick wit but I understand she is plain and has a cough. I have arranged you shall meet the lady now the duke and duchess are willing...

Such a great family would not approve of a bastard as a match for their daughter. Jem knew in his heart Lady Knowles was right. He would be his father's heir, but at a price. He stared at the words 'plain' and 'a cough'. So Miss Celia was sick also. Perhaps they could find no other who would wed her? This would be a marriage of convenience for the parents—but what about the girl? Jem could not imagine himself a married man. What he had done with Miss Pussy last night had been enough to satisfy him—but children? What would a man make of children? He closed the letter—and his eyes... His ride from 'The Angel' with Humphrey had left Devon close to him as it always did. There would be no views in town like he had seen from the ridge; trees sweeping in waves, a thousand white sheep driving across the barren country and such a sky that told of the wild sea beyond the moors. He would choke in London as he breathed in her chimney fogs. And his companions? They were simple lads, sons of squires and vicars, of tenant farmers and yeomen. They respected him now and he would not find their like in the callous city. He wondered if a man could be sick for home before he left it. He thought of Pussy and her claws. She had sheathed them well while she stroked his back and purred; there was no lechery in her—she was all warmth.

He thought too of the girl he had saved from Humphrey Moon. Would he see her like in London ever? She had been too proud to be tumbled in the ditch; she had about her the air of a lady although she was a serving girl.

And Humphrey? He was a thoughtless fool, but his badness could be cured. All he needed was someone to teach him manners. He craved to be a gentleman... Jem opened his eyes. All this was Devon—Mary and Humphrey both. He had told the farmer's son in jest, he would take him to the capital. Why should he not? He would bring part of the country with him to remind him of its laughter. As Jem thought seriously about taking Humphrey to St. James's the prospect seemed more pleasant —and even bearable...

Mistress Moon was beside herself. Outside in the yard, the pigs were screaming for skimmed milk. Inside, the fires were flaming fiercely and the loaves not ready to be shoved in. Little George could not be consoled even when she stuck a fat finger into his gums, while Humphrey was seated in the parlour still wearing his dirty boots. She hoped he would not provoke Mr Moon any more. Since the palaver with Mary, his mood had been foul. Added to this, he had just received a visit from Minister Strong who had chided them severely on Humphrey's looseness.

Mrs Moon's cheeks flamed as she burnt her fingers on the oven, not only at the scorching , but at the thought of Humphrey and Miss Betty Bly. Mr Moon had chased his son around the yard with a stick.

'Did I educate you for this? So you could dally with a wench who pulls ale? You are a scandal, sir, about this country!' Humphrey had ducked then which was a good thing as his other eye would have closed under a cracked skull. Mrs Moon had managed to calm Frederic down, got him to see reason. After all, Humphrey was young and youth was precious. She had pointed out to Mr Moon that they were lucky Humphrey was still with them after his near escape in Exeter. Their wild young son had been drinking when he had almost been pressed into the Navy to fight the French. She was grateful to Mr Farr for that anyway. Why the boy would have had a life much worse than the Brushford pigs, guarding England's shores on one of His Majesty's ships. Mr Farr had taken some punishment that time, but the gang had left him and Humphrey alone when he told them he was the son of Lord Castel. Why, all of England had heard of that lord's regiment and Mrs Moon thought it a great pity he was not out in the Peninsula with Wellington. If he had been, that foreign war might have ended sooner!

As Mistress Moon sucked her fingers where the blisters were appearing, she thought what a shocking thing it was to be born out of wedlock. 'Poor Mr Farr,' she said to herself, 'and he is such a gentleman.' She had one great fear—that Humphrey should get a bastard upon some village girl and bring home the bird to roost. That was why Mr Moon belaboured him so for his lewdness, being of a similar opinion.

The last loaf was in so the farmer's wife sat down and gave weakly George the breast. She was afraid the little dove would not live long. It was a sad thing bringing a child into the world when a woman was past forty. She had not the heart for it. George was contented for a moment, then squalling again.

'Oh, Mary Willcocks,' she groaned as she rocked him to and fro. 'Would you were here to take this baby on your hip and give me some peace!' She had given the girl what was owed from her wages—seen her go with a sinking heart. Mary had been biddable although her father had not given her a good character. Mrs Moon remembered the cobbler's words.

'My girl is given to strange fancies. She has been so since the day she took brain fever after sleeping in wet straw. I give you leave to beat her when you will. She needs such notions knocking from her empty head!'

Mistress Moon had soon found Mary's head was full and forgave her for dreaming because she was good in the house and an angel to Georgie. And now she was gone and Mr Moon had sent to the village for another girl, who would scarce have Mary's brains. Mistress Moon sighed, remembering the events of yesterday.

. What a spread the cunning girl placed before them. She had had it in her mind then to ask Mr Moon to raise her wages. She did not know that her master was in a foul mood having already been warned in the market place of Minister Strong's impending visit. Mary had picked strawberries, made a soft pudding, brought out the butter she had fashioned herself and bread kneaded and shaped the way they both liked.

'Mary Willcocks,' Frederic had snarled. 'Come in and stop dreaming at the parlour door!' When she had asked, his face was purple. 'What, girl? Did I hear right? One shilling! You hussy! I'll take the stick to you.' Mary had ducked and Mistress Moon had rushed at Frederic to stay his arm. But Mary had been stubborner than her mistress had ever seen.

'Only a shilling, sir,' she had persisted. Mistress Moon had noticed how she had put on her best dress and clean apron. It was then that Frederic had lost his temper completely.

'Get out of my sight, girl,' he had thundered. As Mary retreated, he hollered, 'and you can start packing.' Mrs Moon had begged him to let Mary stay. She remembered how upset she had been. She had cried even.

'What shall I do without Mary? I have so many house duties!' He had been as stubborn as his maid, turned his back on her saying,

'I'll get ye another girl, Charlotte, and that fanciful hussy will return straight to the Witherage cobbler!' So Mrs Moon and Mary had lost to the might of a man once more. She had hustled Mary from the room, chided her for approaching her master when he was out of sorts. But Mary was beside herself, had pulled off her cap and apron saying,

'Give me what I am owed. I don't want to stay here any longer!' Mrs Moon had been terrified the girl would be ravished on the way home. It was late afternoon and miles to Witherage.

'But, Mary,' she had said, 'leave in the morning when Mr Moon's temper has abated. He may change his mind.'

'Give me my money,' the girl had said, pulling her black brows straight across flashing eyes. 'I am sorry to leave you, mistress, you have been good to me.' There had been tears in her eyes...

Mrs Moon brushed away the salt drops from her own. The morn had come and Mary Willcocks was gone. As she was calling Walter Megs in to take the milk to the pigs, she heard a clatter of hooves.

'Heavens!' she said, raising her hands. 'Not another visitor! When shall I get this baking done?'

Jem Farr did not hinder her long. As she fetched him home-brewed wine from the cool dairy, she straightened her cap and paused to see her reflection in the window pane. It was her delight when he came to see Humphrey. She would be well satisfied if her son learned some manners off Mr Farr. She would encourage the friendship as long as she was able. Mrs Moon waited while Jem tasted the wine. He looked like a great lord with his snowy shirt frill, blue tail coat and elogant close-fitting breeches. She placed a great slice of ham before him, a piece of poultry, cheese and the remains of Mary's pudding. She stared at it dumbly, thinking of the girl. When Mr Farr finished, he was off to Humphrey...

As the chiming clock struck two, Humphrey burst from the parlour whooping joyfully. He caught his astonished mother round the waist, kissed her on both cheeks and lifted her upon the great elm table. Jem Farr, amused, leaned upon the lintel.

'What ails you, Humphrey? Put me down.' She was cross and tired.

'Be glad, mother, and I will tell you a secret.' She tried to be joyful. He bent and whispered in her ear. It was all she ever wanted—her Humphrey to go to London with Mr Farr. She cried a little as she had done yesterday—and it was only when she was in bed she cried even more beside the snoring frame of her farmer husband.

'Humphrey and Mary gone in a week!' she said, staring gloomily up at the beams, where the candles threw threatening shadows. 'Whatever shall I do without them, Frederic?' But the master did not hear only bellowed the more, while Mistress Moon pulled her nightdress below her knees and tried to warm herself to sleep...

CHAPTER 3

The cart clipped smartly round a bend where the river wound itself in a distant loop across the valley. Mary was looking at the clouds, their silver shrouds reminding her of the last laying under the yew she had witnessed in Witherage Churchyard. Dame Ellen had been a fine corpse who had saved enough in her life for a silken shroud fashioned with Chinese embroidery about her eggshell skull and wizened forehead.

It was then Mary came out of her dream; the wagon was careering to a crunching halt and Mary found herself thrown on the road, staring at two bottle-shaped, bare, brown legs, streaked and grimed with the dust of the road.

'Bejasus, the wench has fallen on the ground!'

'Hold the nag, Paddy, whiles I drag her up!'

Two more ugly feet were planted before Mary. She covered her ears with her hands at their accents. She was a victim of papists! She felt a huge, beefy hand about her wrist and being set on her feet again. Where was the carter? She dared not look. Head broken and murdered? She heard their loud laughter pierce through her terror:

'We won't eat ye, girlie! Look up!' She squinted into the sky from which a freckled face, topped with a thatch of flaming red hair like the stack outside Moon's barn, thrust into hers.

'Get off me, murderers!'

'Murder, is it? It will be if you don't stop that wingeing!' The speaker had curls as black as her own and only one arm. Yet the two men and Mary managed to rebalance the cart and mend the carter's leg.

And that was how Mary met the Irish gypsies, deserters from the old 88th, two of the fearsome Connaught Rangers, who fought with no shoes on their feet and went into battle, merry as larks. At least, that was their story to which Mary was forced to listen. She sat between them, still as a stone, while they sang blustery songs in their fine voices. She could not get rid of them, even though she lied to them calling the injured carter her father. But she was soon found out when the horse bolted for home and the farm dog almost ate the three of them.

She had to confess finally to being a servant turned off from her situation and seeking her fortune in Exeter. She had done the right thing! They, suddenly, became her friends because she had known injustice. Mary walked on silently between them. How she was going to escape she didn't know. She was remembering Mistress Moon's words warning her about the terrible Irish. So far neither had done her harm, but it could only be a matter of time.

The one-armed boy had a very fine voice and sang a song about 'Mary of the West'. Where was that West? She had thought Ireland to be a terrible place like its people, dark, boggy and savage. They were only rough and merry, with none of the slyness of Humphrey Moon. She had never met Irish before, but had seen them with their pandy bats, laying out all and sundry after harvest home. They drank beer like goldfishes in a cistern and lay with the roughest maids. They babbled heathen prayers in a Popish tongue and, according to Milly Cater, ate old women and babies.

Still, so far they had not knocked her in the ditch or stole her money or her virtue. Mary was getting hungry. She had her carrots and bread in the bundle but, if she shared it with these two, there would be none left. She couldn't wait.

'Stop, Irish,' she said, 'while I open my bundle.' The trio stood while she got out the carrots. The men asked for nothing, only stared. 'Here, lads,' she said, offering a piece and a bunch of three sweet roots with light feathered tops.

'Thank you, my lady,' they mocked, but took them eagerly.

'How far to Exeter now, do you think?' she asked, nibbling and looking across the green country. It was a breezy day and suddenly Mary felt blithe and free.

The red-haired man stood up and pointed:

'We have ate of your carrots and now we will repay your charity. You see over yonder. The covert next to the field?'

'Yes.' She could see smoke.

'Our journey's end, for the night at least. You can stay with us.' Mary was afraid. Was it some hidden cottage where they would murder her for the pin and sixpence?

'Thank you, no. I must get to Exeter before night falls.'

'We'll do you no harm. Molly at home would strike me off if I tempted a lonesome maid,' said Redhead and Brown Shamus laughed. Mary's colour rose.

'Tis the gypsies you'll be seeing, Mary, not the length of our breeches!' Her cheeks scarlet, Mary looked into the man's mischievous eyes. This was no Irishman surely, but a gypsy.

'Are you one of the travelling folk?'

'No, Mary, but I have a sister married into the clan. Come on and meet her. You can dine tonight on rabbit meat and barley bread!'

The smoke was rising in a lazy spiral, thick from the brushwood. It couldn't be a cottage, but a camp, because there were flashes of silver water and red among the trees.

She looked at Paddy Redhead, who laughed:

'So, Mary, you're afraid like my Molly was when she lay behind the Spanish lines. Her heart was beating as fast as yours. Now she is safe with a fine babby to show for it back in Exeter!'

'Will you swear a papist oath that you'll not hurt me?' cried Mary.

'By the body of Our Lord; on the crook of Holy St. Peter, you will be safe with us! Come on!' Shamus was running swiftly towards the trees. Mary could hear dogs barking.

She put out her hand to Paddy Redhead and he lifted her over the broken stile, set her down behind a sweet clump of shepherd's roses, which were nodding their pink flower heads in agreement.

'Well, Mary,' she whispered to herself, 'whatever black work comes of this, you have only yourself to blame.'

Rosa Kelly was not fearsome, nor were the others. They made her very welcome. She was safe in a little van, unhurt. Her best dress would never get over the journey unless it saw a flat iron. As for her petticoat! Then she put her hand in her bodice to feel for the shilling warm between her breasts —and the pin—all part of him, near to her. Her cheeks burned as she thought of his touch; she could almost smell the perfumed linen and tobacco as her hand lingered on the coin.

Then a scream rose in her throat. A man had entered, was staring at her greedily. He came towards her and put his hand in her bodice. He was grasping Jem's shilling and her breasts!

She fought him off in terror. All she had feared was happening:

'Take your hands off me,' she screamed and twisted out of his grasp. She could see the knife glinting on the small dresser. In a moment, it was in her hand. 'Come no nearer,' she gasped. Whether she would have the nerve to cut him she didn't know, but there was no need. Another man was grabbing at the gypsy's shoulders and pulling him away from her:

'Touch her again, Dow and I'll break your neck!'

Mary stuffed the pin back in her bodice and covered herself. The man was looking. He was lean and tanned with narrow brown eyes. Mary suddenly thought of the cruel ferret Walter Megs had thrust down the leverets' holes in Brushford spinney.

'Hear this,' said the man, 'I am Tod—and I say leave this fine girl alone. Dow, get out and fetch some water for the maid you've bruised.'

The gypsy ducked his head and was out of the van in a trice. 'Rosa, come in and look after this girl. She needs your protection.' He looked at Mary.

'I beg your pardon for what has happened here. I am the king and Dow will be punished. We pride ourselves on our hospitality and want no part in such a welcome. From now on, you will be safe in the camp of Tod, the Fox.' He pulled his cloak about him, turned and left.

So Mary found the gypsy camp a convenient refuge if not quite a safe one. In the dark of the evening, she stood on the steps of the van and Tod was beckoning her into the firelight. He was so much like the crafty animal which strayed out in the night for easy pickings. There was something about him she could scarcely trust, but he had protected her. His eyes were sly and reminded her something of Humphrey Moon.

'Come on, Mary,' he said, 'Rosa is going to tell you your fortune.' He turned to the assembled gypsies. 'In this way we shall make Mary Baker welcome!' Mary started guiltily every time she heard the unfamiliar surname. She had wanted to forget she was a Willcocks and the daughter of the Witherage cobbler. So she had chosen 'Baker' as a safe, warm name and added 'from Crediton' to it, in case the squire got wind of her flight and sent a constable to find her. She would not go back to Witherage to be a slave to a cruel father. After all, wasn't she out to seek her fortune? When she was a lady, dressed up in finery, she would return to the village and Jem would fall in love with her and claim her for his own.

She stepped out of the gaily painted *vardo* and Shamus Kelly slipped from the shadows and escorted her to the camp fire, holding her hand prisoner in his one set of fingers. The wood smoke made a cloudy roof above the watchers' heads, blowing down crazily as the wind gusted and tangled itself in their mouths and clothes. Sparks showered as the flaming branch resettled itself in the embers. The fire was burning Mary's neck and face but she didn't dare draw back as all eyes were fixed upon her. Rosa squatted by her side, her breasts straining against the knotted blouse. Mary had seen none so dark in Witherage—except Jem Farr. She put a hand to her bodice, imagining the feel of his hand as he clipped the jewel to cover her breasts. The pin was still safe with his shilling next to her throbbing heart. She had always wanted her fortune told by a gypsy woman and now another dream was about to come true.

Rosa swung from side to side, her glass beads catching the firelight, her hooped earrings making circles of light in the night air. She was a different woman now from the one who let herself be ordered about by that rough gypsy man, Black Dow, who had done mischief to Mary. He was seated the other side of the fire, his eyes fixed on Mary still.

Tod was beside her too, half lying in an idle way. He yawned, then sat up impatiently, shouting to Rosa:

'Hurry, woman, the fire is sinking. Tell Mary from Crediton her fortune before you have only the stars for light. She is dying to hear it as we all are!' The gypsies murmured.

They had not the courage of Tod, the fox. He was their king, wore a brocaded waistcoat and coins about his neck. The old spirits dare not touch him in his brightness, were only such raggle-taggle as they.

Mary *was* dying with impatience—and fear. If Minister Strong had seen her, he would have called her a sinful wench, said she was selling her coal-black soul to the Devil in Hell. The minister knew all about the devil. That was all Mary had ever listened to in his sermons. She shivered at the picture of Satan striding along the ridge in his great black shoes, his belly full of papists.

Rosa was moaning now, stretching out her hands, while her husband Black Dow, sat mutely opposite.

'Stir, Pan, stir,' shouted Tod, the king. The old man struggled to his feet, ready with the poker. He shoved it in the fire and its iron showered in a thousand sparks where Rosa gazed. She stared into the redness, then up at the stars. Mary looked up too, a coldness falling on her face. She felt again for the pin, now hard at her breast. Mary did not know if it was the wind, or the gypsies moaning. 'Stir, stir,' commanded the gypsy king. Pan raked at the glow. Rosa was unheeding now, like the mad woman at Exeter fair who fell in a fit in front of the serving girls' astonished eyes and foamed at the mouth.

The moaning grew louder. Mary knew Rosa was speaking within it.

'I see—' she looked up and down '—pictures of greatness.' Mary's face was burning again with eagerness to listen.

'A carriage—and gold. A land—' the gypsy hesitated, 'a great land—bright—and diamonds.' The ash flew up in the summer dark and Mary stopped the cry rising in her throat. The moaning was coming again. She could feel the gypsy king moving beside her, his leg close to hers.

'It is darker now,' cried Rosa. The fire was dying. 'Dark like a man, very dark, smiling—and full to the brim.'

Mary's heart leaped like the spring frog did from under the stone at Brushford when it gave her a fright. Her mind was away and over the fire, far from Tod, across Witherage, to Birt and Jem. The ash branch crumbled, leaving the clearing dismal. And Rosa's voice was deep with sorrow. 'Sadness, sadness, all weeping and pain.' But Mary did not care, she was riding with Jem. 'Wake,' screamed Rosa, drawing herself up, catching Mary's sleeve, stretching to the sky, 'wake to the sadness,

Mary Baker.' Mary started quickly as she heard the name she had made for herself. Tod was on his feet too.

'Enough of that, woman.' He kicked at her and the fire with his foot. The old man tottered back and Rosa swayed dazedly and her gypsy man caught her in his arms as she fell. 'Quit moaning. The girl will not rest in this camp if you frighten her. Is not everything sadness in this world?'

Mary caught his arm.

'She spoke of greatness, Mr Tod and I thank her for it. I have know sadness already!' He looked at the girl his men had brought in off the road. She had spirit.

'You are pale like a *gorgio* but you have the heart of a gypsy.'

'What is a *gorgio*?' Mary asked.

'It is one who is not Romany; who has not our blood. One who lives in a house, is no traveller.'

'And where do the gypsies come from?'

'With the East winds!' said Tod. 'From the country of Caspar!'

'Not from France and Boney?'

'No, Mary Baker. From the lands where your Christian Jesus set his foot—and beyond.'

'What is beyond that?'

'Did you not go to school?' He laughed, drawing his cloak about him. It was a fine one with a scarlet lining.

'I was too busy driving the horses and wooding.' She did not intend to tell this strange foreigner about her dreaming while others sat learning.

'So now you have your fortune, Mary, talk of diamonds, dark man and all. What will you make of that?' She shook her head.

'What I can.'

'And that will be much, I tell you.' He put a hand under her chin to lift her blazing face. 'This is another to be watched—like Humphrey Moon,' thought Mary. She looked across at Shamus Kelly, who was sitting, propped against a fallen elm. Tod followed the glance.

'Shamus!' he called. The man stood up. 'Redhead!' The crooked shape stole from the shadows to stand beside him. Mary looked at the wild companions. 'Mary, go to the van with Rosa! This is man's talk. Dow!' He slipped towards them. 'You sleep under the stars—away from this maid, who will share Rosa's bed tonight!' Mary obeyed and walked towards the caravan, sensible of four pairs of eyes upon her. There were now only men in the clearing, all the women had disappeared.

'What a find you had,' said Tod. The Irishmen grinned.

'Just sitting solemnly in a cart—until the wheel fell off and it overturned,' said Paddy Redhead.

'Pinning the carter beneath,' smiled Shamus. He had seen many fine lads trapped under wheels on the battlefield. The carter had been lucky a French devil had not crept up to blow off his head.

'She was mighty frightened at the sight of us,' said Paddy proudly.

'And who would not be?' said Tod, smiling grimly at the lad with one arm and the bent shape of the other. 'You have very fine figures!' They cared not for his mockery, but dared not show it. If they had no home in the gypsy camp they would be in a poor way, having deserted an English army which embraced any kind of man who would throw in his lot with England in her fight to drive Napoleon from Europe. And Tod's work needed someone like them, fresh from the murdering Connaught Rangers. Robbing in England was a dangerous game and still could mean the hangman's noose. When Paddy and Shamus picked up with the Portuguese gypsies, they were soon at home, twisting chickens' necks, spiriting plate from sacked houses deserted by the French. Besides, Shamus was almost one of them with his dark looks come down from Queen Elizabeth's time, when his woman ancestor had set herself up with an Armada gypsy. He had only to mention his sister, Rosa, wedded to Dow in the tribe of Tod in England and he and Paddy were swallowed into the clan.

They had left the Portuguese at Lisbon, clambered on a fast merchantman bound for Bristol and made themselves useful to the captain. Soon the two of them were on the English roads, living and robbing as they could. Shamus had the strength of five men in the one arm he had left; Paddy, the cunning to twist his crooked back into any open window. After an early haymaking, they had melted into the crowds of itinerant Irish labourers, clawing for work in the wheatlands and made their way towards the city of Exeter where they knew Rosa, Dow and baby Zak to be. They knew too there would be even finer pickings with English gypsies than in the ravaged Peninsula or Holy Ireland.

They had enjoyed maids by the score, had given up counting, talking of them even. This one was different.

Shamus desired her—Paddy knew. He was careful in this part of the country lest his woman, Molly o' the Lines got wind of it. She would have flayed him worse than stern Wellington had when he stole the food and cracked the skull of the young lord sleeping against his saddle. If it had not been for Shamus Kelly, he would have still been a Connaught Ranger—but the lad had been fearful sick after losing his arm, craving for food and drink. Paddy sighed as the gypsies huddled into a circle. He would never be a proper man again since his bones had split under the whips and his muscles broken like worn-out hempen rope. He felt the weals on his skin as he scratched his back, prickly with woodsmoke.

Shamus's eyes glittered under a sky cleared by the wind now, with the moon in full-blown sail. Coach robbing was more to his taste. It gave him the chance to feel a horse beneath him, to renew the wildness of youth racing a Connemara pony, which by now was but a bag of bones. He spat on the floor as he listened to Tod's plan. Anything that would repay the murdering English gentlemen for their wickedness in Ireland, was suitable for him. He might have fought for them in the Peninsula but it was only to put some bread in an empty belly or to listen to the screams of those he rammed with the bayonet. Why, Boney's guard were but another breed of masters rampaging over the whole of Europe.

'The coach will be making fast pace by then,' said Tod, his cunning face alight. It was tanned like oakwood and in the moonlight, his narrow, brown eyes twinkled unmercifully. 'There will be rich pickings.' He swung back his great cloak and checked the pistol in his belt. 'Come on—or we will not make the plain in time!' He whistled and a boy ran forward leading a plunging horse. Behind, the gypsy ponies walked sedately. 'By *Duvel*, Pegasus, you are a wild piece of horseflesh!' The stallion whinnied; he was frisky, longing for a mare. As Tod got his foot in the stirrup, he was chafing at the bit, his head pulling for freedom.

Back in the little van, Mary was undressing, casting her eyes modestly down as Mistress Moon had taught her. All was peace until she heard the sound of hooves. She was up to the door, but Rosa pulled her down.

'See nothing, Mary. It is safer. If you have no knowledge of what goes on here you cannot reveal it. It is Tod and the ponies you can hear. He is bedding them for the night!' Mary thought of the man who issued the orders and of the look he gave her. Should she fear his interference in her sleep?

'Has he a wife?' she asked. Rosa laughed, settling baby Zak at her breast.

'Tod will jump over the fire with no one but a queen; he is our king; he has not chosen a woman yet!' Mary shivered thinking of the girl's fate. 'Oh, Lord,' she thought, 'that girl will have a painful time!' She would never forget Milly Cater's excited explanations about wedding nights.

She lay in the narrow bunk, thinking of how she had come. It had been a risky thing picking up with such fellows. But when the wagon broke, she could only look for help and they had not harmed her in spite of their ugly looks. It was when they had led her, protesting, through the moon daises and into the wood, she had feared most. There had been nothing like the relief she felt when she had heard the dogs barking, smelled meat wrapped in woodsmoke and seen the cluster of vans.

She watched Rosa feeding the baby beside the table where the candle flickered. Its soft light warmed the copper pans, horseshoes and china. Rosa's feet were bare upon the carpet. Mary had seen such a fine one at Squire Birt's when she took the chickens from Brushford for harvest home. 'How do these travellers come by their wealth?' Her heavy eyes were closing as she planned tomorrow's journey. She must go then; she had been too long with the gypsies and it was dangerous. Soon she was dreaming sweetly, riding with Jem over the fences, clad in a green hunting gown with a curled feather in her hat; dancing at Birt—but there was darkness then as she struggled on to Witherage, slipped through the gate to fall begging upon her knees before her father...

The chaise bowled down the street with Witherage wives agog. They had all heard of Matt Willcocks's outburst on Mr James Farr. Now Mrs Birt had come to send him packing.

He heard the rapping and tumbled down the bare stairs, pulling on his smock. 'Devil take Mary,' he cursed, 'for careering off with care for no one!' He wrenched open the door... Alice Birt's dressmaker was the best. She had insisted that the squire's wife should wear a train in keeping with the fashion but Alice had demurred. Therefore, Mrs Birt wore a round gown that morning to satisfy the woman. It was slightly trained yet its skirt was decorated with as many trimmings as the dressmaker could cram from knee to hem. From Mrs Birt's neck cascaded a five-tiered lace collorette, while perched on her head she wore a silk poke bonnet, wonderfully quilted... The squire's wife threw up her lace veil before the astonished cobbler's eyes.

He bowed his head and shuffled.

'Good morning to you, Willcocks. Will you leave me standing at the door?' A small crowd was collecting in the street; Matt Willcocks reddened and backed her in, bowing. She stared around the room, noting the poverty.

'My wife is with her sick sister in Crediton—' he began.

'I am looking for Mary, man!' She cut him short with the tone.

'The worthless ja— my daughter is gone, milady!' He shuffled miserably.

'Gone where?' She arched her eyebrows at the cobbler. He shrugged, then picked up the paper Mary had left on the dresser and handed it to Mrs Birt, who drew a pair of spectacles from her indispensable. 'So,' she drew in her breath, 'the bird has flown—not back to Brushford, I'll be bound!'

'What has my girl been up to?' he snarled. Alice Birt looked into the man's face, despising the rough tone and the semblance of dutiful father. He lowered his eyes furtively.

'Nothing I know of, Willcocks, except she was turned from a good situation—assaulted on the king's highway—and is wandering now!'

'Who attempted her, milady?' His face was dull red with anger. Fine folks were all the same. If Mrs Birt was out to protect young Mr Farr he would still charge him, gentleman or not.

'I hear it was young Mr Moon up to his mischief again. If it had not been for Mr Farr's intervention, who knows what would have happened to your daughter. But you are her father, Willcocks. Did she not speak to you on the matter?' Mrs Birt watched his face keenly. It was all too plain, there was no real love between this father and his headstrong daughter. Matt shook his head, thinking of Moon. What had the rogue done? 'I see by your expression, Willcocks, you were ignorant in this matter. So now Mary is wandering alone. Well, well—I shall alert the constable and when she is discovered she will be bound to the parish until I can secure a new situation for her!'

'Thank you, milady,' muttered Matt, touching his greasy hair.

'I fear you have not treated her well, Willcocks!' said Alice Birt. 'If a child is used badly in her own home, where else will she find kindness? Good day to you, cobbler!' With the reproof ringing in his ears, Matt bowed the squire's wife to the door and up the garden path. He watched the coachman hand her into the chaise like the rest of his neighbours. With flaming cheeks, he took the basket which the coachman handed down from the box and dropped—at his feet—and the two horses sprang on their way.

Matt swore under his breath as the chaise bowled off, then out loud at the grinning villagers. Still cursing, he picked up the provisions, ran in the gate and down the path.

As he slammed the cottage door behind him on the curious crowds, he was vowing Hell's vengeance on Humphrey Moon...

Above, the night clouds chased the moon madly across the sky. Below, the traveller might have thought the cloud had come to earth as a thousand sheep drifted across the ancient plain.

There was no such peace inside the Salisbury coach. Mr Jem Farr and his companion rattled and swayed uncomfortably as the vehicle dashed on making eight miles an hour on the bad parts of the road and twelve on the good.

'I should have brought Sweetbriar,' grumbled Humphrey, flicking one of the night insects off his skintight breeches. 'The mare would have carried me to London in half the time!'

'I think not, Humphrey,' said Jem. 'You would have broken her neck with the ride. She is happier at Brushford.' He, too, was wishing Star was between his legs and the fresh air blowing in his face. The stench in the coach was foul and when the wheels bumped in the potholes, the two young men were thrown against two other passengers, one, a minister with a nose like a sickle; the other, an elderly man who had slept through it all.

'By God, Jem, I wish I was up beside the driver or on the box with the guard. This air is foul!' Jem looked at him reprovingly and Humphrey knew that manners forbade such remarks about other persons. The farmer's son lay back on the cushions and tipped his hat over his eyes in a gesture of excessive boredom. Jem wondered too how he could fare for another fifteen hours in the cumbersome conveyance.

The guard on the box peered into the night, straining his ears for the sound of hooves. He would be glad when he saw the needle spire of the cathedral piercing the night sky.

There was no comfort up on top where a man was an open target for every highwayman in the county of Wiltshire.

The driver handled the ribbons of the four bays skilfully. He would be glad when his treasures hauled the coach out of Rushy Bottom and over the crossroads. The road was stretching like a stream of milk, formed by two straight tracks making a cross in the moonlight.

'Get that pistol primed, Jack,' he growled. 'Who knows what is lurking in Rushy Clump!' It was a notorious spot for footpads and felons on horses, who were intent on robbery. The coach dashed through with never a hint of trouble, over the brow and along the ridge.

Five hundred yards distant, the four were waiting! The guard would have relaxed thinking danger was past, would be chewing his tobacco, maybe drinking from his flask. As the coach hit the skyline, the dark shapes were galloping in unison.

Jem heard the thunder of horses first and the harsh shout roused Humphrey like a gunshot. The minister cowered and the fat man slept. But Jem and Humphrey had their hands inside their great cloaks—pulling out loaded pistols. Jem looked meaningly at his friend, whose face was bright with the excitement of it all.

'Shall we teach these "gentlemen of the road" a lesson they won't forget, Jem?'

For answer, Jem threw back his great coat and hugged into the window shadows. As the first, dark shape came dashing beside them, another was grabbing the lead horse's reins. Jem and Humphrey were ready. The guard on the box was fumbling with his gun but dropped it as he stared into the barrel of another.

'Stand!' came that hoarse voice again as the coach came wrenching to a halt. The dark figure at the window was reining in his animal, pulling it back and away from the door. With a roar, Humphrey thrust his pistol out of the window and squeezed the trigger. The noise and smoke brought the fat gentleman to his senses. The minister was clasping his hands, while Humphrey's ball ripped into a swarthy shoulder smashing the bone. Screaming in pain, the highwayman reeled and his frightened pony plunged away into smoky darkness. Jem was leaning through the other window aiming upwards where a frantic shadow was struggling with the guard. About his head waved a cloak with a scarlet lining. He dared not shoot, and turned his head just as a bullet flew by, missing his skull by inches and embedding itself in the buttoned seat. Humphrey roared again and let fly with his second pistol. Up on the box, the guard had recovered and was shooting back. The driver had beaten off the robber who held the horse's head and the coach was moving. Then, Jem heard the curses uttered in a foreign tongue, the sound of horses wheeling. He thrust his head hastily out of the other window to see three men pulling another behind them, with a fainting body in the saddle.

'They're on the run, gentlemen,' the driver sang out and Humphrey whooped and fired again, followed by the guard. 'You've given them the slip, lads,' shouted the man on the box. 'It's a good thing that ye were gentlemen instead of ladies or we should have been goners!'

'Is it a good thing, Jem, there are no ladies here?' asked Humphrey with mischief in his voice. 'Why we shall have no more excitement until we reach London town!' Jem laughed out loud at his friend's expression.

'I tell you, Moon, you will have enough excitement in the Royal West to make up for twelve highwaymen.' He leaned back and, taking the fine cambric handkerchief from his waistcoat, began to wipe the blood that was oozing from the scratch where the bullet had missed...

Mary woke with a start when the dawn was breaking to the sound of horses wheeling outside. Rosa was sleeping with Zak snuggled to her breasts, so she climbed up to the window. In the pink of the clearing, four horses were steaming. The men were clustered about a pony, busily hoisting a limp figure from the saddle. As they stretched up to bring him down, the fiery dawn flamed on their pistol barrels. Mary put her hand to her mouth to stop the scream ready in her throat, then she slid down again.

She crept back to the narrow bunk, shivering and wondering how she would ever get away from the camp full of robbers. 'Oh, Lord,' she prayed. 'Please get me to Exeter safely. Let me find work away from this world of men. Amen.' Then she thought of Mr Farr. He was not bad. He had saved her from harm. She wished she knew where he was now, imagining him seated in the drawing-room at Birt, or sleeping in a big four poster. After, she thought of Miss Pussy. With a heavy heart, she turned towards the painted wooden wall, forcing her eyes to shut and erase such painful pictures.

There was no sign of any injured man next morning. Mary was not sure if she had dreamed it all but, as she walked past pots and kettles slung in a heap for soldering, females raking over the embers of the fire and bringing wood for the morning's tinkering, the magic of the night before, when Rosa had told her fortune, had dissipated like the mists which were chased by the sun's rays into insignificant wisps. Yet, when she glanced over to where the ponies were tethered, she could see three of them caked with mud to their necks.

Suddenly, Rosa was beside her, Zak asleep on her hip.

'You have some good ponies,' said Mary to cover her curiosity. Rosa looked at her with expressionless eyes.

'Do you know about horses?' Mary shrugged.

'As much as anyone brought up near the moors. Thank you for your hospitality, Rosa, but I must be off!'

'Without the men? I can't let you.'

'I was alone before—and it is not far to Exeter!' She was afraid she would be unable to escape.

'It is not—but Tod has forbidden me to let you. Get back to the van and I'll get you some food. They'll be up before long—then they'll take you.' Mary felt like a prisoner.

She ate well on that summer morning. Goat's milk cheese, wild strawberries, a chicken breast and white flat bread, hammered upon a stone. Rosa offered her dark meat with the white, but Mary was suddenly afraid it might be drugged. Had not her mother and Mistress Moon always warned her to keep away from the gypsies?

'It's venison!' said Rosa. Mary shook her head, only half-believing. Besides, she loved the shy beasts and imagined them wandering free.

'You eat well!' Rosa smiled crookedly at the words:

'Beggars must eat!' Suddenly, there were men all around, fastening their breeches. Mary turned her eyes away, thinking about Minister Strong's words on temptation. Then Tod was towering above her.

'So you must go, Mary!' She nodded.

'Thank you kindly for the night's shelter!'

'Did you sleep well?' he asked. A sixth sense warned her to be careful.

'I slept like the dead!' she lied. She looked up at Shamus Kelly, whose face was dark and suspicious. Tod bent and hauled her to her feet.

'You will be safe on the Exeter road with these two to guide you!'

'I need no one. I have walked that road often and nothing has happened to me!' cried Mary, realising she was still not free.

'Not yet, Mary—and Shamus and Paddy will be there to prevent it. They have business in Exeter!' Rosa laughed out loud, then shut up at Tod's scowl. Mary shrank back from its fierceness, but he caught her by the hand. 'If you were a Romany woman, we might lie under the stars together—with the fire to come!' She blushed at his meaning. Then the dark gypsy turned to his men. 'See no trouble touches this spit of a Mary.' He was still holding her hand. Turning to look into her eyes, he said:

'Come back one day, Mary. You will be welcome in our camp!' Then he was gone, striding across the clearing.

The whole camp turned out to see them leave. The last Mary saw of it was a fluttering scrap of red where a scarlet-lined cloak had been hung to dry on a branch in the willow wood. She looked towards her wild companions. Between here and Exeter she must give them the slip or into what danger would she be dragged. As the three of them pushed waist high through the uncut grass, full of pale moon daisies, she was planning her next move. As they reached the stile in the hedge, thick with shepherd's roses, Paddy Redhead picked her up and sat her on the top.

'Now, Mary—whatever your name is—' he said with a sly grin, 'you are in our protection. Don't try and give us the slip, will you?' Shamus Kelly climbed past her and put up his arms to lift her down.

'Why should I?' asked Mary, faintly. 'I am only too glad to go along with you!'

'Good!' said Shamus, delicately unpicking her dress from the thorns. 'Into my arms, your ladyship!' Howling with laughter, they carried her, protesting, towards the road. Then the two men set her down, straightened her dress, linked their arms about her waist and Mary, her feet scarcely touching the ground, was escorted on towards Exeter in the company of two of the bloodiest rogues who ever deserted the Connaught Rangers and Wellington.

CHAPTER 4

Would the boy come? Robert Castel was used to giving orders and having them obeyed. He had given sterner ones than calling his bastard in from Devonshire. Men had lain like worthless animals, heaped in red jackets which had soaked their blood gaily, doing what Robert Castel had decreed they should do.

He looked at his emaciated hands, black with liver spots, which had done so much damage to others—and himself. He stared at his rings, loose on the joints; those heirlooms which represented a line of aristocrats sprung from the soil of Gloucestershire. Now there was but one Castel left whose blood was pure English. The next—Castel winced—had the crushed vine of France in his veins.

If Robert had married the Duchess of Barton, it would have been a different story. They would have been bright flowers together, Western hawthorn and Yorkshire rose! Robert spat upon the Turkish carpet at the bizarre fancy. The duchess might have looked like a rose in her slim girlhood when he and she had sprung into bed to cuckold Tom; now she was red and fat like the overblown peonies in his Sussex gardens. He wondered if the girl was like her in spirit, if not in looks. Celia Barton's plainness had been proclaimed in whispers at Court, while her health was a source of prayer to a thousand peasants grubbing for bread in that wild Yorkshire landscape. Whether she would have the stamina for his French bastard was a matter of some interest to him.

He had to admit that he wanted to see if the boy still looked like Marie with those soulful eyes, full of pain. Perhaps Harry Birt had transformed him into some thick dolt of a country squire only fit for riding to hounds. Was there a chance he might be like Robert himself with a sharp wit and a taste for the fight? That would be too much to hope for. Not every Frenchman took after Buonaparte; the most were like that sickly Louis they had dared to rid themselves of in the Terror. But French women were pure passion.

Robert was persecuted by sharp pains in his groin when he thought of the music of love he and Marie had played so sweetly. He, himself, could not have dreamed of the satisfaction he had had from the French girl he had stolen out of the arms of her marquis and spirited away to the London house.

Castel groaned as he pressed at the pain in his belly. He realised, like many other unfortunate gentlemen, the torments love could bring. Told to abstain by a succession of dry physicians, he had persisted and finally had ended his sexual career confined to a chair in the drawing-room, half-poisoned by evil smelling medicines, half-crippled by the lancing of the cruel buboes which had gathered of late.

'Damn you!' groaned Robert Castel at his ill-used body. 'You are not fit for soldiering nor women any more!' Which of the two had been his greatest passion would be difficult to say. If a man put begetting and death side by side he would be hard pressed to tell the difference. Robert saw both as one. All those he had admired were gone; Nelson at Trafalgar and Moore at Corunna—all England had left was a prince as debauched as any man in the kingdom; a king, devoid of his senses and a duke, almost too big for his boots, careering over the Peninsula with his fellow generals, young puppies all, towing Thomas behind them.

Robert had known Tom, Duke of Barton for years. What he respected in the man most was his ingenuousness. When the two of them had taken split leaves and Tom had returned to the Regiment, he had never suspected where his dear friend, Robert had flown, nor that his several stillborn sons had been Castel's. Yet he had a live daughter. Robert knew she was Tom's because he himself had been away in France when she was conceived. He grinned at the thought. What match could be more suitable than Celia Barton and his son? It would almost be a family matter and the duchess had agreed very readily in the hope that a male heir would take his place in a line which had none. It was all very convenient—as long as Tom agreed; but they were still waiting for the letter from the Peninsula where he stubbornly refused to give up playing soldiers with Picton.

Lord Castel sat, motionless, thinking of the grizzled general dicing in that eternal game of life and death.

It would take many lives to rid Europe of Buonaparte. Echoes of past drums battered in his aching skull as he re-lived that last American campaign when the heavy smoke drifted across the sky. Washington's guns had battered Yorktown for five whole days until Cornwallis asked for surrender terms. It had been the worst day in Robert's life when he had seen his General make the fatal mistake which caused eight thousand men to be taken prisoner. He had vowed vengeance on the French when he rode, defeated, out of green Virginia. 'Perhaps that is why I made Marie suffer so!' were words that resounded in his brain, bouncing out hollowly, echoing against the patterned walls, wreathed in dragons, which were a feature of the great house in St. James's.

When the footman entered to light the candles he was sure his master was dead, but Robert Castel kept on living in order to see Master James Farr whom he had called post-haste from Devon to take a bride and his inheritance...

Mary's head was nodding in front of the range. It had been a tiring walk to Exeter, especially as she had been planning all the time how she could escape from the Irish gypsies. She had had no success; Shamus had watched her unmercifully; his eyes as keen as the hawk which hovered over the moorland. They had come through that part of the city Mary hardly knew —a poor place it was, with women leaning from the windows and dirty children playing in the gutters.

In that tiny back-to-back house she had collapsed in the chair and been fed bread and tea by Paddy's woman. The redheaded man was yawning too but his one-armed friend still seemed watchful. Paddy pulled his shirt over his head and Mary gasped in horror at the snake-like scars tangled on his back.

'He got that fighting for you English!' swore Molly, pointing an accusing finger at the shivering Mary.

'What do you mean?' It was the safest question the girl could think of. The woman's looks told her to take care in the face of such an enemy to the English.

'Why, Arthur gave him that—the devil take him!' Molly cried into the girl's puzzled face. 'Your precious Duke of Wellington, who was told of my Paddy stealing some bread, had him strung between two trees and flayed. It is a wonder he is still alive after that torture!'

Mary was sick at the thought and at being in the company of these wild people. All she wanted to do was get away safely, but there was fascination in the tales they could tell.

'And was that in America?' Molly burst into raucous laughter.

'Do you hear that, lads? No, it was on the Peninsula. Did ye never go to school?'

Mary reddened. She had hated the dame and the gabbling by heart. There was no happiness in learning such. She had craved for stories of foreign places and people. In Witherage, there had been none.

'And women go to war?' Mary's eyes were wide.

'We Irish do!' said Molly proudly. 'We follow our men behind the lines to give them comfort. They get none from your stern duke.' Molly pointed accusingly again as if Mary was responsible for Wellington's behaviour. Mary could hardly bear to look at the Irishwoman's face. There was a scar stretching from eyebrow to chin. The woman followed her eyes, put up a finger to trace the line of the cut. 'Yes, Mary, you can look, I got this fighting for England!'

'And I,' echoed Shamus, pointing to the space beneath his shoulder blade.

'How?' asked Mary faintly, trying not to look.

'I was wriggling on my belly behind the lines,' said Molly. 'Men were crying out all around and the smoke from the cannon covered us all. It's a terrible thing, Mary, to hear the screams of dying men and the whine of shell in the air. My heart was beating fit to burst when I crawled to my Paddy on the cannon, clutching his bottle of drink to my breast. I had good friends behind me. Another two girls—God rest their souls—they were dragging up the iron balls when a shell blew the two of them away, leaving a piece of shrap in my face, torn to the bone!'

Mary stared at her dumbly, imagining it all.

'And I pulled it out from her face,' said Paddy softly, 'and as she lay unconscious, she was still clutching my bottle!'

'And—Shamus?' asked Mary. She had to hear it all.

'That was when I was with the doctor, recovering. They carried him in with his poor arm hanging by its skin. I could see there was no way Burgess had time to bother with him. He had his hands full with the dying.'

'Burgess?' asked Mary.

'The doctor—and a great man too—not a butcher!' said Molly. 'So I stood myself up in the slippery blood and took up the shears—' Mary hung on her words, her bright eyes staring at Shamus. 'Then I clipped it off!'

'The arm?' asked Mary.

'Yes,' said Shamus. 'And do you know, she never picked it up! Just left it on the ground for a Spanish dog!'

'Quit grumbling!' spat Paddy. 'If Molly had not done it—and used the poker on you after, you would have taken gangrene and mortified!' They faced each other hotly while Mary shrank back. Why had she stayed to hear such things? What was she doing in this dark little hovel in Exeter when she should be seeking her fortune?

'Stop it, you two!' commanded Molly. She turned to Mary. 'My Paddy has seen soldiering all over the world, but after the flaying he had enough and took to tinkering.'

'I was in America even,' said Paddy proudly.

'Oh, that is where I want to go!' said Mary. She had heard they were all ladies and gentlemen there.

'And you are right!' said Molly. 'When we have enough saved we shall go to the quay at Bristol and take ship.'

'Not back to your home in Ireland?' asked Mary.

'No! Folks are dying there from hunger too. But to the Americas where poor people can make heaps of coin in the furnaces honestly!' Molly glanced at Shamus.

'Instead of stealing!' said Mary suddenly, thinking of the night in the gypsy camp. She wished then she had swallowed the words; Shamus Kelly was staring at her curiously.

'Whist, Mary Baker, or you might find your pretty throat cut one fine night!'

'Enough of that murdering talk, Shamus!' said Paddy. 'If Mary wants, she can ship with us. I have a mind to be back in Virginia where I was as a lad with General Cornwallis. What a day that was when we marched through the line of Frenchies and Americans. They never jeered at us, just kept quiet because they knew what kind of enemies we were!

To tell you the truth, the lads and I were glad to be beaten. We had all had enough of that five days slaughter. But our lords were not! Cornwallis was too ashamed to turn up for the surrender, and Castel—he had that dark look on his ugly face—'

'Castel?' interrupted Mary, heart leaping at the name of her dear.

'Have you heard of that bastard?' Paddy spat on the floor. Mary had only known another. She shook her head.

'He had a black heart with his men—and his women!' She hardly heard the rest of Paddy's words. She was thinking the man could have nothing to do with Jem; was not 'her lord' the sweetest and kindest in the world?

There was nothing in his father's emaciated body Jem could recognise as the strong man who had turned him out to Birt, except the sarcastic curl of the lips. He tried to conceal his revulsion as he faced the motionless figure seated in the high-backed chair like a carved statue.

Jem felt the familiar coldness of the room. When he had been a child he had always hated it because of its darkness and fearful dragons, grimacing fiercely from the walls. He approached the chair slowly until the figure raised its hand warning him to go no further.

'Who is it?' The voice was thin.

'James, my lord. Come in from Devon.' The word, 'father' would have stuck in his throat, but Lord Castel beckoned him and peered into his face. Jem almost recoiled when he saw the livid features and smelled the foul breath.

'Yes—like your mother. The very image.' It seemed impossible to the young man that a seed from this human stick had issued to fashion him. He was the nearest thing to a corpse that Jem had ever seen.

Throughout their conversation, Jem was disgusted more and more by his corruptness and cruelty. He spoke of Celia Barton as if she were a bitch to be brought to litter by his son.

'I have made up my mind that you will make the marriage I never did!' Jem wanted to rush and shake the truth out of him as to why he had never married Jem's mother, but he held back. Then his father made one surprising movement, grasping Jem's ruffled sleeve with a bony hand:

'I must have your word you will marry the girl and get some children!'

'Why?' The question was an accusation.

'So you will be Lord Castel. There must be someone to carry on the name!'

'And that is the price I must pay?' asked Jem bitterly.

'It is!' His father was relaxing his grip.

'Why this girl?'

'She is rich, James.' He showed a ghastly grin. 'Mind you, she's plain. Her face is of no account. Look in other places for her beauty!' Jem was full of contempt. 'The dowry she brings is priceless and remember—the Bartons have no other heir—nor will they now as the duchess is past fifty. But I tell you, lad, she was a bright one once.' Jem remained silent.

'Nothing to say? Can't you face such a task? She's a weak, little thing—and she may die. And then *you* will be the sole heir to half the Northern Counties. How would you like that? All yours—imagine—the son of my little French whore!' Jem raised his hand in anger and his father shrank back. Then it came to him the old man was but a shrivelled evil who could hurt him no more. Without Jem, the great Lord Castel had nothing. At least if he legitimated him, Jem would have something that was rightfully his own and which should have been his mother's.

'Don't ever speak of my mother like that again!' he cried, lowering his hand.

'You *are* like her! All passion and flashing brown eyes!' Castel was recovering his courage. 'Don't go too far, boy! Remember I'm offering you my name—and a seat in the House of Lords!'

'I don't care for that—only about the wrong you've done!' Jem had not meant to burst out like an angry child; he hated himself for breaking his reserve before such a man.

'You young fool,' said his father. 'You'll see it my way before long. Love is nothing. It's only land that counts and an aristocratic name! Well, you won't be a bastard much longer. That should put it right. But you have to marry the Barton girl.'

'I'll see,' said Jem. 'Perhaps she has no stomach for me either.' His father smiled:

'She has. She's panting after you or so her mother told me!'

'And the duke?' Jem couldn't imagine his reaction.

'I'm waiting for a letter from him. He'll come round.

He won't be against it. I know. He was always easy to convince!'

Jem looked into his father's cunning eyes:

'All right, I'll see her—but I cannot promise to marry her.' It was all he could think of to say in revenge. He knew his father had won the day. Without legitimacy he would wander through the world alone.

'Now you're being sensible,' said the old man. 'Well, James, maybe you're more like me than you've realised.'

Jem bowed a trifle, then looked straight into his face and said, slowly and clearly:

'I would be a bastard to my death rather than be anything like you!' As he walked out of the gloomy room, his cheeks flaming, he could hear his father chuckling...

Celia paused on the stairs, caught a glimpse of her frightened face in the oval mirror, surrounded by tiny mocking Cupids, and took a deep breath to calm herself. How many years had she dreaded the day when she would be forced to marry a man she did not know. Its coming was inevitable as she knew it was her duty to perpetuate the Barton blood if not in name, and bear sons who would strengthen their Yorkshire fortunes.

When the footman opened the tall doors and stood to announce her, Celia's heart was pounding like the frenzied sea which battered the northern coastline. She hoped the dabs of rouge she had been forced to use to heighten her colour, were not too scarlet, nor that her neck would blaze like a turkey's. She had heard that he was wildly handsome—and she was plain. She lowered her eyes quickly, almost afraid to look at his face as he strode forward and bent over her hand to kiss it. She saw the thick curls, slightly longer than the fashion, touching his velvet collar.

When he looked up she was near swooning; her heart skipped and that vile cough rose in her throat, causing her to open her 'indispensable' with trembling fingers and draw out a lace handkerchief to stifle it in her mouth. He took her hand again in his strong fingers and she was sure he would sense her trembling.

'Celia—I'm so happy to meet you at last.' She smiled but her mind was whispering, 'Men who look so have many whores—they are never faithful to their wives—especially a plain one.' Jem Farr had wide shoulders and narrow thighs; his tail coat was blue and nipped in at the waist and his breeches were tight, smooth cream. She looked away from his manhood and into his eyes, which were serious and kind. 'I must be dreaming,' thought Celia, 'that this man is going to be my—husband!'

'My mother tells me you have not been in London long?' she said politely.

'That's true. And I miss the County of Devonshire.'

'And I, Yorkshire—although I'm returning soon.'

'Then we're exiles together—for a while.' She blushed and his words rang in her ears. After a dozen more pleasantries she was in love with him already.

Jem stayed longer than he expected. Celia was as fond of country life as he was. They had, at least, something in common. She was also very well educated for a woman, having spent much time reading, owing to illness. They talked of politics and poetry, but there was one thing neither spoke of—love.

Humphrey Moon was sprawled across the sofa when Jem returned to the great house in St. James's. The farmer's son made no attempt to move, just grinned. Suddenly, Jem found his presence irritating.

'Well?' asked Humphrey.

'Well what?'

'Is she as plain as they say?'

'No. She is fragile—and has elegant conversation.'

'Pooh!' scorned Humphrey. 'She must be plain because, if she was beautiful, you would be shouting it from the rooftops!'

'This is not Betty Bly, Humphrey! This is a duchess's daughter.'

'Beneath their gowns all women are the same,' replied Humphrey comfortably. He was sure at least of this.

'You have a dirty tongue!' said Jem. 'A gentleman would never speak so—not even in private!'

'Well, I've met some London gentlemen already and they are worse than any Brushford farm hand,' replied the other.

'Then you've met the wrong kind,' retorted Jem, remembering his father. He turned to look through the window into the square, thinking of his wedding day to come...

Jem stared at his gilt buttons, but he did not see them. He knew the heart that beat beneath the quilted, white velvet waistcoat was not that of an eager bridegroom. It held no desire in its frenzied beating, only a cold anxiety. He let his dress gloves lie quietly upon the knee of his buff pantaloons.

'Why, cheer up, man, the bride is here!' whispered George Meredith in his ear. He was an Earl's son, but his parents couldn't make him a match like this. The countess, his mother, was an old friend of Lord Castel's and my lord had chosen George as his son's groomsman. George knew him little, was rather a companion of Moon's. Jem nodded, wishing Earle Grant was standing beside him to give him heart. He had never lacked courage, but this day had no equal in his life. Before, Jem had no knowledge of equality, being only a bastard. That was why he'd wanted Earle, who understood and had become his great friend in London. Earle was a misfit of another kind, being half black.

Jem had thought himself badly off being half French, but it was nothing to the social misery Earle had endured having a black mother, who had been raised up to the status of planter's mistress and whose son had willingly been given the name of his father.

The old man sat stiff and proud. He had forbidden Jem to ask Earle to the wedding even—and there was nothing his son could do about it.

Jem looked up grimly to the vaulted roof, criss-crossed by fanlike arches; to the golden stars enmeshed in the plastered ceiling. It was a fair place in which to marry. Both sets of parents had insisted the wedding be in London and the Court invited. Jem could see the prince's fat face, dabbing the perspiration from his brow, shifting his great bulk endlessly upon the chair beside the altar.

If Jem had had any of his way he would have married in the Roman Catholic Church which had been his mother's. He knew little of it, but it would have been a defiance against those who always had their will. Jem remembered his father's face when he had suggested it:

'What? My son married as a papist? I would be laughed out of town—perhaps even the country! The Bartons would not countenance such nonsense. Don't worry about it, lad. It will not affect your immortal soul!'

As the organ pealed for Celia, Jem wondered if there was anything he might ever do against his father's wishes. He was just as much a slave as his mother had been. This wedding could never be a true one; it was a compromise. Riches for morality—a suitable husband for Celia and legitimacy for Jem. Perhaps there *was* something of his father in him that what he should have done for love was being done for gain. He pitied his bride then. 'I don't love you,' he whispered as she started from the door. 'May God have mercy on us both!'

Even Celia did not recognise herself when she saw her slim figure weighed down under the heavy silk worked with the Barton crest. She fingered the shield on her dress as she began to walk down the aisle. Earlier, when she had looked at herself in the shimmering veil she had felt another girl rather than plain Celia Barton, who sauntered through the corridors in an untrimmed dress, curls flowing free.

Celia put a hand up to her veil. Her mother had insisted on the hairstyle, although she had begged to keep her curls.

'My dear,' the duchess had said, 'all the Court will be there. You can't disgrace the Barton name with a hairstyle like a serving maid. You will like it, I promise. Why, *à la victime* is fresh from France. Although these French are constantly at war, it doesn't stop their women leading the fashion for the whole of Europe!'

Celia sighed as she smiled at her kin from all over England, crammed in the pews. She could see the prince now, grinning broadly and her knees began to shake. Her close-cut head was light from excitement. If the style was from France then she was the picture of Joan the Maid, her head like a small boy's which gave her a look more fragile than usual. Would he like it? She could see him turn to her. All her suffering under the scissors had been for him.

Her hands were damp with perspiration as she felt the Barton rose embroidered on her breast. Her hand under the pretty nosegay could feel its sharp wires, which Jennie Marden of Barton village had tormented her eyes over in the candlelight. The villagers had been angels, turning out from their beds when she made her last journey to London as a maid. If it had been in Celia's power they would have been treated kindly instead of being forced to send their young into the factories, where the desire for iron was so strong that half the North could hardly feed the furnaces' gaping mouths.

Celia could see her mother's ostrich feathers, garishly nodding. She had once been the toast of London.

She looked across into her father's face. If he had always been home to cheer her, she could have borne life with her mother, but she hated his long absences, had always done so even as a child when so many gentlemen came riding up country to see her mother, the duchess—including Lord Castel.

Celia had prayed to God about it; now she was sure that Jem wasn't like him. Even to speak that dear name in her heart made it flutter. She would be very kind to him, as his father had been cruel. If Jem and she had a son, they would love him dearly, until he was old enough to go to a great college in Cambridge and take his rightful seat in the House of Lords.

As the high fanfare ceased, Celia fingered the lace square in her bouquet, hidden close in case she needed it to quench her cough. Jem was more handsome on his wedding day than in the last green spring time when he bent over her hand and touched it with his lips. She shivered and Tom Barton felt her tremble and tightened his grip for support. Then Jem was taking her hand—and her father's reign was over.

For a moment he felt the thrill of the bridegroom as their eyes met. He hardly recognised her shrouded under the rich veil, any more than he knew all her gathered kinsmen. He took her small hand in his own and they moved towards the bishop.

'If only it was for love!' thought Jem as he began to make his vows. His heart was aching as Celia looked trustingly into his eyes while the ceremony slipped on…

Mary made for the place she knew best of all. She followed the twisting little way, coming out of Fore Street, thinking of all the old times at Brushford, when she, Milly and Walter had come to see the mummers and carol singers performing in front of the cathedral. It seemed so long ago. Before she came from between the houses into the open square, she peeped around the corner. It was a habit she could not break since she escaped from the Irish house and the clutches of Shamus Kelly. If she had not given him the slip then, what would have become of her? 'I might be dandling some Irish baby on my knee, a captive of that robber, Shamus!' she thought wryly. If she had not escaped through the window and over the roofs, while he was battering at her door drunkenly, he would have done her as much mischief as Humphrey Moon intended. And there would have been no Jem Farr to rescue her! She thought of him with an ache in her breast. Since she had cut herself off from Witherage and her parents, there was no chance of news of Birt Park. But she liked to think of him riding to hounds down the village street, but Mary's mind cut out that picture of her love standing with Miss Pussy at the inn door.

Mary felt older and wise. She had never given up the idea that one day she might meet Jem Farr on equal terms. Why, weren't the papers full of marriages made between servants and their betters?' But how would she ever meet him or find him even, tied as she was to Mistress Moore, the tanner's wife and all her brood of troublesome children. Mary had once thought Georgie Moon a handful, but the noisy Moores—and Humphrey. She had forgotten him as well. He went with those things parcelled up like a bundle and pushed to the back of her mind, things that Milly Cater dragged always to the fore in whispers of bedding and getting with child. At that very moment, Mary was wishing she might never see an infant again.

She came out into the sunlight and a Close, crammed full with carriages. Gentlemen in tall hats were handing their ladies down. Mary loved the new bonnets they were all wearing, helmet shapes decked with flowers—and small ringletted hairstyles.

'Was there ever such a place as Exeter for finery?' sighed Mary to herself, looking sadly at her plain stuff dress.

'The groom, the groom!' came a cry from a knot of people and Mary pushed forward. 'God bless the groom!' croaked an old wife in scarlet cloak and bonnet.

'Who is it?' asked Mary.

'Don't you read the paper? Why it's the finest wedding Exeter will see this year. Young "Turkey Watt" has got himself a lady. I knew him too when he was but a common sailor. Now he has found himself a countess.' Mary could not wait to see him—he had a breezy look and hair brushed back severely; he rolled a little as he stood beside his groomsman.

'Why, that is a clever fellow,' said a servant girl. 'They say she saw nothing else but his features and fine clothes!'

'And now he is married into money. Well, well!' Mary stood until the bride arrived. She did not see her wrinkles, nor her powdered cheeks—only the gown that fell straight to the ground in elegant lines.

'God save you, madam!' shouted the crowd. Mary stared on at the embroidered over-panels which swept like curtains, held in place by a belt with a winking diamond. The sleeves fell over the elbow, their creamy lace secured by the bluest ribbons. On the shoulders were diamond clasps and about the neck small jewels.

All her servant's dreams were in that gown. She put up her hand as if she could feel her ostrich feathers waving in the breeze already. At last she had found a way to see Jem...

Nearly all the guests had gone. Celia and Jem had decided against a tour as she was in delicate health and would have found the travelling too much. When they had danced together in the quadrille, he had noticed her heightened colour and the perspiration on her brow. She had been forced to withdraw from the dance and fan herself. She sat beside her handsome husband listening to the full orchestra her mother had hired for the wedding, but she had been glad when the musicians dispersed and the guests made their farewells. Celia had been almost too tired to look over the wonderful presents, but her mother had reminded her sharply of her manners and that the night to come was the most important in any woman's life.

When Jem had held Celia to him in the dance, he had felt no warmth from her slight body although the rooms were unbearably hot. Neither did he think of bed until Humphrey strode up to him and his wife and offered them a toast.

'To Jem and Celia. May this be the night you are jolliest; the finest sport you have ever—' He had been drinking too much and Jem gave him a warning glance. Celia was colouring more and clutching at his sleeve.

'I beg your pardon, Celia!' he said gently, 'but I must have a word with my friend.' He caught Humphrey's shoulder and guided him towards an ante-room.

'You've had too much to drink, Humphrey. Mind your tongue in front of Celia!' To his amusement, Humphrey put up his fists. 'Don't be silly, Moon. No bridegroom fights at his wedding!' There was a sneer about Humphrey's mouth.

'By God, Jem, I don't envy you even though she is a duchess's daughter. She's as plain as the cow—' Jem caught his shoulder angrily.

'Haven't you any manners, farmer's boy?' he said.

'Tch, tch,' said Humphrey nastily. 'Still when you have done your duty, you can be off elsewhere. Your fortune's safe now—!'

'Get out,' said Jem, contemptuously, beckoning a footman. 'Show Master Moon the door.' The footman called another and the two of them hauled him away, protesting loudly.

'What is the matter, Jem?' asked Celia, seeing the dark look on his face as he returned to her side.

'Humphrey had had too much wine, that's all!' She sensed she should ask no more.

Jem watched her go upstairs with her mother and her maids. His father walked slowly from the dining room supported by two servants.

'Make her a true wife, Jem!' he croaked and there was still a glint in his eye. Soon the duchess came down to join them. Her fat cheeks glistened and she laid a hand on Robert Castel's black sleeve and he leaned heavily on her as the servant stepped back. She turned to Jem.

'See you treat my poor lamb kindly. Oh la! you are so like your dear father.'

'Yes, your Grace,' murmured Jem, trying not to see his father's ghastly grin. 'I will.'

'You may call me mother now!' Jem could not. He watched them handed into their carriages, contempt in his heart.

The last person he saw downstairs was a maid who came over shyly to pour him more wine.

'Thank you!' She had dark curls and red cheeks and a freshness about her which did not smack of the tired town. 'Where are you from?' He could see she was trembling because such a great lord spoke to her kindly.

'From Somerset, my lord.' The soft burr in her voice reminded him of someone he knew.

'What's your name?'

'Maria, sir,' she curtsied.

'Here.' He felt in his pocket and produced a handful of gold. 'Take this—and remember my wedding day.'

'Thank you, my lord!' Her delighted eyes ate up his coins; she bobbed and ran off quickly. Jem leaned back, trying to remember what other brows had been so black, what other lips so full and red. 'Good night, sir!' She was peeping round the door, then fled, ashamed.

Suddenly, he was back in the dusky night near Witherage barrow. How could he have forgotten sweet Mary Willcocks with her bright eyes and honest heart? She was Devon to him as she rode behind in the saddle; as she clasped his shilling tightly. Where was Mary now?

'Oh, Mary,' he sighed softly, 'it would have been a warmer wedding if you and I were to lie together. But no, I have a duchess's daughter, who must be colder. I'll never be as free as I was with you.' He could see Celia's maid upon the stairs, giggling and beckoning. He put down his glass, strode over to the carved staircase and slowly climbed towards Celia and his marriage bed...

The thought of fine 'Turkey' Watt and his success with a fine lady, gave Mary courage. She peeped out of the curtained alcove and saw the haughty shop woman hovering over the dresses.

'Fetch me the silk!' ordered Mary imperiously. The woman hurried forward with the dress laid across her arms. She had done everything she could to please Mary since she had seen the small bag of coins Mary had been saving for months. At least Mrs Moore paid her eight pounds a year to relieve her of her screaming children. Mary had saved all day and night until she had enough to return to Birt. She had told herself so many times that if she looked a lady she could win Jem's heart. He would surely notice her once more! She felt sure there could be love in his heart too for her, because he had cared enough to save her from Humphrey Moon; to visit Brushford many times and spend the day hanging over the wall watching her churn butter and clean like a true housewife. If 'Turkey' Watt could do it, so could she! Hadn't he only been a common sailor who had captured a great lady? Sometimes, Mary hardly thought her plan would work, but anything was worth a try!

She looked at the silk, which was far too expensive. The woman was holding it up against her.

'Take it away! It doesn't suit my complexion.' She waved her hand disdainfully. 'Bring me the muslin!' It was a delicate white with strange foreign animals and hunting scenes embroidered on the sleeves. 'I'll try it.'

'I sold a similar to Miss Fane, the lawyer's daughter and—'

'Did you dress Mr Watt's bride?' challenged Mary.

'No, madam, but I hear the gown was—'

'Exquisite! But so were all we guests!' She could see the woman believed she had been there. Mary turned in front of the mirror with the white dress falling straight from her firm breasts. It didn't shimmer; there were no diamonds, but it was fit for a lady. 'I'll take it! And a cluster of feathers to match.' She had seen those from the peacock hung in the window and noted their price.

'Madam has taste,' cooed the woman. 'An indispensable to match perhaps?'

'I have far too many already,' replied Mary with some haughtiness. 'Undress me!'

When she returned to Moore's, she barricaded herself in her bedroom lest the children enter. Then she lay on the straw mattress with her boxes beside her. Throwing her arms behind her head, she planned how she would soon take leave of this dull house and return to Birt to steal Jem's heart...

She was tired after the long walk, putting out of her mind that again she had left a good situation. She spread the contents of her bundle under cover of some trees, laid out the muslin lovingly and smoothed its creases. Then out came the feathered plumes which she arranged carefully in her curls.

In the shade of an oak, which dipped its mesh of black branches like a thick maze, she stepped out of her old black dress, folded it and put it away in her bundle, which she concealed behind a tree. She stood, stretching her naked shoulders under the muslin until the white dress hung perfectly upon her figure.

'No one will see me except Flora Jessup,' decided Mary. The cook had been a good friend of hers and had fed her often, letting her slip up the passageway to Squire Birt's library to look at the picture books.

'Then, afterwards, I'll find Jem!' she sang high-spiritedly. She walked on through the wood watching her dress did not catch on any thorns. At the fringe of the trees, she cleaned her clogs, which she had painted with hearth whitening.

Then she emerged from the undergrowth, like an apparition in the wood. She looked across to the house with its turrets and spires. Birt had never looked more beautiful to Mary Willcocks, who had hope in her heart. She had saved every penny for that dress and feathers. She knew the haughty shopkeeper had thought her a princess in disguise when she paid for it with all the grace of a lady. Now she felt like one— and Jem could not fail to love her when he saw her. Mary knew it in her heart. She was unsure how she would reach him, but she could wait.

Mary ran from tree to tree across the drive and into the kitchen garden. She was sure Flora Jessup, the Scottish cook, still worked there. She knew she would receive her. Mary stopped to set her headdress right beside the carp pond. She looked at herself, adjusting her dress. A queenly image stared back through the spongy spawn. Throwing back her head haughtily as she had seen the Misses Birt do, she rapped on the kitchen door.

'Oh, Lord!' screamed Flora Jessup at the white-gowned figure.

'Don't scream, Flora,' said Mary. 'It is only Princess Mary coming visiting the Birts!' She giggled.

'My God, girl, are you mad coming here pranked up like a lady?' Mary was surprised to see there were tears in Flora's eyes. 'What's the matter with you frightening ordinary folks so? Where have you been all this time? Why my lady even has been searching for you!'

'I am a lady now, Flora,' answered Mary, smoothing down the muslin.

'A lady, is it?' The Scotswoman's eyes narrowed in an unfamiliar way.

'I got this honestly. I saved for it, Flora. Do you like it? It came from the finest maker in Exeter!'

'You are mad!' Flora was staring at her. 'Turning up at my kitchen door, dressed in finery like the Misses Jemima and Emma!'

'Ah, but Flora, doesn't it suit me better?'

'It may, but however you came by it, it is not honest, Mary. What does the daughter of a poor cobbler want with a lady's finery?' Suddenly, Mary's eyes were full of tears.

'I tell you what she wants, Flora, what she has never had! But she will, I promise you!'

'She will not when her father hears of it—and the master and mistress. Do not let Lady Birt see you in feathers and white! The squire might blow your head off with his pistol!'

'Oh, stop sporting, Flora.' Mary was helping herself to a piece of game pie. 'I'm famished!' The Scotswoman watched her, hands on hips.

'Eat it up then—and don't drop it down that gown. If you hear the footman coming, run into the coal hole!'

'And dirty this? No thank you,' said Mary, stoutly, her mouth full of pie. She looked at Flora. 'Is Master Jem at home?'

'Ah, that's it!' said Flora, triumphantly. 'It's our young master you're after, Mary. You've missed him—I'm afraid. He went up to London months ago!'

'London?' The pie turned on her stomach. Jem had gone.

'Yes—and you know what else?' Mary shook her head. 'Dick, the new footman, the rest of the servants, and I myself are all alone. You needn't fear the squire will blow your head off. He has gone with the missis to—' Flora thrust her face into Mary's '—Master Farr's wedding.' Mary gave a little cry.

'Why,' said Flora triumphantly, 'I wouldn't be surprised if he is sprawling in bed this very minute!'

'Don't, Flora,' moaned Mary. Flora shook her.

'You've always been a dreamer, Mary. You're looking for the moon. A girl like you for a great lord's son? No, my Mary, you will have to settle for a labourer, who will strap you into sense and get some bairns upon you—'

'Not me, Flora Jessup!' shouted Mary, tearing off her peacock feathers. 'I will be a lady—maybe a princess too!'

'You're crazy!' said the astonished Flora.

'Perhaps I am—but I tell you—it is true. I've seen it—in my dreams—in the fire—'

'Get out of my kitchen, Mary Willcocks. Don't come back till you are sane again!'

'And that will be never!' cried Mary. 'Wait and see, cook!'

'I will wait for that day!' was the last scornful remark Mary ever heard from Flora Jessup...

They lay in each other's arms drowsily. Celia was full of loving for him. She had never felt such happiness as when Jem had entered her; now he had claim to all her secrets. She had worried a little that she had not been strong enough to take too much of him; but he seemed satisfied, murmuring endearments and caressing her quiet body. It had been nothing like she feared nor near as dreadful as the old maid had told her it would be, when she had prepared her clothes for her journey to London. Before he came up she had taken lemon juice, honey and sugar candy for her cough. Still afraid she would be unable to stand him, she had drunk a little opiate to calm her. This had made her drowsy, but easy. He must have liked her too as he was as gallant as any gentleman should be with never a hint of roughness.

Jem stared at the heavy drapes, making that four poster a love nest where no secrets could be spilled. He looked at his bride's sleeping face, her hair, severely cropped was just a wisp upon his own luxuriant chest curls. It had been like violating some brittle temple that shattered at its opening, that cried out at being ravaged. He had done his duty, which was a sweet one, but there had been no soul in it. She had had no fire for him either. Their coming together had been as children do at play.

'Oh, poor Celia,' he whispered. 'You think that is all it is. Maybe you are right and passion is wrong.' But, as Jem closed his sad morning eyes, he realised that all he had been dreading was come about and this was his wedded life beginning...

Mary walked away from Witherage the way she had come, looking at no one. She had collected her bundle, taken off her muslin and feathers and climbed back into her black stuff dress with the fraying wrists.

She looked up at a sky which smiled no more. A black despair took her heart as she set off into a wind, which smelled more of winter than of spring. All her work and longing had been for nothing. What could she do now? How far *was* London? Beyond Crediton, Tavistock, Honiton, where my Lady Birt got lace? She furrowed her brow as she thought of those unopened school books with queer-sounding names. She must not follow the setting sun, only the rising. She could hardly see his watery face for tears. Turning to where she believed the eastern sky to be, Mary Willcocks looked down at her clogs, noting the broken heel and started off along the high road.

CHAPTER 5

The doctor stood quietly by the side of the restless girl. She had taken the last of his beds that night, which were always filled by the piteous and starving. London was full of unfortunates; those who had lost all self-respect owing to suffering and starvation; who wandered the streets with neither the skill nor experience to equip themselves for survival in this monster of a city, which was stretching farther every day gobbling up the lands of the poor.

Ned Burgess felt her forehead. She was full of fever and raving in her sleep. Her voice had the burr of the West Country, which he recognised with a pang. Was he not from a country town himself with its quiet ways and peaceful stone? For the hundredth time, he questioned the ways of the wealthy and powerful, which caused girls like this patient to come into the city seeking work, when they should have stayed content with their families at home. He turned to Mrs Gall, who was wearing a sour look. She seemed displeased always without a cheery word even for the dying. Two minutes ago, she had scolded a fresh-faced nurse, who had made a simple mistake and in her confusion had added to it by almost scalding herself as she tipped up the boiling kettle.

'Have you tried to get the girl's name?'

'We did but she was raving!' answered Mrs Gall ungraciously. She had never worked with such a doctor. He took everything to heart. They had buried four children that very day and she could have sworn he had tears in his eyes when the youngest went. Sarah Gall had no time for sentiment. She had a job to do and often it was a ghastly one. If she broke into tears each time a patient died she would have been weeping all day. She looked at Dr Burgess coldly, wondering how he had fared in the army fighting Boney. He must have seen some blood then.

The youngest nurse approached, having refilled the kettle.

'Excuse me, sir!' Mrs Gall nodded her head, piercing the girl with a razor-sharp glance. 'I'm sure I know her name. I heard her shouting in the night. She said "I am no man's Mary"!'

'Well, that's not much to go on!' said the young doctor. 'But thank you—at least it's something. She probably has parents looking for her now. Perhaps we can get her history—*if* she survives!' He had seen fevers like that too often. If it was coming from the lungs it could be fatal. Ned wondered at his anxiety for seeing innocent youngsters suffer. He had endured so much sickness and butchery. Why hadn't he lifted twenty good limbs a day on the battlefield? But somehow back home, it all seemed worse. Then, London had been a good dream, now, it was a nightmare with its people starved of fresh air and sunlight.

Mary knew there was someone kind beside her bed, yet she could hardly see him, because her head throbbed unbearably and her eyes were almost blind. She cried out even more when that kind presence was withdrawn and a woman came out of the mist of heat and cruelly stuck a straw hard in her nostril, which made her choke on the blood in her throat. She shouted at her when she could speak, screamed to be back on the road to London again in the covered wagon. She could see her companions' faces, but could not recognise them as Witherage folk. She must have met them upon that terrible plain where she had wandered, weeping for Jem and home.

The ward reeled as Mary slipped in and out of unconsciousness. When she woke and looked at the fire at the end of the room and the other white beds, she knew she was in some hospital; then she was glad to slip into darkness again as she remembered the evil thing she had almost managed... It had been a very fine gate with an oak tree leaning over it. She had climbed the bars meaning to get over—and then those wicked thoughts had come. She had not meant to do it but she had been in such despair. No-one would ever love Mary Willcocks—Jem was gone—her father beat her cruelly—she was the laughing stock of the village—and Humphrey Moon? Was he not like every man out to tumble her in the ditch—and she would see Jem no more—so what was left in the world for Mary. She had balanced on the top bar of the gate and tied her apron strings around the branch. Then she had put her head in the noose of her pinafore. It had been only one step to the bright next world. As she jumped from the gate all Mary could feel were the strong arms of the carter close about her dragging her back from eternity...

Ned watched the girl struggling in the nurses' arms as they heaped the clothes upon her so she could sweat out the fever. He had been watching for any sign of change since he had been called into the ward to see a consumptive case who was approaching her end. The woman had lost all her strength and could not swallow, her eyes had sunk deep in her head and she was getting colder. After she died, Ned sat for a while with his chin in his hands. Then he had pulled himself together and directed his compassion towards the living. Since he had ordered

Mrs Gall to push the straw into Mary's nose, it seemed to relieve the pressure for the girl showed several signs of coming to. He felt her pulse which was still low.

'The leeches, Mrs Gall!' They lifted them one by one out of the bowl and Mary screamed each time she felt one fasten on her temples. Ned watched them working upon the affected part. He was glad because she seemed quieter. Mary could feel her life blood draining away. She was dreaming of such a long time ago at the little school...

'You're a quick girl, Mary,' said the dame, 'but how can I teach a girl who is never on her stool? Where were you yesterday?'

'I was driving the horses, ma'am.'

'And what good will that be, Mary, when you are called upon to be a good wife and order your man's affairs?'

'I wish I was a man, instead of having to wear this ugly pinafore!'

'Take that for your sauce, girl!' cried the old lady, giving Mary a clout on the head...

'Unfasten the leeches!' ordered the doctor. 'She has had enough! Look at her pallor!' Mrs Gall pulled off their clinging mouths.

Mary put up her hand to stop the pricking...Milly Cater was a devil for that and her spitefulness made Mary howl, 'I'll bite you, Milly, if you pinch me again!'

'Oh,' screamed Milly. 'I was only joking!'

'What kind of joke is it to pinch like that?' asked Mary, putting her hand up to her cheek.

'If it was Walter, then it would be different!' teased Milly.

'Don't be stupid. What do I care for him? Let him pinch you instead. I shall have a wondrous man, a gentleman with curls and lace, with a velvet coat and silk breeches!' Milly's mouth dropped open at the words. Mary loved to see her and the girls hang on to her stories breathlessly.

'And will he—?' Milly jerked her head towards Walter Megs.

'No, not in the straw with Walter, but in a fine bed with silken sheets. I shall marry the gentleman first, of course and we—'

'Go on, Mary!' breathed Milly, drawing closer... and Mary saw her face was a kind man's and knew it had been another dream. Ned Burgess looked down.

'Prepare the poultices, Mrs Gall. I think we're getting to her now.'

'If you say so, sir!' said the nurse glumly. She was disappointed that she could not show the younger nurses how to bleed a patient from the back, or put clysters inside. She had seen it done before with much success. It never failed in cases of brain-fever such as this one. She had no faith in poulticing.

'I shall stay with her for a while and bathe her temples with vinegar and rose water,' said Ned, sitting beside the bed.

'You, sir?' gasped Mrs Gall.

'And why not, Mrs Gall? Haven't I lost four little souls today? I hope I shall not lose another!' He bent his head over Mary. Mrs Gall shook her head in disbelief. Dr Burgess must be losing his senses like the patient, in undertaking such a menial task.

Ned was tired of being cheated by death. 'Oh, God,' he said to himself, as he bathed Mary's temples gently, 'we have to learn more—or we'll lose the whole world!' The country girl was stretching out her hands to him for help. He took them in his own. 'Don't be afraid, Mary,' he said. 'We'll cheat the reaper. I shan't be fetching the Reverend Mr Pattendean just yet!' Mary stirred under his soothing touch.

'Why, Jem?' she said, staring vacantly into Ned's face.

'Not Jem—but Dr Burgess of St Giles.' He knew she could not understand; she was feeling around her breast with wild hands.

'Gone, all gone!' she cried and sat up wildly. The doctor laid her down.

'Don't use up the little strength you have left, Mary. Lie still!' Mary knew the pin and the shilling were gone.

'I have betrayed you, Jem, darling.' She was sobbing terribly. Ned Burgess shook his head as the fever rushed in again. Mrs Gall had heard her cries. She came hurrying across, a triumphant look upon her face, when she saw what little use the bathing had been.

'Shall we bleed her again, sir?'

'No—but poultice her feet. The warmth will ease her.'

When they applied the bread and boiling milk, Mary cried out fearfully as her father pushed her to the fire...

'Please, don't push me into the coals!'

'Step in the cinders, Mary!' urged the brute. 'Then you can dance all you want!'

'No, father, I beg you!'

'The dame said you were dancing in the yard, when you should have been learning!'

'I only saw the lovely maypole!' she pleaded, remembering the straight ash pole and the gay ribbons.

'You should have been quiet on your stool like the others. Not in the yard like a dunce! Now dance, thick head!' Mary could feel the searing pain.

'I will dance no more, father!' She gave a terrible cry...

'Stop poulticing!' ordered Ned. 'Let me see her feet! Why, the poor girl's been burned. Look at the scars!' He choked on the words.

'Haven't you seen men burned?' asked Mrs Gall, who could keep quiet no longer.

'I cauterized men, women, but never a maid!' Ned lost his temper completely. 'No more poultices! And if you question my authority again, I will have you brought before the Reverend, who is a charitable man and would not stand your cruelty!' Mrs Gall gave a frightened bob, picked up the bread and milk and swept off, driving her nurses before her.

Mary was left in peace for a while. She lay gasping for breath, sometimes putting her hands up to her ears to try and deafen their buzzing; other times, beating her poor aching head against the pillow. As that weary London day dropped into sleep, taking its impoverished people into their foul back-to-back houses or into the streets, Mary Willcocks was fighting for her life with as much will as she had tried to lose it.

The two men stood at the end of the ward. Ned Burgess looked white with tiredness. He was ready to drop asleep also after an exhausting day with only a young trainee to help him.

'You need a rest, Ned,' said the other. The Reverend Mr Pattendean was a good man, who found his duties at St Giles not only heavy but a blessing. To him fell the task of tracing those nameless beings who were carried in and out alive and dead. He had witnessed many horrors in the time of his governorship. His long shadow stretched itself in the firelight, up and across the mantelshelf to hover on the ceiling and stare down at another unknown female tossed on the London scrap heap.

Mr Pattendean turned his black hat in his hand and stared inside as if it might give him inspiration. Ned looked into the worried face, framed by powdered grey hair.

'She is called Mary. That is all I have been able to find out. And she is fond of a man called Jem.' The minister shrugged his shoulders.

'The two commonest names in this city.'

'She is from the West Country. I recognise the accent.' Mr Pattendean put a white hand on the doctor's sleeve. He could hear a note of homesickness in his young friend's voice.

'Ah! Had she any money or possessions?'

'A bundle. It was lying beside her on the steps. There was the usual in it, although—' he paused, 'one of the dresses had cost something. Probably given it by some lady she served. But there was something of interest.' He beckoned a nurse, who caught up a small iron box from the table and brought it to them. Ned turned the key and handed the minister the shilling upon a leather thong and the diamond pin. Pattendean turned the latter over.

'A thief—perhaps?' Ned looked across at the pale girl. He had seen women with sweet looks perform unspeakable actions, women who lifted men's arms from their bodies, as he had seen the Irishwoman do who had shrap in the face. He shuddered.

'We have no proof, Reverend.' The doctor did not profess any knowledge of men's souls, only their bodies.

'Could she have come by this honestly?' asked the clergyman wryly.

'You're the minister,' answered Ned, shrugging.

'I am—and often sorry for it.' That very day he had visited two unfortunate men sentenced to transportation for petty theft and who had cursed him and God for the injustice. 'I have grown too suspicious, Ned, in my old age. Will she live, do you think?'

'I don't know,' answered the doctor, wearily. 'But she has spirit and youth. If I do save her, I wouldn't like to see her turned over to the justices.'

'She will have a chance to explain,' said the minister. 'If she recovers, I will do what I can and find her a place in some honest house.'

'Oh, bless you, Pattendean. Well, I must be getting to my bed. It has been a hard day.' He took the shilling and placed it in the box.

'Goodnight, Ned.' The clergyman turned from the fire and Ned watched his black figure walk slowly across the ward. The doctor looked at the diamond pin the minister had handed to him. He had seen one like it taken from a dead French officer. He looked towards Mary.

'Perhaps Jem is a soldier, eh? Did he leave you wandering, poor little girl?' He locked her treasures away and gave them back to the nurse for safe keeping. Then he yawned, stretched his tired limbs and headed for his room.

They fetched him at three when the London sky was still yellow—black from its million fires.

'The young woman is dying, sir.' The messenger's face was ashen.

'When did she get worse?' asked Ned, shaking the sleep from his head and reaching for his breeches. He threw off his nightshirt and was still tucking in his clothes when he strode across the courtyard and up the stairs. The trainee was just as pale, part from lack of sleep and part from anxiety.

'I'm sorry, sir, but the girl is worse. I thought it best to send for you!' He slapped the boy on the shoulder and stared through the candlelight at Mary's face. This was the time of night when most were fetched to their heavenly home; when their spirits seemed weak and light, like morning birds for flight.

'Shave her head!' Mrs Gall hurried for the razor, her night bonnet flying wildly. If Burgess had blistered her earlier, the girl might have lived! 'The blistering-plaster?' he said to his junior, who rushed to prepare it. Ned hated doing this, but it was her only chance. If the disease had spread from the lungs to the brain, there was no hope.

It took some time to shear Mary's heavy curls, but they fell to the floor through Mrs Gall's fingers, leaving her like a shorn sheep under the woman's hands. The two men watched in silence. When it was done her small skull looked ridiculously white crowning such a red and swollen face.

'The plaster!' said Ned. They strapped it on and on. An hour later the blisters were rising—and another, ready to burst. Mary babbled like a mad thing, but she did not die...

She was under the open sky, driving Brushford horses through the rain which was hot and burned her face. Then she was diving in the carp pond at Birt, gasping as the water changed her peacock feathers to foamy bubbles. She was choking with the water in her lungs, but she rose to the surface again. In the cloudy sky above, she could see Flora Jessup's face, framed by the night-bonnet.

'I only want to see him!' she screamed, but Flora was pushing her down and away...

'She wants the minister,' said Mrs Gall, drawing back.

'Where is he?' cried Mary, catching a glimpse of frilled shirt. 'I will see him, I will!'

'Yes, you will,' soothed the man's voice. She lay, exhausted, as the prayers were read...

She could not see Jem in the pew between Squire Birt and his dark little wife. Instead a great fair fellow with a slouch hat and leather breeches was leering at her.

'Moon, Moon, be off with you!' screamed Mary...

Doctors and nurses stared.

'It is nearly dawn, my dear,' said Ned. 'There is no moon; only the sun waiting to rise.' She clutched at his hand and he gave it her gladly.

The fever broke in the quiet ward as day was breaking. Mary was drowning wet—and calm. The young nurse looked up and rang the bell. Ned Burgess came.

'I think—' she said, leading him to Mary's bed, '—she is gone, sir!' He leaned over, putting an ear to her breast. Then he took a small glass from his pocket and held it over her mouth.

'No, girl!' he squatted back on his heels. 'She's alive! The fever has broken!' He turned from Mary's bed, full of new hope. At least, the body was safe—now let the soul take care of itself.

Across the city in the great bedroom of Farr House, another girl was propped against her pillows, praying the night away and begging the dawn to come quickly and ease her pain.

Jem opened the door and glanced in to see if Celia was asleep. As usual he had left it late to come to bed. He found that if he did, Celia's drugs helped her on into the morning without the two of them being awake all night. But she was stirring. He entered, closing the door behind him, noting the pale, exhausted face with open eyes staring into the gloom. He approached the four poster quietly.

'What are you doing, love?' she asked in a hoarse voice.

'Getting ready for bed. And Celia—I've been thinking. Perhaps we should take a trip?'

'Not to the waters at Bath, Jem. It'd kill me. Nor Brighton. I couldn't bear the sea.' She was even afraid to return to Yorkshire where the cold wind swept across the moors and made her terrible cough worse.

'No, Celia, to Birt where the air is fine. It will do you good—and they are precious people.'

'I know, Jem, but I'm not well enough.' Her tone was pleading. 'I want to stay here with those I know.' She coughed. Hope was disappearing fast for both of them. Each night was worse than the last. It had been a weary marriage.

'Do you think we should sleep apart? Then you can rest.' He hated hurting her, but was at the end of what he could do.

'No, Jem, please stay! I'm afraid of the dark!' Her eyes were full of tears. He took her into gentle arms as if she was his sister. 'You don't have to kiss me. You can turn away when I cough,' she said anxiously. 'I'm afraid of passing you the disease. Perhaps we shouldn't sleep together any more?' Her expression begged for a lie.

'The physician says there's no harm in it. But, all right, I won't kiss you.' He could see her happiness at the falsehood. 'It is an obstinate cough, but it can be cured!' Jem couldn't bear to tell her what the doctor had really said with a grave look on his face.

'Then it isn't consumption?' She had feared so much when the surgeon had asked to see him.

'No, Celia. You know you're better than when he spread the pitch between your shoulders.' That treatment had been frightful. She shivered, remembering it, and clung to him greatly.

'Oh, it was awful, Jem!'

'I know, but you *are* somewhat better.' It comforted them both when he repeated the words. He had never loved Celia as a man should a woman, but he pitied her helplessness.

'Yes, I am, Jem—if only—' she hesitated, looking into his strong face, wishing he could pour that strength into her, '—if I could give you a son, you wouldn't be so sad, would you?' She traced the serious lines of his mouth with her finger.

'Don't worry about it, Celia. I'm satisfied as I am. There's plenty of time.' She lay quiet in his arms, remembering her mother's sly questions as to whether she was breeding yet. Then the coughing started.

Two hours later they had had no sleep and Celia was quite exhausted. To save waking her maid, Jem prepared an infusion of poppy leaves and roots that the physician had ordered. She was so weak he had to prop her up and hold the bowl to her lips. He watched her fall asleep soothed by the opiate.

He walked over to the window, stood watching the dawn streak the sky with pink. He closed his eyes. He could almost transfer himself away from this miserable city towards Devon, but not quite. The morning glow was pouring fire on the domes of London; touching porticos, bridges and balustrades with its warmth. Jem shivered and drew his robe about him. Then he sat down in a chair beside the bed, trying to remember the young man that once he'd been...

Through the good offices of Reverend Pattendean, the chaplain, Mary had been found a good situation with Mrs Matthews of 1, Clapham Place. The house was very different from any Mary had known in Devon; Mrs Matthews was exceptionally pious and spared no effort in training Mary in the ways of the Lord. If it had not been for Mrs Matthews's daughter, Betsy, life would have been very dull indeed. Betsy had a fine walk, an elegant figure and hair the colour of ripe Witherage corn. She had taken it on herself to teach Mary to write and read, in fact, to do all the things she had neglected in the past. After a long time in the Matthews's house, Mary was becoming quite accomplished.

'You've learned very quickly, Mary. I can't believe you never went to school!'

'Thank you, Miss, but it's true. I used to go dibbling and I drove the horses. But the dame didn't like me, so I ran away!' Miss Betsy laughed out loud. She was glad Mary had come to the house. She was always cheerful, except when she was thinking of home and her dead parents. She had told Betsy all about their funeral in Crediton. It had been so touching Betsy had cried when she heard of it.

'You know you'll soon have a hand like mine,' said Betsy, examining Mary's work. 'I must show Mother. It's so extraordinarily clever!'

Mary went out into the garden tying her apron strings. She loved Miss Betsy and, sometimes, regretted she'd had to tell her lies about her parents being dead. If she had given her real name, Mrs Matthews would have insisted on writing to Witherage. Then she would be forced to go home. So she was going to stay plain Mary Baker, the orphan from Crediton.

That morning, Mary had plenty to think about. She and Esther, the Jew's cook from next door had been planning the escapade for quite a time. They had even confided in Lucy Tippet, the milliner from whom Miss Betsy bought her hats and of whom Mary had become very fond.

The plans were laid at last and only the finer points had to be hammered out. Mary had been excited ever since Esther had invited her to Mr David Lear's wedding in Kennington. She just had to have some fun. She couldn't be reading the Bible the whole time. And she had played fair. She had asked Mrs Matthews for permission, but her employer had turned quite white at the thought.

'A Jew's wedding! Indeed you can't go. A Christian girl attending such a ceremony! You're far too young and inexperienced!' So that was it. Mrs Matthews never changed her mind.

As Mary walked slowly down the path, she paused to look at the flowers wilting under the frost. She bent to straighten one deadened head, feeling morbid and alone. What was it like in Witherage now? The ice would be drawing its veil over Squire Birt's pond and they'd be riding to hounds. Could three years have passed since she left all that? And Jemmy? Where was he now?

She was soon jolted out of her reverie by Esther's loud hissing. The Jewess was comical with two heavy lines for eyebrows and a hook of a nose. She soon cheered Mary up. Her chattering reminded Mary of those raucous crows which spread their gossip noisily through the churchyard elms at Witherage Church.

When their conversation was finished, Mary had the plan firmly in her head...

'I have a letter, Mistress,' said Mary, offering it. 'From Mrs Baynes. I think I know what it's about.'

'Well—' Mrs Matthews pursed her lips as she read it. Then she looked at Mary, who flushed. '—this invitation. Do you want to go to the christening?' Mary nodded.

'I'm friends with the lady's cook, Mistress. I should like to go and help.'

'Let her, mother,' said Betsy, reading the message. 'She works hard—and I told you about the lessons.'

'It would be more suitable than the other invitation, of course.' Mrs Matthews smiled rarely, but the corners of her mouth turned upwards for one moment. 'She is a good girl, I suppose. She has a good eye for the needle and quick wits!'

'Thank you, Mistress,' said Mary, relieved the plan was working...

Mrs Matthews looked her over carefully. Mary was afraid she would glimpse the red dress Lucy Tippet had lent her and which she was wearing under her sober Sunday blue chintz.

'Good!' said the mistress. 'You look decent enough. You must be back by eight. I can't have my servants wandering all over town in the night hours. And don't forget the baby's name!'

'I won't!' said Mary, itching to go because Esther and her man friend were waiting round the corner and would leave if she was late!

'No strong drink, mind. If you must taste it, make sure it's only a small port or lemon juice in water!'

'Yes, Mistress.'

'And taste the syllabub. Mrs Baynes makes an excellent brew.'

Mary finally made it. As she passed down the hall towards the back stairs, Betsy was watching her.

'Oh dear, Mary,' she said under her breath, 'what are you up to?' She turned back to the drawing-room, trying to think why Mary should be wearing red silk beneath the blue chintz...

They shook hands like two adventuresses outside the garden wall. If Mary had thought about it, she would have realised what a dangerous course she was taking, throwing off her blue dress in the protecting shade of the arched gate and opening her cloak to show off her red.

Yet, with her curls flying wild and the new gown, she felt freer than she had done since she first came to London. With the discarded dress bundled into the back of the waiting cart, she was ready to see what a great city was really like. She had had no chance at all to see the capital. First, she had been ill, then she had been in Mrs Matthews's claws. She laughed out loud.

'Your friend's in a good mood,' said the driver, looking at Mary with admiring eyes.

'Keep your glances for me,' said impudent Esther, throwing her arms round his neck. That brought Mary a little to her senses. However she was feeling she could never be as free as that with a man.

'I have to be back by eight,' was all she could think of to say. Her two companions laughed and looked at each other. Suddenly, Mary was reminded of that frightening journey she had first made to London with the carter and his companions. The two women, Horse-Teeth and Blue-Dress! She'd almost forgotten them. They had been a dangerous pair too, dragging her between them and dropping her on the steps of the hospital. She had never trusted them either. What was she doing deceiving her mistress?

'You're not regretting it?' said Esther.

'Of course I'm not.' Mary spent the rest of the time looking at the quality passing. Her eyes followed each dark young man who passed by on a horse. It gave her something to do while Esther and the driver behaved indiscreetly—and it made her think of Jem. He was somewhere up West, but where?

'What's the matter, Mary?' asked Esther boldly. 'Are you thinking you want a man like this one? He's a great hand at lots of things!'

Mary felt her cheeks go red, but something was throbbing within her. Was she longing for a man? She didn't know, because she'd always been faithful to Jemmy and thought nothing of anyone.

'Aren't you ever goin' to marry?'

'I expect so, but he'll be a Christian gentleman.'

'And where are you going to find one of those? Most likely it'll be a lad who humps milk or carries a coal hod!'

'I do love—' Mary was angry, then remembered what she was saying. She broke off.

'He's bedded you?' shrilled Esther.

'No! And he won't until we're wed!' The driver stared at her red cheeks.

'I think this Jewess is no companion for you, girl, if you feel like that. You'd best get down before she leads you into some devilry!' Esther turned and slapped him. He grasped her to him, then kissed her full on the lips.

'See what you're missin', Mary?' purred Esther...

Mary didn't miss anything. She stared at it all and stored it away in her memory. She had come into another world, full of black-haired men with wild eyes, black coats and aprons. The girls had covered heads and kept their eyes down.

It was all so new she asked question after question.

'Do you never hold your tongue, Mary?' asked Esther sharply. 'You will see Master David and his bride soon—when they return from the synagogue. Then we'll feast like queens!'

'Is a synagogue your church?'

'Yes. We've had a fine new one built. Jews set much store by their religion and marriage.'

'So do we!' cried Mary, thinking of the minister at Witherage. Like Mrs Matthews he would never have approved of her attending a Jew's wedding.

'Your gentlemen have many whores!' tormented Esther.

'I don't know what you mean,' retorted Mary, thinking of Jem.

Then she heard the music, thin and merry like the Brushford shepherd at his pipe.

'Come on,' said the cook to Esther. 'Take your friend upstairs. She wants to see the Kallah and the Chatan!'

'Bride and groom!' explained Esther pertly.

The bride was so beautiful it made Mary gasp. Her small features were perfect; when she moved, gold rattled on her waistcoat. David dealt in jewels and coin and he brought his bride a magnificent heritage. The Lears had been goldsmiths for centuries and this match was what he had wanted most. He was getting a rarer gem than any in his shops. He looked at her lovingly. Mary watched them from her corner and the feelings were stirring within her once more.

'Why've you such a long face?' asked Esther grinning. 'I'll find you a Jew to cheer you up as soon as the feast begins. Come on!' She pulled at Mary's sleeve.

She was as good as her word, bringing over a dark young man with a sad look. He had an air of Jem about him, so Mary was polite.

'Your curls are lovely. You should always let them free,' he said.

'Your women don't.'

'Daughters of Jewry must cover their heads.'

'What? Even in the house?'

'Men can see their hair sometimes.' He smiled. 'We have to wear a hat too.'

'You wear cloaks,' she said, 'like we do, but you have hoods with points!'

'You ask a lot of questions.'

'How else should I learn things then?' She looked him full in the eyes.

'My, you are innocent for a Christian,' he replied softly, nearing her, 'and I wish you were a Jew.'

She blushed at his nearness. 'Haven't you ever met a woman of our race?'

'In the streets—but never spoken.' He said it so slyly she was sure he was mocking her.

'Will you show me some of your language?' She had been hearing it for hours and it annoyed her because she knew nothing.

'You want to learn the Torah? You're a strange one!'

'I don't know what you mean, but I'm going to try my hand at it.' She found a stick of charcoal and sat down. Esther danced by the two of them.

'Have you forgotten this is a wedding, Mary?' She was clinging to a young man who was making great eyes at her.

'Have you forgotten the driver?' retorted Mary sharply, taking no notice. She was engrossed in what he showed her. Yet as the hours wore on, the music fired her blood as much as the wine had done. There was the clapping of hands, the sound of strange instruments, the men servants were whirling about the room, crying out in Hebrew; the old folk were sitting in the corners, using their hands for talking and making their rings flash diamond fire.

The heavy curtains had been drawn early, so she and the boy were almost masked from view. Mary's face was burning with her eagerness to learn and the heat of the room. Suddenly he had his arms about her.

'Let me make your face burn more with my kisses!' She could smell the wine on his breath.

'I thought you were a good Jew, sir,' she shouted, pushing him from her.

'I thought you were a good Christian,' he replied with a sneer. She had to struggle with him; she had been mistaken. He was not like Jemmy at all!

'Esther, where are you?' She was looking for her friend. She found her half-asleep in a lad's arms. 'Get up, will you. I have to go home! It's past eight and we'll have to walk. Wake up!'

'Let me be,' slurred Esther. 'You go yourself.'

'For pity's sake,' cried Mary, 'I don't even know where we are.' She dragged Esther to her feet, looking round all the time in case the boy was following. At last they were free of the house. Mary hailed a passing cart. The man took them for street wenches, saying things that set Mary's cheeks flaming. Esther was coming to by the time they reached a great square.

'Esther, how far is it to Clapham Place? I have to go home!' The Jewess yawned widely.

'Don't take on so! You haven't been out like this for three years—or so you told me! We might as make the best of it. You're always going on about your fine gentleman. Now I'll show you some!' She took Mary's arm. 'This way—come on! The Royal West. It's fine at this time of the night. Let's go and look at the quality.' There were fine folks now all around them, mixing with the poor. Mary's eyes were dazzled by the lights but, although she was afraid, she was becoming excited again...

While Jem Farr fought courageously against his wife's sickness and his own growing melancholy, his mother's countrymen were pushing on into Russia to frighten the Czar, who did not relish a war.

In that spring of 1812, the *Grande Armée* was already at the Polish border and the young ruler of Russia was facing destiny and preparing his army. He was also fortifying the road to St Petersburg.

In London, news was sporadic and gentlemen, including Lord Castel were prophesying an end to Napoleonic nonsense. In the Peninsula,

Wellington too, was on the offensive and marching south to Badajoz. Twice the British had tried to take the fortress but had been forced to withdraw. This time, Wellington had hope. The clubs and coffee houses saw spring as a time of renewed vigour for England and Englishmen; but there were the heedless few, who only had pleasure on their minds.

When Humphrey Moon had first come to London with Jem Farr, the farmer's son had been an uncouth young man whose former recreations were cock fighting in barns and gulping ale in the kitchens of village inns. To him, Exeter had been the wildest place he had ever seen before the kindness of his lordly friend had provided the means of introducing him to a society, whose pleasures were openly sophisticated but secretly much more dangerous.

Jem had given him lavish rooms adjoining Farr House in the corner of the square. In the beginning Humphrey had been delighted with his apartments, but as his tastes changed and his vices increased, he became rapacious, contrasting his quarters with the spacious rooms and staircases of his aristocratic benefactor. To placate himself, he filled his rooms with luxuries, furnished by Jem's purse; invited fops, scoundrels and silly, elegant young men, who praised him to his face, but whispered behind his back that they suffered him only because he was a country clown with an amusing accent and the strength of a Devon bull.

Yet Humphrey was no fool! He despised them all for their womanish ways and manners; used their names to ingratiate himself with others more important than they and gained entrance by this, and his association with Jem Farr, to the smartest set in town.

The hope Jem had of bringing Devon to London in the shape of Humphrey Moon, had been abandoned as their difference in temperament; Jem's marriage and sadness and Humphrey's looseness, drove them apart. Humphrey tossed the remembrance of home aside like a worn-out boot and assumed the unscrupulous role of gamester, cad and lecher.

Yet Humphrey was in a strange mood that day; the chirping of nest-building starlings was suddenly reminding him of home. It had been a tedious winter in London and that green morning saw the farmer's son impatiently slapping his thigh, encased in fashionable breeches, with his horsewhip. If only his mother could see him now in smart riding clothes, she would hardly believe him her son, such a great gentleman he had become and with grand friends. It would take a catastrophe to get Humphrey back to dull old Brushford. He was finished with it all, but the farmer within him stirred occasionally when Witherage spring tumbled back in his consciousness.

'By God, are you ready yet, Meredith?' The earl's son yawned and his fat cheeks wobbled. George would rather have been snug in bed sipping his morning chocolate than riding in the Row with Moon. But the man was a comical fellow and was doing well for himself. Besides, his lady mother had charged George to be civil to any friend or kin of the Castel family. In fact, she had been a trifle distracted after Lord Robert had arrived and ensconced himself with her in the drawing-room for an hour and when George had casually asked her what the old cad wanted, she had been almost hysterical when she had given her son the orders. George had often wondered about his mother and that man, on account of the bad reputation he had with women, but he soon put it out of his mind, having far jollier things to do like chasing maids and dabbling in politics.

He looked at Humphrey, resplendent in stiff-crowned cap and popular Hessians. George preferred his own hussar boots as he felt tassels on one's shoes seemed slightly idiotic. He had wondered often how serious Jem Farr, the nicest Castel he knew, could love Humphrey Moon, and treat him so well, keeping him in good pocket in spite of the fact he had a sick wife to cope with, who grew sicker every month. George pitied Jem more now than he had done when he had been his groomsman. He hoped with all his heart, his lady mother would find him a healthier bride, but unfortunately, never a richer—George sighed; he had been overspending at the races of late and she had called him to task the very week before Castel came. George blamed the family lack of money on his worthless father, an earl who had got the mania for palace—building and squandered the Meredith fortune on follies and mock-Gothic.

'Ready,' he bumbled, tucking his frilled shirt into skin-tight breeches.

'Good!' Humphrey turned on his heel, cursing the fat aristocrat, who bored him to death. Jem had been the kind of companion he liked, but his benefactor had no time for anything now. Humphrey had tried to remind him how it used to be, but he had pretended not to listen. Besides, the only friend who ever dined with him now was 'the chocolate fellow' Grant, who was abhorred by society and only stuck to Jem because he himself was an outcast. And there was Celia—the farmer's son wished fervently that no woman ever got her real claws in him. With George puffing behind him, he strode to the stables, where the lad had saddled a fine piece of horseflesh.

As he and George turned their horses out of the gates, for some strange reason, Humphrey suddenly mourned Sweetbriar, whom his father had probably turned out to grass or was using to pull the small chaise. With the morning wind in his face, Humphrey headed for his ride in The Rows, remembering Witherage.

They jogged stiffly along, sweeping their caps to every sweet-faced girl they met. They made coarse jokes together while the grooms led their sweating mounts back to the stables, then they strode back to their rooms to change for the day's business at their favourite coffee house. Humphrey was not fond of politics. Indeed he would have been entirely ignorant of the Prime Minister's assassination, if George had not made such a fuss about it. Humphrey was sure it was because the Earl's son had a rightful seat in the House of Lords and liked to advertise the fact to a friend, who after all was only a farmer's son. Humphrey would not have cared if a dozen Spencer Percevals had ended their miserable lives in the House of Commons that May as long as it did not affect Jem's aristocratic purse, which was a continuous source of revenue.

The day wended its merry way through to evening where they danced in the hot Assembly Rooms and had their eager fingers smacked by countless fans. Finally—sprawling in one of Jem's carriages, Humphrey said goodbye to an exhausted George and set off for his favourite club, the notorious Brooks's where a man could lay a bet on anything even to the length of the jades' skirts, as they paced continually up and down outside on the pavement.

He ate too well and had the heaviness come on him which he had often felt in Brushford when he had raided his mother's dairy and stuffed himself with Mary Willcocks's butter and barley loaves. As he picked up his wineglass for a refill, he wondered why he kept thinking of home. It had been the same all day although he had not the slightest intention of returning there ever and could not be pining for Devon acres.

He tipped the liquid to and fro morosely, squinting through the cut glass towards those common noses pressed to the windows of the club. So many folks came to peer at the celebrities within and Humphrey felt superior again not knowing how foul it was to be poor and on the outside looking in. Through the shining opacity, he was suddenly conscious of a face. He put down the wine and looked at the window straight.

His heart gave a mighty lurch. If he had been superstitious he would have said it was witchcraft. He had had Witherage on his mind all day and now it was here—standing with nose pressed to the window! She was here whom he had not met since he pressed his hot body on hers in the mucky ditch.

'Humphrey, lad, it's your lucky night!' he muttered happily as he stared, only half-believing, at the pretty features of his mother's former maid, Mary Willcocks. She was standing open-mouthed watching her betters at play in Brooks's…

Mary stared up at the building with its white fluted arch and handsome windows. The pillars were almost like the Greek capitals which supported the front of Birt Park, but this was not creamy Devon stone only white brick. The five square-headed windows were blazing with light.

'Look at them gaming,' said Esther. Mary craned her neck.

'What's the place called, Esther?'

A man on her left laughed. 'Have you never heard of Brooks's, wench? Nor Whigs? Nor the Prince of Wales?'

Mary knew he meant to offend her. 'Of course,' she replied, turning her head to the windows. The men inside were all she'd ever imagined. The tables were loaded with victuals, custards, sweetbreads, peaches. The diners' clothes gleamed under the chandeliers. There was a young man near the window, with close-cut hair, biting through a peach skin.

'That'd make you forget your gentleman!' gesticulated Esther.

'It would not, but I grant you, he is fine!'

'You've hit it,' said the man who was still at her elbow. 'He's the lion of London—the talk of the town—and he champions the people. Why, he spoke up for us in the House of Lords!'

'Who is he?' asked Mary. She was thinking of Jem again and how be believed in good.

'Lord Byron, wench. He's also the scandal of this town.' At that moment, the young lord stretched himself lazily and looked into the crowd. Mary, like all the women around her, thought he was staring at her alone.

'He has an eye for every woman,' said another voice from the crowd. It was as if he heard. Lord Byron stood, was up from the table and walking out of sight.

'What a dream!' cried a woman. 'Would he take me to bed!' There was laughter that made Mary's cheeks flame.

'Doesn't that beat Mrs Matthews and her pious cant?' whispered Esther mischievously.

They had some trouble getting rid of the man who had first spoken to them. Eventually, they gave him the slip at the far side of the square…

The heavily-built fair man stumbled from Brooks's, determined to keep Mary in sight. 'It's a miracle,' he kept saying to himself, 'or it's that damned port! I know it's her. Thinner than when she was in Brushford, but what a figure!' His carriage dawdled on behind him, while he shouted instructions to the driver as to whom he was following. Finally, he climbed in and sat back against the cushions.

'If you lose them,' he screamed at his coachman, 'you'll be out on your ear.' Humphrey knew he had no need to worry. The man would be too frightened to let the girls out of sight. 'Now, Mary,' he said out loud, 'this time I've really got you. Once I find out where you live, who knows?' The idea put him in a good mood and he spent the next hour imagining what it would really be like having Mary at last and doing what he wanted with her…

'The baby's name, if you please!' She had waited up for Mary's return. When the girl hadn't come home, she had sent the cook round to Mrs Baynes. The woman had come home, red-faced and eager to carry the tale that Mary Baker had been lying; the baby had died at birth and there had never been any christening.

Mary twisted her fingers in her dress. She felt too tired to brazen it out. The mistress knew it had all been a falsehood. She might as well face up to it. Still, there was just a chance!

'Edward Francis,' she lied. It was no use.

'And was there feasting and dancing?' There was an ugly deep line at the corner of her mistress's mouth.

'Yes, but I only—'

'Don't say another word, Mary. You've broken my heart with your lies!'

'Who says I'm lying?' asked Mary recklessly.

Mrs Matthews jumped up and boxed her ears. 'Take that, and that!' She was raining blows one after the other and Mary was ducking to avoid them. Suddenly, Miss Betsy was between them.

'Stop it, Mother. What has Mary done?'

'She has openly disobeyed me, Betsy. She has been to a Jew's wedding!' Mrs Matthews staggered back to her chair.

'Mother, you've overdone yourself. What have you to say, Mary?'

'Who said I'd been to the wedding?' challenged Mary, her tiredness leaving her.

'The cook,' panted Mrs Matthews. 'I have it all.'

'Have you, Mary?' asked Miss Betsy sternly. Mary was sorry to have offended her.

'I wanted to so much. I'm sorry, Miss. I did no harm.'

'After midnight? I warrant she's lost her virtue,' wailed the mother.

'I haven't. I only danced, Miss Betsy.'

'With a man!' cried Mrs Matthews. 'Imagine sporting with the other sex, unchaperoned!'

'Oh, Mary,' said Miss Betsy, knowing now why the girl had been wearing red under her dress. 'You have made me sad.' Her blonde hair fell about her shoulders. Mary thought she looked as pure as an angel.

'I did no harm, Miss. The Jew boy was showing me how to write his language. I've the piece of charcoal in my pocket. Look!'

'Don't show me any more,' cried Mrs Matthews. 'She's a lost soul. I know it!'

'Don't take on so, Mother. Mary's come home safe.' Miss Betsy was looking for the smelling salts.

'All lost, lost,' moaned the old lady. Mary was just about to escape, when she pushed her daughter aside. 'Don't slink off like the night cat you are! You'll be locked into your room until I can fetch the Reverend Pattendean to speak to you.'

Mary couldn't stand the thought of his great solemn face thrust into hers.

'Lock me up, Mistress,' she pleaded, 'but don't send for that man of God!'

'Upstairs, you wicked girl,' were the last words Mary heard from her mistress.

She lay on the bed, tears rolling down her cheeks. She'd only wanted to see the wedding. What had she done? Frowning, she took a piece of paper and stubbornly formed the words she had learned. She had stored it all perfectly. There were the Kallah and the Chatan, all remembered:

'When I am a princess,' she said, lapsing into dreams. 'I shall sleep under a golden canopy and wear gold coins in my turban. I shall speak a very strange language, something like this one. It won't be ugly like the words of Mrs Matthews, neither will it be solemn like Mr Pattendean, but it will have gypsy music in it.' She closed her eyes, worn out by the day's happenings. She imagined herself surrounded by slaves. She would never box their ears, but be kind to them—and seated on the throne beside her would be a man as dark as Master David Lear, except he wouldn't be a Jew, but have eyes as dark as a Spanish gentleman and wear a diamond pin in his cravat...

She woke at five to a click. She was sure it was the key turning. She was right. The door stood ajar. She suspected it was Miss Betsy who had freed her. She put on all her dresses, one after the other, tied the rest of her things into a bundle and made sure Jem's pin and shilling were close to her breast. Peeping round the door and seeing no one, she ran down the backstairs, drew back the bolts and slipped into the lane...

The coachman had been ordered to wait for as long as it took for the girl to emerge. There was no way he could question Mr. Moon, who was a pig of a master if thwarted. So he had spent a terrible cold night up on the box while Moon snored on inside. How many times had the coachman wished he had never been put into that wild young man's service, but he was only a servant after all. He had seen things since working for him that had made him sick. He was sorry for the girl whoever she was or whatever she'd done to cross Moon.

The driver was almost asleep and half-frozen when he jarred into wakefulness. Their quarry was coming out and into the lane. As she passed the coach she glanced at him in a frightened way. He thought she had probably finished her night's work and was scared of being discovered. He shook his head and blew out his breath into the freezing air. 'God, these women of the streets; they must have a constitution like the devil.' Still, he couldn't let her get away or he would suffer for it.

When she was out of earshot, he bent down and shouted, 'Sir, sir, wake up. The woman's on the move again!'

He was rewarded by curses and Mr Moon's thick voice: 'All right, you lout, stir the beasts and yourself. Get after her!' The coachman pulled his clothes straight, wiped his running nose on his sleeve and twitched up the bays, who were still as stones.

With Humphrey throwing himself about inside to shake off a murderous mood, the coach and its occupants swayed sedately behind at a respectable distance...

Mary was hot even though the morn was freezing. She had put on all her dresses to save carrying baggage. It was the only way to travel when you were in a hurry. She had done it before and doubtless, would do so again. Mary had no illusions about her plight. Once more she was alone and friendless in London but, at the moment, all she cared about was putting a great distance between herself and Mrs Matthews. She imagined the old lady's reaction when she awoke and found her gone. Mary smiled at the thought but she was sober again soon when she remembered Miss Betsy. The lady had been very good to her indeed, even in this last act of setting her free. One day, she would write to Miss Betsy in the fine hand she had taught her to let her know Mary was settled at last.

Mary hesitated at a street crossing. Which way? East seemed the only possibility. She had followed this road before once when Mrs Matthews's cook had taken her to see her sister beyond Blackfriars Bridge.

As Mary pushed past the early morning risers, she was wondering how she would find another situation without references or money, which was worse! Suddenly, she had a glimpse of the dome of St Paul's.

It did her good to see it. A church ought to give comfort to the poor! She could do with meeting some kind folk like those in St Giles'. Ned Burgess had been an angel. Yet, there was no way she could return because of Reverend Pattendean.

She paused to look in a baker's window. The sight of bread made her stomach turn but, here, there was no kindly Witherage baker, only a scowling face thrusting at the window and signing her to be off!

It was then she remembered that journey she had made with the cook. The woman had said something. But what? Mary paused again to think. Wasn't there a place somewhere round that took women in? She was sure of it but she couldn't remember the name! Mary had asked the cook if it was a nunnery.

That was right! And she had said, 'Aye, it's a nunnery, sure enough. Full of chaste women!' And she had laughed as if it was funny. Mary had meant to ask her why, but she had forgotten. A nunnery was exactly what she wanted. Of course she didn't want to be a sister, but she wanted food and shelter. She'd try it. When Mary made up her mind, she carried on with the plan as quickly as possible. The traffic was heavy now, a bedlam of carriages and carts. There were street cries tearing through her ears and all was noise and bustle. Who could she ask?

There was a middle-aged man looking into a draper's window. He looked kind and approachable.

'Sir,' said Mary, '—can you direct me to the nunnery in Blackfriars Road?' To her amazement, he pulled up his coat collar and ignored her.

She shrugged and approached another man, who was selling hot chestnuts: 'Can you direct me to the nunnery in the Blackfriars Road?' He spat on the pavement.

'What? Are you worn out by your night's work?'

'What do you mean?' She was angry that he thought she was a street woman.

'Get off and ply your trade somewhere else!' She was about to retort rudely when a woman in a shawl, wearing two bedraggled feathers in her hair, stepped right in front of her on the pavement.

'Get going!' she said. 'This is my patch. Get off or I'll box your ears!'

'Look,' said Mary, 'I was only asking for the Blackfriars nunnery!'

'Were you?' asked the woman sneeringly. 'Then it's the best place for you.'

'You know it?' cried Mary, thinking about breakfast.

'You're artful,' said the woman, 'I know it as well as you do. And on the right day too.'

'What day?' The woman laughed at the question.

'The first Wednesday of the month. What else?'

'Yes, the first Wednesday of November, that's right!'

'You are cunning,' repeated the woman. Mary didn't know why she was, but the woman was still smiling, so she smiled back. 'Some will do anything when it's cold and trade's falling off. Come on then, walk along with me. I'm going past there!'

Humphrey had been watching Mary from behind the curtains. He had been right all along. Mary Willcocks had taken the job he had always imagined she would. A man would do anything to get hold of her even on the farm. 'Well, Mary,' he said under his breath, 'if you'd asked me just what you'd asked those two I wouldn't refuse you!' He grinned. All he had to do was get rid of the old whore and reveal himself to Mary. Suddenly the coach came to a jarring halt.

'What's up?' he shouted. 'You haven't lost them, you fool?'

'No, master, but look where we are!' The driver was delighted; the devil seemed to be on the girl's side instead of his usual place, at Humphrey's. 'The Magdalen!'

'What?'

'Yes, sir, she's going in!'

'Never!'

'She is!' Humphrey couldn't believe it. After waiting all that time and all night, he'd been cheated again.

The coach and bays stood still, the coachman waiting for orders. Humphrey was drumming his fists together trying to think what to do. She would be in there for some time. They always were until they tired of it and wanted the free life of the streets. There was nothing for it but to go back.

The coachman heard his grunted orders with relief. Now he and the mares could eat. As the bays wheeled their way towards Farr House, Humphrey sat there silently planning how he could go about getting Mary Willcocks out of that prison.

CHAPTER 6

A grille in the middle of the door of that dismal building slid open.

'Yes, what's your business?'

'I'd like to come in.'

'You're too late!'

'What do you mean?'

'We took the others in over an hour ago!'

'I'm sorry,' said Mary, not understanding, 'but I've come a long way. I'm very tired and much distressed.' She had to play up.

'Wait,' said the woman. Mary sat on the top step, then she heard the door bolts sliding. There were two women in the doorway. One was the portress, the other looked like a lady in a black silk gown. Mary curtsied, thinking it was the proper thing to do. She didn't know how to treat sisters having never met them before. Somehow she had imagined they would be like nuns she had seen in picture books.

Suddenly the lady stretched out her arms. Mary hung her head.

'No, don't hang back from the Lord's forgiveness.' To Mary's embarrassment she saw the lady had tears in her eyes. So they were going to let her enter! Mary was so happy to be out of that noisy street and into warmth and breakfast! Yet there seemed to be no comfort. The great hall was bare; no chandeliers nor drapes; only long cotton at the windows, hanging stiff and straight and there were candles burning in iron sconces to light that wintry morning.

She was led across the echoing space to a small room with a fire in the grate.

'Undress,' the portress said.

'Why?' asked Mary, thinking of all the dresses she was wearing.

'If you wish to enter this place, you do as you are told,' said the lady. Mary nodded. She could see a carved kneeler with a straw sack. She supposed she had to undress to pray. She stood by the fire and was as far as her petticoat and drawers when the door opened. Mary looked into the woman's face, which was surrounded by plaiting descending from the plain, bordered cap she wore. 'This must be a nun,' thought Mary.

'Good morning, sister,' said Mary politely. The woman was staring at her, then her face was smiling. She had the most enormous teeth like the horse at Brushford. Suddenly, she grabbed Mary and kissed her.

'Don't you know me? I'm Jenny, who was in the cart with you. You remember? When you tried—' her voice sank low and she was looking about as though she was afraid of being overheard.

'I can't believe it,' replied Mary. 'The London road—outside Calne, when I was sick.'

'Shhh. If you come in here, you're not allowed to speak anything of wickedness.'

'Beg pardon,' said Mary. It was a miracle to see the woman again and in here. Mary hadn't liked either of them then, but she could have kissed this one now.

'Are those all your clothes?' asked Jenny, indicating the heap. Mary nodded and the woman shook her head in a surprised and sorrowful way. 'You have to take them all off!'

'Even these?' said Mary, shivering. She wasn't too keen on standing naked before this strange woman. She had been taught by Mistress Moon never to be seen without drawers.

'Even those.' The woman nodded, 'You will be clothed in righteousness from now on.' Then she picked up Mary's dresses, tut-tutting at the red silk from Lucy Tippet's.

'You're not taking them away?'

'You'll have to dress like the rest of us while—you're in here,' said Jenny. 'If you leave, you can have them back.'

'Oh,' said Mary, satisfied. She shivered again from cold and embarrassment as she stood naked before the fire. Then Jenny disappeared only to reappear with two more women, one dragging a bath tub and one with pitcher and towels. Then they brought kettles in from the kitchen and poured icy water in to cool the boiling.

Mary stood still, trying to cover her breasts with one arm and the private place with the other.

'No need to be shamed in the sight of your sisters. We are all naked in the sight of the Lord!' canted Jenny and the rest.

'Amen!' said Mary.

'Get in!' Mary put the tip of a toe into the water. She hadn't bathed for six moons at least. She was used to casting off her clothes in the Brushford woods and sporting in the lake, but not in a bath! However, when she did get in the water was soothing.

'Now—I'm charged,' said Jenny, 'to ask you if you are clean?'

'I've only just got in,' replied Mary.

'I mean of disease!'

'Yes, I never have to go to the doctor!'

'And you've come here of your own free will?'

'I certainly have,' said Mary, wondering what to make of this strange examination. She stroked herself tenderly with the smooth rainwater.

'Now—your hair!' Suddenly, Jenny had a great pair of shears in her hand.

'No, please,' shouted Mary, trying to rise and slipping about. 'Not blistered again!'

'Not bald,' said Jenny, 'just a precaution against lice.'

'I don't have lice,' said Mary. Her curls were thick and luxurious. They had grown more since they had been shaved off in St Giles three long years ago.

'It doesn't matter,' said Jenny. 'It's the rule!' She began clipping them over the side of the bath. 'So perish all vain and wicked ways,' she muttered as mounds of curls fell to the floor. Mary moaned. Then, suddenly, Jenny had her by the shoulders and was pushing her head down in the water.

Mary thought she was drowning and began to struggle, splashing water everywhere. Jenny, who was a strong woman with arms like a prizefighter, let her head up then.

'What were you doing?' spluttered Mary, her eyes stinging.

'First your body, then your head, now your heart,' said Jenny. 'The dirt of the streets is off your frame. Now you're really my sister.' It was then that Mary began to see much of Mrs Matthews in the grinning Horse-Teeth. The latter hoisted her up and began to towel her body roughly. Mary stooped for her underthings but they were disappearing.

'Stop. I have some valuables!' She remembered Jemmy's pin and the shilling.

'Sinful wages. They'll be safe here in the Magdalen,' sighed Jenny.

'This is what I'm afraid of losing,' said Mary, taking hold of them.

Jenny put up her hand as if to ward off the evil. 'Poor little sister,' she said. 'They'll be safe here.' She stretched out her hand and Mary gave them up. It seemed an honest place, but if she lost them she'd have the justices in!

Mary put up a hand to her head. 'Have you a glass so I can see?'

'There isn't one in the whole place. We don't need them in here.'

'Oh,' said Mary, wondering where she had come. The door opened again and another sister handed her clothes. There was a grey stuff dress and a white tippet, but no ugly cap to put on. Mary had always hated wearing a servant's cap, which made her look bald. While the other watched she dressed herself in the new clothes.

Then she was taken out again into the dark corridor lighted only by two candles. Mary could smell beeswax and knew that someone had sweated a great deal to bring up a polish which showed even in that dim light. Finally she was ushered into a room.

The lady whom she had seen earlier, was seated at a table. With her was another woman and a man in a black coat, whom Mary knew was a minister by his grave look.

'Be seated,' said the lady. 'I am the superintendent of this institution.'

'Yes, ma'am,' said Mary solemnly but, all the time, afraid that her stomach would rumble and break the quiet spell of the place.

The man stood and pointed at Mary. 'So young and so depraved.' It was a new word for Mary, but she could see it was a bad one by their faces. She held her tongue, thinking of breakfast. He was coming round the table towards her. He put a hand on her shoulder. Mary could feel its coldness through the stuff dress. He reminded her of Reverend Pattendean. She could feel him looking across at the seated company.

'We should make merry and be glad,' he said, 'for this is our brother who was dead and is come to life again. He was lost and he is found!' Mary wasn't sure if she was supposed to reply 'Amen!' but she did.

It had been the right move; the superintendent was smiling. 'Good girl. You know your scripture. You must have had some upbringing.' Mary realised she was supposed to open up then and tell them who she was and where she came from, but she kept quiet remembering Mrs Matthews. 'You were tempted?' The lady's voice was sad. Mary decided it was best not to upset her or she wouldn't get any food. She nodded. 'And fallen?'

Mary certainly had—under Humphrey Moon! She shut her eyes, hearing the other woman say quietly, 'The poor girl can't stand the remembrance of her own wickedness.' Mary would have liked to ask her what she meant by it, but didn't dare.

'I shan't press you more today,' said the minister, withdrawing his hand, 'because I know what a wicked world we live in. Are you sorry for all you have done?'

'I am!' said Mary truthfully. If she hadn't gone to the Jew's wedding, her stomach would have been full. The thought of food made her head dizzy.

'Careful, she's swooning,' cried the superintendent.

'It's the Devil going out of her,' said the minister.

'The form! Give it to her,' said the other woman.

'Can you read?' asked the superintendent when Mary was coming to.

'A little,' said Mary, her wits returning.

'It's a petition,' said the minister. 'In it is a request to enter this house of God. There are blanks throughout for your name, your original parish and address. That is if you had any!' He looked most severe.

'I did,' said Mary indignantly. She wasn't having anyone think she was a beggar woman. 'I came from Crediton in the County of Devonshire. My parents are dead. I have no home in London.' She was hoping they'd believe her lies. Anyway, how could they check up? It wasn't really right to deceive them but, if she did not, they'd throw her back in the gutter. She answered the rest of the questions glibly, wondering how she had such a capacity for lying and making it seem all truth. When they were finished and she had signed the petition, she spoke of her own accord. They stared in amazement.

'Your Reverence and good mistresses, what do I do here in the Magdalen?' She had to find out.

'Why, girl,' the minister replied, 'be cleansed of your sins and learn to be useful again by earning honest bread.'

'Oh, praise God,' said Mary, meaning it with all her heart. She had been afraid it might be wearisome work like scrubbing, only fit for an Irish labourer.

'There is one thing,' said the superintendent, 'you are never allowed to speak of your former life. All of it must be forgotten.' It was wonderful! Much better than she had dreamed. She didn't want to speak of anything that concerned her personally.

She was taken afterwards and given bread, milk and meat. There were others eating and mighty rough some of them appeared. Mary was glad she didn't have to talk to them. After, she was shown to a dormitory by the portress.

'That is your bed! May you never share it with another!'

'I won't,' Mary replied, 'besides, there's no room!' She wanted to giggle. The woman looked sharp at her and Mary stopped sporting. She was shown extra clothes hanging in a long cupboard, then taken back into the hall, which was full of girls in pale grey dresses bending silently over long tables. At the end was a dais where a dame was seated.

'And what can you do, girl?'

'I'm a fair hand at cooking. I can look after young ones and babies. I can drive horses, dibble and weed. I've milked cows and goats. I drive sheep —' Mary was determined to make a real job of it. She was sure she could hear faint whispers, even giggles again.

The dame looked angry. 'Household tasks—' She was looking at a paper. 'Mary Baker. Nothing else.'

'I see,' said Mary, thinking.

'Embroidery?' The dame's voice was cold.

'No, ma'am.'

'Gloving?' Mary shook her head.

'The making of gowns?'

'No, ma'am,' Mary was feeling rather foolish, knowing sixty pairs of eyes were fast on her from behind.

'The loom?' Mary nodded, looking bright.

'Yes, ma'am. I can use the shuttle, but I drop it very easy!'

'So, Mary Baker, you can do something useful after all. Here, everything is done for God's glory.' The dame signed to the woman seated below her. It was Jenny Horse-Teeth! 'Take this girl and show her some fine needlework.' Jenny showed Mary to a vacant seat, threaded a strand of silk and began some simple stitches on the back of an old glove.

Mary sat quietly and watched with her usual concentration. Then she picked up the needle and began to copy Jenny's work with her usual dexterity.

Later, when Mary looked back to her time in the Magdalen, she would have said it was a happy time but too dull for her liking. Some of the other girls called it a 'blessed place' and hoped to stay a lifetime, but Mary was hankering for life outside. Remembering the Magdalen was different to being in there and, in the light of experience, Mary could see that it was male company she was missing.

However, then, she was only dreaming of Jem Farr and hoping to see him. So she could not agree to stay a lifetime in the sober Institution. Christmas had come and gone.

There had been carols in the hall but it was then she wanted Devonshire and its snow, the hot-spiced punch, the mummers and the kissing-bushes. Posset in the Magdalen was weak and the roast beef dry. The girls had sung a dreary hymn on New Year's Eve, instead of toasting the horse and his right ear, while on the twelfth night of Christmas there were no fires nor happy singing. Mary was truly bored. She stood at one of the lower windows, staring through the glass like a caged bird, weak for want of flying.

Annie, the whore was feeling the pinch. Sometimes she regretted walking the streets, especially when it was mizzling and miserable. She felt jealous of the women who had a permanent place in Number One Court, those who were kept constantly engaged by their gentlemen. She had never been so lucky. She pulled her shawl about her and stamped her feet. Today she could almost envy that stupid sister of hers shut up in the Magdalen. At least she was warm and fed. Jenny had never had any real feeling for whoring. She had had to be constrained to it in the beginning. Annie knew she was different; she had it in her. It gave her satisfaction to take money from gentlemen. She spat on the ground. She had never found one of them to be gentle. There were some brutes who came to Mrs Smith's for pleasure. One thing about being out on the street. You could choose who you took and who you duped. She sniffed, then sneezed as a drop of moisture fell off one of her bedraggled feathers.

'Bless you!' said a voice. 'How goes it, Blue-Dress?'

'No better for seeing you.' Annie didn't like the woman. She was always after the best custom. If the two of them were seen together it would be harder to get a gentleman.

'Be like that then—but you'll be keener when you hear the news.' 'You're lucky, you've a sister.'

'What do you mean?'

'In the Magdalen.'

'Eh?'

'It's worth money,' said the other, peering into Annie's face. 'And if I tell you, I'll expect something.'

'Get off,' said Annie.

'I mean it. There's money in it.' Annie could tell she was serious by the look on her face.

'Go on then.'

'Promise you'll give me some if you get any. Or I'll—'

'Don't threaten me,' said Annie. The other backed away frightened. Annie grasped her by the front of her dress. 'Go on, tell me!'

'You know Moon?' Annie spat again. Who didn't know that murdering swine? There were girls who would stick a knife through his ribs without even thinking of the drop, just to get even with him.

'What about him?'

'He's after this whore. She went inside and he wants her out. He'll pay gold to have her. Annie, if you could get to your sister and make her help—'

'She wouldn't,' said Annie, but she was thinking already how she could make her. 'How much will he pay?'

'He's in Number Two Court now, roaring with drink. He has said he's always had a passion for this whore and he has to have her back.'

'Who is she?' asked Annie.

'Search me, but they say she is all passion too. She must be to stand him!'

'Right,' said Annie, her brain working quickly. 'I'll be coming along in a minute or two. Number Two Court you said?' The other nodded. She hadn't spotted the carriage dawdling across the road. 'Tell Moon I'm on my way,' shouted Annie, beginning to run. She was grinning at the coachman and nodding. Then she was up swinging on the step, looking back at the other. 'You'll have to be quicker than that, Straw-Hair,' she grinned. The other shook her fist as Annie began opening the door and climbed inside. As the carriage gathered speed, Annie hung out and shouted back:

'Tell Moon I shan't be long and—' the rest of her words could not be heard as she was pulled backwards and out of sight...

'I'm having a visitor,' said Jenny to Mary, who was finishing a wonderful seam.

'Is it because you're being confirmed?' asked Mary. She wished there was someone to visit her too. The only bit of excitement she had had of late was when the superintendent had called her before the Board and told her that her work and behaviour were excellent and her reward was to be confirmation. The idea of the Bishop of London coming to the Magdalen had almost turned Mary's head. It had been so long since she had seen any man except for the chaplain minister.

'You'll know who it is,' said Jenny grinning. For the hundredth time Mary thought how like the Brushford horse her sister was.

'Will I?'

'She was in the cart with us,' whispered Jenny, looking around fearfully in case someone was listening...

When Mary saw Annie she remembered how she had disliked her even in that short time they had spent together. There was something sinister about her and she brought a boldness into the room, which challenged Mary.

Annie looked at all the girls with interest. She had had a full description from Mr Moon. She had been charged by him to find out the whore on the pain of her neck being snapped. And he wasn't joking. He had said the girl was dark, slim and had been wearing red under her dress when she had come in. Annie was near despairing because all were dressed the same in pale grey stuff. However, there was one thing in her favour. That stupid sister of hers was the one who washed the whores when they entered. She must have seen the clothes. She tried to question Jenny but the fool would not be drawn to speak anything of former times.

It was then her luck turned!

'Mary?' Annie looked across at the girl coming to meet them. 'This is my sister of whom I told you.'

'In the cart,' said Mary, looking at the bedraggled blue dress. The woman evidently had done no good for herself wherever she worked.

'You're staring,' said Annie. 'Do you like my clothes?' Mary swallowed back the rude remark. 'I suppose,' Annie continued, 'you wished you weren't dressed in grey all the time.' She was determined that for gold she would ask every reformed whore in the place if she had a preference for red silk.

Mary looked down at the sober colours:

'I miss the brightness of other clothes—'

'Shhh,' warned Jenny, 'you mustn't speak of anything, remember.'

'Oh, why not?' said Mary impatiently. She was truly angry with them all. However this woman looked she had come from the outside. The Devil was getting at Mary's tongue. Sometimes she wanted to shock her sisters just so she could see their faces.

'Right,' said Annie. This was a woman of spirit. 'Where do you come from? I think it's amazing we should meet again, don't you?' Mr Moon had said the wench came from Devon. Hadn't this one come from that direction Wiltshire was on the way.

'I come from Crediton,' lied Mary and Jenny covered her ears, while the other girls looked on astonished.

'From Devon then?' asked Annie, thrilling a little. The Devil was with her that morning.

'Yes—and I do miss my finery!' declared Mary defiantly. Sometimes she had just had enough of being good!

'Red? Do you like red?' questioned Annie. The girl fitted the description, she came from Devon and —

'I love it,' said Mary. 'And I had on a lovely red silk dress when I came in.'

'That's enough!' cried Jenny. 'No more, no more.' Mary knew she had gone too far. Blue-Dress was smiling broadly. It had been easy after all.

'Cheer up, sister,' she said. 'This one knows what life's all about. She has no place in here.' Annie drew a crumpled piece of paper from the bosom of her gown. 'This is where I live,' she said. 'Take it—and if you get fed up with all this, I'll make you welcome.'

Mary closed her eyes as the bishop confirmed her. He was a prince of the Church. That would have to do for the meantime. His hands felt cool and pale. When she was told to sit down, she was glad she had been able to talk her way through it all. Now she had been given the strength to get away from this place and seek her fortune again. She had somewhere to go; whatever she felt about Blue-Dress. Then she remembered the bedraggled feathers and the woman's tawdriness. Did she need her?

As Mary rose from her knees, she was planning her next move.

The following month she obtained her release from the Magdalen in an unexpected way and one over which she had no control. She was called to the superintendent's office.

'Be seated, my dear Mary. You see, we have company.' Mary looked. There was the minister as always but, this time, he was accompanied by several strange ladies.

The superintendent continued, 'You may be wondering why I've brought you here. The truth is we have never had such a girl for learning. I have shown the ladies here specimens of your finest work.' Mary blushed. 'When you were confirmed I was so proud of you. Mary, it matters to us all how the Magdalen prospers and a girl such as you helps in our work. Do you know it takes some thousand or more pounds to keep this place?' Mary gasped at such a sum.

'Naturally we want every one to know about the success we have here—and you are one of those. We need a lot of money to keep going.' She picked up some letters from the table. 'Here are notes from some of our girls who have gained honest employment.' She picked up some more. 'Here are letters written to us glorifying our work. Indeed, what we have done has appeared in newspapers and magazines. Are you surprised?'

'Yes, ma'am.'

'And will you help us?'

'If I can.'

'Good.' There was a little applause.

Mary brightened. 'What would you have me do, ma'am?'

'You write a fine hand. Therefore, we want you to set down your former life—' Mary started. Had they found out about her? Her eyes filled with angry tears.

'It isn't—' She was ready to defend herself.

'My dear, no need to weep. We all know it's hard for you.'

The minister rose from his place behind the table. 'You may write it all down in private if you wish.'

'What shall I write?' sobbed Mary, finding it easy to cry and knowing they would pity her.

'I think you should begin by recounting the dreadful course you took in this city,' answered the superintendent gently.

'At the hospital or Mrs Matthews?'

'I don't know, my dear. It's best to confess everything. Say who brought you into wickedness, who seduced you. Tell what dreadful man forced you into adultery,' the superintendent seemed quite excited.

Then the minister added, 'Tell everything about how you began your life as a whore and faced eternal damnation!'

'Madam!' said Mary, scandalised at hearing a minister use such words. 'I've never done those things. I've never been seduced!' It was nearly true. Could you count Humphrey Moon pulling you into a ditch or rolling you in the corn mill? 'Who said I had?'

One of the ladies who was wearing a fur-trimmed pelisse began to cry. The minister looked white and the superintendent was fanning herself with the letters.

Suddenly the clergyman came to himself. 'God help you, girl, for lying so. You've just been confirmed!'

Mary's face went bright red. 'It's true! I swear it. I've never had a man, I promise! I'm still a maid!'

'And you were never a whore?' asked the superintendent in a small voice.

'Never! I'm a Christian girl, ma'am. How could you think it?' — There was silence. Mary looked from one to the other. If it had not been so serious she could have laughed.

They gaped like the fish in the pond at Birt. They thought she was a woman of the streets. She could hardly believe it, but she was beginning to understand. That was why no one spoke of their life. They were all whores in the Magdalen!

The minister sat down with a thump. 'Here!' he shouted. Jenny came hurrying in, her bonnet askew. 'Take this woman out of here. Summon the physician.'

Jenny pinched Mary's arm as she pulled her from the room. 'What have you been saying? What have you done to those who have looked after you?'

'Nothing,' replied Mary stubbornly.

'How could I have made you into a friend?' asked Jenny with a soulful look on her face. She pushed Mary into the little room she had first entered and locked the door behind her...

The doctor put away his tools. He ignored Mary, who was sweating with embarrassment and went over to the superintendent, whose face was turned away.

'Upon my word, madam, it is the first time I have seen a virgin in the Magdalen.'

'True then?' asked the lady in a low voice.

'Probably untouched.' The superintendent shook her head at his words.

'Thank you for coming. I will deal with her now.'

Two days later, Mary found herself in that small room again. She had been dressed in her gowns and Jemmy's things returned. Then, a free woman, she walked out into the early spring weather. There was a greenness in the air and a smell of new life in the wind. She looked up at the dismal building, thinking of her suffering sisters inside.

'Well,' she said under her breath. 'It seems there's no way a woman can do right. I've been thrown out because I am a virgin, while everyone out here is trying to rip me apart! I've had enough of being a woman to be trodden on. I'm going to change into a footman and hire myself out into service. If I'm in men's clothes, no one will molest me!' Mary had decided earlier that day not to go to Blue-Dress's because, in the light of the last few days, she was sure she knew how the woman lived.

Mary walked on in the notorious district around Tyburn Turnpike. Suddenly, a sign caught her eye. It was written in Hebrew. A closer look revealed a Jewish pawnbroker's, full of the broken ends of people's lives.

The Jew was very glad to pay for female garments. Fine dresses were in much demand in that area of town. Mary stuffed the coins she had been given into the bodice of her old black next to Jemmy's pin and the shilling. Then she looked for a shop that sold men's clothes. On pretence of inquiring for her brother who was about her size, Mary acquired a footman's rig with tight little knee breeches and a coat with a nipped-in waist. She was glad her hair had been kept short in the Magdalen and she bought a hat to completely cover it as she was afraid it would appear too fine for a lad's.

She disguised herself in a church porch, emerging as a pretty footman. What she did not see, as she walked along, was the woman on her tail. If she had she wouldn't have recognised her. The blue dress was gone, replaced by an elegant gown, high-waisted and ribboned, covered with a cloak bought by Castel gold.

Some distance behind trailed a carriage. Inside sat a broad fairheaded man who was happy that soon Mary Willcocks would be at his mercy.

The time was near. Mary found a corner where some other young men were standing for hire. She joined them.

'Is this a good exchange to find work?' she asked the man beside her, hoping her voice would be taken for a lad's. But the young man was pointing:

'You're lucky!' he said. 'Look, someone is beckoning you from that carriage. I reckon a fine lady has taken a fancy to you already!' All Mary could see was the beringed hand waving to her. Then the door of the carriage opened a little and a woman's voice cried:

'Hurry up there, lad, I need a footman!' The man to whom she had spoken, nudged her and gave her a mighty wink of the eye.

'Go on,' he said, 'if you don't, I will!' Mary made her way over to the coach. She didn't mind because it was a lady. What she didn't see was the opposite door open and the lady scramble out!

Then a gentleman's voice said, 'Hurry up, man, we need to question you.' Mary sighed. So there was a gentleman there after all. The door opened wide and Mary climbed in.

The carriage jolted forward and was off with a sudden shock. Mary found herself sprawling, then a strong hand caught at her coat and thrust her down on the seat.

In one terrible second, Mary looked across into the gentleman's face—and screamed.

CHAPTER 7

She stared into his face, half-believing. She'd screamed with shock at seeing him again. Humphrey Moon, her old master. How could it be? It was like a nightmare. And he was staring at her too in the old way. Her hands were wet and she shrank back against the cushions.

'Mary,' he said. 'Not as rosy as in Brushford but just as ticing.' His voice had the smoothness of milk, but the old Devon thickness was rising to the top!

'Humphrey,' her voice faltered. 'How did you know me?'

'It's a long story,' he said, leaning back and away from her. 'But I did.' He was silent, looking her over until Mary got redder under his probing.

'Let me out of this carriage,' she said.

He laughed. 'You think I would after finding you again?'

'Please, Humphrey?'

'Wheedle me more, Mary,' he said and she knew what he meant.

She put up a hand to knock the roof and attract the driver's attention, but he caught her arm in his strong fist holding her prisoner.

'You'll go when I give you leave.' Mary knew she could do nothing; it was like a bad dream that she had to see out.

She tried to divert the conversation. 'Are you in London visiting?' But he could not be; it must have been planned but how and why? Could he turn up like this to take her off the street?

'You've been betrayed,' he said as if reading her thoughts.

'So you've come to fetch me back to the village?' It was a wild hope. He shook his head, looking at her the whole time. There was a fleck of spittle on his full lips and his tongue moved between them like the forked barb of the adder.

'Betrayed by a whore.'

'What?'

'Come on, Mary, be realistic. Why do you think you're in this carriage?'

'I was looking for hire.' How could she explain? To be wearing men's clothes was mighty dangerous.

'That was obvious!' he said. She couldn't mistake his meaning.

'I've only recently left a decent place—'

'The Magdalen!' He laughed out loud and the man up on the box was relieved. If Master Humphrey was in a good temper he wouldn't beat the girl; the driver didn't want any part of murder.

Suddenly Mary was preparing to stand up to him. How he'd come upon her was beyond comprehension; all she knew was she had to fight back. That was all that could be done against Humphrey.

'How dare you say I'm a whore? I left the place because I wasn't!' He roared with laughing.

'You were always a sly one, but you won't dupe me this time.' She could see what was coming and tried to duck.

The next thing she felt was a crash in the head. She could see nothing for a moment.

Humphrey had only meant to land her a stinging blow. He hit women when they asked for it and she'd been asking for it since those Witherage days. Still, he was a bit sorry, because she looked sick. He put out his hand but she shrank from him again.

'Let me down,' she whispered, 'please, Humphrey.'

'No chance, I'm afraid. You're in ill luck tonight, Mary. But if you behave yourself, things'll get better.' He felt delighted because she wasn't sobbing and screaming; it saved him being more violent. There was one thing he was sure of. This time Mary Willcocks would not elude him.

The horses pulled in the opposite direction from Humphrey's rooms in St. James towards poor and mean streets where labourers and mechanics struggled to make their living. On the very borders of Charing Cross, the coachman drove through into a Row, where the houses had a faded but elegant look, their fronts supported by columns.

Humphrey smiled. He hadn't needed to tell the driver where he and Mary were bound; this was a haunt of his and filled with some of his oldest friends. When he was weary of gaming and dancing, he would make for the house of Mistress Smith. There, like so many other London gentlemen, he could find a sympathetic ear.

All the time Mary was planning her escape. Although he'd almost broken her bone he hadn't the better of her yet. Once outside she would scream 'murder' and someone would help her surely. There was another thing; he hadn't been drinking. She could reason with him perhaps. He was dressed in fine clothes now; maybe he had a little grace to go with his apparel. She shut her eyes and prayed.

When the coach stopped and the door opened, she thought there was a chance her prayers were answered. The house didn't look too bad and there was a footman. Mary was very conscious of her male apparel and swelling cheek but the man took no notice. She started to brave it out:

'You've done well, Humphrey,' she said. 'It's not a bit like the farm.' There was a bright chandelier in the hall and scarlet wallpaper.

'Glad you like it,' he said, marvelling at her capacity for play acting. Well, it wouldn't do her any good. If she screamed he'd ram his fist down her throat. A woman was hurrying forward, her lace cap covering a mass of carefully-arranged curls:

'What a charming companion, Master Humphrey. Will you be in for supper?' Mary swallowed. Perhaps it wouldn't be too bad after all and she could get away then.

'I used to know Miss Willcocks from my Devon days,' he answered, but there was sport in his tone.

'I'm sure you'll have lots to talk about then,' said the woman in a most friendly way. Suddenly Mary was surprised to hear a piano. They passed an open door where a plump gentleman was entertaining several young women. Mary was relaxing a little. He couldn't murder her with company about. She'd get to the bottom of it all in the end...

She found out later that she was quite wrong. A maid had brought them meat, but Mary was too afraid to eat. He thrust some beef at her and she refused. He offered her wine but she could drink nothing. The atmosphere was stifling, drawn curtains and no air to breathe. She knew she was trapped.

She spoke of Brushford and his mother, anything she thought might dissuade him from his purpose. Yet she knew it was in vain like every woman knows when a man has her at his mercy.

'Humphrey, please, I beg you, do not—' He had her back against the cushions, on his knees, pressing his body into hers. His thick arms were pushing behind her back, crushing her breasts to his chest.

'I beg you, Moon, don't touch me!' She screamed then, knowing they must hear, but no one came! He had his hand out and was tearing her footman's jacket open. She panicked:

'No, Humphrey, no, I don't want to. Listen, listen!' She was drumming her fists about his head but he seemed to feel nothing or not to care, so intent he was on seeing her body. She thought she would die of fear. 'I don't want to!' she sobbed. He stopped for one moment, looked into her face and said:

'But I do, Mary. I want Witherage in my arms!' Then his mouth was on her neck, his tongue hurting her throbbing throat. 'You'll like me. I'll be better than the others!' He was straddling her half-naked body now. She writhed beneath him to free herself, crying for help. All she could hear was her own frantic breathing and his ugly words.

'You'll love it, love it!' All she could think was she was to be ravished by Moon. She struggled mightily: 'I won't! I won't!' The ceiling whirled above her. If she only had some ornament to knock him on the head— but a searing shock of nerves gripped her as his searching mouth found her nipple and bruised it. She jerked out her legs in agony, screamed inside. This wasn't how she wanted any man. It was a nightmare of revulsion and pain.

He was dragging her across the carpet; she was pulling at his legs begging him but he was deaf to her cries. He had no time for any softness with Mary. He'd been cheated too many times. It was a pity he'd had to rape her in the end; he would have preferred her willing. Now he would feel that heat which had eluded him in the corn mill and the cold mucky ditch. There was madness in his body for the girl. She was putting up a good fight; she might have been a virgin for all the screaming she was doing, but she'd always been a great play actor. It probably satisfied her.

He threw her on the four poster. Humphrey preferred a bed; it was softer than the floor.

Mary had been hurt so much already that she was hardly heedful of what he was doing. She had lost her shoes and her breeches were ripped right down; her breasts were free and she was still trying to cover them. He pulled her poor hands away saying all the time:

'Come on, Mary, play the game. Humphrey doesn't want to fight you.' When he was between her legs he put his mouth to her ear and the words made her vomit.

'Did Jem have you, Mary, that night in Witherage?' He cursed at her sickness, then carried on. She bit his shoulder, but it made only a little difference. He was like a hound, lathered up in the hunt. Then he tore her apart like he had done some pretty little vixen on the Brushford hillside. As it was done, the screaming inside Mary was exhausted.

All she was conscious of was pain in her depths; the terrible sadness at the loss of herself, taken by a man's power. In one thrusting madness she had been like a white rag tossed on the line, dry to the sky.

'God,' she moaned and moaned beneath his body.

'Shut up, girl. Did you feel nothing? Quit crying!'

He sat up astride with a crooked look on his face. 'It wasn't that hard. You couldn't have made more noise if you'd still been a maid.' He ran his fingers through his thick blond hair and stretched. She hated him, more than her father; than the foulest murderer in Newgate! She had always known he was the devil. He had taken her against her will and it meant nothing to him. He got off and stood naked before her. She turned her face into the pillow. He was pouring wine and offered her some. Then he stretched again:

'I'm damn tired after that, Mary. Do you know that you've worn a strong man out? Move over.' And he was in bed again and fondling her. She shuddered, but was too broken beneath to scream. If she had had a knife she would have plunged it in to him.

His eyes were dull with sleep as he countered her look. 'You won't kill me with that look. Be happy, you've found yourself a gentleman. You'll be all right with me. And don't run off when I go to sleep. You'll only be taken in to another court.' He pulled her to him. 'Why, I've a mind to get going again, you stir me all up with those pretty looks. You should have given in years ago at Brushford—like Milly!'

'Milly Cater?'

'Ay, but she had no brain; only fit for tumbling in the hay. And Betty Bly. God, now I have you. Humphrey Moon has a sweet Western whore to match his strength.' When he finally closed his eyes, Mary rolled from the bed and burst into weeping. She had fallen into Humphrey's trap.

She poured some icy water from a pitcher and into the bowl by the bed, washed her limbs, hands and face, then pulled a thin cover from the bed and sat like a statue in the chair.

Later he woke and pulled the exhausted Mary back into bed. She had tried the door several times and found it locked. There had been nowhere to fly. She couldn't even cry the second time. Humphrey looked over her body with shining eyes:

'Mine, all mine to keep and play with. I'll keep you from other men, Mary. You'll have enough from me!' She bit her bitten lips again and again, crying out inwardly, 'Think, this is what poor women of the streets go through all their poor lives!' She said nothing, just closed her eyes, blotting out the wickednesses he did to her strained body, hoping she might die peacefully beneath him…

She slept, not even heard him pull on his boots and dress. He leaned over her and she cried out in her dreams. He grinned: 'You'll be safe here until I come back, Mary. The madam will find you plenty to do while you wait for your master!' He went off, still smiling.

Mistress Smith let herself in to the room and looked down at the girl, spreadeagled on the bed. For one moment she felt pity for those bruises and that wretched woman with years of men to come. She, herself, had once been young and thoughtless. Even the woman's breasts, thighs and belly bore the blue marks of his hands. It seemed the girl from Devon had made a wild night of it. 'You must have some spirit,' said the madam, 'to have stood Mr Moon.' Two of her other girls had run screaming that they would have him no more and she had been forced to find them kinder gentlemen. Mistress Smith leaned forward and shook the girl. She wondered just how long she had been at this game.

Mary woke terrified at the touch. Was it Humphrey again? Never in all her life had she dreamed such fearful things. She stared vacantly into the bland face of Mistress Smith, then she sat up and drew the sheets about her.

'Why didn't you stop him?' she said coldly. 'Do you know what I've been through?'

'He's a rough one all right. Devon Bull, that's what they call him downstairs. Still, you'd know all about that, wouldn't you? You best wash and come downstairs for some meat and drink.' Mary stared at her in horror. She was as much a monster as Moon. Shame and evil meant nothing to such a woman. Mistress Smith held her scathing glance.

'Take that look off your face. You should be used to it by now. You knew him, he said.' Mary broke into hysterical tears, throwing her head back against the pillow and screwing the bedclothes in her fingers. The madam caught her by the shoulders and shook her. Mary cried out in pain.

'Stop that, do you hear. You'll make yourself sick and be good to no one!'

'Where am I?' cried Mary. 'Where is this horrible place?' Mistress Smith seemed not to notice. She was looking inside a tall robe. She turned, holding a pretty dress with lace sleeves and a fine ribbon under the bust.

'You're in Court Number One. And count yourself lucky. We have only gentlemen here. Those who eat well, pay accordingly. Put these on!' She handed Mary a *zona*, helped her put the silk bands about her top half so they supported her breasts. Mary cried out at the pressure. The madam felt about her ribs.

'Has he cracked one? No, I don't think so. Just bruising.' Mary couldn't bear the shoulder straps to be added because they cut into the scratches his nails had made. She let the woman help her on with long wide linen drawers after she had soothed away the soreness with tepid water. Mary's head was dizzy from Humphrey's blows and she felt a shadow.

'There,' said the madam, 'you're finished. Feel better now?' She took Mary's torn footman's clothes. 'You won't need these,' she said, smiling. 'There's only one kind of man here!' Then she handed Mary a pair of slippers with rounded toes.

'I have to go,' said Mary dully.

'You can't. I'm ordered not to let you. You'll be safer here than trying to make a living on the streets.'

'Safe?' whispered Mary, feeling the tears come.

'Well-clothed, well-fed and loved! What more could a wench want?' asked the madam drily, holding the door open, yet, as the girl passed through, she was wondering on the wickedness of a world where a poor woman like herself was constrained to make such a living.

Christmas of 1812 had come and gone in a flurry of excitement. Since the news of the French retreat from Russia which had broken in the second week of December, all London had been a whirl of madness. Trade which had fallen off with the ports of Europe closed, was flourishing again and Celia was hoping that her Yorkshire peasant families were looking to better times than in that year before when several young men she knew had taken to battering down the mill owner's door from sheer necessity. She had cried when she had heard of the cruel sentences passed on the rioters, death and transportation. When she had talked it over with Jem, he had spoken passionately about their responsibilities towards the poor and she was proud of him. Yet they were powerless; the land was in her parents' hands and her father was in Portugal, her mother in sole charge.

Not only did Celia feel anxiety for the peasants' lot, but also for her father, who had been wounded at the Battle of Salamanca, having been with Cole's 4th Division and caught in the leg by a sabre when the Portuguese had fallen back. She had written to him begging he return to his daughter and London and let Wellington's army press on to victory after winning such a decisive battle. Tom Barton did not come being loth to leave the only life he knew; so Celia kept on worrying.

And there was Jem. Celia sighed. She knew what he had to endure—a sick wife and not even children for consolation. She was desperate when she knew she had failed in her duty, but in the bleak month after Christmas when she saw other young women with babies and small darlings walking in the square at playing with Christmas toys; a quiet numbness had taken away the motherly ache within her. She knew too it was because she would never hold one of her own to her breast. But could he bear it while she lived?

She wished he would go out to friends or invite them even. There seemed a dullness in his eyes not caused only by lack of sleep and the foul weather. She had suggested he go skating on the frozen Thames, but he had refused that like everything else. She saw his morose face when he read of the plight of the French—and although her mother and his father could never understand why he should regard himself any part a Frenchman, she did. Her husband had loved his mother greatly and was still grieving for her albeit ten years or more. If Celia could have kissed away those sad lines about his mouth, she would. In fact she wished anything might happen to raise her handsome husband from his fit of despair.

Celia looked across at him as he stood with Earle Grant. The half-caste was the only real friend Jem had in London now, as he and the farmer's son he had brought with him from Devon, were merely on speaking terms. Only twice since Christmas had Jem dined at his club and then it was alone. Suddenly Celia thanked God for sending Earle to them.

'Shall I play the harp, gentlemen?' she called. Jem smiled at this effort to please them.

'Yes, Celia, it might lift our spirits.'

'Come, Jem,' said Earle. 'Mine are buoyant now that trade is good again. My sugar and coffee can roll out of the Caribbean and end up for sweetmeats in the Courts of Sweden and Russia.' Jem laughed in spite of himself. Celia heard the sound with relief and seated herself to play a light tune which filled the room with cascading notes of music. Earle walked over and stood beside her while she played.

'Jem is in better spirits now,' he said, looking down on Jem's wife. Her exposed shoulders were beautiful rising from the low-cut gown, but there were deep recesses each side of her throat where the coughing had taken its toll. The narrow ribbon under her small breasts accentuated the thin body and, when she smiled at his words, there were no dimples, only the skin stretching over the bones severely. Celia was in bad health—and it showed.

Earle thought of his own mistress, Juba as he watched the white girl plucking the strings. There was a rich strength about her; her skin glowed like ebony wood and she was always laughing. Often, he thought, he should make her his wife, but there was time as Earle had no aristocratic father like Jem to constrain him to a marriage of convenience. He was a rich merchant who had found Jamaican life much to his taste and who rarely returned to London, letting his son carry on his business there. However, Earle himself was not on the best of terms with old Mr Grant, who still kept slaves on his plantation. Although there had been general emancipation, his father still made use of their bodies to work the land; and they were no freer now than they were when his own mother had been brought up to the great house to share his father's bed. Yet she had been treated well because Mr Grant was still a Christian gentleman. As to the rest of his lineage, Earle knew practically nothing except what the old mammy cook had told him as he scuttled about her kitchen dressed in young gentleman's European clothes.

It seemed that when Mrs Grant was raving in childbed fever after bringing forth another still-born son, the mulatto girl had been brought with her new baby, to whom she had given birth in the slave sheds, and the child had been wrapped in linen and placed in the empty cradle. Mrs Grant died without ever seeing the tiny usurper in the nursery. The slave girl was charged to keep the fact secret that Earle was her son and to say her child had died at birth. She, herself, was the child of a French pirate and a negress and pale in colour. She stayed to 'wet nurse' her own son and give his true father, Mr Grant, comfort after his wife died.

Richard Grant spread the rumour about that his boy was his wife's son, after one terrible night when Bella Grant had been ravished by a run-away slave, intent on making a white woman suffer. He saw it as his duty; a Christian gentleman must at least acknowledge this dusky son as half his. As Earle looked down at Celia's pale face, he thought of the black cook who was whipped cruelly for saying the mulatto was Earle's true mother, of the way the English ladies lifted their brows when as a child he was brought into tea and about the 'virtue' of Mrs Grant, which was in question having none to defend her name after death. Of the sweet-faced mulatto, who had shared Mr Grant's bed and who was his true mother, he preferred not to think, because what she had suffered made Earle very angry. When he was a man, he had removed himself from the plantation accompanied by coloured friends, not servants, and settled in London's Bedford Square, where he kept a house as near to Jamaican ways as he could.

He looked across at Jem, thinking how much of his history was like his friend's and knowing that this had been what first had brought them together, besides a love of swordsmanship and horses.

Celia glanced up at Earle, whose complexion was like a polished oak beam. He had even features which gave him more of a look like carved wood and long jet black hair, brushed severely behind and tied with a dark ribbon. About him was that foreign air which no famous tailor nor hatter could erase. Neither Jem's father nor her mother could bear to have him in the house, but Celia knew how he and Jem were together and was content to love him too.

'Fie, Mr Grant,' said Celia, finishing the tune, 'your thoughts were not upon my music. Both you and Jem are far away!' It was a joke with anxiety in it.

'I beg you pardon, Celia,' he replied, bowing. 'I am distracted today owing to business.' Celia was glad, hoping this might be what was the matter with Jem too.

'I see. Coffee and muffins?' she asked, brightening. The men helped themselves while she presided over the pot. They walked to the fire where they were out of Celia's hearing.

'Well, Jem, Celia is a picture of an English wife,' said Earle.

'She is very sick, Earle.'

'I know. I can see by her colour. She is sweet, Jem.'

'She is—and I stay for that!' He knew Earle understood; they had exchanged enough confidences.

'Still starved of love, old friend?'

'I give her all I can,' said Jem passionately—and Celia looked up from her embroidery. He looked down in the fire, answering softly: 'I don't know if I understand the word any more. I have had many mistresses, Earle. Now I have a dear wife—but I have not found love.'

'Poor Jem,' said Earle. 'Would you if you could find it?'

'I'll not take another mistress—while Celia lives.' Earle laid his hand on his friend's arm sympathetically.

'It would ease you, Jem.'

'My body—but not my conscience. I went into this marriage with eyes open. Celia thinks the world of me and I cannot disillusion her.'

'Well, Jem, I don't know if I could stand it.' Earle was thinking of Juba and her warmth.

'You have the tropics in your blood!' said Jem.

'And you have Spain.'

'No, Earle, that's one thing I never told you. My mother was French—like your grandfather!' So they joked on—and Celia relaxed, thrusting her needle in and out of the heart of a flower.

'Don't breathe a word about your birth, Jem,' said Earle, suddenly serious. 'Buonaparte is falling everywhere in Europe and you must stand upright here otherwise you'll be hunted down in every part of this city like King Joseph hunts down all his Spanish enemies in the name of France!'

'No one knows outside my family except you.'

'Well, keep on letting them think you are one of our glorious Spanish allies!' He clapped Jem on the shoulder. Celia's heart went out to the two of them. 'Thank God,' she thought, 'I've been given a sweet husband, who does his best to make me happy—and his good friends are around me.'

Earle turned to the window, his arms about Jem's shoulders. 'I wish you were happy.'

'Never mind,' replied Jem in a low voice. 'Sometimes I wish I could get away from London. In Devon, I might feel different.'

'One day we'll go together,' said Earle. 'Perhaps when I come back from Brighton. You can show me your valleys and fields—and fresh women.'

'You're going away?'

'Business, my friend, in the Regent's kitchens. He must eat!' Earle grinned. 'Why don't you come?'

'I wish I could.' Jem thought of Celia's refusal to leave London.

'Well, think of it. And meet me at Brooks's tonight. We'll talk more about it!'

'Are you going to try again?' asked Jem, thinking about the last time Earle had been forbidden entrance.

'Why not? Isn't one of the greatest young lords in England a member—and my best friend?' Jem smiled. Together, they could beat the world. Suddenly, a shaft of wintry sun pierced into the room making the flames of the fire and the ashes dull white. When he had bidden Earle farewell at the door, he returned to Celia, who was seated peacefully embroidering a Barton rose.

'Celia,' he said. 'Earle wants me to dine with him tonight at Brooks's. I think I may go.'

'Oh, do, Jem. You've been out far too little lately.' She got up and came over to the fire, glancing at her pale, plain face beside her handsome husband's, outlined in the tall mirror.

'Perhaps I should go out more—if you don't mind.'

'Well, I cannot go myself in this cold weather.'

'Come, Celia, look at the square.' He took her hand to lead her to the window. 'Life still goes on while we are buried inside by the fire.' He laughed and pointed at a young woman, dressed in a taffeta riding habit, her hat adorned by a nodding ostrich plume, pulling her frisky horse about on the grass to wait for a handsome lad in black riding clothes, who was spurring to reach her.

Celia saw the look on Jem's face. It was open longing. She had wanted to raise his spirits but hers were sinking lower. There was a strange feeling in the pit of her stomach. Then a sudden thought struck her like a bolt, the same she had feared when she had first set eyes on sweet Jem Farr.

'The time has come, my dear,' it said. 'Aren't you afraid? Your husband is ready to spread his wings...'

Jem had almost forgotten what it was like to be part of the world again. He stared through Brooks's bow window at people and carriages all intent on the business of pleasure. Jem felt part of that excitement, a feeling he could hardly recognise after so many weary months. When he had left the house he had known that Celia was hurt but something inside was stirring him on. He knew in his heart that he had had enough of playing the game of marriage, a game where his father had the upper hand.

George Meredith was seated in a curtained alcove. He was surprised to see Jem Farr, pouring out wine and letting the world pass by. He seemed to be waiting for someone so George got up and went over.

'Good evening, Jem, what brings you here?'

'George.' Jem looked at his groomsman. George was not Jem's kind of friend. He wished that Earle would come as he had promised. Meredith was the kind of man Jem had avoided so carefully when he was illegitimate; a man who would challenge another to a fight or a duel; bet on a first rate race horse or on the sharp spurs of a cock.

'Will you take a drink with me?' asked Jem, out of politeness. George had a pleasant face when it was flushed with wine, he also had some pretty conversation to hold a person for an idle hour or so. He was full of stories of the tour of Italy which he had made a few months ago with his brother, Lord William. And Earle still did not come. Then George began to speak of cock fighting and wenching. Another young man joined them.

He turned to Jem and said, 'Do you go to the cock pit, sir?'

'I have been melancholy lately,' answered Jem. 'I have had no taste for that!'

'Then you should look for other pleasures, sir! Racing, perhaps?'

'Yes!' answered Jem, feeling his old self almost. 'I am fond of spirit in a horse!'

'And, by God, so am I!' cried George. 'There is nothing to beat handling the ribbons, ripping along fast, drawn by a bloodhorse in a chaise.' The three of them had found some common ground. And so the talk progressed. As they drank more wine, George became excited.

'I have a taste for women, who kick well too!' he drawled. 'What would I give for an English Rose with flaxen hair and eyes the colour of speedwells right now?' Jem laughed. He knew that he was behaving out of character, but somehow the wine was going to his head.

'I go for dark women,' he said, 'with curls and eyes like chestnuts!' He suddenly felt guilt about Celia then.

'You will not make a poet, Jem, with your chestnuts! Why didn't you use the nightingale? That's a far prettier bird!' laughed George falsely. And there was no sign of Earle! Suddenly Jem felt bereft of true friends. These were stupid fellows all of them with vacant faces and affected manners. He drained a fourth glass of wine. Why had Earle not come? It was then he saw the small chaise arrive with Earle's arms in gilt upon its side. No one alighted except the man from the box. He was black and dressed in full livery. Jem watched him hand in a note at the door. It was meant for him and as he slit it open, the boy was climbing back on the box to wait.

I am prevented from our meeting by pressing business. I leave the
carriage for you. Come to me at eight. Earle G.

Three more gentleman joined them while Jem was staring at the note.
George could see the familiar seriousness returning to Jem's face.

'How say you, Jem, we leave this damn place and find us one of
these fair creatures to sport with?'

'I don't think so, George,' said Jem.

'Come on, lad,' answered George, pulling him by the sleeve. The
other laughed too.

The one who had joined them first said, 'Mr Farr has both chaise
and carriage. Let us all pile in and make our way to some place where
we can find a pretty bed tonight?'

Jem could see the drunkenness in their eyes, and he wished he was
as drunk as they. He looked into their grinning faces. Half of him
wanted to go with them, half wished to stay. When he had told Celia he
was dining with Earle at Brooks's, that was all he had wished to do;
now he had been drawn into a more dangerous game. He could not
cheapen his marriage so.

Suddenly George wanted to make Jem Farr laugh again. He was
determined to take the man with him; also Jem's carriage and chaise
would be to his advantage. Besides, he felt aggrieved that Humphrey
Moon should be so wrapped up in his new whore that he had no time
for his old friends. George wanted to pay him out, was hoping that he
might see him in The Rows. It would give Humphrey a shock to see
George with his benefactor.

George looked so ridiculously eager that Jem could not refuse him.
As the young men picked up their hats, Jem was lying to himself even
more. After all, he could not be a prisoner throughout his life. He would
tell Celia that he had been to a cock fight which had kept him late.
Surely he could enjoy some little relaxation. Suddenly, desire like a
weight was dragging him down from the pedestal where he had sat
like a monk for months.

The six young men strode out of Brooks's and only one of them was
sober. Jem hailed his coachman, then turned to the black boy who was
driving Earle's chaise. His companions climbed up into the carriages,
laughing and cursing. It was only when he was seated among the
cushions that he was feeling shame to be going whoring with George
and his crew.

Jem's coachman waited for his orders, while Earle's servant sat
mutely at the reins; then George stuck out his curly head:

'The Rows. Come on, man, and hurry!' The coachman was used to
taking Master Moon to that address, but had not taken Jem there

before. He spurred the bays and the chaise followed hard with the young men hanging out of the windows, calling to any young woman who was walking on the street. Jem leaned back, his face hot from the wine. He had been a married man for some time but he was still ashamed of their behaviour. Besides George was joking continually and his language was coarse.

Suddenly Jem was sick of it all. He knew what he ought to do; he should knock on the roof, call the mad chase to a halt and tip them out on the footway. But something prevented him. It was a strange and sinister feeling as if a hand had him by the collar, stopping him from moving. He let the coach dash on, stayed by the icy touch. He was cold now with perspiration—he couldn't stop it. The two carriages hastened into the maze of streets, which were pressed full of folk stumbling drunkenly through the late hours; men and women lolling in doorways, children who should be sleeping, tottering and playing in the gutters. George, who had been swaying sleepily beside Jem, suddenly revived as they swung into The Rows. As he sprang into life, Jem sunk into lethargy, wrestling with his conscience which was behaving far too gallantly. The coachman brought the carriage to a smart halt and, behind, the young men were already tumbling from the chaise. They had all disappeared into Row No. 1, when Jem got out slowly. He looked up at the coachman:

'Take the carriage home, man. I am going on to Earle Grant. Please tell my lady's maid that I shall not be returning tonight!' The coachman grinned. He would make the excuse as Mr Farr wanted. He did not blame him for taking a little pleasure, away from the gloomy house and an ailing lady. He liked madam well enough, but had often wondered at the faithfulness of her young husband. Jem walked back to the chaise and its black driver, who stared ahead inscrutably.

'Wait—for a while!' he commanded as he stepped into the chaise.

George appeared between two of the house pillars, with a girl on each arm. He brought them over to the chaise, seeing that the carriage had gone. He was still determined to get Jem inside, thrusting the blowsy girls forward in an effort to attract him. Jem looked into their pretty, smiling faces and saw nothing familiar there. All he could think of was the pale sad face of Celia as she had watched him go from the upstairs window. He looked again, saw the full breasts straining against the low-cut blouses, felt the heat they exuded, ached for their comfort—but would not get out.

'One for you, Jem,' tempted George, his fat face glistening with perspiration. 'Come on, man, there is no one to teach you your duty now,' he added rudely. Jem glowered. How dared the drunken young aristocrat taunt him so?

'Keep them for yourself, George,' he said coldly, drawing back the curtains. George retreated, smarting under the insult, feeling he had been treated badly by this insolent young man who thought himself better than he was. Perhaps he did prefer Humphrey Moon. He stalked off into the whorehouse grumbling, dragging the two girls behind him.

Jem sat, wrestling with his own hot feelings, blaming Earle for letting him down, uncertain still as to what he should do, while down the street behind him came a girl in a muslin dress, covered by a fine cloak; she was walking slowly, head bent, unseeing of passers-by. Several young men tried to detain her, catching at her sleeve, but she brushed them off impatiently and sauntered on. There was about her an air of loneliness, on her face a lost look when she stared in to the shop windows. Before she reached Row No. 1. She hesitated, then stepping out boldly, approached the carriage...

For countless mornings after Humphrey had ravished Mary, she dreamed of escape from his heavy coarse body and his callous ways. She had cried often, pleaded with him to let her go, reminded him of his mother at Brushford, but all to no avail. She was his whore and so she would remain. It was a terrible life for a woman with a man she hated. If it had not been for Blondie, another whore, Mary might have taken the road to eternal damnation. Many times when she lay with Humphrey Moon, she wished she had thrown herself off the five-barred gate and been hanged by her own apron strings. Humphrey was a cruel lover, but when he had gone she was ministered to by her new friend.

'It cannot last for ever, Mary,' said Blondie. 'I'm sure he'll tire of you—and if he drinks enough he might choke himself in his sleep. I promise you it will end!' It was a shocking life too in the whorehouse. She had seen girls die because they would not seek a doctor's help, many taken off for lying-in, to return crying for their children who were gone to the Foundling Hospital. But the Lord had heard Mary's prayers and had not made her pregnant by Humphrey Moon.

On the days Humphrey did not come, Mrs Smith put her to scrubbing the rooms.

'If you cannot be a whore today, then you must be a maid!' she had joked. As the days passed Mary's strength seemed to be returning, especially when she saw the pale London sun peeping in at the window. After all, it was the same sun that rose over Witherage Barrow and Birt Park. She had to get away somehow.

She had spoken to Blondie seriously about it many times.

'Would you be able to help me leave this place?'

'Leave?'

'So I shall never see Humphrey again!' Mary spoke desperately.

'You'll never get rid of him,' said Blondie with a wisdom far beyond her years. 'Though you hate him, he still possesses your body!'

'But not my spirit!' said Mary. 'That is free yet!'

'Still dreaming, Mary!' Blondie had listened to many of her fancies when they had lain together, tired by the day's work.

'I shall do that always!' said Mary. 'It is the only thing that can take me away from this world. Some day I shall see Jem, Blondie!' She had told her friend all about the gentleman she dreamed of.

'What would this Jem say, Mary, if he knew you were a whore?' Mary's eyes filled with tears at the thought.

'I don't know, Blondie!'

'You will never get a husband, Mary—after this life!' Mary feared what Blondie said was true. She could never return to Witherage because of Humphrey Moon. Wherever she hid in Devonshire he would find her. Blondie had looked at her friend affectionately.

'If I can ever help you, Mary, I will. I promise!'

'Thank you!' Mary threw her arms about her friend, and kissed her on the cheek.

She began to play Humphrey at his own game. One week he had cursed her for not laying out his breeches properly.

'You idle fool!' he spat. 'You still have as much mischief in you as you had on Brushford Farm!'

'Well, why don't you go then, Humphrey?' replied Mary tartly, ducking to avoid the blow he aimed at her with his fist.

'So you've still some spirit after two long months?'

'Yes, I have, and I always will!' Humphrey faced Mary, who had a mighty temper when she was roused. Perhaps he should have found some gentle little whore to spend his time with, instead of this dratted girl with a viper's tongue? 'Here, Humphrey, have a swig from this bottle!' Mary ducked again as he twisted it from her hand and flung it across the room.

'Don't cheek me, girl, or I will get Mrs Smith to beat you!'

'Yes, Humphrey!' mimicked Mary, seeing the fight was dying in him. If she kept this up, perhaps she would be rid of him in a week.

That week had seen the beginning of the greatest trouble of all. The signs seemed unmistakable.

'Oh, Blondie,' cried Mary. 'Do you think that I am pregnant?'

'Perhaps!' replied Blondie with a serious face. 'But I can't tell you—you must go to a doctor!'

'I have no money!'

'Go to Mrs Smith and ask her. She keeps some coins by for such!'

Mary collapsed, her head in her hands. 'Don't despair, Mary dear, remember, it's part of our game!'

'Oh, what am I going to do?' cried Mary. 'I wish I was in my grave!'

The doctor could not tell her either. He said it was too early and to come back in another month. She walked slowly from his house, trying to imagine what it meant to bear a child. The whole of London seemed to be looking at her, pointing to her disgrace, tormenting her with the evil she had done. There was no place anywhere for Mary Willcocks now and she felt more dejected than the first day she had come from Brushford when Farmer Moon had turned her off and that was a long time ago. She began to plan as she walked. She must escape from Humphrey Moon now whatever happened; she would rather risk her life than lie with him again and bear his child. She stared in surprise as she saw the chaise standing outside The Rows. It was highly polished, bearing arms on the side and up on the box was a black boy in green-gold livery and wearing a powdered wig. She knew it was a gentleman come looking for women...

Still unsure as to what to do, Jem glimpsed the girl idly, then took up his cane about to knock on the roof with the command to start. Suddenly, something made him look again. The cold feeling at the back of his neck was waning; the warmth returning. Surely he knew her, but how could he? He watched as she was passing the carriage. He wasn't wrong—he couldn't be!

'Where are you going?' Wondering, Mary heard the warm and mellow tone. She thought she knew it, but she could not be sure. The door of the chaise was opening; it *was* a gentleman and Mary wanted nothing to do with it. She suddenly saw two of her fellow whores peering through the windows. If they told Humphrey Moon what would become of her? Suddenly, the young man was on the steps of the chaise.

'Sweet Lord!' cried Mary, her stomach turning and everything was black around her. The man was out with an agile leap and lifted her swooning body into his arms. He carried her back in and knocked on the roof.

'To Mr Grant's, driver, as fast as you can!' Jem laid Mary's slight body upon the cushions and knelt down beside her, chafing her hands. Mary woke to the scent of gentleman, all leather, tobacco and perfumed linen.

'Jem? Is it really you?' She was looking into the dark brown eyes which she had thought she would see no more. They were kind as ever—and they were brimming with tears. With one swift and helpless movement, Mary put her arms around his neck to cling to him close. Nestled into his warmth, she drowned in his nearness and he bent and kissed her lips. She did not know if it was a dream; neither did she care; she only knew she was safe in his arms. Jem's lips were warm. He ceased the kissing, stared in her eyes.

'Is it a miracle, Mary? That *you* are here!' He was holding her hands fast. 'It must be! Have you come up from Devon to comfort my loneliness?' She let him keep her fingers prisoner.

'How did you come here, sir?'

'It doesn't matter, Mary,' he replied, 'but how did you?' She stared into his eyes hoping the tears wouldn't show. Was it possible that Moon had told him where to find her? Could it be chance that had brought him to the how? But his eyes were kind as they looked at her.

'I was hoping to find a situation in London. I've come in from Devon looking for work.' She hoped the lie sounded convincing.

'It's a miracle that we met, Mary. I've been longing for Devon and I've found you. But—I'm sorry for kissing you. I beg your pardon—I was beside myself with joy.'

'There's nothing to forgive, sir.' She had been waiting for his kiss for years. 'Look, sir, I have something here. I always remembered you.' She put her hand inside her dress and brought out the coin tied on a leather thong. 'Your shilling, sir, which you gave me on that blessed night in Witherage. I never used it.'

'Oh, Mary,' said Jem, 'you have been true. How many times have you needed a shilling?'

'Never more than I needed you, sir—' she suddenly realised what she had said—and to a great lord too. 'Oh, Mr Farr—please forgive me—I quite forgot myself. You're a great man now and I'm only a—' He broke in and saved her.

'Very sweet girl,' he finished softly. Of all the women he had known, Mary Willcocks touched him most. When he had kissed Mary's lips again he had thought of the strangest things; of the country and Brushford; the warmth of home— almost satisfaction that told him he was doing right. That kiss had jarred him out of his lethargy, told him he loved his wife from duty only, but without the feeling this girl Mary could wreak in him. When he embraced Mary he could feel the youth stirring once more, an experience unfelt since Witherage days.

'And this, sir, I kept this!' She brought out his pin. 'It's yours, sir. You should take it back now. I don't need it any more.' Now Jem had kissed her it was all she desired in the world. Her life with Moon had floated away—and Jem knew nothing of it. To him she was just a maid.

'No, Mary, take it back. It's yours!' Jem put out his hand and pinned it to her bodice. She was dizzy under that touch. Her body woke madly at the caress, because she was imagining what this man would be like to love. He did not withdraw his hand so she took his other and pressed them close to her heart so he could feel it beating. At this response he stared at her dumbly. Every thought he had had of loving Mary Willcocks rushed into his mind. He was recalling riding into Brushford, leaning on the gate watching Mary about the house. Why, he'd always thought of her like a lady instead of a country girl. There had never been coarseness on her lips—like some of the village wenches, only a wild and pretty fancy that flew from her lips and made a man want to taste the words. She was like the larks that rose brown and bright, full of lightness and truth. Suddenly, it was a delicacy that Jem felt he must recapture and hold close to before he became bitter and weary of life. With Celia he had become an old man at twenty-three. He needed a girl like Mary to show him life again.

So his hand stayed there and his eyes told her what he thought. She drank in their depths as if she had dived into the pool where the golden carp lay like fairy monsters; she could drown in Jem's eyes if he let her stare on. While he gazed, the colour rose in her cheeks.

'You have lost some of those roses you had in Brushford!' said Jem tenderly, removing his quiet hand and lifting it to touch her burning cheek. She shivered at the caress.

'That was a long time ago, sir, and I—am a woman now!' She hesitated in case her experience showed. He laughed.

'Are you, Mary?'

'Don't ask me, sir, I beg you—'

'Ssh, Mary, I have no need to know anything unless you wish it so!' His finger strayed to her lips to prevent the spell being broken. She let the bow of her mouth brush his skin and it was his turn to shiver.

'We are together now, sir, as I have dreamed.'

'Did you dream that, Mary? I didn't know!' It was an honest answer as he had only thought of Mary when Devon came in his mind and when he had seen that bright little maid who served him at his wedding. The thought of that unhappy day creased his forehead in a frown.

'You look so sad, sir.' She was staring into his face, creased or smooth, it was the face of an angel. 'Don't be! I'm here to comfort you!'

'That would take a great deal, Mary.' His smile was exactly as she remembered. She wanted to be fast in his arms and kiss the clear-cut corners of his mouth to keep that smile for ever.

'My heart is racing, sir. Can you feel it?' The sound of Devon in her voice made his own heart sing.

'How did it happen, Mary, that we should meet? I can't believe it!'

'Neither can I. It must have been God who sent you to me, sir.'

'You haven't forgotten your village faith then, Mary?' She knew he wasn't mocking her because of the softness in his voice.

'I have tried not to,' answered Mary in a small voice. At least she had remembered how to pray—for escape from Humphrey Moon. She dreaded even thinking about him. She must get away from the subject of what she was doing here in London. 'Have you been in the city long?' she asked, desperate to know what he had been doing.

'I have been in London for many weary months, Mary!' If she had to hear about his marriage, then she must. He had used the word, 'weary', that must mean that he was unhappy. She could see by his face that thinking about those months had brought a melancholy look. Suddenly there was hope in her heart. Perhaps Humphrey Moon had been lying when he had said Jem was wed?

She had to know, so she said, 'Why don't you return to Birt if you are not fond of London?' She steeled herself for his answer.

'Mary—' he paused, looking at her from serious eyes, 'I am a married man now and London is my home.' She showed no sign of surprise, only closed her hand over his more tightly.

'And you are not happy, sir?' She was holding on to him tightly now and he was grasping her fingers. She looked into his eyes again. 'Forgive me asking you that. It was impertinent.'

'No, Mary, I am not happy, but it is my fault, not my wife's. She has a sweet temper but I—'

'No, sir, you have the sweetest!' gasped Mary indignantly. There was no one within ten miles of Witherage who was such a gentleman.

'Do you think so? You flatter me, my Devon Mary. I have caused some pain to Celia.'

'She has a pretty name,' said Mary, thinking of her own plain one.

'No, Mary is the Queen of Heaven!' he said, and she went dizzy at his words. What man except 'her Jem' could speak such language? They stared into each other's faces, feeling the heat in the atmosphere. Then Jem let go her hands and leaned back against the buttoned seat.

'Yes, Mary, I *am* unhappy, but I have not looked at another woman—until now.' She blushed. 'I'm sorry, I should not speak like this before a maid. You know, Mary, when I look at you, it seems I am hardly married at all.' She had never seen that look in his eyes before.

'Don't you, sir?' she asked, wonderingly.

'Do you know what my marriage has done for me, Mary?' She shook her head at the words. 'It has given me an appetite for—love. Another thing, Mary, which I should not tell you, is that in this marriage of mine I have not tasted love.' Her eyes were wide. 'Imagine that, Mary. Jem Farr does not know what it means to *love*.' All Mary had ever imagined about him was how he could love. She did not understand. His eyes were even darker now—and wild. She had to tell him what was in her heart.

'And, Jem—' she dared to use this familiarity. 'I do not know about

125

love either.' It was not a lie—what she had done with Humphrey Moon had nothing to do with love. Suddenly Jem was beside her.

'Mary, would you mind it greatly—if I was to kiss you?' She put up her small hands and stroked his dear face.

'If I was to burn in hell, sir, for all eternity, it would not stop me kissing you!'

She heard the catch in his voice as he crushed her lips to his. It was a kiss that made up for years of yearning and emptiness, a kiss when two equals meet, not servant and master. So fast were they in each other's arms that they did not notice the carriage slow up, nor hear the coloured boy jump off the box. The first they knew was when the door was opened and a voice was heard, soft like the taste of sloes and gin, warm like Jamaica rum.

'Why, Jem, you seem to have kept a sweeter appointment than mine!' Earle Grant put out a hand and took Jem by the shoulder. 'Wake up from drowning in that kiss. You are here in Bedford Square!' Mary clung on to Jem afraid to lose him again, frightened to look at the owner of the voice. Jem lifted her head gently. She opened her eyes.

The man was dark and handsome, black eyes glittering in a sunburnt skin. His lips were full and sensuous; parted in laughter. She longed to shout out, 'I am no whore, but Mary, Jem's true beloved!' Jem broke from her clinging arms, and taking her hand, he placed it to his lips. Earle Grant stepped back and Jem was up and out. Mary hesitated as he turned and handed her down like the greatest lady.

'Mary, this is Earle Grant, my dearest friend!' The man was bowing.

'Where are we, Jem?' She looked up at the lighted windows.

'In Bedford Square. Earle, this is my darling Mary Willcocks of Witherage, Devon, whom I have known for many years. She has made my sad heart happier this night than in three long years.' Mary gasped. The coloured man indicated the steps.

'Welcome to Bedford Square, Miss Willcocks. Come in, you and your fine *stoshy* and sample our hospitality!'

'Thank you, sir!' answered Mary, looking into Jem's eyes, too dazzled to think of her old muslin. 'What does he mean, Jem?' Earle Grant stopped and smiled.

'*Stoshy* is the Jamaican name for lover!' His eyes were bright. Mary put out her trembling hand and Jem took it in his own. Escorted by Earle and her own true love, Mary passed under the arch surrounded by fine Coade stone, into a lighted hall which was as fine as any she had ever seen...

CHAPTER 8

Mary forgot the cold London world outside; in Earle Grant's house she felt the heat of the tropics. Behind the tall sash windows, the mysterious island of Jamaica beckoned her dazzled eyes. What she saw there was carved on her heart like the Grants carved their tattoos upon the slaves on the plantation. In Earle's house there were no servants and Mary became part of a freedom she had never known. Black and white, master and servant were as one, all equal.

Earle Grant had a mistress, Juba, who did not wear the elegant silk of a lady, but an embroidered tunic that hugged her to the middle of her thighs. Beneath it a billowing skirt which opened when she walked and parted to disclose legs, strong like those Amazons Mary had seen in the pages of books, which she had stolen in to take from the shelves in Squire Birt's library. Juba had taken her upstairs and shown her a line of mahogany cabinets, filled with the finest clothes. Mary had taken out the dresses reverently; fine cotton, lawn, cambric, lace. She had held them to her skin savouring the feeling. Juba had dressed her in the most beautiful and taken her down to dinner. They had eaten 'angel-food', well-named because Jem fed her dainty bits from a golden spoon. She and Juba seemed like protected birds in a strong nest made by those who wished to cherish them.

'This is "matrimony"!' said Earle quaintly, lifting the cover from one of the dishes. The word for 'wedding' made Mary's heart jump and her breasts rise and fall above the low-cut neckline of the gown she had chosen. It was a pudding made in the old way, star-apples and oranges, spiced and sweetened. The taste slipped over her tongue and down her throat like honey, soothing away the saucy pimentade they had eaten with their meat.

'How do you feel after taking the sauce?' whispered Juba to Mary, while their men joked on.

'Why?' she asked innocently.

'Because it is pure cassava and gives you good dreams!' Juba laughed.

'This can't be true,' murmured Mary; it seemed as if she would wake up soon and be alone with Humphrey Moon again.

During that strange meal she learned many things; of how Earle had taken Juba to protect her from a cruel overseer on his father's plantation; of his disgust at the treatment of slaves; of his love for a mother who was never recognised by his father and of the cruel life black men and girls had suffered. When the stories were over Earle turned to Mary.

'What do you think, Mary, of such cruelty done to your Christian brothers and sisters across the seas?' Mary shook her head sadly.

'I am sorry for it, Earle,' she said, her eyes bright with tears. Jem put his arm about her waist and pulled her to him.

'It is not your fault, Mary, nor mine!' he said. Earle smiled.

'And something else, Mary, there are Christians in this town who will not sit, eat, nor drink with me because of my colour!' He put a hand to his face.

'Not me, Earle!' cried Mary, distressed. 'I love your ways—and Juba's!'

'I can see that, Mary!' said Earle, standing. He pushed back his carved chair, came round the table, bent and kissed Mary on the cheek gently. 'This is a brother's embrace, Mary; white or black, it feels the same. And now—we are going to bed!' He called Juba to him and she nestled close. 'Jem? Remember how fortunate you and your race have been. Make love always—not torment!' Mary and Jem watched Earle and Juba walk out of the door across the wide hall and up the staircase. Jem caught her hands and looked into her eyes, which reflected the bright lights from the candles on the chandelier.

'Well, Mary?' he was stroking her cheek. 'What shall we do?'

'I am yours, Jem,' she said softly. Her past life was far away now.

'Do you mind that I am married?' he asked.

'No!'

'I will not hurt you, Mary, but—always love you!'

'I know, Jem.' Jem drew her head against his velvet shoulder. Hiding her face against him, she let Jem Farr take her up the staircase, kissing her as he went. Mary's eyes were closed as her dreams began in truth.

He laid her gently upon the bed Earle had brought with him from the West Indies. Around them he drew the drapes, beautifully embroidered with scenes of native love. When she felt his strong body against her own, she was almost fainting with joy; his skin was smooth like the silken sheets, shoulders broad enough to cling to in her delight; hair, thick enough to twine her hands in joy. There was in her a wildness she had not felt since she plunged behind him through the Devon lanes. He guided her with a skill he was learning afresh. She twisted and turned at his dear commands as he pressed her more and more—

and then they were riding together to a dizzy height where all was panting agony.

She thought she would break in two upon his spurring and when the dark world of loving burst they fell madly down and down, drowning in their love as sweet relief flooded their frenzied senses and gave them peace. She held on to him in her delight, knowing he had never ridden away from her on that night in Witherage, but taken her with him then to Heaven close to the Devon earth. To Jem, that taking was more than love. It was the planting of new life in him and her, the closest sweetness he had ever known. He had thought nothing of Celia then; no regret but had been swept away on a ride so passionate that he could never remember one the same. Mary's climax was full of years of waiting and wanting Jem. They had both been lonely.

'Such a coming together never was, my Mary!' he murmured as they lay, sated with breathless passion. They fell asleep and Mary rode in dreams over the moors; madly threw out her arms and clasped him again. He woke and kissed her breasts and all the secret places until she was his once more. It was a wondrous bed; its strength had embraced their wild lovemaking; its curtains safely keeping their most intimate secrets. It was a place for love and Mary learned to be a princess there.

. In the darkness before dawn, Mary woke to trace a delicate love picture with a gentle finger upon Jem's chest between the manly hair and around the little nipple. He smiled and caught her hand, stopping its boldness. Then he put out his and returned the caress. Her limbs felt like water under his touch and the fires stirred up again. They did not see the dawn fire the sky nor Juba step silently into their room and retreat with a delighted expression on her face.

'Come, Earle, look at these two!' She stretched out her hand and Earle grasped it, lifting it to his lips. She had given him untold pleasure throughout the night—and he was glad Jem had found the same. 'Dear Gem,' thought Earle, 'the best friend I have in the world. You have found love after all!' He held Juba's hand.

'Come, Juba, leave them to their dreams in this happy bed!' It was meant to be a bed for loving; he had brought it back to remind himself of his own birth and breeding. When his mother had forsaken her poor bed made from bulrushes to feed him in this great one, it had been the beginning of a better life, master's woman or not. He had never known pale Mrs Grant, but he knew in his heart that the mulatto girl with a sweet face had borne him truly. Juba and Earle walked out as silently as they had come.

The late morning sun woke Mary with a start; she stretched her limbs deliciously as if waiting to feel Jem's body upon hers once more.

The warmth caressed her like Jem's touch; she hardly remembered where she was, only that she had loved him. She turned to look for fear it was a dream like all the others. But he was there, his curls dark on the pillow, his body smooth against the sheets. Her eyes travelled over its strong lines. 'To think that any man could give so much pleasure!' thought Mary, wondering. 'How could I ever have believed that those things Moon did to me were anything to do with love? Why, love is all sweetness and joy!' She drew back the drapes with the strange foreign scenes. She had seen nothing of the fine room last night, only gazed up at the candles' light as he carried her to the bed, and drunk in their reflection from his eyes until that sweet time when he had closed the curtains about them.

The furniture was tall, fashioned of strange woods. At first she thought it was black poplar, but its hardness was such that she knew it was a foreign tree. Some of the deep drawers were open, inviting her to look. Within, the clothes were beautiful. The naked Mary stepped from the bed, walked over to the cabinet and took out a brocaded turban and set it on her curls, like the women wore who adorned the drapes of the bed. She stood before the mirror looking at her own strange reflection, stroking her body lovingly. Here he had touched it—and here.

'Oh, Mary, you are beautiful!' Her heart lurched at his voice and the consciousness of her nakedness. Jem was up and out of the curtains with the white sheet about his brown loins. 'Are you playing at being a Jamaican girl?' She put her hands across her to try and cover herself from his gaze. He laughed sweetly. 'No, Mary. Don't cover yourself up. Let me see you again.' He was close and she felt the sheets slip down and his warmth…

When they had loved again, they sat on red cushions and strewed the fine clothes about the floor. Jem dressed her in silk and lace; she donned trousers open like Juba's and he kissed her white legs about the thigh. He clad her feet in silver slippers, then took them off to caress her toes. She put him in a billowing shirt and laced it. It was then they heard Earle's voice:

'God bless you, Jem—and Mary! Come out and eat the feast we have prepared for lovers!' Mary and Jem came down the staircase, their arms entwined. They were gazing in each other's eyes and spoke loving words. Juba ran across the hall—and kissed Mary on both her cheeks. She led the girl on to the drawing-room while Earle pulled Jem by the arm. Juba sat on the drawing-room floor, cocked her head on one side and Mary blushed.

'Was it beautiful with Jem, then?'

'Wonderful, Juba!'

The girl rocked with delight.'And so it was with Earle. The *duppy* is laid, Mary!'

Mary looked puzzled. 'I don't understand what you mean, Juba.'

'It's a kind of ghost—in the Caribbean—he knows what is in our hearts. What is done cannot be undone!' Mary shivered suddenly as if a cold shaft had struck her heart. Juba looked at her sympathetically.

'One day Jem will return to his wife, Mary. It's cruel, but true. He must although he loves you. But she is sick and—she will die!' Mary shivered again, thinking of poor Celia.

'No, Juba, she will live!'

'No!' said the negress calmly, 'the *duppy* say she must go!'

'Not witchcraft, Juba!' Mary remembered the strange scenes about their bed, where lovers made their potions and wise women their spells.

'No *ju-ju*, Mary—only true love!' said the girl lightly and then she smiled. 'But Jem will not go yet—until he has left a seed in you which will blossom and be cultivated!' Mary shook her head at Juba's talk. 'Why, Mary, nothing but a little child which will grow in your womb and be part of him!' Mary felt faint; she was remembering the month she had been told to wait.

'Don't faint, Mary!' went on Juba, 'it is the most natural thing in the world. Isn't it what you want with Jem?' Juba's face was serious.

'I don't know,' said Mary. 'I hadn't thought about it!' She wondered at her ability to lie to herself as well. The only thing she could think of at that moment was her life with Humphrey and the terrible knowledge she might be carrying his child. The thought made her feel sick; she knew her face was white, so she looked down quickly to hide her pallor.

However, Juba did not continue the conversation, only rose from the cross-legged position, stood for a moment, then came and laid her hand on Mary's arm. In that light touch, Mary felt sympathy and understanding, which she had found only rarely in her life. They started as the doors sprang open and Jem stood there. There was anxiety written in his face.

'You're not sad, Mary? What's the matter? Didn't I make you happy?' He lifted her pale face and stared into her eyes. He turned to Juba. 'Have you been saying something to upset her?'

'No, Jem, she hasn't! T'was only women's talk!' cried Mary. Juba smiled, but there was a wariness about her.

'All right, Juba, you can go,' he said.

'I'm not sad, Jem, truly I'm not!' If her heart had been breaking she wouldn't have let him know. He was too dear to her. 'I'm tired, I think and—' He imprisoned her in his arms once more.

'And so am I after such a night!' She blushed. 'Mary, if I hadn't to go—' She put up her hands and pulled his mouth down to hers. When they ceased kissing, she said:

'Do you have to, Jem?' She marvelled at her boldness. She had only been with him for a night and all she could think of was how to keep him for ever. She kept thrusting down the thought. that he might not feel like she did.

'It won't be for long,' he said. 'I'll be back tonight and the next—and the next!' He wanted to tell her then that she had no peer; that between him and his wife there was none of the passion he felt for her. With Mary he had tasted such physical satisfaction of which he had never dreamed. He had been a bastard for so long; hardly remembered any woman's touch could be this sweet; had been farmed out as a child; lost a mother whom he loved. As Jem held Mary and felt her body against his; her fast-beating heart; her firm and lovely breasts; all those lost feelings welled up inside. One night had made her all those things to him. If this was love, then he wanted it for ever.

As she snuggled against him and he brought her to a chair and drew her on his knee, he was wondering himself why Mary meant this to him. He thought it must be because he had been lonely and longing for comfort; that she represented the only comfort he had known which was his life in Devon with the Birts. It seemed that with Mary he could be himself, not someone else like he was with Celia.

All these thoughts rushed through his head as he felt her softness again; knew each burning touch and kiss was reciprocated by one who was feeling the same.

'Yes, Mary, I'll be back again,' he murmured, savouring her taste. 'For more and more.'

'You won't get tired of me?' The tone had such pleading that he smothered its doubt with another kiss—and another. But all the time reality was forcing them apart—for a while. It seemed that when he held Mary tight, Celia did not exist—but when he and they drew apart, the shadow of his wife was thrown upon them.

'I do have to go, Mary,' he said, but she buried her face against his shoulder. 'Celia will wonder what has happened to me. You see, I had stayed in of late and last night was—'

'Yes, Jem?' Mary raised her head. 'Was what?'

'Wonderful, my darling!' He kissed the corners of her mouth to frighten away that woebegone look. How could he tell her that he had been like a monk for so long that Celia might think him a dead man if he did not return.

Mary hated herself for making it so hard for him; the fact was she had never felt so jealous and selfish. She could not, would not pity that lady wife in St James's. If she had made Jem happy, he would not be with Mary now. She did not deserve him.

'Mary,' he said, 'your eyes are as quick and fiery as when you denied me that kiss in the garden at Brushford. Do you remember?' She had never forgotten how she had run in confusion from a laughing Jem Farr who had demanded a kiss as well as apple cake.

'How could I ever forget that day, sir—Jem. You know—I loved you then!' He just could not break away, until the arrival of Earle made it easier. He stood up and his friend put out a strong brown hand. Jem took it.

'How can I thank you?' he said. Earle smiled.

'I need no other thanks except to look in your face, my friend. I am happy for you—both.'

'Mary, Earle and Juba will look after you. They want you here with them—and so do I, my love. You will be safe here. No more walking the streets, Mary.' He shook his head at the thought, but Mary shivered inside as she saw the meaning of the words in a very different way. 'God, Earle, what a country this is where little girls can wander all alone without protection.' Earle nodded and threw an arm about Mary's shoulders. She was afraid he would feel her trembling.

'Mary will be fine with us, Jem. Don't worry—and hurry back. We shall all be glad to see you—but this one—' he looked into Mary's face, 'will be overjoyed.'

With one last quick movement, Jem stooped and kissed Mary's lips.

'It won't be long, my love,' he said. 'Try not to worry.' As he strode from the room, Mary clung to Earle and he turned her face to his shoulder to drown her tears...

Those early months of 1813 seemed the longest Celia had ever known. Yet her sad mood did not match London's, as the capital was full of hope now Buonaparte was on the run. Scarcely a day went by when she did not look out of the window and see the scarlet jackets of the guards as they marched out to Portsmouth, Plymouth or other harbours to join Wellington's ever-increasing army. He was bringing together the greatest force England could muster to bring the war in the Peninsula to an end. Soon he would have eighty thousand British and Portuguese troops ready to face the French.

The only good news that came to St James's that spring for Celia Farr was that Tom Barton, crippled from his wound and unable to stand the rigours of a soldier's life any more, was to return to his daughter's London home. Yet sometimes when she was really low,

Celia worried she would not live to see her beloved father again; the cough was getting worse and she was using more and more opiate.

The doctor had warned her about it.

'Be careful with the potion, my lady. You'll get too used to the drug and it can fetch you off unawares. Remember, it's a long sleep in eternity.' She had thought he showed a great indelicacy in mentioning death before her. Jem never did!

As she lay in the dusk waiting for her husband, her eyes were full of tears. She should have been happy that he was to spend a rare night in the house. How many times had she regretted her words urging him to go out and enjoy himself by mixing with other people besides her? He had taken her advice too seriously—and now she was sure he had another woman. Yet he had not ridden off the whole of that day but wandered about the house with a grim look upon his face.

Celia had longed to run to him and make him tell her what was the matter. She had hoped it was because he had broken off with the whore perhaps and was feeling bad about it. But when he looked at her, she was sure she was wrong and that whatever was worrying him was something to do with her. She plucked at the counterpane with anxious fingers as her mind roved over all the possibilities any frankness might bring.

Finally, she heard his step along the corridor, heard his valet close the dressing-room door. When it opened, her heart was beating as madly as it had done on her wedding night when she first beheld her handsome husband.

Jem walked into the bedroom, clad in a green silk robe, belted at the waist. Celia drew in her breath; once she had dreamed that those looks might be only hers; that wonderful body for her pleasure alone. Now she knew that had been pure fancy. Her anxiety brought on her cough and she looked at the opiate. He picked it up; stared at the poppy draught with serious eyes.

'You're taking too much, Celia,' he said. 'You know as I do how bad it is for you.'

'I must have it tonight,' she said. Something had to take away the pain that racked her breast. It was agony just having him stand there and knowing he did not wish to be near to her.

He handed her the drug without a word. He did not beg her to try and do without it; he felt her agony but there was nothing he could do to allay her fears. He had done all he could and now he was finished. Jem knew how she felt about him; what she wanted from him. He could give it no more than he could stop deceiving her every blessed day with Mary Willcocks.

'Why shouldn't I take it, Jem?' she asked, forcing him to give her some kind of answer. It could not be the one she craved—that he loved her above everything and must keep her with him in this world for ever.

'It is bad for your health,' he replied. At least that was a true answer.

'What health?' she asked and he caught the bitterness in the tone.

'You must have faith,' he continued lamely. That he had never lacked as he had always believed that somewhere happiness might be waiting for him.

He had never 'loved' Celia in the sense a man should love his wife. Between them there had been friendship and companionship. He had wanted to do his best for her; to help her. At least in that he had been honourable, shown loyalty. That gallantry he knew he had for women had shown itself in his ministrations to Celia, but there had not been love between them—not on his part anyway.

With Mary he had found physical satisfaction; the joy of bedding an equal in health who was full of the lust for living; who had journeyed with him to the height of pleasure. Even when he and Celia had first come together it had been nothing in comparison with this madness he felt for Mary. There was in him almost revulsion for Celia's sickness. When he looked at her white face with its blazing cheekbones, her wasted body; he could not stomach lying with her when not so far away his beautiful Mary lay waiting for him to return and love her passionately.

'Don't look at me so, Jem,' whispered his wife and he averted his eyes. 'You're angry with me, aren't you,' cried Celia. 'What have I done? What's the matter?' She hated herself for being so weak; but she would have done anything in the world to be in his arms again. It seemed that the weaker she became, the more she burned for him to drag her back into his bright life out of the darkness which waited hungrily for her poor body. She wanted to howl at him, batter his wide chest with her frail arms, ask him where he had been that month of nights when she had retched out her heart in a lonely bedroom. But she had not the strength. There was so much difference between them like spring and winter; he, so full of life and she withered and cold. That someone who had brought him such vitality was stronger than she!

'You have done nothing to me, Celia,' he answered. 'Only good!'

'Then why—' she cried. 'I have faith in you, Jem, you know I have—and in myself—if only you still love me! Come here, my darling and hold me close. We've been apart too long.' Her body was aching for him. 'Kiss me, Jem, please!' She was catching at his hands desperately.

From where he stood he could smell the drug about her and it made him recoil. He let her hold his hand, wring it in hers, but he knew his fingers were cold. He could not make love to Celia any more, but he pitied her with all his heart. There was still integrity within him that would not allow more lies. Mary had begged him to tell Celia about them; to leave her. There were other ways than words. Celia knew already—and it was a cursed business, but he could not give up such happiness for sainthood.

'Oh, God, Jem, don't you understand I want you?' She despised herself for begging; it was almost like the small bitch tied in the yard, howling for relief.

'I know it, Celia, but—'tis no use,' he said, looking in her eyes. She burst into tears, turning her face to the pillow, her breath coming in struggling gasps, the pulse throbbing madly in her neck. But he had no way to comfort her. 'Celia! Celia!' he said, hopelessly. She controlled herself then, fearing he would walk out and be gone for ever.

'Jem,' she said, coming to herself a little, mastering the mad despair which had almost overtaken her. 'Will you listen for a while?' He nodded, conscious of the hurt he had done her. 'Let's speak of this no more. I know now that you don't want me; that you have—' She shivered, drawing the bedclothes about her shoulders; hunching herself so that her shadow was thrown by the candles into stiff angular shapes about the room. 'You must do what makes you happy, but I beg you—let us stop as dear brother and sister in this world. As we have been friends, let us stay so—'

'Celia—'

'No, hear me out. I will not beg you again to be my husband, but I'll never forget what you've been to me and —if there is justice in Heaven above, then you'll be only mine in that bright place!'

'Forgive me, Celia!' The words broke from him in spite of himself. He wanted to do nothing that would betray the great love he felt for Mary.

'For what, Jem? For needing the kind of love I have never been able to give you? For wanting the child I cannot bear? I do forgive you, Jem, although it is murder to me to know you are going somewhere else!' She turned her face to the wall then and he stood by dumbly, until he put out a hand and pressed her shoulder.

'Celia, listen. I am going to Brighton with Earle. I've made up my mind. If you need me, I will return. I think it's better this way—that we're apart. I will write, I promise—and you'll let me know if—'

'Go, Jem, please go,' she sobbed. 'I don't want to hear any more!'

He walked out into his dressing room, threw off his robe and stood naked and free before the window. He closed the doors so he could not hear her sobbing nor see the great four poster where he had spent so many miserable nights. He entered the adjoining bedroom and turned down the sheets.

He could have called the maid to do so for him, but he just wanted to be alone until he was with Mary again. One night away from her was Purgatory. He had forgotten to pull the drapes, so he lay in his single bed looking up at the cold spring moon until his mind flew fast to Mary of his dreams whom he made his wife again...

Celia's face was wan as she watched her husband ride away. She wondered if she would ever see him again; knew he was taking the woman with him to Brighton; knew she had lost him for ever. He had told her he would return if she needed him. Perhaps she should have pleaded madly for herself, begged him not to leave her to die alone; to help her like a husband should. But in her heart she knew it was no use. Nothing would change; he loved someone else.

Celia stood mutely as Jem rode out of the courtyard. She saw him pause, look back fleetingly, so she lifted her hand in a tiny movement, then withdrew behind the heavy drapes, struggling with her tears...

She had more to endure later on in the morning when her lady mother arrived.

'You let him go!' The duchess's tone was incredulous. She had ferreted out the trouble with bright little eyes, which roved cruelly over Celia's shrinking body. 'What else could you expect, daughter? Jem's a man. If you can't satisfy him, he *will* go elsewhere. He has his father's appetites!' Celia's colour rose at the words; first, in defence of Jem; secondly, because she despised her mother for what she had been.

'No, mother, Jem is not like Robert Castel! He's a fine man. I love him!'

'You fool, girl. You haven't loved him enough! Where's the son he yearned for?'

'You are cruel, mother,' cried poor Celia.

'He is gone because he can get no children on you!' continued the duchess mercilessly, turning from her pale daughter.

'Is it my fault I am so ill?' asked Celia, wounded to the heart.

The duchess wagged a fat finger. 'Sick or not, you should keep him in your bed, girl! Or he will get a permanent taste for other women!'

Celia was terrified then what would happen if her mother found out what had passed between her and Jem; what would she do or say if she found Celia and Jem were to sleep together no more; that they would never have children; that Jem had gone off with his whore. Her hand trembled as she took the cup of tea that the maid had poured from the silver pot. Her mother's stern eyes fixed upon her then and she quailed the more. When she watched the cold woman climb into her carriage, Celia returned to the house, thinking the most miserable thoughts ever. 'I might as well be dead now Jem is gone and I have no one to turn to!'

She passed through the corridors with dragging steps that kept pace with her heart...

Humphrey stood, one booted foot resting on a velvet chair, flicking off the mud from his morning's ride. He had hoped the fresh air might soothe his temper. He hated the empty cheated feeling he knew so well since he had lost Mary Willcocks to some aristocratic coxcomb who had made her his own and hidden her somewhere for his pleasure. How many times had he sifted the little knowledge he had, looking for clues. He had been sure that the whores watching could give some description of Mary's abductor, but the stupid fools had as much chaff in their heads as that simpleton, Milly Cater of Brushford, had in hers.

He had been in such a rage when they refused to help him that he had thrown a pewter tankard and cut the face of one, who had immediately threatened him with the tipstaffs until he offered her a gaudy to shut her mouth. He was sorry he had marred her face, but when Humphrey lost his temper he could not control himself. It had always been so and would probably remain so.

Humphrey knew he could have what whores he wanted but there was no one like Mary. Her quick and viperous tongue had relieved London's daily boredom.

He put down his foot and roared for his servant to remove his boots. As he sat in the chair, thrusting his leg against the man's chest, he wondered why he had ever thought London to be wonderful. It was not that he craved for Brushford in the least, but he missed what he had been when he had come up with Jem Farr. He was jaded with loose living; had satisfied all his worst appetites; had enough coins to do as he pleased; fine rooms and whorehouses by the dozen to visit; but it was only when he met Mary again that he had perked up and seen the old Humphrey appear. Now she was gone and he was faced with the daily round of pleasure once more.

As the man toppled backwards, Humphrey scowled and ordered his day-clothes brought quickly. If he could not have Mary, then he would go and find Jem Farr, who had grown cold to him of late and who had buried himself like a monk in his dreary marriage. Perhaps he could tice his old friend out again, away from the clinging Celia and they would bring a new meaning to whoring.

As he stood to be dressed, he considered whether to tell Jem about Mary. So out of sorts had he become, he was almost of a mind to enlighten Jem as to how he had found the minx and enlist his help in the quest. As he settled his cravat, he cursed himself for thinking of it.

Why, Farr would want her for himself, Celia or not, and that wouldn't suit Humphrey. Not at all!

He decided there and then that he would take a turn round the square and call upon young Lord Castel. There was only one thing that made Humphrey uncertain whether his benefactor would be in the frame of mind to see him; he had been out a lot of late and thick with the chocolate fellow whom Humphrey abhorred. 'Still,' thought Humphrey Moon as he blundered along aimlessly tapping the railings with his cane, 'he might want a change of friends again and take to old Humph after all.' So wallowing in self-pity, the farmer's son made his way to the opposite end of Farr House, which stretched itself around the square as befitted the great home of a London gentleman.

When he reached the portico, his mood had changed to savagery as he thought once more of how Mary had given him the slip and he cursed all aristocrats who could buy and sell bodies at will with the heaps of coin they had never earned. His face was deep red with anger as he snarled at the footman who answered the door.

'Pray tell the young lord his oldest friend is here!' The man hurried off, his face a frightened mask, to return with

'Madam will see you, sir!' So Jem was out again! Humphrey suddenly wondered if he kept a whore like Humphrey did not! He followed the footman, who threw open the doors of the morning-room in haste.

Celia was bowed over embroidery. She looked up at his entrance and Humphrey could see she was paler and plainer than ever. If he had been Jem and faced with such a wife, he too would be out each day, thought Humphrey nastily.

Jem's one-time friend was the last person Celia wanted to see that morning. His face was flushed and she feared he had been drinking. She would never understand why Jem kept Humphrey Moon in idleness.

'Good day, Humphrey,' she said and her voice was thin and cold.

'I was looking for Jem.' His words were pointedly insulting. Her colour rose, making two red spots on her cheeks.

'You've missed him, I'm afraid,' she answered, glad it was so. Humphrey growled impolitely and slapped his thigh with an impatient hand.

'Do you know where he is?' She shook her head; she wasn't going to tell Moon that he was with Earle Grant, nor that they were going to Brighton together. She would not give him that satisfaction.

The farmer's son jerked his cravat straight, bowed his head, turned on his heel and strode out through the doors. As Celia watched him go she thought the labourers on her Yorkshire estates had better manners.

Humphrey loitered outside thinking. He was sure now that Jem Farr had tired of his grey life with an ailing wife. Suddenly he burned with curiosity to know what Jem was up to. He walked round to the Mews and was successful in frightening the stable lad to death, from which he ascertained Jem was gone again to Grant's.

Then he went to find the evil-looking fellow who swept up Jem's stables and whose services he had gained before. The man looked at the gold coins, then ducked his head respectfully. He risked his neck working for Mr Moon especially if it was likely to bring trouble to his young master, who was kind and thus his servants' favourite.

'If you can find the information I want,' snarled Humphrey, 'there will be more where this came from. I want you to discover where young my lord is going; whose bed he shares and when he will return. Tell anyone about our conversation and I will break your neck!' The man shivered; he had felt Mr Moon's wrath before and he could imagine his bones cracking in a vice-like grip.

He jerked his head, looked round and over his shoulder, then whispered:

'I'll bring you all the news I can, sir, you can depend on that.'

'Make sure you do or it will be the worse for you!' threatened Humphrey with a cruel smile. Then he hurried through the stables to rig himself out in riding clothes intending to have the friskiest horse saddled so that he could gallop away his anger in a mad ride through Hyde Park...

Those few weeks with Jem had made Mary a different woman. When she thought of her former life as Humphrey's whore, she thrust the thoughts away and fixed them upon the man she loved. Nothing seemed to exist for Mary outside the Jamaican house in Bedford Square. She forgot the ugliness of the streets beyond its walls; the poverty she had known, but enjoyed a life she had only dreamed of. In Juba, she found a happy companion who had also known a crueller way of life and been scarred by it, but who was putting it all behind her in the secure love of a man.

It was only when the dark moods came upon her when Jem left for St James's that she put down her head and cried, imagining him in the arms of the pale cold wife who waited for him. She loathed that daughter of a great house and wife of a noble man, whom she loved more than Celia did. She had begged Jem not to return to her, but he had always gone; spoke of duty and loyalty. Finally, Mary had wept and beseeched him to tell Celia he would go home no more, but he had stared at her with serious dark eyes and she had loathed her selfishness and thrown herself into his arms, begging forgiveness.

Sometimes she thought that perhaps he did not love her truly; that she was still to him the serving-maid he had first known; that she could never be his equal, but those fancies faded away fast when he returned to take her in his arms.

Yet when she was in a sweet temper there was plenty to amuse her in Earle Grant's company. He had taught her what it was like to live the life of the Indies; talked with her in the quaint pidgin dialect of the island which she had picked up quickly; and how he had roared with laughter when he found out she had always longed to fence like a man.

Mary did not know that Earle was one of the finest swordsmen in London, but she knew that when they donned their masks and he taught her to fence in the Jamaican fashion, she longed for a man's freedom to fight and win what he desired. So the long days passed and the nights in Jem's arms were all too short. Mary had taken to wearing the tunic and breeches of a Jamaican girl and a brocaded turban upon her curly tresses. Jem said it suited her being wild and free, but that spring morning she felt imprisoned within herself.

Jem had told her that when he returned he would be hers alone. She had stared at him wishing it was true, but she dared not believe it. She could not imagine he would leave Celia for her although it was her dearest wish. But he had said so and she wanted it to be the truth.

The thought of what had passed between Jem and Celia had tormented Mary the whole of the night. Besides she did not feel well and thought she had taken too rich food at dinner. Desperate to chase away the gloomy night, she had asked Earle if he would fence with her at an early hour and, somehow, it did her good to hear the bright blades clash and grate; their fiery chatter vanquishing the drab night ghosts.

It was only when Jem did not return early that she was plagued with doubts that he was going to tell her they must part. At ten, she was practising her cuts when she saw him appear above her in the gallery. Her stomach was churning; her nerves on edge as she heard him come clattering down the stone stairs. By the time he reached the last step, she was determined to brave it out and fight for her love, whatever he had to tell her.

Suddenly and irrationally, she lifted her rapier as he approached her, arms outstretched and smiling. He stopped, puzzled by her action. She pointed to the line of swords.

'Mary?'

'Come on, Jem, see what I've learned with Earle!' He put up his hands in a gesture of surrender. He wanted to humour her, seeing what a strange mood she was in.

'All right, Mary, but you know I need only one weapon for you!' His forwardness made her heart lurch.

'I mean it, Jem. I want to show you.' He turned to look at the sword rack. 'Any one will do,' said Mary and he could see the fire in her eyes.

'I've never fought a woman before. Not with swords anyway,' he joked, wondering what was behind her strange behaviour.

'Well, now you can try,' said Mary.

'One minute,' he replied, taking up a blade to please her. 'Before we start we must make a wager. I know, if you win, you can do your worst!' He laughed and his eyes sparkled. 'If I do, you will be sorry!' He was into a fighting stance as quickly as a cat. Suddenly Mary had the devil in her.

'Did you ever fence with Celia, my lord?' she asked as she circled, but inside she was cursing herself for the sarcasm. He did not deserve it; he was never mean to her. Jem didn't answer, just followed her with his eyes and the quivering sword. She wanted to drop her weapon then and run into his arms, but she could not as she had made the wager.

That lost moment of concentration was nearly the end of her, because he flicked her guarded breast with the shielded tip of his sword.

'Didn't Earle warn you never to be off guard?' he said and she could hear the hard tone in his voice.

'You won't disarm me,' she said and drew the small dagger with the emerald hilt from the hidden place in her breeches. With sword in her right and dagger in her left she closed upon him.

Neither of them saw Earle and Juba standing in the gallery as they fought each other for supremacy.

'You are doing well as a man, Mary, but I like you better as a maid,' he joked, but Jem's breath was coming fast and his eyes were very bright as he pursued her.

Once, she almost had him, and was ready to fling down her weapon and fly into his arms, but the play-acting had grown deadly serious upon his side. He was driving her back inch by inch and she was weakening. She wanted to cry 'Quarter!' but it was all in fun, so she kept on brazening it out.

He put up his velvet-covered arm and blocked her cut; she almost forgot herself and struck at him with the dagger, but his other hand was swift. He grasped the little weapon and twisted it from her until it clattered upon the floor. She knew now she had made a mistake; that she'd gone too far; that a fit of pique had brought on something so earnest and deadly she was very frightened.

'Now, Mary,' he said softly, 'what will you do?' He broke her grip— and her arm almost. Her sword spun away and over the polished floor. With the tip of his sword, he forced her to her knees; then she was on her back and his length was heavy on her.

'I win!' he said and her gentle Jem was gone. He put his hard mouth over hers—then Mary could feel her head reeling and everything go black. With a terrible heave she was pushing him away and trying to rise as the sickness came upon her. With a tiny scream she turned her head to one side and vomited...

He carried her up the stairs, panting. The perspiration ran down his face as Earle and Juba met him and helped carry Mary to the bedroom. Jem stood back, trembling as Juba leaned over Mary with anxious eyes.

'Earle, what have I done to her?' cried Jem. Juba turned:

'Don't worry, Jem, she'll be all right. Leave her with Juba. The play was too much, that's all. Take him away, Earle and give him some wine. I'll look after her.' Jem was still turning to look at the bed as Earle led him through the door.

Mary put her two hands to her face and shivered.

'God, Juba, I am sick!' she moaned. The girl looked at her keenly as she unlaced her blouse and breeches.

'Remember, Mary—it is morning!'

'What do you mean?'

'Our conversation? Mary, the time has come!'

'You mean—the baby!' gasped Mary, realising the truth. 'Oh, no!'

'Don't be afraid. You'll be fine—but you must play men's games no more if you want Jem's baby to be safe.'

'Oh, Juba,' sobbed Mary and the girl stared at her, a puzzled look on her kind face as Mary continued to cry uncontrollably...

'How are you, Mary?' he asked, his face full of anxiety as he hurried towards the four poster. 'What happened?' She looked at him uncertain as to how she should begin. If her love had been the only man she had known it would have been easy to blurt out she was pregnant and wait to be cosseted and spoiled. On account of her fears, the words came haltingly:

'I think—I'm better now—did Juba—' He stared at her and she knew she was not making sense. 'Jem, I'm sure I'm—pregnant!' She waited—then he was on his knees beside her, cradling her body in his arms.

'Oh, Mary, I love you. That's wonderful—a baby!'

So many thoughts rushed into his mind. It seemed as if the whole of his passion for Mary had centred itself upon this one beautiful thing—that she and he had made a new life, which was part of them alone!

'You're happy, Jem?' she asked and there was a tremor in her voice. He kissed her tenderly, then with a greater hunger, but she held him off. 'What did *she* say?' Jem had forgotten to tell her and she had to know.

'What do you mean?' She wondered how he could detach his mind and only think of one thing at once, when she was tormented by so many.

'Celia. What did she say?' He didn't want to remember his wife, because his joy in Mary's news was rushing like a fountain-head and welling throughout his body. But he could see Mary was in deadly earnest.

He put out a hand and stroked her curls back from her brow. 'She was—distraught.' He was afraid to upset Mary with the details. He was dismayed to see tears start in her eyes. Mary herself didn't know why she was crying. After all, hadn't this been for what she had prayed all these weeks? It seemed now a little thing in comparison with the baby. 'I'm sorry, Mary, I didn't want to upset you.'

'I know that, Jem. I was just thinking that we are so happy and she—'

'Don't, Mary,' he said. 'Celia understands about—us.'

'How could she?' asked Mary. 'I couldn't if I was in her place!'

'Thank God you are not,' he whispered, burying his face in her soft neck. 'When will it be?'

'What?' asked Mary.

'The baby? You're sure, aren't you?'

'Not quite, but I think so.' If it hadn't all been so serious she would have laughed at his innocence. What did a man know about a child anyway? Plenty about getting it, but bearing was a woman's business.

'Imagine—my baby,' he murmured.

'Ours!' she corrected gently but, all the time, she was thinking of her visit to the old doctor and his not being sure. Perhaps this child could be Jem's after all? Suddenly a worse thought struck her. It would be a bastard, whoever its father was!

He could see by her face something was wrong.

'Are you afeard of having the child, Mary?'

'Isn't any woman?' she said quietly. 'But I'm more afraid of it being a bastard.' The shock struck him too. He had been so happy with the news he had almost forgotten she was not his wife. 'You know what it means, Jem, don't you?' she said, looking at him with honest eyes.

Within himself, he could not imagine this child to be illegitimate, because he could never have offspring by Celia. Fate had ordained her lot, however cruel.

'I'll marry you,' he said. In all his exuberance and joy of that moment, he was ready to step over the boundary of irresponsibility. Hadn't he cut himself off from his life with Celia? He kissed away the wonder in Mary's face until she was breathless.

'How can you?' she gasped. He placed a finger against her lips.

144

'I'll find a way. The only thing you need worry about is—the baby!' He laughed out loud and she saw the Jem she had always loved. Gone was the serious frown; the melancholy look. He was the old Jem Farr who had teased her at Brushford, then had treated her so gallantly her heart went out to him as being able to do anything in the world.

Mary still held the hope that he could work a miracle—but would the babe be like him? He was so dark and Humphrey was fair!

'Mary!' he chided. 'You're worrying again. What you need is care and rest—and I can give you both! Nothing is going to stop my baby being born! Now, here's some exciting news for you. I am going to take you away from London; to somewhere that will do you good.

'You like the sea, don't you? Every Devon man and woman loves the shore. Not to the West Country, Mary, but to the most fashionable place on earth. You'll love it. All those gowns and fine gentlemen and ladies—' She laughed with him then, catching his spirit. 'And uniforms, Mary, you know how you like those!'

'Where, Jem?'

'Brighton! With Earle and Juba. While they sell sugar to His Portly Highness, we will stroll down the Steine and I will buy you everything you wish—' She loved him so much then, it hurt. The sickness had left her and she was ready for the adventure. At that moment, safe in his arms, she could have faced a dozen Celias but as she clung to him—she still thought she could stomach only one Humphrey Moon.

CHAPTER 9

Royal Crescent had proved to be a charming place from which to enjoy Brighton's many pleasures. It was very fashionable which was a bonus from Mary's point of view. She declared to Jem that she had never seen such dresses and style. He'd laughed fondly at such a frivolous attitude, but she knew he was so delighted at the idea of being a father that he wouldn't have cared whatever she said. In fact, he was willing to give her absolutely anything. Sometimes, when she thought about it, she felt she had to tell him about her former life but, when it came to it, she hadn't the courage.

'I can spoil you as much as I like here,' was what he said as he rubbed her aching back. She was now heavily pregnant and quite uncomfortable, but his attentions did her so much good. She knew she was luckier than she'd ever dreamed she could be but, behind it all, there was the nagging remembrance that the child would be a bastard.

'Jem, I'm so happy,' she whispered, but the thought was always there. So she let him spoil her as if to make up for it. Brighton was, after all, London-by-the-Sea with all the capital's excitement and none of the dangers Mary feared. Here there was no Celia and no chance of meeting Humphrey.

Rather, she was likely to be confronted by the advent of another new and accomplished dressmaker or milliner. There were tailors and breeches-makers coming in every day, so the men were well suited too. Earle, who took a great interest in his appearance was forever telling Juba that the money he was making from his negotiations in the Regent's kitchens, was flowing into the tradesmen's pockets as fast as the outgoing tide.

Yet he, too, was delighted with their joint apartments. He said he felt at home there as the Crescent had actually been built by a plantation owner. Mary added this knowledge to all the rest she had learned from the coloured man and his mistress. She knew Jem took his advice daily; she must do the same.

There was another advantage to the Crescent. There were Mews where Jem and Earle could keep their horses. But Mary liked the bow windows best. There she could sit and look out to sea imagining far-off lands. She looked across at him one morning when the sun was reflected in the glassy surface of the waves and striking the white house with its glare.

'You like it here, don't you?' He nodded in answer to her question. What he liked most was the added beauty of she who was carrying his child. 'I'm glad you're happy,' she added.

'You are too?' His anxious face made her curse herself for being so tactless.

'Of course, but I wasn't born to such finery. Remember I was a simple villager.'

'You were never simple,' he said. 'There was always too much going on in that sweet head of yours.' She laughed and he was glad of the easy familiarity he felt in living with Mary Willcocks. With her he could be just Jem.

He liked Brighton. It had none of London's coarseness nor extremes of poverty. Here his conscience as to the miseries of the poor was easier. In this graceful Crescent there seemed to be only affluence. He cared about the less fortunate but, now, it was his chance to have some happiness.

'What are you thinking?' Mary said.

He smiled. 'Only about how lucky I am—having you and him.'

'What else?' She knew him so well now.

'Is there anything else?' He was thinking how little she really knew about his life—farmed out at three and educated.

Mary had expected that answer from him. He was a sophisticated man.

'No, why should there be? Come here. Why are you wearing this old jacket?' She brushed a mote of dust from the velvet.

He marvelled at her wisdom. He understood her too. She believed that because he came from the highest echelons of society it was best to trust him. She could never realise what evils wealth brought ; all the riches of the Castels and Bartons could never make up for this simple and joyous life with Mary. She was everything to him. He had known his mother only for a short time, then he had been taken from her like a discarded puppy. The Birts had been very kind, but he had not been theirs. How could he acknowledge a man like Robert Castel as his father? He didn't want to be a part of him. As for Celia—through no fault of her own she'd never been a true wife to him.

He sighed, then saw her worried face. 'It's all right, Mary. I'm quite content.' He didn't want to lose that trust she had in him.

'Jem, I hate to say it but—' Her fear was bursting from her.

'What?'

'The baby. It'll be a bastard.' She began to cry. Jem was shocked. He had never seen her weep like that.

'Shhh, love.' He cradled her in his arms, but what could he say? It was the truth.

'I don't want him to be,' sobbed Mary, allowing herself the luxury of being cosseted. Somewhere, inside, she was hoping he might have an answer. She stood, her feathered plumes drooping over her curls.

'Hush, Mary, 'twill come all right, I promise you.' He held her to him. He knew what it was like being a bastard and he had come to pity the child kicking lustily inside her. But what could he do?

As the time for the birth was approaching, Mary knew she was demanding too much from Jem; her daily heaviness made her irritable and unreasonable. And she kept on thinking about Celia. If she hadn't been up there in London, it would have been only her, Jem and the baby to come. She didn't want to hate that shadow, which seemed to be continually thrusting between them, but she was learning how to!

Jem seemed to be able to read her thoughts. She knew he had never wished the marriage concocted by his father and the duchess, so she kept on pressing him. She hated herself for it because he was always kind to her and courteous.

The matter came to a head one morning when a visitor arrived asking for James Farr. The housekeeper showed the gentleman in. He was older than Jem, quite elegant and evidently making the call out of pure courtesy.

The Marquis of Salisbury bowed over Mary's hand, but his eyes were cold and scathing. She felt extraordinarily sensitive that moment and fought to withhold the tears. Salisbury was perfectly polite as a gentleman should be, but Mary knew that he scorned her for being Jem's whore. With all the emotion that was in her, she vowed she would never have anything to do with that lord again. When he left, she went to the bedroom and cried.

Jem bent over her anxiously. She could see the strain in his face. She stared at him wanly.

'That Salisbury—he cut me dead, Jem, you know he did.'

'It's not true, love, he was most perfectly mannered.'

'It's because I'm your—' She couldn't utter that foul word that meant so much in her past. That was what she was; all she was. And she had so wanted to be a lady!

'Don't, Mary, you're not that!'

'What am I then?' She despised herself for continuing to hurt him. 'I'm not your *wife*, am I?' She wished she was back in the farm garden waiting for his horse to come skittering through the yard; then she had been untouched and still his!

'Not in name, love, but—' he sighed, soothing her with stroking.

'That's the trouble,' she said.

'Salisbury is sure to have a mistress. They all have. I expect that's why he's in Brighton.' He was trying to please her; she didn't want to know.

'I wonder if they are as miserable as I am,' she cried, burying her face in the pillows. Mary realised how badly she was behaving but, however much she loved Jem, she somehow wanted to pay him out for what a man had done to her.

And it was not his fault! She was sorry after and clung to him, kissing away his sad looks.

'Mary, Mary,' he said, 'you're all fire and sweetness.'

Then he was kissing her too and they were taking from each other what comfort they could...

Jem talked to Earle about it. He had never seen anyone as determined as Mary when she wanted something. He had lain all night wondering what he could do. It was so bad for her and the child to be in this state— and he wanted nothing to happen to either. He knew little of women's moods before childbearing, but he was sure such anxiety would do Mary no good.

Earle shook his head and smiled. 'Women have always been so, Jem.'

'But you've never experienced it?'

'I haven't been so lucky.' His face was serious.

'I'm sorry, Earle,' said Jem, cursing himself for the remark.

'Don't be, lad. It's the way we live—and Juba can have no children.'

'What will you do?'

'Who knows? But we're not discussing my son-to-be, but yours.'

'Earle, when we were in London I told Mary I would marry her. It was a wild thing to say but—'

'You wish you could?' Earle was sorry for Jem with all his heart.

'I have a wife!' Jem set his teeth and ran his hand through his curls. 'I wanted no wife; now I have to have Mary. She's the mother of my child. And he'll be a bastard like his father!' At that moment Jem could have destroyed anything within his reach because of the passion he was feeling. Earle was silent, letting his friend pour out the anger within, knowing the torment Jem was experiencing.

'There is no choice for me is there, Earle? I got myself into this. God knows I don't want Mary to be this unhappy and—I can't wish ill on Celia! But I have to do something!'

'Do as you feel, Jem.' Earle was so sorry for him, could appreciate those feelings, but it was Jem's decision. 'All I can say is that in our culture things are different. There we 'marry' as we will. We call our women 'friends' which makes them our wives. You know it is only in your society's eyes that whores are made.'

'I wish your creed was mine,' said Jem bitterly.

'But, lad, you wouldn't want to be black,' said Earle quizzically. 'Count your blessings—they are Mary and your child. Forget all the hypocrisy of wealth and position. If you have faith it will all come right. Anyway, I know it will!'

'How?' cried Jem, but there was no hint of what Earle meant in his unfathomable eyes.

'Juba said the *duppy* told her it will all come to pass.' The words were so strange that Jem felt a coldness in him. 'Make Brighton a honeymoon to last you through the bad times.'

'Can you tell the future?' Jem was about to cross himself; he had almost forgotten how. 'Have faith,' Earle had said. He finished the cross. Earle was smiling.

'Not I, Jem, but Juba is a seer. Everything will come to you in time.'

'If I could believe that, I'd be happier than I am now!'

That conversation with his friend had set him thinking of things long forgotten. He had been forced to marry Celia, there was no doubt about that. It was a legal union but they had hardly consummated the marriage. Besides, he had married her in a faith that was not his or his dead mother's. She had taught him to be a good Catholic and he had made vows in another church.

As Jem turned all these things over in his mind, a plan was forming. What if he married Mary in secret. When they had been in London, he had recklessly promised such a marriage to her. She believed in him implicitly and it might satisfy her. She wouldn't understand the legality of it all; she trusted him. And he was only doing it for her. If something happened to Celia then—

He hated himself for thinking that. He was behaving like a rogue. His wife had been so good and he loved her like a sister. She would never know what he had done. After all, Mary was his wife in all but name. But who could he find to marry them? Greater folk than he had managed such things before. He could find a priest, a foreigner, a Frenchman like himself. No one would know he had married Mary! The more he thought of it, the more attractive the idea became. At the finish he was convinced it was the only answer. In any case he intended to stay with Mary for ever.

It turned out that Brighton was the perfect place to find such a cleric. The town had been the refuge for many exiled clergy from

France. Quite a few had stayed on there whereas many had returned home after the Terror and others had gone inland.

Abbé Carfour, formerly of the Diocese of Nantes, lived in a small house in the village of Rottingdean. He kept a chapel there which was often attended by other exiles. He was well thought of in the village, as the Protestant pastor there was a good man who expected his parishioners to care for others. Abbé Carfour was allowed to practise the Faith with his own faithful until, one by one, they dispersed to return to France less afraid than when they fled that country. Soon, there were only a few left. So the Abbé was very happy to welcome a newcomer.

'Father?'

The priest shaded his eyes from the sun which was glinting on the sea making it glassy jade. 'May we speak together?' The dark young Frenchman seemed troubled and nervous. All the signs of a soul in agony showed in his face.

'Of course, my son.' The Abbé could see that the man was an aristocrat and, when he heard his story, he was overjoyed at the idea of bringing two more souls to salvation.

'Put your heart at rest,' the priest said to Jem. 'I will do everything I can to help you. I can't say I approve of what you have done but you're doing the right thing now, marrying the girl. But, first, you must make your peace with God!'

As Jem knelt before him, he trembled inside knowing he was making a false confession.

By mid-August, the Abbé promised to marry them. Jem kept telling himself that it was for Mary's sake and the child's he was doing this. His heart had thudded madly when the priest had given him the answer he wanted that it was his duty to marry her and make the child his. Carfour had not the smallest notion that Jem was married already. He had told the old man his name was Jacques Farré and that he was a French exile who was staying in Brighton waiting for the chance to return to France like the Abbé himself. Why should the Abbé think he was lying? He had promised that after the private ceremony in his rooms he would go along to a Protestant pastor in Brighton and fulfil his duty in the Established Church of England.

Jem hated all the pretence but he had to do it for Mary's sake. He had told the Abbé too that she was not fit to meet the priest and that he must be the one to arrange all.

The morning he had agreed with Carfour was very near indeed. It was hot weather and Mary had been finding it hard to sleep in the heat. She was very sad at losing Earle and Juba who had had to return

151

to London on pressing business. There was also the fact she was great and uncomfortable. She turned from side to side to ease herself.

He put his arms about her. 'I'm sorry you feel like this, Mary, but you'll cheer up when you hear my surprise.'

She heaved herself over and looked at him with puzzled eyes. 'What is it? Tell me.'

He got out of bed, walked to the window so she should not see his face. 'Is it another dress for after the baby?' He smiled at her vanity. 'Look at the state I'm in now!'

'I thought you loved finery above everything.'

'No, I love you best, Jem,' she called, sorry for being so ungrateful. Hadn't he given her everything she wanted?

He turned, came over, extending two hands to pull her up.

'And I love you,' he replied. 'Come here and look at this beautiful morning.' The mist over the South Coast was rising above Brighton and disappearing.

'What's the surprise, Jem?' She looked full into his eyes.

'We're going to be married!' He had imagined saying it so often; now it just slipped out. Her lips opened in amazement; she gave a little gasp and leaned against him.

He held her tight. 'Don't faint, Mary, please!' He could feel her trembling.

'When?' He swallowed at the question.

'Later this morning.'

'This morning,' she repeated, 'but how can we?'

'I've arranged it all.'

'You have?'

He nodded. 'Priest—and everything.'

'But who will marry us? You're married already!'

'Do you think I've forgotten?'

'Oh, Jem,' she cried wildly, putting her arms about him.

He could feel his child kicking within her. He put his hand on her belly. 'I told you he'd be a Castel.'

'Not a bastard,' she whispered. She couldn't reason it out, but Jem was a great man and power could do anything. For one inexplicable moment the thunderous face of the Witherage minister burst into her consciousness, ranting on hell fire. If it was wrong it couldn't be helped. It was what she had always dreamed of, to be wife to Jemmy Farr.

'Are you pleased?' he asked.

Mary wondered at his foolishness. He was like all men.

'How can you ask me that? Sometimes you are more like Walter Megs at Brushford than the great lord you are.' She put her hand to her mouth. 'This morning? What will I wear?'

'Mary, Mary, will I ever understand you or any woman? Here I've been worrying myself sick over how I was going to tell you and all you care about is having a wedding dress. Perhaps you shan't have one, comparing me to Walter!' He loved teasing her, safe in the knowledge that he had prepared everything.

'Jem, what shall I do?' A man could never understand how much something like this meant to a woman.

'You have it, my love,' he said and strode off. He returned from his dressing-room with an armful of boxes, which he strewed across the bed. 'All there. From the finest maker in Brighton. And it will fit!'

'Jem, I love you,' she said. He held her close. 'Are you as happy as I am?'

'Happier than I've ever been in the whole of my life!' he answered, lifting her mouth to his.

As he possessed her lips as he had her body, he was thinking that, if this secret marriage was regarded as evil in the eyes of society, then men were false and he would be answerable to no one but his God...

Mary tried to curtsy before the priest but found it most difficult. But the Abbé kindly raised her, seeming to take no notice of her condition. Mary couldn't understand that but, again, it was not for her to question. Jem had taken care of everything.

Carfour smiled at the woman's prettiness; he could not be sad in spite of her sin. Wasn't he going to join a young couple in matrimony? He was glad that one more heedless young man had repented of a sin only too prevalent in the frivolous society of that South Coast town.

'You have no need to curtsy to me, my dear,' he said in his broken English. 'Save your genuflections for your Creator.'

Both she and Jem trembled a little when the ring was placed on her finger. Mary was remembering the old life; not with Humphrey, but those past Sunday mornings in Witherage Church when the dark boy had stared at her from the pew where the gentry sat. This morning had made her one of them. She couldn't get over her wonderful luck. As the French priest uttered the musical Latin, she was reminded of the wedding of Mr David Lear. That had been the beginning of it all. Whatever was to happen in the future, she'd never forget this simple ceremony when Jem Farr made her his wife.

Jem's heart was beating fast when he looked into her happy face. It was a new life for him. He was remembering when he made vows that weren't so true. His heart had battered then, but not for the same reason. He would never regret this action but he was praying God would understand it.

Their servants stood as witnesses; Mrs Mayne the housekeeper and

Mary's maid. He had rewarded them with gold and they would never speak of it.

When that summer day was over and dusk was coming on, Mary and Jem lay side by side. It didn't matter that they had lived together for months, knew each other's bodies so well, because there was a bond between them now which gave them on-going strength. They could not be passionate on their wedding night because of Mary's awkwardness, but they enjoyed it in their hearts.

The last thing Mary savoured before she fell asleep was Jem's gentle hands caressing her tired body and sending her into the sweetest dreams.

Tom Barton looked across at his daughter. She was paler in complexion than ever and he was tormented by her sad look. He cursed his son-in-law for what he was doing to Celia. How could he leave her in this condition?

'Will you call Jem back?' he asked point blank. He had wanted to say it for days, but he feared to upset her more. Now it had to be said. He couldn't watch her pining like this. She was growing weaker while the other love of his life, the British Army, strengthened by its June success at Vittoria and its victory at Sorauren in July, was storming on to the summit of the Pyrenees.

If only Tom was with Cole and Picton. He would have been happier to face death on the battlefield than stare it in the eyes at home. He seemed to be surrounded by anguish. His war wound was painful and Celia was wasting away.

He waited for her reply.

'No, I can't. He'll come, I know he will.'

Tom swore at her patience. 'God knows why I consented to the marriage. He's like his father!' He grimaced with pain. The sabre had thrust very deep.

Celia, an anxious look on her face, hurried over. 'Sit down, please. I'll pour you some wine.'

'It's not wine I want. 'Tis him back here. You can't go on protecting him. He's like his father, I tell you!'

'He's not. I know him. I understand Jem. He'll come back to me.'

'*I* understand him!' said Tom bitterly.

'He's a good man, father and I love him.'

'Celia!' he said, looking into her face. 'I understand you no more than I understand any woman. How can you talk like that? He has been gone some time and he should come back. I'll fetch him.'

'No, you will not, father,' cried Celia. 'It's our business, not yours!'

What could he do? She was hurrying out of the room trying to hide her tears. He sat, staring at the floor, thinking of all the mistakes he'd made. He was a soldier, not a lady's man. He should never have allowed Celia to marry Castel's bastard. He passed his hands through his hair. If he'd been as strong with his wife as he was on the battlefield, he would have said no, but she had so much hold over him. If he had not done so their name would have been pulled through the mire.

He'd always known about his lady wife and Robert Castel, even when they thought he didn't. He had been prepared to stay quiet about the affair; he wanted no scandal and, in any case, he was always away soldiering. He himself had made a bad marriage; his wife had never been faithful. There were reasons, he supposed, as he was away so much but he still had the Barton pride. He hated scandal and the blight it threw upon a noble family.

Tom shifted in the chair, stood up and walked about the room, trying to think what to do. Robert had been cunning, insinuating that should Tom not agree to marry Celia to his bastard, he might take up his old liaison with the duchess again. He had implied she might even take up residence with him which would have tainted them all with London mire.

So he had agreed—now Celia was paying for it! When he first met Jem he had thought him to be an honest young man. Evidently he had been mistaken.

Although Celia didn't want him to interfere he felt he must. But how?

An hour later he was decided. He would send for Humphrey Moon, the most available of his son-in-law's friends. The rascal was living in the house; he was kept by Barton money and he would have to do something in return for that keep. Tom despised Humphrey as just another example of the effeminate young man of the time, who had nothing to do except enjoy himself and had no sense of responsibility. He thought that if such a one was shipped to the Peninsula and given a good trouncing by Wellington, it would do him much good.

But knowing Humphrey, the duke was inclined to think he would never reform. And as for James Farr? Tom grunted with annoyance. What could anyone expect from the son of a French whore anyway?

Humphrey was almost glad to learn that the Duke of Barton wanted him. He was sure he knew why. Ever since his spy had brought him the news that it was Jem who had taken Mary Willcocks, he had been smouldering with rage. Everything was so clear. All the time he'd been keeping Mary with him at the Row, Jem must have known. And he'd been playing the saint ministering to his wife while he was planning to steal Mary away from Humphrey. The farmer's son had cursed them both; the girl for escaping him and his former friend for taking her. Humphrey was sure now that, after their fight on the road to Witherage, Mary had let Jem do what he wanted.

The thought of that drove Humphrey out of his mind. If it had been any other man, any other girl, but her and him! He couldn't stand it. He had asked himself why. In one stupid moment he believed he really cared for his mother's former maid. It was true that when he was with her he forgot every woman he had ever been with. And he was bewitched by her moods, her talk, her wit, her violence even—but now Jem had her and Humphrey was beaten again.

He'd taken his rage out on every one near him. There was no servant that didn't run to him quaking with fear. There wasn't a whore in Number One Court that didn't shy away from him and not one of his so-called friends came to visit in his present mood. Not even that fool, Meredith.

So the summons from the duke was, at least, a relief from himself. As Humphrey put on his coat he was thinking that surely the old man had found out about Jem's whoring in Brighton. It served him right and, if he could, he'd help Celia's father to break up the liaison and get Mary back.

He wasn't disappointed.

'Your Grace?' The old man was seated at his desk. He looked tired. Humphrey didn't care about how he was feeling. He was only thinking of how he felt at that moment. He had never liked taking favours from gentry. Years ago he would have been satisfied doing the things he always did, riding to hounds and spending his nights with barmaids. But his father had spent money in making him into a gentleman, had given him an aristocratic fellow to play with—and now he was used to the life. He didn't want to jeopardise his position. He had to appear deferential.

The old man stared at the farmer's son, wishing he might never see the man again. Ever since James Farr and his wild companion had come into his daughter's life they had brought nothing but sorrow to her. The duke noted Humphrey's fashionable clothes with contempt. It was Barton money that bought a 'Polish' greatcoat with loops, frogs and lambskin facings. In London, all was foppishness and ridicule. Why, the rascal was wearing spurs and boot garters!

'So—you're here at last!' It had taken the man one hour to get dressed up like that. 'I'm going to be blunt about the matter on which you are called. My son-in-law is in Brighton. And I want him in London. As you are his friend, I assume you know what is his business on the South Coast. Do you?'

'Perhaps, Your Grace,' answered Humphrey carefully. He didn't want to upset the old man too much.

'None of your "perhaps", man,' said the duke. 'I'm a soldier and say what I mean. Do you know what James is doing down there?'

'He has gone with friends.'

'I suppose you mean Grant?'

'And others,' said Humphrey suavely.

'Do you mean a woman?'

'It's possible,' replied Humphrey, not risking 'perhaps' again. The duke stood up and walked round the desk.

'I want a straight answer, Moon, or you'll be out of this house on your ear and without a pence coin in your pocket!'

'I understand, Your Grace.' Humphrey could see the threat was meant. 'I think Jem is gone with a woman.'

The duke's face was flushed with anger. 'He's as much a rascal as you are. Aren't you ashamed, Moon? Lady Farr is keeping you in luxury and she is repaid like this.' The duke flicked a finger at Humphrey's coat.

'May I remind you, sir, that I am not married to Lady Farr. You should be saying this to James!'

'You're insolent, Moon. It is my money that keeps you in these clothes. And don't refer to my daughter without leave!'

'I'm sorry if you feel like that, Your Grace, but Jem has always supported me. Don't you know I'm the last link with his life in Devon?'

'Have you forgotten to whom are you speaking?'

'You called me, sir,' replied Humphrey. He could see the duke's cheek working with emotion. He turned.

'I'll give you one last chance to stay in this house, Moon. If it had not been for Barton gold, your precious playmate and yourself would still be knocking about the moors. But I'm not going to discuss my personal affairs with you. I order you to go down to Brighton and bring James back!'

'I? How could I make him come? I'm very sensible of Lady Farr's goodness to me. She's a wonderful woman. If I'd had the luck—'

'Sir, you go too far!' shouted Tom Barton. 'I don't care to hear your opinion of my daughter!'

'I'm only saying this because it's true. How can I get Jem to leave his whore?' Humphrey realised that he was beginning to enjoy the conversation. The old man was quite ridiculous. 'You should go, Your Grace, that would frighten him!'

'I cannot. It all must be kept from Celia. I can't fetch the rogue. She'll guess!'

'I could take a letter, Your Grace,' suggested Humphrey, relieved that the interview was turning in his favour. 'I'd be glad to do that, but not to speak with him.'

'Would you, Moon?' sneered the duke. 'You'd do anything to keep your feet warm in my house. Then you can take a letter.' Tom Barton banged the top of his desk in anger.

Humphrey sat, watching him write. All the time he was scratching the top of his boot with his whip end, thinking of the effect such a letter would have on Jem and how soon Mary could be in his power again.

Jem remembered that moment for years. He took the letter fastened with the Barton seal and stared at it. The comfortable room about him became fixed in his memory. Mary's easy chair in the bow window, where she sat watching the sea; the oval mirror surrounded by Cupids which he had bought her to remind them of love; the mahogany writing desk. All those objects that were common to them both were what he remembered in the days that were to come.

He broke the seal. It was not his wife's writing. He didn't hear Mary come and stand beside him, just stared at the summons, which was clear and threatening. If he did not return to Celia immediately, the duke would come down personally and force him to do so. Added to this, he would, if Jem was not of a mind to act honourably, dispatch the whore to where she belonged and teach her a lesson she would not forget.

The face of Celia's father came into his mind. He was a straight-forward old soldier and would do what he said. The effect on Mary would be devastating. He couldn't let it happen. He didn't blame the duke. Any father would do the same.

'Jem? What is it, love? Is it from Celia?'

He turned quickly. He couldn't let her see it. 'No, Mary. It's from the duke. An ostler brought it from the Brighton mail.'

'Oh!' said Mary. She had known it would come one day. Their happiness could never last. He had a wife!

'It won't make any difference,' he replied. It was a kind lie.

'That's not true, Jem. You'll have to go, won't you?'

'How do you know that's what he wants?'

'Jem, Jem,' she said, 'he's her father. Any father would do the same.' She sighed, remembering the brutal cobbler who had been hers.

'I won't go yet,' he said, holding her close.

'You'll have to, Jem. He's a duke, after all.' She was smiling through her tears.

He held her tighter. 'Mary, a duke isn't God! I can't leave you now.' Her face was buried against his velvet shoulder. 'Mary, are you listening? I can't leave you.'

'You have to go back to your wife,' she said, trying to stop the quiver in her voice.

'But you're my wife.' He felt her move away from him a little. He put down his hand and pulled her face to him. 'You are my wife, remember.'

'Yes, I am and it's enough for now, Jem. But Celia has always been between us. I've thought of nothing but her. You've been so kind; you've loved me so much. And I've been happy, happier than I ever thought I could be. I've had you, Jem, for a while—and that's all I wanted.'

'How can you say that?' He gritted his teeth to stop himself cursing the duke and Celia—'

'No, don't be angry, Jem. I've the child—and you'll come back. And we have a secret. We are married, truly. It didn't matter it was wrong. You'll always be my husband. I'll never want anyone else.'

'Mary,' he said, 'you're an angel!'

'I don't think so,' she answered, holding her breath tightly to steady herself. He mustn't know how she was feeling. What she wanted to do was to cling on to him and beseech him not to leave her, but something was preventing her speech. What she had said had evidently cheered him. She could never keep Jem if he wanted to go anyway; one part of her knew he did not, the rest that he would.

'But will you be all right?' His anxious looks were reassuring. 'How can I leave you, Mary?'

'It isn't due for a month—if the date's right.' She hoped her voice was sounding normal but, inside, she was amazed at her mind's capacity to hold so much. 'I'll be comfortable, Jem, spending all the time thinking about you coming back.'

'Thank you, love,' he answered. She could sense relief in his words. Her intuition had been right then—he was going to go anyway. Mary had always had the power to divine what folk were thinking. 'I promise you I'll be back as soon as I can. They can't keep me away from you.' He held her close.

When she was free of his arms, she looked at him calmly. 'I'll help you pack, Jem. No need for the servant.' That simple statement had been part of her life. She knew her duty. He was a great man, not a simpleton with labouring on his mind. She had been a servant for so long and would have done anything to keep her master near but, if he was determined to go, then she would still wait faithfully for his return.

The farewell nearly broke her heart, but she kept on smiling. His eyes were full of love.

'I promise I'll be back soon. Remember you're mistress now and the housekeeper and servants are ordered by you. If you need me for anything, send a letter by chaise. Take care of him.' He put his hand on the baby's shape. 'Mary, I love you. Remember that. Goodbye, my darling!' He kissed her and, with a glint of spurs, was gone.

She hurried to the window overlooking the Mews. She could see his horse saddled and waiting. He came out, looked up. She opened the window.

'Goodbye, Jem!' and the tears were already rushing into her eyes. She could hardly see him through the haze they made.

'It won't be long, Mary, I promise you,' he shouted as he settled himself in the saddle. Then he was wheeling the horse and trotting away.

Mary withdrew from the window, stood, hand clutching the brocaded drapes. The room had never looked so forlorn; she felt all the life within her becoming cold and numb.

CHAPTER 10

Mary was seated in her usual chair, but she was not behaving as she usually did, exclaiming on the fashions passing by or speculating as to the identities of the wearers.

Her mood was different. A heaviness had fallen upon her which was only partly caused by the thunderous weather. The beach opposite seemed to have caught the atmosphere too as there were only one or two late bathers waiting for their machines to be pulled into the water by the horses.

She closed her eyes wearily. Jem had been gone just a day and it seemed a lifetime. She looked at her bloated body. What would they say in Witherage if they knew? It was a strange thing to have a child growing inside; there was one comfort however; she had no more nightmares as to Humphrey being its father. The baby would be Jem's alone; she was convinced of that. The doctor would have been able to tell!

The thought was meant to comfort her but it kept bringing back the horrors of the day Humphrey took and raped her. If she ever met him again, what would she do? If Jem ever found out—? Mary got up and walked across the room. She felt the nervous tension rising within her. It was bad for her, and the baby, but now Jem wasn't here to comfort her fears. Perhaps the child would be fair? Jem was so dark. If it hadn't been for his wife—she was beginning to hate that shadow. She would never die! Immediately after she had given birth to such a thought, Mary was afraid for thinking so.

The maid entered carrying her morning chocolate. Mary could see by the girl's face she was worried to see her mistress so distracted. When she went out, Mary couldn't stomach the drink. She felt sick with anxiety. She heard the gentle knock.

'Come in,' she called miserably. It was Mrs Mayne. The housekeeper bobbed to her mistress, not failing to notice Mrs Farr's pale looks. Perhaps the visitor would do her good!

'Sorry to disturb you, ma'am, but there's a gentleman asking for you below.'

'A gentleman?' repeated Mary, puzzled. Who could be calling on her? 'Didn't he ask for Mr Farr?'

'No, you, ma'am. He particularly said Mistress Farr.'

'All right, Mrs Mayne, show him up.' Mary would be glad of any company the way she was feeling. As the housekeeper left, Mary rearranged her dress and, walking over to the mirror, patted her curls into shape. What a pity she looked so! She was deciding whether to offer wine or chocolate when there was a sharper knock.

'Come in!' She turned to the door with a smile.

'Mary!'

She stared wide-eyed; the blood draining from her face. 'You!' It didn't sound like her own voice, only hoarse and small!

'Me!'

Mary lunged towards the bell, but he was there first, warding off her helpless hand. 'No, no,' said Mary, shaking her head in disbelief.

'Yes, Humphrey Moon.' His eyes were flicking over her body with contempt, 'so what Mrs Smith said was true. You are with child.' His tone was hard and ugly.

'Don't come near me,' she said. 'Get out of my house!'

'Oh, no, I don't think so, Mary. It took me two whole months to find you and your lover. You little bitch, you always wanted him, didn't you? He had you that night in Witherage lane. Do you think I don't know?'

'Get away from me,' said Mary, drawing in her breath, her lips dry against her teeth, 'I'll scream for Mrs Mayne and she'll have you thrown out.'

'Scream away then. The woman knows a private meeting when she sees one. She wouldn't do a thing.'

Mary opened her mouth. 'Mrs Mayne, Mrs Mayne!' There was no foot on the stairs.

'What did I tell you?' said Humphrey. 'No woman ever refused gold.' Mary made for the door then, but he had her fast in his arms, pressing her against him.

'It's mine,' he said and she felt his weight.

'It's not! It's Jem's. Our baby, not yours. Let me go, you pig.'

'What language for a lady,' he replied, smiling. 'You would have passed it off as his, wouldn't you? And it's mine. That was a nasty thing to do, Mary, whore or not. I'd rather have it in the Foundling Hospital than in his arms!'

She was hearing those words in a daze. This couldn't be real. It was a nightmare. How did he find her? It was what she had dreaded for so long—and it was happening. Her stomach turned and the baby kicked frantically.

He looked at her pale face, glistening with sweat, up to her contemptuous eyes.

'Hate me all you want to, Mary. It won't make any difference. The bastard is mine. I don't care about being a father. I only want what's mine. And when I tell him about us, he'll agree with me. I know Farr; he'd never take to another's child!'

'You wouldn't, you wouldn't!' said Mary, clenching her fists. 'You mustn't tell him!' Her voice was a searing high.

'Wouldn't I just?' said Humphrey.

'Please! Please!' If she had to beg, she would, only he mustn't ever know. She'd kill Humphrey first—or herself.

'Shut your mouth, Mary,' he said cruelly. 'None of it'll do any good. You know that. It's your own fault. You took to the way of it.'

She knew there was no way of dissuading him, nor killing him either. She could feel a sharp pain tugging her inside and gave one little gasp. He pulled her to the chair and set her down.

'That's better,' he said. 'I don't want you having it here.'

She looked up at him with murder in her eyes.

'When Jem knows what you've done to me, he'll run you through.'

'No, that's what he'll do to you, Mary, when he knows the truth.' Humphrey wondered if he had gone too far. She was so pale. But it was her damned fault for standing up to him. Mary's throat was dry; she felt sick inside. If only she had been strong enough to tell Jem. There was no way out, no more then when Moon had raped her. His hateful eyes were still appraising her. How could he ever be anything to her when she knew Jem loved her?

'Whatever you said to him he'd never believe *you*. He loves me and we're married.' Although he didn't reply she knew what she had said had shaken him. Already she wished she had not, but it was too late.

'You're lying. How could he marry you?'

'He has—here; so be careful, Humphrey Moon.' There was still a chance for her by the look on his face.

'You little fool. He's married already.'

'I—' She was going to agree, but held back the words.

'You knew, didn't you, Mary? Do you know what it's called marrying two women? Bigamy, Mary—a crime.' His eyes were cold. She suddenly felt shivery as if she was going to faint. She should never have told Moon. What would he do to Jem?

Suddenly she felt herself fainting—that terrible feeling of helplessness, her head whirling. She bent forward and he had her in his arms. She breathed deeply trying to steady herself, to summon up the strength to break free, but she couldn't.

'Come on, Mary,' she heard him say, 'it isn't that bad. If you come with me I won't tell him, I promise. I won't harm him if I can have you.'

'You promise,' her words were dragged out from deep inside.

'I do what I say. At least you know that, Mary.' He took her chin in his hand and forced up her head. 'If you come with me, Farr will never know. Married, eh?' She couldn't stand looking at him, so she fixed her mind on other things. She let him nuzzle at her neck, the whole of her shivering with disgust.

'Don't worry, Mary,' he said, 'you were only his whore like you are mine. Lord James and a servant? Never. You should have known better. You're only another of his girls.'

'Whatever happens to me, Moon,' she said, jerking back her head, 'I'll make you pay for this. Someone will do to you what you have done to me. Whatever lies you speak, I tell the truth. Jem Farr loves me and always will.' She was away from his hands. 'And I love him, that's all there is to it. I can't fight you but, God knows, I'll make you sorry for what you've done.'

'You have your colour back now,' he said. 'Wipe your face—it's all streaked and worn. Come here.' He stepped forward, but she avoided him, drawing her sleeve across her eyes and cheeks.

'Keep away from me!' He was angry then, the veins standing out on his forehead, his face dull red.

'You'll come to your senses soon when you're back where you belong. You'd better get some things together.'

'I'm going nowhere.'

'You are,' he said, taking her arm. 'You'll go just where I say or it'll be the worse for him.'

She despised him for using such a threat against her. If she had not cared so much for Jem, she would have stood her ground, heavy with child, and screamed until help came.

'Get moving,' he said, 'or I'll make you!'

'No, you'll never make me do anything again,' she replied coldly. 'It's only because I'm like this that I let you do anything with me.'

'Won't I?' It was a flippant answer but his expression showed he knew she spoke the truth. He poured himself wine as she stuffed some things in a bag. As she looked at all the fine dresses Jem had bought her, she thought that he must come and find her. She didn't know what she would do if he did.

The coach was crammed and uncomfortable and Mary's condition made it even worse for her. The coachman had only one interest at heart; getting to London as quickly as possible. Speed was what the passengers expected and what they received. Comfort was lacking.

There was only one other woman in the compartment. Mary was glad, at least, of that. Ever since that sharp pain of earlier on in the day she had felt quite delicate and the occasional griping pains that struck her now and again boded no good.

Humphrey did not speak to her. He had always liked Mary Willcocks's spirit but, now, even that appeared to have deserted her. She was as pale as a corpse and sat with her eyes closed. He hoped she was not going to have the child. He'd delivered many a calf back at Brushford but never a bastard. He drank to steady his nerves. His flask was his comfort. She couldn't escape the coach and so he kept on swigging.

Mary could see Moon was getting drunk; his eyes drooping to the coach's painful rhythm. It had been the most dreadful journey, even worse than the one she first took into London, but now she was a wiser woman.

She was sure they'd reach the turnpike soon. Clapham was near and Lucy Tippet. If only she could give him the slip and find the milliner's shop. He was snoring, but she couldn't move. He had her ankles imprisoned by his boots and, each time she moved, he rolled against her in his drunken sleep.

She looked across at the woman, who had sympathy in her eyes. Mary shrugged miserably and the woman darted a cross glance at Humphrey.

'My ankles are quite swelled, you see,' said Mary. The other occupants ignored her remark. 'I'm very near my time and I didn't wish this journey.'

'I'm sure you didn't, dear,' replied her fellow passenger. 'Men! What a trouble they are!' Suddenly she looked mischievous. She was putting out her foot and jabbing at the side of Humphrey's boot. He stirred uncomfortably and Mary was free.

'Oh, thank you. What a relief,' said Mary attempting to lean and rub her bruises. It was far too much of a strain.

'No trouble at all, dear,' said the woman, 'I've had my fill of men as well.' She glared at the other occupants, who looked out of the windows.

'Are we nearing the turnpike?' asked Mary. 'I shall have to get out and stretch my legs, but *he* won't let me.'

'Almost there,' said the woman, 'and don't worry, my dear. If your husband can't let you have a breath of fresh air in your condition, he isn't worth a fig. I'll see you get out.'

'Thank you, ma'am, I'm very grateful. My back is really aching.' That was not a lie.

The swaying motion ceased. The woman leaned over and stroked

165

Humphrey's lolling hand. He was coming to. Mary was staggering up and thrusting herself through the door. She was so desperate she almost forgot she was pregnant. She could feel a tearing inside as a man pulled her down into the crowd. Then an agonising pain cut right through her. Stifling a cry, she hurried into the mêlée of coaches and people and was lost in the bustle at the Clapham turnpike.

Lucy Tippet was just settling down for a dish of tea when she heard the hammering. She couldn't afford to turn away any customer even if it was not shop hours. She put on her shawl and hurried through the front. There was no one to be seen through the glass. Then she looked down.

She thought a beggar woman had fainted outside her door, so she pushed it partly open to investigate. The woman moved, looked up.

'Lucy, it's me! Help me, please, Lucy, please.'

'Who are you?' cried the milliner.

'Mary! Mary Baker! Please.'

In the last fifty yards Mary had fixed Jem's face in her mind. If she could only imagine him, she would make it. She had brought out her breath in short gasps as she had seen Mistress Moon do when she was having Georgie. How far she was on she didn't know, because it seemed an eternity since the waters had broken and soaked her underthings through.

Lucy caught the girl under her armpits and pulled her inside to lean against the counter. The tall mirror where Lucy's lady customers tried on their hats, reflected Mary's dreadful condition. Lucy chafed her friend's cold fingers and wiped the sweat from her face. Then Mary let out a scream she had been forcing back through her clenched teeth.

'The baby's coming, Lucy, the baby!'

Mary whimpered, moaned, sobbed and screamed for five more hours. At the fourth, Lucy had had to send for the doctor. He and Lucy took it in turns to examine, cajole, instruct and encourage her for the last sixty painful minutes.

Mary had never wanted anything more in her life than that body to be severed from hers. She was almost out of her wits with pain.

When the head appeared, the doctor said, 'What a pity, Miss Tippet. If only women were taught a trade like a lad and apprenticed. Then they would never prostitute themselves for bread!'

It was a boy. He slithered into the world with a rush, his mewling cry like a piteous small cat. Mary could only hear him faintly. It was as if she was soaring above her pain of a body.

'A boy!' said the doctor. 'All over, m'dear, all over!'

He handed the child into Lucy's capable hands and, like a good business woman, she wrapped him in cloth and gave him to Mary. She stared at the screwed-up little face under a thatch of the darkest hair, then burst into tears.

They were seated together before the fire with the baby feeding at the breast. Lucy had asked no questions about his father and Mary was grateful.

'He'll have to have a name, Mary. What will you call him?'

'I've been thinking,' she replied. 'Edward Francis.'

'Why?' Mary smiled at the question. Lucy wanted to know and she would in time. She couldn't call the child James and she wanted to forget Humphrey's existence.

Edward would be for dear Ned Burgess of St Giles who had saved her worthless life. She knew little about Francis, except she liked the name. It had country music in it. Once she had seen a picture in Squire Birt's library of a man with dark eyes like Jem's, seated on a hillside with those natural creatures about him she remembered from Devon days; the quiet vixen, a brown lark and everywhere those woolly fools of sheep. Below the picture, the golden letters said simply, Francis. It had always stayed in her mind. It would do for him.

'Was that *his* name?' asked Lucy. Mary put her finger to her lips.

'Hush. Look, Lucy, he's asleep at the breast.' Then she looked into the eyes of her friend. 'I will tell you, Lucy, I promise, but all I want to do just now is sleep.'

CHAPTER 11

'My lady, my lady, his lordship's here!' Celia's maid was almost running.

'Calm yourself!' chided Celia. If her father saw the girl's unbecoming behaviour he would think his daughter had no control over her servants. Then Celia remembered he was taking his evening exercise and her heartbeat rose in her ears. Jem had come as he promised. Jem had come home.

'Thank you, Lord,' she prayed under her breath, holding the arms of the chair for support. Then she began to cough.

'Shall I fetch your smelling salts, my lady?' asked the girl, but Celia shook her head, trying to suppress the hollow noise.

'No!' He must not have come home to a wife who was near swooning. 'Help me upstairs!' The maid took Lady Farr's weight easily as she led her to the staircase.

While Celia was being helped into the dress she had saved for Jem's return, she was beseeching the Lord again!

'At least let him stay a little. Let me hold him in my arms again. Let him have left her and come home to me!' She was begging to hear the answer but there was only silence in her heart.

She stood passively, worn out, allowing the maid to dress her. All she could think of was defending Jem to her father. He had been wrong because Jem was here of his own accord. The duke must never know he had a mistress.

She had to protect her husband from her father. Celia could never tell him, any more than she could order Jem to stay at home. Her husband must take what course he had chosen. She loved him more than anything and the girl could not harm her. Celia was his wife!

As she came slowly down the staircase she was thinking of that first sweet moment she had seen him. Then it had seemed too good to be true. Whatever was happening now there had been good times. On the bottom stair she was already sure he had left his mistress, had tired of the whore, but when she looked in his eyes she knew he had not!

'How are you, Celia?' His kind tones almost made her weep.

'Tolerable.' It was like meeting a stranger. He took her hand and kissed it. That was all his lips said. A faint brush on her skin. She wanted loving language from him, but none came.

He walked over to her embroidery frame. His broad back was towards her. She waited for him to speak as he looked at the intricate piece she had been working on when he left for Brighton.

'I've nearly finished,' she said, wishing all such mundane things could be pushed aside and she was in his arms once more. 'It's been difficult—'

'I know,' he replied. The pink dog-roses on the frame reminded him of Mary. It was more than difficult. It was going to be impossible. He turned to his wife. 'Celia, I'm here but I—' He had been wrong. There would be no need to explain. She knew what he was going to say.

'You came back. Why? Did she leave you?'

Jem caught his breath. 'No.'

'Why then?' Celia waited.

'I had to.'

'You didn't come to see me. I should have known.' Then all was clear. 'My father! He sent for you. Didn't he, Jem?' His face showed the truth.

Celia's eyes were very bright. 'What did he say to you, Jem? That I'd die without you? Well, I will, I will!' All the hope that had risen within her had died most certainly. 'Go, Jem, back to her. I don't want you if *he* made you!' The exertion of the speech was making her cough. She gasped for breath. He went towards her awkwardly, but all he was wishing for was Mary's arms. He was sorry for her but what could he do?

'What's she like, Jem?' gasped Celia as she tried to control the spasm. 'Is she beautiful and elegant? I'm plain, but have a heart!'

'Stop it, Celia, you'll make yourself worse!'

'No, don't come near me, don't, I beg you!' She was near hysterics.

'Celia, you'll do yourself some harm!'

'And what do you care?'

'I do.'

'But not enough. You come back for my father, but not for me. And I love you, Jem, more than she ever could. I need you more than she!'

'She needs me too. She's—' He had almost given away that Mary was pregnant.

'What, Jem? She's what?' Jem could never tell her.

'Jem, tell me! Is she with child?'

'Yes.' There was no other way but the truth.

'Oh, Jem. Jem!' She sat down trembling.

'I didn't want to tell you, Celia.' He put a hand on her shoulder, but she recoiled.

'You have though—and now you feel better.' It was too much for them both. He sat down beside her, but she turned from him. He caught her hands and pulled her to face him.

'Celia, listen. Whatever you think of me, I still care for you, but I can't help loving her. God help me, but I do. And I always will.' His voice was quiet. 'There's nothing else I can say.' They sat motionless, Celia's eyes puffed and red from weeping; Jem's face grim.

She pulled her hands away, stood, small body tense. 'All right, Jem, I'm not so unfeeling as to harm any child. Go back to her. She needs you now. At least part of the child is yours.' She put her hand to her mouth, her knuckles showing taut and white. It was as if she was preventing herself from speech. In a moment she was calmer. Celia looked into his eyes. She had always known he was honest.

'Jem, I told you once that I didn't blame you. And now I'm even older and wiser. I hope that she will be kinder to you than you have been to me. Goodbye, Jem, I'll pray for you.' She picked up her skirts and walked to the door. The last picture she had of him stayed in her mind; his bow as she passed out of the room.

When Celia had gone he ordered meat and wine. He was mad to get back to Mary. It didn't matter that he was tired and the Brighton road was wearisome, nor that the last wedge had been driven between him and Celia. Barton would never do anything to him or Mary. He would take her away to safety, perhaps to another country where they could be happy together.

As he clattered out of the great courtyard of Farr House, Jem wished he would never live in its gloom again. He was dog-tired but he would have made the journey a hundred times if Mary was waiting for him at the end.

Mrs Mayne described the kidnapper so well that Jem was sure it was Moon. How he had got to Mary and why she had gone with him was more than Jem could understand. He only knew that the duke of Barton and Humphrey had somehow contrived to do away with his love. But what had they done and where had they taken her?

Half-mad with worry Jem found the ostler who had delivered the letter. The man told of how he had been given coins to say the news had come in the Brighton mail. Afterwards Jem learned from several people that they had seen a girl, great with child and as pale as death, get up in the stage in the company of a man with shining fair hair and rough manners.

Where could they hide her in London? Nowhere because he would have the truth from both of them. Although he was quite exhausted he hired a new horse and set back on the road to the capital.

Those who saw Jem that day hardly knew him. He looked fifty instead of his twenty-four years and his sweet expression was changed to one of misery. The groom who led his horse away in the dark morning hours trembled in case the young lord discovered who had given Master Moon the information.

'I've never seen him ride a horse that hard,' said the stable lad as he threw a blanket over Jem's mount. 'He must have ridden like a madman!'

'Where's he come from?' asked the groom.

'Why, Brighton, man,' said the lad and the groom was gone as quick as he could to convey the information to Moon.

Humphrey was drinking to steady his nerves. The night was full of discordant laughter and Blondie passed him by hanging on her gentleman's arm.

'Are you still mourning Mary, sir? May you never find her!' Humphrey clenched his fist, but the whore was well protected. He hated her and swore out loud that every woman was a jade!

Mrs Smith watched him carefully. He was giving her house a bad name with his evil temper and violent ways. She was hoping that one of his great friends would come along and carry him off home.

That thought was fate because at that very moment the drawing-room door crashed open with a frightened footman bowing before the stranger. The man was enveloped in a cloak and he still was wearing spurs.

Mrs Smith had been long enough in the game to recognise trouble when she saw it. She hurried forward to greet the gentleman, noting the strained expression on his face.

'Sir?' She curtsied, looking up into the darkest eyes, intimidated by the feeling of power he exuded.

'I'm looking for Humphrey Moon!'

'I'm not sure if he's in, sir.' Mrs Smith had summed up the situation. She sensed there was going to be a fight and she didn't want it in the house. While she was hoping that the stranger wouldn't recognise Moon, another part of her was wishing justice on a man who had caused her and her girls so much anguish. She stepped aside as the man suddenly strode forward. It was too late—he had evidently found whom he wanted.

Humphrey sat still, a bottle of wine before him. Now the moment he had expected was here, he felt a tingling in his body. There had been no doubt that Farr would find him. He was no fool. Humphrey even surprised himself in the knowledge that what he would have to tell Jem would be his real revenge. A sense of excitement was coupling with fear as Jem strode across the room. The aggressive urge to wound the nobleman was rising in Humphrey. It didn't matter that they had grown from boys into men together—what mattered most was that Jem Farr was just an aristocratic bastard, who thought he had the right to everything, including wife and whore.

Several of the girls looked frightened; some of the gentlemen adjusted their jackets and collars. There was a murmur of conversation, then silence.

Jem thrust his hands hard down on to the table and stared into Humphrey's face.

'You'd best stand, man. We have a score to settle!' Humphrey stood up abruptly and the chair crashed down behind him. A girl cried out and Mrs Smith signed to the footmen.

She was determined there would be no brawling in her best rooms. If this wild pair wanted to murder each other, then it would be done outside.

'So you made it at last, did you, Farr?' smiled Humphrey, but there was perspiration on his brow. Jem breathed deeply, trying to control the anger which, when it came, was so violent that it frightened him. Through set teeth he could see the madam bustling over, flanked by her servants.

'I want no trouble here,' she cried. Jem looked at her coldly.

'Then find us a place where we can do what we want.' The footmen were already at Jem's side, waiting. Humphrey moved closer. He was slightly unsteady with all the drink he had taken in the last few hours, but that didn't prevent him from recognising the situation. One footman slipped between Jem and himself.

Mrs Smith caught him by the arm. 'Mr Moon, I beg you, go to your rooms.' She was directing him towards the door.

Jem made as if to follow but another servant placed himself in front. 'Will you follow him quietly, sir?'

'I will. Stand aside, footman.' He felt calmer and Humphrey must not escape. Mrs Smith breathed deep in relief and fanned herself when the two men were out of the room.

'At the first hint of breakage, get yourselves together and throw them out in the mire,' she hissed to her servants. 'Now get after and see what they are doing!' But when the footmen followed, they already found the door to Master Moon's rooms fast shut.

They had stood without speaking for several moments. Then Jem said bitterly, 'You know why I'm here, don't you? To think I ever called you a friend.'

'Why should I know?' asked Humphrey, playing for time.

'You took her, didn't you? You and the duke?'

'Who?'

'Mary!' It hurt Jem even to say her name, to think what they had done to her. 'You came to Brighton and you took her away!'

'Mary who?' Humphrey feigned a puzzled look. Then Jem was right against him, standing up to him like when they used to fight as youngsters.

'You know what Mary! Mary Willcocks!' Humphrey almost lost his balance as a chair was close behind him. He was suddenly more sober than he had been since he had lost her.

'That whore!' Jem had him by the lapels but he twisted free, stood gasping, waiting for Jem to come at him again.

'What did you call her, Moon?'

Humphrey backed away, put his hands up. 'No need for fighting, Jem, lad, if you listen to what really happened—'

'Why should I listen to your filth?'

'Don't you want the truth?' Jem stood still. He didn't know why; he wanted to murder Moon there and then, but he had to know the truth.

'When did you ever speak truth? If you have done anything to her—'

'I did that a long time ago,' said Humphrey suddenly. He was like that; he could go on lying, but suddenly the words came out.

'What do you mean?'

'Remember that day, Jem, when you were in the carriage and she was coming down the road?' The words hit Jem more surely than any Humphrey could give him. How did Moon know about that day? 'Where was she going, Jem? Where had she been?'

'How did you know her after Devon?' Jem could hear his words but they seemed far away. All the time he was following Humphrey who was avoiding him.

'Why did she get in your carriage, Jem? Shall I tell you, Farr? Do you want to hear?'

Suddenly, Jem lurched and struck him a blow on the mouth.

'You're afraid to hear, aren't you, Jem? That's why you hit me, isn't it?' Humphrey felt the salty taste on his lip, which he wiped with the back of his hand.

'Where is she, you liar?'

'Careful, careful,' cried Humphrey, picking up a chair to hold him off. 'I don't know, do you hear, I don't know!' He didn't really want a fight. He had been drinking and would get the worse of it.

'You know!' said Jem, trying to get him. Humphrey choked. 'If you won't tell me where she is, I'll make you!'

'I *don't know!*' shouted Humphrey, backing into the bedroom. All the time Jem was after him. 'If you stop, I'll tell you. It'll do us no good sparring. She isn't worth it, Farr! Back off, man and I'll tell you the truth!'

Jem stopped. He hated the hot temper of his that snapped out his reason. It just came flooding over him and took his senses with it. He'd have to hear Moon out; then he could find Mary.

'That's better,' said Humphrey, straightening his back. 'We shouldn't quarrel over her.'

'Just get on,' said Jem, despising the oaf.

'That's where I had her, lad, in there.'

'What?' Jem didn't understand.

'Don't look like that. I'm as mad as you at losing her. She was my whore first.'

'What did you say?' He heard the words but they didn't make sense.

'I found her out in the street, dressed up as a footman. She'd put herself up for hire. Mind you, I'd seen her before on the street—then, when she had been in the Magdalen—'

'Mary,' said Jem under his breath.

'I took her. She was better with me. Don't look like that, Jem, it was my turn. You had her in Witherage.'

'What?' Jem was staring at Humphrey, his face creased as if he did not understand. 'What do you mean?'

'She was on that course then, you know that. Artful vixen.'

Then Jem was on him. He laid Humphrey out with full force and the two of them were sprawling. Outside the door the footmen got ready.

'You're lying, say you're lying!'

'I'm not,' shouted Humphrey, half-smothered below. 'I lived with her, I swear I did. Willcocks was my whore here in this very house.'

'I'll break your neck for lying!'

Humphrey could see Farr was in dead earnest, so he threw himself up and butted the man in the face. Jem staggered back and Humphrey was crawling out across the carpet trying to rise.

The footmen were trying the door.

'Ready!' shouted Mrs Smith. The door burst open and the servants were dragging at their arms. Jem tried to shake them off but he found he was blind with tears. Humphrey was standing leaning against the robe, but his eyes were bright with triumph. He tried to laugh but there was the feel of blood in his throat.

'Now, sirs, out with you,' cried Mrs Smith. 'I won't have this house made into a boxing ring!' Jem felt himself freeze. It was fear that took him, not of anyone, but of his thoughts. He was thinking of the child.

'Yes, you're quiet now,' said Moon, dabbing at his mouth with a handkerchief, 'but Mrs Smith will swear to it too. Hadn't I a whore

174

come in from Devon, madam? Tell this gentleman the truth. Did she not have a country look about her and a merry sharp voice—?'

'Enough!' said Jem. At that moment he cared for nothing. She would have told him, she must have told him, she wouldn't have deceived him. He knew!

'Yes, Farr, that had you, didn't it? And Mrs Smith, didn't the girl attend the doctor's? Was she with child?' Jem closed his eyes in agony. He would hear no more. All he wanted was to stop Humphrey's mouth for ever. That was the only thing that could ever give him satisfaction.

'She gave me the slip. On the coach, but she'll come crawling back—'

'Shut your mouth, Moon. You've done yourself the worst service taunting me.' Jem shook free of the footmen's arms. 'This brawl is over. You'll never speak like that again. I'll have my satisfaction.'

There were girls and men staring in at the door, listening to his wild words.

'Yes, look at me,' Jem said, 'look at him. And listen! This thing has deprived me of my wife and child. He'll pay for it.' He stared at Humphrey and through him. 'At dawn you can choose your weapons.' A thrill ran through the company at his words. Humphrey struggled out of the footmen's grasp and faced Jem.

'Suits me, Farr! Where can I blow your head off?'

'A carriage will come and take you there. Be ready.'

Blondie looked up to the ceiling. It was the finest thing she had ever heard—if only Mary could have been there to see it. Jem was pulling his mud-stained cloak about him.

'And if you do not come, I'll hunt you down!' He was already pushing through the crowded doorway, along the blood-red corridor and into the dark night.

They used no lanterns for fear of discovery. The men and the carriage huddled under the protection of the trees, where the unsuspecting birds were beginning to twitter in the dawn.

Earle's hat was pulled over his eyes, but he was still watching the set face of his companion. He had tried to warn Jem of the consequences; what would happen if they were discovered fighting illegally, but there was no telling him anything in such a black mood.

Earle blamed himself for leaving Brighton early. If he and Juba had remained, this might not have happened. He couldn't understand why the girl had gone off with Humphrey Moon or what she had been to that man. All he really cared about was Jem's happiness. And he couldn't believe Mary was false. She doted on Jem, who had poured out his heart to Earle all through that long night in Bedford Square.

It was then Earle learned that Jem had married Mary. Doubtless Humphrey and the duke knew of the ceremony, which was ill luck for his friend and even more so now he believed Mary had deceived him. That was the thing Jem could never stomach and what had prompted the duel. Earle had tried to comfort Jem; tell him there was an explanation, but the young man seemed unwilling to listen, but Earle knew Jem well. He would never believe that Mary was untrue without her explanation.

Yet he would not be dissuaded from the folly of a duel. It seemed that all his revenge must be wreaked on Moon and Earle couldn't blame Jem for that. He would have felt the same. Hadn't he been through it all with Juba and the *busha*? He too, had murdered that man just as easily.

Earle had let Jem's grief pour upon him. He had hoped he would cry himself empty, but he had been wrong. Jem was almost mad. Earle looked at his drawn face. He would look worse should he add murder to bigamy and what was more, perhaps lose life itself! It was then he heard the carriage.

'Here he is, Jem, he's coming!' The rattling wheels brought the enemy fast towards them. Hyde Park had been an obvious choice for such a meeting. There were many wild places in it which Princess Caroline had failed to tame. In the distance and direction of the carriage, Earle could see the glint of the Serpentine.

The gig came to a halt in the clearing and Humphrey jumped down. He was followed by a less agile second, although George Meredith had stirred himself pretty quickly when he heard that Moon was about to blow off that arrogant Castel head.

Mustering all the elegance he could, the Earl's son approached Grant. 'Mr Moon chooses pistols.'

'Pistols, old friend,' said Earle, returning to Jem. 'Did you want swords?' Jem shrugged.

'It makes no difference. Any weapon will kill a dog!' Earle was sorry to hear such reckless words. He was hoping rashness wouldn't take its toll and spoil Jem's aim. He walked on to the chaise and withdrew a finely-ornamented box.

As he opened it, the pinkness of the dawn exposed a pair of the finest French pistols any gentleman could own. They were so beautiful in that early light, their golden hilts enamelled in wonderful shapes, but as he carried them over, there was no beauty in them for the coloured man. To him, they were simply instruments of death.

Earle showed them to George, who, in turn, demonstrated Humphrey's weapons. They were plain, dull English, but from the finest maker. The seconds made the arrangements coldly; twenty paces, then turn right-angled and fire.

Jem struggled against the desire to get even with Humphrey. He was experienced enough to know all that mattered now was a steady hand and brain. He let Earle take off his jacket so his aim should not be hampered. He could see the perspiration standing on his friend's forehead.

'Don't worry, friend, I'm almost myself.' It was true, but he did not want to be Jem Farr, just some unknown man who had a task to accomplish and would do so without flinching.

As he faced the lumbering farmer's son, Earle thought what an aristocratic figure he made. His curls, although tied back by a ribbon, were somewhat ruffled by an early morning breeze that had come to cool the hotheads.

Humphrey's fair hair was dull red in the dawn. He found that his hands were trembling when he held the pistol.

Jem thought of Mary. She would tell him the truth. It was inconceivable that she would have gone with Moon of her own free will. Jem would have to seek out the reason and thus, he had to survive. The thought steadied his hand. Humphrey thought of Mary too; it made the blood start up in his face and he was still trembling. Jem was remembering Witherage and honesty; Humphrey remembered Devon with contempt. What inequality had been bred there between master and servant!

As Jem turned to walk the paces, he fixed Mary's face in his mind. He had to live on and prove that her love was true. He pivoted, his right arm stretched out; his elegant pistol pointed full on at Humphrey's face. He was almost light-headed as he fired—and realised he was still alive in the midst of noise and smoke.

Humphrey was reeling and Jem watched him fall in a misty dream. Then Earle's arm was about his shoulders, pulling him close.

'It's over, Jem! You had him in the face!' Jem turned slowly and together they walked towards the kneeling figures of George Meredith and the doctor. George's fat face was pale and quivering with shock. He looked up at Jem.

'You've done for him, Farr. You've killed him!' Jem could hardly believe he could have done such horror. His ball had caught Humphrey on the right side of his face, blowing the cheekbone away. There was nothing but a mass of destroyed flesh and bone—and blood everywhere, coursing down his linen, ghastly scarlet.

Earle looked at Jem's white face. He could not hear the birds singing to the dawn; they had been frightened away. The wood was silent, waiting for death.

A dizzy Jem ran from the scene and vomited. The doctor put his ear to Humphrey's breast, then took a small glass from his pocket and held it to his mouth. He looked up.

'He isn't dead, but near it! I can't do much, but I'll try.' George and the doctor, in company with the coachman struggled to lift up Humphrey's heavy frame. Then they carried him towards the gig.

Jem stood shaking until Earle led him to their carriage. Now he knew what he had done; killed Humphrey, removed the man who had given him such pain—but there was no triumph only an empty feeling—almost worse than the one before.

They sat together. Earle with his hand on his friend's shoulder trying to comfort him; Jem, his head hanging. Earle clapped Jem's back.

'At least you're alive, thank God!'

Jem straightened. 'I meant to do it, Earle, I meant to kill him. I was mad when he said those things about Mary but, you know, I think I was mad when I first found her gone. I wanted nothing else but to kill that swine!'

'I know, my friend, I know!'

'How? Have you ever fought a duel?' The coloured man cared for Jem then, more than he'd ever done.

'Yes, Jem, if it'll make you feel better, I've killed a man. And it was because I loved a woman. But it did no good, man, in the end; no good at all. I did it for Juba—on the island. The *busha*, you would call him "overseer" tore her virginity from her. She was but a little thing and I loved her even then. She was thirteen! What he did to her should never be done to a woman—but he paid. I broke his neck with my hands!' Earle stared at his strong fingers. 'Does that make you feel better, friend?' Earle closed his eyes.

'No!' cried Jem, ashamed, 'but, at least you know how I feel!'

'Man, you're distraught; you need rest—and peace!'

'I'll never rest without her!'

'And you'll find her, I tell you. Remember what I said in Brighton, Jem, it is only in the eyes of society that whores are made. You will find her and she will tell you the truth. If he had hidden her, it wouldn't have come to this. He was as mad as you at losing her. She might even come to us. She knows where to find you, Jem!'

'But where is she?'

'I guess she is gone somewhere safe and will return in her own good time. I'm speaking sense, lad. You may not be so lucky!'

'Lucky?' Jem rounded on him.

'No, Jem, I'm not your enemy. But you have some. The duke who will make you pay. He may charge bigamy upon you; and Celia—'

'She is not my enemy.'

'Oh, Jem, Jem. All this could kill her if she knows.'

'Stop it, Earle,' groaned Jem.

'Man, this is only sense. And Humphrey? Can you cope with it all? And Mary? And the child?'

'Don't, Earle!'

'What will happen to them if the world finds out? Mark me, it will! You're a great man and great men's pleasures belong to the world. Mary would be hunted all over London.'

'What shall I do, Earle?'

'Go quickly somewhere—and leave me to find Mary. Quit the country—give yourself space and air to breathe. You can sort things out when you're together again.' Earle leaned back against the cushions, knocking on the roof to alert Quao. As he gave the orders to drive to St James's, he studied his friend's face. He looked a little brighter and more hopeful. Earle marvelled at youth's capacity for rallying.

'Well, man,' he said, 'do I talk sense or not?'

'But how can I leave her here in London, without knowing how she is and what—'

'I told you, Jem, Mary can reach you when she wants—and I am sure she will.'

'I shall wait for her, Earle.'

'You will not if you have sense.'

As the chaise neared Farr House, Jem shivered. Full day was breaking on London and soon he would be a wanted man.

'Where shall I go, Earle?'

'The Americas? The Caribee?'

'But they're at war with England!'

'And so are you, man!' It was no time to joke but it lightened the atmosphere.

'Mary always said she wanted to go to the New World. She thought everyone was equal there.' It was so painful thinking about her.

'Well, when I find her, she can join you.'

'If you find her, I'll come and fetch her.'

'Then you're going to take my advice, Jem?'

'Yes, there's nothing here for me now.'

'And no one can touch you in the Americas. No Bartons nor Castels.'

'I'll take the name I used when I married Mary. I'll be plain Jacques Farré. But I will miss England.' He was thinking of Devon. 'And Earle, will you swear to look everywhere for Mary?'

'If I must,' he answered. 'I swear it on my word as a gentleman—but I'm afraid we're going to have swifter news of Humphrey Moon. That's why you must make ready at once. And I will resolve your affairs, your money and such. You won't be without.'

'You're a good man, Earle,' said Jem in a low voice. There had never been a friendship such as this.

As Jem alighted from the chaise and was swallowed into the house's gloom, all he could think of was Mary and the child. He had to hear her story from her lips and he would never rest until he did.

Celia tried to bear the shock. She stared in surprise when she knew his servants were packing. But she had never thought he was leaving the country. She kept away from him because she thought he was returning to Brighton to his woman. She was afraid to tell her father in case he had Jem followed and brought back, so she bore the added burden of that secret. It was not until she read the letter he left her that she collapsed crying in her chair.

Jem bade her goodbye as gallantly as he had always treated her; he didn't speak of love, only respect; about her fairness and his guilt; he reminded her of her own words when she had begged they should act as dear sister and brother in this world. He assured her he would never forget her, would always hold her in regard, but that he could not help what he had done or tell her how he felt. He added there were several other pressing reasons for his quick departure...

When she found out what they were she took to her bed. Humphrey had been cruel enough to pen a letter before the duel. He had it delivered two days after. It pointed out that Lady Farr had been much deceived and that Jem had married the whore in Brighton.

Celia tore his letter into tiny fragments and burnt the pieces. She felt a strange sense of relief as their ashes blew in the fireplace. She sent a message to Moon's rooms telling him to make a speedy departure and never bother her or her husband again—but the maid returned in a very great state crying that Master Humphrey and my lord had fought a duel and the former was near death.

After she had heard that, Celia became worse. A deep lethargy overtook her, deeper than she had ever known.

It was whispered gossip in the servants' hall that Lady Farr was surely on her way to Heaven, which would be the only true comfort accorded to her in such a short and unfortunate life.

180

CHAPTER 12

Edward was quiet at last. He was as worn out with crying as his mother who sat beside him rocking the wooden cradle Lucy had bought for the baby from the market.

Mary never stopped looking at the boy who was now the only love she had left in the world. She was afraid for him. He was no great feeder and would take little contentment from the breast. Instead he seemed to mimic her moods, first lethargy, then wild longings for other times.

Mary cared for Edward more than herself, as quite often she wished she had jumped off the five-barred gate and been hung by her apron strings.

Lucy told her that women often felt so after a birth and she had consulted the doctor who had brought Edward into the world. He had examined Mary and tut-tutted anxiously.

'Give her panado and gruel, Miss Tippet. Now, Mary, you must try to be easy and not fret. It's bad for you. Take a glass of wine sometimes and a morsel of chicken.'

It would have been a simple answer, but that was not what was the matter with Mary. She wanted to see Jem. However, a weakness had come all over her body and she hadn't the nerve nor energy. Whatever the doctor said, it was more from worrying about what course of action to take, rather than childbirth.

Finally she had decided and that was why she was seated beside Edward weeping and rocking the cradle. Lucy had been gone an hour already. Did it really take so long to deliver a letter to the house in St James's. Half an hour after that, Mary was wishing she'd made the decision earlier as, by then, Jem might have decided too to stay faithful to his wife.

Mary had worried so much about what to put in the letter. She was so frightened that Humphrey had carried out his threat and told Jem about her life with him. But she had to take that chance.

She had done her best. She said how much she loved him; that she would explain everything when she met him and then she told him the child was born and dark like him. She added that if anyone spoke evil of her, he must not believe it, but give her the chance to explain.

How many times had she blessed Miss Betsy Matthews teaching as she struggled with that letter. She wrote the words over and over again and even then she'd torn them.

At last it had been sealed and was gone!

Mary rocked throughout the whole afternoon. Finally, Edward was sleeping like an angel, until she heard the key in the shop lock.

'Lucy, Lucy, have you seen him? Is he well? What did he say?' There was no reply, so Mary rushed into the front to see the milliner slowly hanging up her bonnet.

'You didn't see him?' she faltered. The milliner took her arm and led her back.

'I will make a brew,' she said.

'I'll never taste drink again, Lucy, until you tell me,' insisted Mary, pulling Lucy into a seat. The woman put her hand inside her bodice and withdrew—the letter. Mary stared at it.

'What happened?'

'He's gone.'

'Gone? What wicked man told you such a lie?'

'It's no lie, Mary. Your Jem took ship—to the Americas—'

'No!' cried Mary, rushing to Edward, who stirred and moaned at the cold draught of his mother's skirts.

She put out her hand and plucked him from sleep, held his tiny frame close to her and hugged him, moaning, 'He's gone, my darling, gone, gone. Moon told him, told him—'

'No, Mary, Master Moon is near to death.'

'Death?'

'I can't tell you any more—'

'Tell me!' said Mary in an awful voice and the baby began to cry.

'I can't, Mary!'

'Tell me!'

'Your Jem fought a duel with him and—'

'Oh, God!' cried Mary, rushing into her friend's arms and hiding her face.

'And—' Lucy hesitated.

Mary lifted her face. 'There's more?' she asked dully.

'Lady Farr is very ill—from grief—and that is all!'

'All, all?' cried Mary. 'It's all my fault. I've brought this on Jem and her. I've lost him, Lucy!'

'Perhaps,' said Lucy, trying to find some comfort, 'but you have his son to care for. Think of that, Mary Baker.'

'I think of it till it drives me mad,' sobbed Mary. 'Help me, Lucy, please!' Lucy took a handkerchief and began to dab at the tears. Then she took Edward from his mother's arms and placed him back in his cot, where he continued to howl dismally.

'See, Mary, what you've done. The poor mite is beside himself. Come here, love.' Lucy drew Mary to kneel beside her and patted her on the back. 'It will come right, I tell you, if it is to be. Just stay here safe with Lucy until we decide what is to be done.'

As the old year passed into 1814, Matt Willcocks had become more and more resentful towards fat farmers like Frederic Moon. He was recovering some of that early spirit he had enjoyed as a young man, when he passionately declared himself as the local labourers' spokesman. His wife had warned him of rashness ever since he had affronted Master Farr in the inn kitchen, but he snapped his fingers at her.

It made him sick to see poor labourers walking the roads and squatting with their families, while a man like Moon, who had been too niggardly to raise a good girl's wages, could sell each one of his cattle for fifteen pounds or his land at any price he desired. Mary had never been seen since she left the Witherage cottage to seek her fortune and that, too, had been the fault of a Moon. Matt saw no blame in himself for Mary's departure but he had grinned broadly in the inn kitchen when all the talk was of that blackguard, Humphrey's fate. He had been conveyed from London in a fast chaise and ever since, had skulked, a broken man, about his father's farm, hiding his ugly looks from all.

Betty Bly had heaved at the sight of his face although she had been prepared for it by Milly Cater, who was doing housework at the farm and had reported that Humphrey Moon looked like the Devil himself.

Matt was glad that someone had given the man his just desserts. He had been asking for it for years. Gossip said that his horrific disfigurement was the result of a duel with a great man whom Humphrey had wronged. Matt had roundly cursed that unknown lord for not ridding the world of another worthless rogue of a master.

Matt stared into his ale, his sodden brain tinkering with the plans he'd made to get his own back on the Moons of Brushford. Cobbling paid better since the great Duke of Wellington had learned of Boney's defeat at Leipzig in October last, and had pushed on to strike at Soult on the Gave du Pau in mid-February. Folks needed slippers to dance in to celebrate such victories, while the English weather had been foul with deep snow drifts. Devon village folk needed their thick leather shoes mended continually and studded with nails.

A month ago he had been given a great commission to make two pairs of fur-lined boots each, for Lady Birt and the Misses Emma and

Jemima. When he ducked his head to the squire's wife, he still felt himself reddening when he remembered how she had swept up to his cottage and tried to teach him the way to treat his daughter.

Yet besides no dearth of business, there was still in Matt Willcocks a desire for revenge. That night he was waiting for Jawn, the rat-catcher, who had once been a civil fellow, but now had grown rough and ruthless too, having six children and a wife to support and all the vermin dying in the cold. Jawn's cottage lay four miles from Brushford near to where Birt and Moon land met. The two rich masters had joined forces to produce wonderful game. Matt was sick of skinning rabbits to line females' boots; he had other quarry in mind. He had had the luck to meet a London poulterer's man who would pay the price of twenty pairs of shoes for fresh partridge and pheasant. There was venison too—the list was endless. Poaching paid—until one was caught and severely punished.

It was a strange sight to see the men in their gaiters stealing through the trees and setting their snares. Matt leaned back on his heels to survey the neatest one he had ever set. It was near the fence where the hunt passed. Soon a gaudy pheasant would strut there for cover. Well satisfied with his night work, Matt emptied yesterday's spoils from the traps and the two men clumped off home through the wintry mud and water.

Mistress Moon threw her apron over her head and sobbed as she had done so many times since they had brought Humphrey home. She had screamed out loud when she saw his face so terribly marred, but it seemed he was lucky to be alive at all after that criminal had delivered him such a violent ball in the side of the face. The doctor wrote to say he'd lost much blood, and it was only in God's mercy he had survived.

But Humphrey had—and she prayed every day to thank her dear Creator. What wicked man could have done such a dreadful deed and left a young strong fellow a blind and helpless cripple? Humphrey could see—but only in one eye. His speech was slurred and his neck bowed like an old man's. What he said when he did manage to speak was not pretty. He had just railed at his mother because she had told him not to ride out on such a dangerous morning. She had begged him to take the gig, the wagon, or the chaise even. It did not matter—as long as he would not try Sweetbriar. She had been out to grass and had been used constantly for pulling the chaise, rather than riding free. Sweetbriar had once been a patient mare, but she hated rough work—and showed it. Whatever Humphrey's condition, he was still itching to be out and down to 'The Angel'.

Mrs Moon sobbed on, imagining folk's reaction to that sightless face and horrid leer. He could hardly walk, never mind ride; and was heedless of any warning of hers. She only wished Frederic was there to settle him. She was sure her husband would take him to the inn if he wished to go that much. February had struck them that year with a spate of murderous weather, and the roads were awash after the heavy snow. Witherage high road was worse than ever, broken in craters and holes. Mistress Moon was so afraid that Humphrey would take Sweetbriar and kill himself.

Humphrey drew the deep brim of the slouch hat over his brow, pulled on his muffler, which hid his scars, piled on waistcoat, jacket and riding cloak. He had had enough of a crying parent—and life was calling him. He longed for the warmth of a woman after those cold months of nothing since he had lain sick and maimed.

It was only when he put his hand to his face that he remembered the scars with loathing. His vital parts were still intact; he had the tool for loving and he needed comfort so much. He had seen Milly Cater run screaming at the sight of him, but the jade was a simpleton. Betty Bly had wed some crass labourer and was great with child, but Miss Pussy Clara was still free with her claws and a tongue. She would not see any man's face—only use him. Humphrey had waited for his father to leave for the fields. He had business at the lake shooting wild duck. There was no one to stop him now—only a crying dame.

He appeared at the kitchen door and his mother was rushing at him. 'Don't go, Humphrey, I beg you! You are not well!'

'Pack up the screaming, mother. I have only half a face—but I am still a man!' She drew back, afraid of his bitter tongue.

'Then go in the gig, if you must—but don't saddle the mare!' She cried again. He hated the whining voice, but he crept over to her slowly and slapped her on the back.

'What's done cannot be undone, mother!' His voice was hollow like the cold wind outside. 'There are more cheery places than Brushford these days! Goodbye!'

She watched him ride out of the yard, leaning dangerously to the side. She picked up her skirts and called for the idle girl, who had been the bane of her life since Mary Willcocks's departure, to don her cloak and boots and bring the master back to follow Humphrey...

Sweetbriar was free again like the swift mare she had once been. Now there were no shafts to bind her; no rattling harness on her sides, no cracking whip to flick her ears. Before her lay open land—and freedom.

Humphrey could feel the bit slipping as the mare dashed on madly, unmindful of his directing hands. The wind seared his scarred face like a knife and blew off his broad-brimmed hat. His one eye smarted with the intense cold and tears were blurring it. He had a dizzy head as Sweetbriar found hers and took the bit in her teeth.

She careered madly down the slope fancying she was back in the Brushford hunt when her master had whooped her on wildly before the hounds and riders had murdered that pretty vixen upon the hill. It was a stout fence hewn by a Devon craftsman, who knew his art. Its top bar touched Sweetbriar's belly as she cleared it awkwardly. As her hooves brushed the ground, the snare's wire gripped the mare and tightened on her leg in pincered agony. With a scream, Sweetbriar fell head first, breaking her neck, and her rider hit the ground beneath with a thud; his frantic cry cut short as his back broke right in two...

Mary Willcocks watched the eight-horse wagon pull away. The driver had business in Salisbury and could take her no further. He had shown her the direction of the standing stones and assured her there was an inn nearby which would afford any traveller shelter for the night, however poor.

Mary sat down on an upturned branch in that hollow between two hills. She hated Wiltshire and its bleakness as much as she had before when she passed through it to London that first time long ago. Then, as now, she still was without money. If one had coins then the plain could be crossed in a flash unless one was accosted by highwaymen! As she chafed her cold legs, she was wishing she might see the gypsies again, but she knew it was a vain hope after five years' passage.

After the news of her love's departure, Lucy had begged her to make her home with her in Clapham, using her nimble fingers to stick feathers into hat bands. She had agreed, caring for nothing except Edward and the knowledge Jem had of her life with Humphrey Moon. But it was the baby's death that had changed her mind. She had cried for him bitterly on that terrible day his little mouth dropped from the nipple and he fell into a quiet sleep from which he never woke.

Her little son had been the only link with her past life and when it was severed so brutally, she decided to begin afresh searching for a new and better way. She still wanted to be a lady and make her fortune. With Jem she had tasted the sweetness of a station she craved—and somewhere inside she believed she would meet him again—as an equal. If she did not, then it would be her lot to have loved truly once.

She had no desire to meet any other man because he still filled her dreams; but her great sadness was that he might have believed her untrue. She had thought of contacting him through the Birts at Witherage, but she dare not return there lest her former life came into light. In any case, she could never go near Brushford again; after Lucy had brought such news of Humphrey. Whether he was dead or no, she hardly cared, but she could not risk that either.

She had left Lucy's shop disguised as a man, feeling happier in male apparel. In that way she would not be attempted; it was her one great fear she be touched again. In such a dress she might reach where she wanted. She was still unsure of where that was—but she had a yearning within for the sea—perhaps Bristol port. There was something inside calling her back to the old West Country which she had to see again before she left England's shores and unhappiness behind. Knowing he had gone to a New World, she fancied she might go there too. She still remembered Molly o' the Lines and her tales of the Americas. In that far place a woman might be a princess rather than a servant. With Jem she had been so, but that was over.

She stood up and looked around. Settling her jacket and smoothing down her thick cloth breeches, she rubbed her legs again which were sore from the coarse threads. She settled her hat over her shorn curls; its wide brim hiding her fine brows. She stooped and caught up some dusty earth to smear her face before she reached the inn and met company.

She began to climb out of the hollow and into the wind. Across an expanse of country, she struck, following the carter's directions. Where he had turned south, she went to the West, keeping to the dirt tracks which were pale with chalky clay.

She was breathing hard when she saw the dark spots looking like pebbles dangled on strings. There was nothing to do but follow the tracks towards the circle, although her head was aching from the constant rolling of vale into sky. As she got nearer she could see the massive stones where the tracks converged and some distance over the next hill she saw a thin stream of smoke twisting itself up and disappearing into the clouds. Her head was bursting with effort and relief. It had to be the inn which hid itself from prying eyes in the depth of Rushy Bottom. She was so tired she could hardly make the last few steps.

Its kitchen smelled foul and, to Mary's relief, was empty of other travellers. A dirty lad was turning a spit; and the bar maid grinned to see a good-looking young man.

'A pint, if you please,' said Mary in her deepest voice.

The barmaid hurried to fetch the ale calling, 'You're out late, sir!'

When she returned and poured the brew, it was as foul as the kitchen, and Mary almost spat it out; but she was thirsty and it would do. She leaned her weary head down after giving her last coin away to the maid. It was then the door flung open, and two cloaked men rushed in. Mary sat up, head dazed with the noise.

'Hey, lad,' shouted the smallest, 'there are two mounts outside. Do you want to earn a coin?' She did; but almost thought they spoke to another as she had forgotten her man's clothes. 'Do you want the job or don't you?' repeated the man. She could see an earring glinting in the firelight. There was a darkness in his face that made her pull herself to her senses. The stranger was offering work and she needed it.

They stared as she stood hesitantly.

'Are you deaf—and mute?'

She shook her head wearily, then answered, 'Neither, sirs, only weak from walking.'

It was as manful a voice as she could muster; she hoped it worked. 'All right! I'll look after your horses, but how much will you pay?' He laughed and threw a coin upon the table, which clattered and fell to the floor. Mary dived and retrieved it. She touched her forehead and shot through the door, to discover two steaming horses wandering outside. She led them round the back of the inn to where she thought the trough would be and let them drown their noses. She stood by their sides, taking in their warmth; using their bodies to shield her from the wind. Finally the men emerged. She was about to curtsey, when she remembered—and bowed.

The man, who had spoken, looked down at her. 'You seem a useful kind of lad. Are you in someone's employ?' Mary shook her head. 'Do you want to be?' She nodded, ready to do anything for money.

'Come up then,' he said. 'We are looking for the right kind of lad. Our business needs a skilful horse-handler!' He pushed her up into the saddle then sprang in front. Immediately they were off and galloping into the darkness.

She bent her head against the man's back, not wishing to know where she was bound. She sensed it must be west, but was not sure until she saw the standing stones fall fast behind her. At least, wherever the men were going, it was on her way. She was almost asleep, when she saw the lighted window of a cottage.

When they were very near she saw it was protected by a thin wood—and was poor indeed. Her heart sank; but the knowledge she was dressed as a man gave her courage.

Once inside, she saw the house was mean, no rug, only a cold stone floor; no sturdy furniture like in ordinary cottage dwellings, only a settle and a poor stick of a table. In one corner there was a heap of sacking made into a rough bed; in another, old apparel piled haphazardly. Mary knew that no woman worked in this filthy hut; that it was the hide of men who needed cover quickly. She hesitated after following them through the door.

'Stop loitering, lad!' said the man with the earring, thrusting off his cloak. Only Mary's eyes stared, surprised, as he lit a candle. The man was wearing heavy pistols and he was unbuckling his belt in which was thrust a curved knife. 'Come over here and stoke the fire!' He pointed to a heap of wood.

Trembling all over and casting down her eyes, Mary hurried and threw on some logs. The other man collapsed on the sacking and pointed her to come and sit beside him, as his fellow pulled out a bottle and took a swig. As Mary made her way towards the sacks, her heart was fluttering for fear her sex would be discovered at such close quarters. She sat down.

'You're a pretty lad,' laughed the man on the sacks, catching the bottle the other flung at him, 'if somewhat dirty! Take a gulp of this—then get out to the horses!' Mary felt the spirit burning her throat, but swallowed it managing not to cough.

'That's put some colour into your lily-white face!' the earring fellow joked.

'Now get outside!'

Shivering, and with her belly rumbling full from the drink, she unsaddled the beasts and led them away to a rough shelter at the back of the cottage, where there were oats and hay. She was glad then she had been taught to drive Brushford horses, because the creatures had taken to her and had not kicked the legs from under her.

When she returned, the men were squatting on the settle before the fire.

'Done it?' She nodded.

'You're a useful lad,' growled the dark man, who had the flashing teeth of a foreigner. 'You can manage the horses. But what else?' Mary shrugged, trying not to get too near the fire nor them in case the flames gave her away. 'Can you handle a pistol?'

Her heart was racing. Why did they need pistols? She knew they must be up to no good, probably robbers or highwaymen. She tried to make the pitch of her voice as low as possible.

'I am adept with sword and dagger!' They roared with laughter, looking her up and down.

'What, you?' She nodded. 'You're a fine one!'

'Who taught a dirty lad like you to use a sword and dagger?' said the man with the earring.

'I was in service in a great house, where the butler had seen foreign wars!' Mary still knew how to lie easily.

'Well, we have no swords and daggers here, only a knife!' grinned the man, taking it from his belt.

Mary stared fascinated as the flames were reflected in its shining edge. 'You are well armed, sir!' she said innocently.

'Here,' laughed the other man, who had been drinking copious amounts from the nearly empty bottle. 'Take this pistol in your hand and get some practice!' He threw it to her and it was a mercy she did not drop it. The butt lay heavily in her small hand. The man with the earring was up on his feet and striding to the door.

'Come here, lad, if you are to stay with us, you will need to shoot!'

'At what?' faltered Mary, wishing she had not uttered such words because the man was staring at her keenly. He poked his head out into the darkness.

'No one here except the dead! Point the pistol out—and fire!' She extended her arm as she had seen Earle and Jem do when they were having shooting practice in the walled garden in Bedford Square. The other man had scrambled up and was now standing beside her.

'Why, the lad's hand is trembling!' There was an edge to his voice that Mary did not like. Thrusting down her fear of the weapon, she squeezed the trigger. She thought it had exploded in her hand and could not stifle the scream that flew from her lips as she dropped the pistol and fled back into the room. The man with the earring slammed the door shut and the two of them tackled her and threw her on the sacking. She saw with horror the glint of his knife, as he held it above her.

'Mercy, sir,' she shrieked, forgetting her man's voice. 'The noise fair startled me out of my wits!' The man lowered his knife and looked at the other.

'I think we have a lily-livered poltroon here, do we not?'

Mary could hear the scorn in his voice. As she opened her eyes, she saw the man's face. She looked down and to her horror saw her jacket had come undone and that he had noticed her bosoms. The silence between the three of them seemed to last an eternity.

'A maid!'

'A spy!' That voice was the man with the earring.

'Not a spy, sir, only a maid journeying across the plain towards Bristol.'

'A woman! In men's clothes?' The knife was out again. 'Who sent you here?'

'No one!' screamed Mary, terrified now death was staring her in the face.

'Before we kill her,' said the man with the earring, 'we shall have some sport!' He put a brown hand beneath Mary's neck and ripped open her shirt.

'Help!' screamed Mary, not expecting her prayers to be answered. Then there was a terrific crash, and the cottage door flew open to reveal four cloaked men, the first of whom had tawny hair slicked back smoothly and who was coming over, appraising her body with narrow crafty eyes. She screamed again—and looked up into the face of Tod, the fox.

In that terrible moment he flung the men aside and stood over her.

'By *Duvel*, it is Mary Baker from Crediton!'

The man with the earring was cowering as Tod, the gypsy king caught him by the throat. 'Were you going to do some mischief to my friend, whom I have not seen for five long years!' The man shivered and shook his bead.

Tod turned to Mary. 'I told you, Mary Baker, that you should be careful travelling with rough men. So—you are back in the West Country again?' He laughed suddenly, '—and you are welcome!'

Mary staggered as he pulled her to her feet. It was a miracle—they were highwaymen gypsies! He turned to the men who had almost done her harm. 'Have you lost your wits?' he growled. 'Shooting off a weapon? You will bring the justices on our tails. Get your horses and back to camp!'

He turned to Mary, who was still trembling from her near escape. 'Shut your eyes to all this nonsense, Mary, you have never seen these two now nor their weapons. There are sweeter places for a maid to lie.' His crafty eyes looked at the sacking and his silver buttons made from coins, dangled and flashed in the last flames of the dying wood. 'Come with me back to the camp—and forget all this; and we will sit before the fire together and you can tell me stories about your wanderings...'

Six horses swept up the ridge, their shadows thrown behind as they disappeared, plunging down to the valley below. They carried Mary Willcocks and her wild companions on to the West, away from that expanse of plain and the weird circle of standing stones.

By morning light, Mary was peeping over Tod's shoulder at distant spiralling smoke which told her the gypsy camp was near.

Miles away, Matt Willcocks sat in his thatched cottage, banging nails into the sole of a poor labourer's shoes and whistling cheerfully to drown the sound of the tolling bell of Witherage Church which pounded his ears in pace with his guilty heart.

On silent Brushford Farm, the builder slammed the last nail into the wood coffin and they carried Humphrey Moon north across the fields; not to the kitchen of 'The Angel' but to his last resting place near

191

the church in the village square. There were few to mourn the farmer's son except for his mother, who had seen him only as a heedless child. She wept uncontrollably as they lowered him into the Devon earth, his half-face quiet and white upon the straw pillow.

When Mary fell asleep in the gaily-painted van, it was to the sound of icicles melting into a day of winter sunshine creeping from the east; her cheek was pressed against a pillow stuffed with feathers pulled from the stolen goose, which had rashly strayed away from its Honiton pen.

She smiled as she slept, her head full of dreams of the only man she had ever loved.

CHAPTER 13

The rain cascaded off the ancient inn sign, while the crazy wind rattled the chains wildly, swinging the board so much that any lost traveller would have had little chance to read its legend. The 'Thelbridge Cross' was as decrepit as its sign; unable to hold its own against the worst summer in living memory. Its thatch was mouldy damp, its windows rotting; about its rooms the stench of wet clothes and unwashed bodies; while its sanded floor was dirtied with mire from the roads and moorland.

1814 had been an evil year for its surly landlord who swore continually, calling down vengeance from Heaven at parliament's lack of care or interest for the suffering poor of Devon. So dear had ale become, that each pint he sold to the labourers cost his customers three pence in taxes, which fell straight into the pockets of the London usurers, who held English gentry to ransom. However, that sodden day had been brightened somewhat by the arrival of a carriage and its occupants, who had taken shelter and produced gold to pay for it. The landlord had bitten the piece offered for meat to see it was not faery. When his stumps of teeth proved the coin's hardness, he savoured its feel in a dirty hand, which was more conversant with worthless paper money than true currency.

The inn keeper did not care about the strange folks' colour, only that they brought money with them. Yet he shook his head dolefully over affairs, when men as black as pitch, once white men's servants, had gold in their pockets, while English men had none. There were two chocolate fellows in fine cloaks seated before his kitchen fire watching the spit turn with great round eyes, while their master feasted above on game, for which the landlord had risked his neck. The only two subjects under discussion beneath his roof that day were the strangers within and the foul weather. It was the talk of farmer, labourer and any traveller who stopped at the 'Thelbridge Cross'.

Conscious of the stir his arrival had made, Earle Grant sat on the narrow bed. He stared at his dirty apparel, then stripped to his fine shirt and breeches and shivered before the bedroom fire. The roads in Devon were worse than the mud traps of Jamaica; the wind keener, the crops mouldier and the folk uncouth. He shook his head as he felt for Jem's letter in the discarded waistcoat. Could three years have passed since he had stood in the drawing-room of Farr House and laughingly promised his friend he would accompany him to the West Country? Now he could hardly believe why he had chosen to visit this God-forsaken shire, where the valleys were afloat with rain; the harvest washed away and the peasants starving. He had hardly seen worse in the slave-sheds of the Indies; thin women clutching babies to their empty breasts; towns full of soldiers discharged by a government, which would not further foreign commitment, half of them the wounded heroes who had won themselves glory in the long French wars. Earle viewed the demise of his adopted country with mixed feelings. Owing to the Corn Laws, his export position was low, and besides some great commissions he found the passage of his merchantmen impeded. He had thought seriously of returning to the Indies, where he would be free of murderous economies and English rain.

'Oh, Jem,' he sighed. 'If only you could see your sunny Devon! Where are those girls and hearty young men you spoke of? You wouldn't know it now!' Earle had been served by a scrawny wench, who had been so frightened by his looks that she had hidden her eyes in her hands and rushed from the room, almost knocking over the pitcher she had brought for him to wash in.

He felt for the other letter he carried, which was addressed to the Birts of Witherage. He knew what it contained; his introduction from Jem and the plea to help him all they could in his search for Mary Willcocks. In his latest correspondence Jem had promised Earle he would be received kindly at Birt and would gain the squire's sympathy, because his foster father truly cared about the villagers and their welfare.

All those months away from England Jem had written frequently and he appeared to be losing hope that Mary could be found. Sometimes it seemed he believed that she did not wish to find him ever again, but in other letters he begged Earle to continue with the search for his wife and son. The girl was Jem's real wife now; Celia Farr had been lowered into her grave months ago and had been followed hastily by her grief-stricken father, who had been suffering so long with a war wound that had never healed and festered finally.

Earle had thought then that Jem would return, but it was either the thought of Mary's disappearance for whatever reason; or the knowledge that the Duchess of Barton and his own father had taken residence together, which had kept him fast in the city of Philadelphia, breathing air as putrid as any in London town. So the great Castel and Barton fortunes waited for their young lord who ignored their brazen call, because all he longed for was a true, warm heart, which he once believed he had found in Mary Willcocks. When all had failed, he had prevailed upon Earle to travel to Devon in the hope she had journeyed back to their dear West Country. He had added in the very letter that Earle kept next to his breast, that he never would come back to England unless he could meet Mary again and hear her story from her lips!

Earle sighed, placed both letters in his reticule and stretched full-length on his back, staring at the smoke-blackened ceiling. He covered his mouth with a cotton handkerchief to ward off the foulest air he had experienced since he had left the foggy smoke of London.

Mary had vanished without trace. It had taken Earle's men, Quao and Mustee six months and more to visit all the refuges for vagrants and their children; orphanages and workhouses, places of authorities which held registers. Juba had asked at many lying-in places and every hospital; he himself had advertised in newspapers and ladies' magazines, set notices in coffee houses and travelling libraries; had lads walk the streets shouting her name—had even been to each sleazy whorehouse in London town. Now he was sure Mary had holed up with someone, who was familiar to her, and been sheltered by them.

Once Celia had died, he had gone to Farr House and questioned the servants; there was only one lead! A maid had told him that one day after Lord James had left, a woman had come bearing a letter for him; but had gone without leaving her name. The description of the messenger did not fit Mary, but Earle was sure it came from her. Whatever that letter contained, he was sure Mary had tried to find him; and when she knew he had departed, decided she should not be found.

Earle kept this fact from Jem; to give her chance to come forward again, but she never did. He had almost given up many times, weary of England's coldness, longing for the warmth of his tropical island, but he had promised Jem and would not fail him. He was also curious as to Mary's fate, because he had always liked the girl's spirit when she stayed with him in Bedford Square and wanted to prove her true.

He hoped he would find her in the country; that he could take her to Jem and save his friend from falling into illness and melancholy which he suspected was happening to Castel, when he read between the lines of his lengthy letters.

Quite often Earle feared the child was dead; and that was why he could not find Mary. He had visited the Foundling Hospital but there was no clue to follow. So all that was left was the County of Devonshire and Humphrey Moon. He had been right when he had told Jem he would send quicker news of him! The farmer's son's great strength had saved his life—and the physician who tended him had sent him back to

Devon, half-blind and crippled. Earle had been planning his tactics for a long time concerning Moon. In his carriage was hidden gold, not paper money, which was losing its value fast. When Humphrey saw it, he might be bribed to give some inkling where Mary could be. There were many knots that the scoundrel could tie for Earle—and the Jamaican was sure he could buy a better man than the farmer's son!

Yet how would he ever reach the farm across a soggy moor? His map showed Brushford village and stream, but he would need a guide when he struck off the road.

In the kitchen below, Quao, the coachman, looked up to the ceiling, wondering when his dear master would descend. He pulled his cloak about him, and the young manservant, Mustee, did the same. Neither would ever become accustomed to the vagaries of the English weather—summer and winter seemed the same these days, whereas their island had been always fair and temperate.

Quao looked across to the other customers huddled around the fire. They gazed back, their faces a mixture of curiosity and hostility. The black servants were used to such receptions; such looks meant nothing to Quao. Here no white man was master over himself and Mustee. There was no snaking whip to rip his back; no terrible iron collar to prevent him lying down.

He put up a broad hand and loosened the ruffled cravat, almost fancying he felt again the tortuous weight which had scarred his neck during those ten long days when he had suffered. Neither Quao nor Mustee would ever forget how they had been treated by white men; but they obeyed Mr Grant and tolerated them for his sake. He healed the breach between black and white and they respected him greatly for it.

'Hey, you!' said a rough voice. 'How come you're whiter than he is?' Quao knew the question was addressed to Mustee; once the older man had envied him his complexion of dark cream, but this was when he had been at the mercy of white men—now he was happy to be pure negro.

'Because I have white forbears,' answered Mustee civilly and a whisper ran around the room. There was no one that day in the 'Thelbridge Cross' who wanted to take on fine gentlemen, who carried gold.

'Quiet, you clod,' growled the small dark man from the corner. He was swathed in his cloaks. 'Be civil to our visitors!' The disgruntled labourer drew back and swallowed the last gulp of ale.

'Foreigners!' he muttered, then picked up his heavy staff and plunged across the kitchen to the outer door.

As their defender approached, Quao could see earrings glinting under the black-raven hair.

'Thank you, sir,' he said, making room for him on the settle. 'Come you nearer to the fire. I think you are used to a warmer climate than this!'

'Aye, Portugal was my birth place—and a much warmer one.' The man grinned showing his white teeth.

The landlord watched uneasily. Should he warn his guests that they might find themselves quickly relieved of their gold if they befriended the travelling gypsy? The men were shaking hands.

'Quao—and this is Mustee!' The earrings glinted as the small man bowed.

'Manuel Eynesso—at your service. Will you take a drink with me? Where are you headed?' The queries came thick and fast, but Quao and Mustee were well used to white men's cunning.

'I think, sir,' answered Quao, rising, 'you had best ask Mr Grant.' He and Mustee stood, straight and dark in the fire light, as the masterful figure of Earle appeared through the door leading from the bedrooms. Eynesso smiled but his eyes were sweeping hungrily over the well-cut jacket and embroidered waistcoat, the fine breeches and shoes.

'I shall, indeed!' he answered, bowing once more. 'Please introduce me to your master...'

Manuel wheeled his pony round as Farmer Moon's land gave way to the Birt estate. He had not needed to rob the coloured folks of their gold; they had paid him well for his guidance. The rain had made the going to Brushford a filthy nightmare; even worse than when the swollen river of his native place had swamped the plain and left mud holes, dead cattle and homeless villagers, to whom even the war had not seemed so disastrous.

Manuel scorned all dwellers in houses. Whatever the weather, he was free to wander the world and meet whom he chose. The only authority he bowed to was their king, who ruled sternly but with fairness. Gypsies were not so oppressed as other labouring folk; they used their brains to prosper instead of losing all when landlords tipped them out on the roads. He felt for the gold again—all safe—and there was more to come—and all to find a cursed female and her child, who had been stupid enough to wander away from those who had treated her well.

The gentleman from the Indies had begged him to ask his fellow travellers to look for any woman who had wandered alone into the area. Manuel spat on the ground. It seemed an impossible task; the roads were full of vagrants. Yet the man, Grant had told him her name and father's trade and that she came from Witherage. If he or his people could find her, either here or in Exeter or elsewhere, then they would receive gold beyond their dreams. Manuel had been given no picture of her; only words of description and he was sure of one thing, that if this Mary could be found then he and his tribe would wheedle out her whereabouts even if it meant searching through the petticoats of every woman in the West Country.

Earle watched the gypsy's pony dash along, a disappearing figure, into the drab mist. His spirits were low; when they had visited that cold and dreary farm they had found nothing but death; learned Moon was mouldering in his coffin—that Jem's best hope was gone.

Earle did not relish the task of explaining it all to the Birts; he was unsure if they would see him even; yet he determined to suggest to the squire he searched for Mary Willcocks throughout the whole of Devon. The knowledge he was bringing that she had borne Jem's child would hurt them and her parents, but it might make it easier to find her. He was only afraid that she would be frightened off by this advertisement of her shame—and that she would never reappear. Jem had faith in his foster parents but it was up to Earle how much to tell them. He sighed at the thought of it all. The coach was slowing.

'Mustee!' he called. 'Are we here?'

''Tis the lodge, Mr Grant!' He could see the small leaded windows. Adjusting his stock and jacket, Earle sat stiffly as the surprised lodge keeper and his wife appeared at their door to challenge the driver of the coach, which was so splashed with mire that they could hardly divine the colour or the arms set in gilt upon the side...

The gypsies had kept near the sea shore until that foul summer; at least, there were still rich folk along the coastline—and great houses hidden by sheltering cliffs. They had begged bravely at doors until dogs were set upon them; waded through the deep-cut narrow lane and ditches; knocked on the doors of isolated cob cottages asking for pans to tinker. They struck south always to shelter from those westerlies, which stunted men and trees in exposed places. In that terrible summer of 1816 Devon's red soil was mudwash and regretfully they moved inland for protection. They followed the wild course of the Exe up from the coast until it gave way to the humbler River Creedy. Then northeast of Crediton they nestled above Cheriton Fitzpaine with its thatched buildings and sturdy church.

They had had some luck at the almshouses there, where some old wives had been agog to hear their fortune—but the gypsies had lost their most skilful seer.

The one-armed gypsy stiffened on watch as he peered down to the mists towards the village. Any loose horseman could spell trouble to travelling folk—or rich pickings. Shamus could hear the galloping hooves approaching and drew a pistol from his belt, retreating towards the ring of vans. The rider was approaching the circle fast as if he knew his way, but Shamus had already alerted the camp, and its dirty men and women were standing morosely at their doors as the pony hustled in between and the rider threw himself out of the saddle and on to the ground.

'Bejasus!' swore Shamus when he recognised the man's small stature and the piebald pony. "Tis Eynesso—back from the Witherage road—and I was thinking you were the military!'

'If I was,' growled the little man in answer, 'I should see you hanged for deserting, Brownie!' There was venom in his tone and excitement in his eyes, which communicated itself to Shamus, who had been longing for sport to set his body on fire again; to heave his heavy limbs from this wet and dragging world and raise him up again.

'Where is Tod?' asked the Portuguese, looking round. 'I have news— and gold!' Then there was a great clamour and men and women were down into the mud and pulling at his cloak. Suddenly they fell silent as their tawny-headed king stood at the door of his *vardo*. There was anger in his face at the disturbance.

'What news? What gold?' His tone made them shiver and disappear into the murk of the afternoon. Only Shamus stood fast. They walked together.

'Of a maid—and men as black as we are!' grinned Eynesso, producing the leather bag.

When Shamus heard about the woman, he felt the old tickling in his thighs. He needed arousing from miserable dreams of that girl whom he had desired since he had mended the carter's wheel and whom his sister, Rose, had taught her art.

Mary Baker had learned fast from Rosa; was a cunning female, who played the hearts of men by plucking at the strings until they broke. Her capricious nature had held them all enchanted—especially the Fox. How many times could Shamus have taken Mary to his bed except that Tod was always by—and he dared not touch her. Whether the king himself had taken her virtue yet, was what no one knew. But he had not jumped through the fire and made her his woman—and that was what gnawed at Tod's vitals since Mary had gone.

When Rosa had found her bunk empty that night they had all drunk too much cider. Tod had sworn to break his sister's neck for letting her go—but Shamus knew Rosa could not have stopped Mary Baker because there was a determination in that English woman that beat them all. She had vanished into the rain in the space of ten hours and neither Tod nor the rest could find her.

If Paddy Redhead had been with them still, he would have relished the spirit Mary Baker showed in thrusting off their king and finding a new life. But he and Molly were grubbing in Bristol to save for passage to the Americas. Sometimes Shamus thought he would follow them, but the easy savagery of the tribe was hard to break from and had always suited him, yet since Tod had become surly, the lure of the life was waning...

Tod pushed back the cloak which hung, bedraggled, behind the door, its red, ragged and worn.

'Women!' he muttered. Eynesso's tale disgusted him—they were all faithless jades, fit for nothing but heavy work and breeding—but as he lay on his bed, listening to the rain dripping down the roof, he was thinking of Mary Baker. Why had she given him the slip? He thought of her warmth, her determined eyes and her haughty air, which disdained the common and drove him mad to take her as his queen. He cursed as he remembered how many times she had spurned him, running mischievously for the safety of Rosa's *vardo* .Tod could not ravish the girl if she was to queen with him; she must come willingly or it would be bad luck—yet she had avoided him always and his heat like the pretty filly cavorted before his stallion, Pegasus, but there was sweat under the fine coat before the horse coupled with her finally.

There had been an uneasiness about Mary when the camp had moved near Crediton from where she pretended to originate. Tod had known for many changes of the moon, it was pretence; that she knew the area well he did not doubt, but as for finding from where she really came it was as unfathomable as the dark skies and stars of winter.

Since she had vanished, he had sworn to find her and wrest the truth from her lips. And now Eynesso was come with news of another wandering woman. Well, he would find that one and her child for the rich gentleman's gold if they still lived—and Mary for himself even if he combed the pagan earth until his tawniness had gone and his hair was streaked with age...

Eynesso stood furtively in his caravan, then drew his curtains carefully after ordering his woman to leave. He put a heavy chair across the door, then withdrew the small pouch from his underclothes. He stared at the gold, winking in the stove light. He had taken a risk transferring some of the black man's coins to his own pouch. If Tod discovered it, then the king would kill him. All the gypsies had, they shared; but Eynesso was tiring of his brothers of the tribe.

Now the war was over, he had a mind to return to the Peninsula and live as another gypsy king among the groves, where there was no mist nor damp; where blood ran warm and women's heat was fiercer than in cold England. If he could find this woman and her child, he could cut out Tod and the tribe and take the rewards for himself...

The young woman walked swiftly as if there was some purpose in her errand. Whatever that was, had brought her early to the quay. She might have been taken for a person of quality except she had no companion—and it was not a suitable place to be walking unaccompanied. There was nothing of a servant's mien about her; neither was she a woman of the streets. It was hard to tell her station in life, except she stood out from passers-by with her graceful deportment and quick light steps.

She paused to look at a row of seagulls perched on the stony wall and when they flew away startled and screaming, she watched their easy flight over the waters so intently it made one think she longed to follow them.

Then the girl drew her cloak about her and secured her bonnet strings as she stared up at the masts of the sailing ships. She breathed in the sea air, savouring its salt, which made the flame within her heart burn cold and bright. However long it took, she would gain passage on one such ship to seek a New World far from the old which had treated her so cruelly.

She turned away then, back up that Bristol street, her head full of dreams of the man she loved. Somehow, some day, she would meet Jem again as lover and equal but, until then, she must seek the strange fortune Rosa had foretold that first time in the gypsy camp on the Exeter road.

'Diamonds—and a far away land!' she murmured to herself, 'a carriage—' she breathed and knitted her black brows together, making herself remember what it was like to be loved by him, who had treated her like a princess. She would never be Mary again until she had him back. She would make for herself another life, part of her dreams.

'The poor girl is out of her wits?' whispered one old wife to another as Mary Willcocks, her lips moving as in prayer, passed them in the lane. Then she was gone into the maze of streets, and the sky darkened as the fogs from the hills descended to drive away the sun and hide Bristol under their clammy folds.

CHAPTER 14

The seamen scurried down the gangplank like the rats they had had to put up with for weeks on the voyage. The town of Bristol could not have been more inviting with its lamps and torches, gleaming flashes through the fog that was drifting towards the water from the heights above. A bunch of men made a run to the nearest tavern, except for one who stood hesitant, his plaited pigtail glinting oil in the inn's light.

He turned off the quay and made his way into the drifting mists. He had things on his mind other than drink; he had promised himself that this time he would see her. He had been told of her art by a fellow of his, who spoke about it in whispers for fear of her curse.

That sailor had looked Billy Lee up and down and said, 'You'll suit!' and directed him on. That time he had been unsuccessful; this time he would not be, in spite of the fog.

The house was in the heart of the docklands, pressed between a tavern and a Christian church. When the sailor saw the beaded curtains at the window and the lamp behind, he knew he had found her. It was just as the man had said.

When he was let in through the heavy door he saw no one because the corridor was small and dark, smelling of age. If there was a servant he saw no sign—only the brightly-beaded curtain swinging in the draught. His heart thudded as he approached and he was touching the prayer beads he had in his sweating fist. He put his strong ochre fingers up and drew the veil aside.

It was a strange and exotic room that reminded him of home. A pungent smell came into his nostrils making him dizzy. It mingled with the scent of a quartered garlic that hung from a nail and the unmistakable smell of singeing feathers, burnt to ward off devils.

He could see she had been waiting for him. The gypsy woman sat, proud as a queen, in a high-backed chair. Her hypnotic dark eyes fixed him, like a cobra's stare from under perfect straight brows; her hair curled luxuriously and fell to below her waist, crowned by a turban, loosely woven. From her ears dangled golden rings and she was wearing a shawl, decorated with the forest scenes he knew so well.

He was almost ready to kneel because before her lay the Tarot pack.

She stared into his Chinese eyes, limpid pools of darkness. His sailor's coat was old patched velvet and his smooth pigtail, the colour of black poplar, glistened like the perspiration that stood on his smooth skin.

'Come, *beren-engro*, come!' She motioned to a cushion and he squatted before her, cross-legged. She took his hand in hers and he trembled with the shock. He had some of the Romany language and he knew she was no ordinary gypsy...

He paid her in pearls, which he had saved carefully on his body for this very purpose. She gave him a love philtre, a charmed nutmeg to place under his straw pillow so no one could steal away his girl back home—and a dried weasel's liver so he should be safe from drowning.

Her request was not surprising. That fellow sailor had told him what was expected. She would give him back one pearl for a story of the East...

When the pale morning broke through the fog, he put his velvet jacket over his cold skin, bade her goodbye and took the pearl she had returned to him and placed it on the tip of her tongue.

'One for a kiss, two for a lie,' whispered Billy Lee, his Oriental eyes showing none of the emotion he felt. He had done as well as he had been told he would and she would give him good luck to last for ever...

Some months later when his ship put in from the port of Batavia, Billy Lee went to find the gypsy again. They told him it was a mistake to try and his luck be out. It was. There was a new woman in the house pressed between the tavern and the Christian church, who told Billy that the gypsy girl was gone away to a far country and would not be returning.

Book Two

CHAPTER 15

There was a hush in the cottage room. Folk were peeping in at the door, the bolder thrusting themselves right in to stare at the stranger. The news of her arrival had caused such a stir that villagers came hurrying out of one cottage and then another; even from farm rickyards beyond the boundary. The labouring girls giggled and poked each other, staring at her clothes and serious face.

'Who is she?' asked one in wonder.

'They say she don't understand a word we speak—that she comes from foreign parts!' The speaker was red in the face, looking at the others, who stood, mouths open. The whole atmosphere in and around the simple cottage was charged with wonder; every word spoken was questioned; every phrase whispered gossip.

'Ay, oop, he's coming!' came a voice from outside the room and the labourers were moving away in confusion.

John Sterne, the overseer, had been brought the news by a boy. As soon as he had finished his meat he had followed the child down, who said there had never been such excitement in Almondsbury since the great duke had buried Boney deep in the foreign mud at Waterloo.

Sterne was well known for his strict and rigid rule; he was feared but not hated. He had about him the air of authority, which accounted to the master of Knole Park for the labourers' work and behaviour. They stood respectfully aside as he hurried through, led by young John.

Sterne threw off his coat, straightened his jacket and smoothed down his beard. He stooped as he passed through the low door, looking across to the figure seated by the fire. She was certainly the quaintest sight.

He cleared his throat, unsure of how he should address her. He could see she was young and slim; in fact, her body was comely under the plain dress. She wore no apron but, being a man, he dismissed her clothes as of no account, but his eyes were held by the hat, high on her curls. He had never seen its like before and would have been hard put to describe it. From beneath the fabric, his eyes were drawn to hers, which appeared to be speaking to him alone; to communicate some intelligence to him; almost begging his support. He had never experienced such as the hypnotic power of those dark, commanding eyes.

'Miss—um—' he began.

The woman, who owned the cottage, was bobbing before him. 'Tis no use speaking to her, sir; she cannot understand you. She is a pagan, sir!' Somehow, this was not the description he would have put on this damsel.

'Oh, come, Mrs Gaudy, how do you know that?' Heads were straining to listen through the window, necks craning at the door.

'I know it!' replied the woman stoutly. 'She's no Christian woman. Look at them eyes—and under those clothes she has—a knotted cord!'

Someone outside gave a squeal of excitement.

'Mrs Gaudy, she evidently speaks no English—nor understands a word we are saying. Have the kindness to hold onto her while I go up to the park to seek advice of Mr and Mrs Worall.' The faces disappeared at their magistrate's name. If anyone could ascertain the history of such a heathen woman he would...

Samuel Worall stroked his face with a well-kept hand, as he and his wife waited to see this strange female, who was to be brought up by his overseer as soon as possible.

'What are you thinking, Mr Worall?' asked his wife. Hannah had faith in her husband's powers of discernment. He was not taken in easily and would get to the bottom of this unusual business. She knew also that Sterne was his man—in fact, she had never seen Samuel's overseer so voluble. Whoever the woman was, she had the power to loosen the tongue of reticent Sterne. He was a taciturn man, but his every gesture had shown his master and mistress that this female was in need of their interest.

Her husband removed his hand from his pocket and thrust it into his jacket.

'I am thinking, Hannah, that there is probably not a great deal in this matter to worry us. I feel she is some vagrant slipped in from the Continent—perhaps a peasant French or Jewish woman given to fancies and sick with her lot, probably starving and on the look-out for harbour; you know some of these foreigners have a tendency to histrionics!'

'From what Sterne says, Mr Worall, it don't seem she has taken hysterics!' Mr Worall smiled at his wife's rendering of his words. She added, 'He says she is reserved and has the most expressive eyes.' The more Hannah thought about it, the more she longed for the return of her husband's overseer. She wanted to see this girl from a woman's point of view. 'You won't frighten her to death, will you, dear Mr Worall? If she is alone and a foreigner, she may—'

'Just like you, Hannah, a soft-hearted thing!' he said affectionately, kissing the top of her lace cap. Samuel was glad so often he had taken such a pretty, comfortable woman as his mate. He saw enough of the cruelties of life in his capacity as law-dispenser. At least he could rely on Hannah to make his home life perfectly easy.

Knole was a pleasant house, made more pleasing by having a mistress, who besides entertaining well, had a great capacity for sympathy and an interest in the poor. She was perhaps a little too free with the provisions when she visited their cottages, but they loved her, so Samuel did not spend too much care on managing his estate, having also an overseer, who was strict and fair and who carried out his instructions faithfully. Yes, Knole Park was the place where Sam felt easy; so different from the unpleasant tasks forced upon him by repressive law. His daily life was full of sentence and transportation for petty crimes and staring into the grim faces of those who could not cope with their disillusion as to England's plight, nor bear to wait for better times.

'Samuel, my dear, you must ask Alexander to speak with her!' Hannah's eyes were bright as she imagined the conversation between her husband's valet and the strange girl. The Greek was a learned young man, who could spell and recognize most of the languages spoken in the Levant. So if the girl had come further than her husband thought, and Mrs Worall herself suspected it, Alex would find out. Hannah picked up her embroidery, but her mind was not on the difficult pattern. She was planning a scheme. She would alert the clergyman to the strange arrival. Could he speak Hebrew—that is if the girl was Jewish? He was an Oxford man and must have studied it. She rang the bell and ordered her maid to carry a message to him.

'Goodness,' she said as the girl hurried off. 'Wherever is Sterne? I can't wait to see the woman, Mr Worall. I really cannot!' She was not disappointed for too long. Her first impression of the girl was highly favourable.

She wore a black stuff gown with a spotless muslin frill about the neck; around her shoulders was thrown a red and black shawl and on her feet she wore good leather shoes and black worsted stockings. Her head apparel was certainly different. She had twisted a black fine cotton shawl about her head, making it into a turban. The sombre headgear made her wonderful dark eyes and straight brows stand out vividly from her fine complexion.

When Hannah Worall took her hands, she saw they were clean, small and well cared for—not a servant's hands. Her teeth were pearly white and her chin, small and round. When Hannah smiled, the girl seemed to recognise the mark of her affection and showed her wide mouth and full red lips. In her ears there were no rings, but Hannah could see the marks they had left there.

'Sit down, my dear,' she said kindly, while her husband stood, looking the girl over carefully. The woman remained standing, so Hannah led her to a chair beside the window, where she remained, her hands folded in her lap in a praying gesture, completely calm and full of repose.

The Greek below heard his bell ring and knew he was summoned to speak with the stranger. He dried his hands and chewed some lavender to disguise the smell of the wine on his breath. He dared not let the master scent strong drink about him. Alex counted himself lucky to be in service in England. It was far enough from the Ottoman Empire and its cruelties, from which he had escaped but, in the wet English summers he missed the heat of Macedonia and the mizzling West Country rain was nothing in comparison with the beautiful torrents which poured from the mountains and washed away the roads in his native country. How often had he sighed with relief each time he thought of eight years of tempestuous English political dealings which were far better than the sway of the Pashas and their armies.

Alex had been an interpreter at the court of Ali Pasha and had had the honour to be present when the Englishman, Lord Byron, had visited the Mussulman in 1809. It had been that very visit which had spurred him to escape from the stranglehold the Turks had upon him and his country and risk his life to begin anew in that far-off land which bred noble men like the gallant lord.

When the Greek had reached England, he had found little employ or need for his command of language. He was of some use after he came ashore as interpreter for several non-English speaking foreigners, who had recently disembarked; but soon he had travelled on to Bristol, selling the gold and jewels he had filched from the vizier's treasure chest. In that port, he had fallen under the eye of the astute magistrate, Worall and assisted him in his business duties at the docks. He had become indispensable to Samuel and now lived a good life with the Englishman and his wife in the great house, remote upon its knoll, thrusting into the Channel. It suited Alexander well, except for the weather and the English cooking without oil. Alex grimaced as he adjusted his dress before he stood in front of the master. That was why he drank wine—to drown the taste.

He wondered about the female as he walked up from the servants' quarters. He did not rate women highly, having been brought up to watch them beaten like animals, treated as slaves, digging, ploughing, sowing, carrying wood and mending highways. The common English women he had met were a source of amazement to him with their coarse tongues and dominance over their husbands. 'This female,' he thought to himself, 'must be an even stranger one!' He could not imagine she was one of his race; she would never dare behave so…

He spoke to her in Greek first. She did not acknowledge him nor the language. Samuel Worall watched the play between them keenly. He turned to his wife.

'I assume she *can* hear, my dear? And speak?'

'I'm sure she is not a deaf mute, Mr Worall!' cried Hannah. Alex watched his master pick up the heavy paperweight then hurl it to the floor behind the stranger's chair. She jumped from it with a scream. Mr Worall was triumphant.

'There!' said Mrs Worall. 'Now, my dear, sit down again.'

Alex tried all his languages, Albanian, Turkish, Italian, the dialects of the Empire; but the girl sat immobile as a eunuch. He shrugged his shoulders.

'Sorry, madam and sir, it is no use.' He stared into her eyes and felt a strange pang strike at him deep in the breast. He recognised there was loss in those eyes; mute pleading for interpretation, almost a begging for understanding. He probed his memory to reclaim where he had seen other eyes like hers.

'Ah, sir!' he said suddenly. 'I have seen such a complexion in the people from the East Indies; full lips, dark eyes like bursting figs—' Mr Worall was staring at him in surprise. He had never heard his plausible valet speak with such sincerity.

'I told you so, my dear!' burst out Mrs Worall. 'Alex knows the poor girl has troubles. I only wish we could communicate with her!' Mr Worall cleared his throat, took a pinch of snuff—blew his nose. He stepped forward and patted the girl on the shoulder.

'We'll get to the bottom of you, my dear, or—' he added, *sotto voce*, 'knock the bottom out of you.'

They seated the girl at the table and offered her meat. She thrust away all the animal food that was given her and showed disgust at beer and cider.

'My dear Samuel, she will only drink water! *What* does she live on?' asked Mrs Worall in horror. Nonplussed, master and mistress sat staring at each other across the table.

It was a strange meal with the girl maintaining silence, a quaint figure between her hosts. Just as Mrs Worall was leading her to another room, while Samuel drank port, the maid appeared to announce the arrival of Reverend Steele.

The small clergyman hobbled forward, almost invisible behind the huge volumes he was carrying. He gestured to them.

'I have brought good Fry with me—and others. It should do the trick, Mrs Worall! What think you, sir?'

Samuel stared at the huge copy of the *Pantographia*. 'I just don't know,' he shrugged. 'This business will prove harder to crack than any chestnut in my park!' Hannah furnished the vicar with a glass and motioned the footman to relieve him of his massive burden. When the illustrated geography was spread upon the table, she led the quiet stranger towards it and the vicar. When the worthy gentleman spoke to her kindly, the girl uttered not one syllable.

Hannah placed her in a chair at the table beside the two of them and Samuel Worall stood behind. There was no change of expression on the stranger's face as the vicar leafed through the topographical dictionary, but suddenly the girl clapped a hand to her mouth and cried out; smiled and rocked to and fro.

'You poor dear!' said Hannah, observing a tear fall on the book.

''Tis China, Mr Worall!' cried the parson triumphantly. 'And the Chinese!'

'But she hasn't the eyes, man!' said Samuel bluntly. Alexander, who had been seated at the end of the room as ordered by Mr Worall, was bidden forward.

'If I may interrupt, sir,' said the valet. The parson and Worall stared at him. 'China is as near the Indies as makes no matter. I feel my first supposition was right.'

'Are you speaking of Sumatra and those regions?' asked the parson testily. Alex had no wish to argue with such a learned English priest. He had been brought up to respect the monks. He bowed his head and withdrew. But as he returned to his seat he was sure the girl acknowledged his help with her look.

'I think we've hit it! She is a refugee from Asia!'

The parson crowed and Mrs Worall took out her fan to cool herself as she imagined the terrible way her visitor must have taken.

'Well, what are we going to do with her, my dear?' asked Samuel. 'That's your realm tonight!'

'She must stay!' said Hannah promptly.

'I forbid it,' replied Worall. 'That is—until she is proven!'

'Fie, you magistrate!' cried Mrs Worall. 'Very well! I'll have her conveyed to the inn to spend this night, but afterwards—' she paused and Mr Worall inclined his head in agreement. He was all for compromise...

The innkeeper's wife led the way up the stairs followed by her strange visitor. She turned several times as if to check the girl was still behind her, then being satisfied that she was she continued up the narrow stairs until she reached her little daughter's bedroom. As she held open the door for the stranger to enter, the woman's face was white and she appeared ready to faint. So the landlady indicated the bed which was the place she was to lie, but the girl seemed greatly fatigued and was beginning to walk with difficulty. Suddenly she stretched out her hand towards the nearest chair, grabbed it and leaned on it for support; then let it go and collapsed upon the floor.

'Heavens!' cried the good wife. 'She's fainted!' She rushed forward and looked at her charge. The girl was lying looking at her from innocent dark eyes. She had not swooned, nor did she seem afraid; only grateful to lie down somewhere.

'Oh, Lord,' continued her hostess. 'Whatever am I going to do?' She stared into the girl's eyes. 'No, my dear! Not there—on the bed!' She pointed in its direction. The stranger looked uncomprehendingly as if she had never seen a bed before. The innkeeper's wife lifted her hands in surprise. She hadn't any idea what to do! Suddenly she decided to call for help in the shape of her small daughter.

The child strayed into the room uncertainly, staring at the stranger lying on the floor. Her mother beckoned her.

'Now, don't be afraid, Bess! Come here. I want you to do something for me!'

'What, mother?'

'I want you to show this lady what your bed is for!'

The child laughed out loud, clapped her hand to her mouth and giggled. 'That's right, go over there and lie on the counterpane.' The little girl scurried across the room and flung herself upon the iron bedstead which creaked protestingly. She sat cross-legged, staring at everything in surprise.

'Good girl, Bess!' cried her mother. 'Look! Look!' she caught the stranger by the shoulder and turned her. The artful Bess lay down and pressed her head into the pillow. 'Now you!' The stranger seemed to be responding, because she was moving with difficulty. 'Good, good!' said the innkeeper's wife, drawing her close to the bed. 'Now, you lie down on that bed, and I will bring you some meat and drink!' The child was already shifting over, eyeing the woman suspiciously. She stood suddenly and slipped off the bed.

'She won't eat any food, mother,' said the little girl. Her mother turned incredulously.

'What do you mean?'

'I heard them talking downstairs! They say she will only drink water!'

'She won't refuse my meat!' said her mother stoutly, but she was wrong. When the stranger was brought her food, she was fast asleep and could not be wakened.

The innkeeper and his wife slept fitfully, knowing who was in the next room to them. The landlord felt that the stranger might rob them or even murder them in their beds, but his wife had some sympathy with the girl.

'I think she is just some poor crazed creature wandering the roads—she has lost her mind and will not speak to anyone!'

'I don't know about that!' said her husband gruffly.

'She may be gone in the head, but she has an artful look about her that I don't trust!'

'Don't say that, my dear!' cried his wife. 'Perhaps we may be the means to help her. Think of our Bess. Say if she were in that position!' The landlord snorted and turned over into his pillow.

They were wakened in the rosy dawn by the strangest sound they had ever heard in their lives.

'Listen!' cried the wife, clutching at the sleeve of her husband's nightshirt. He came to with a start and groped for the candle. 'No, no, don't light it! It might be robbers!'

'Felons don't make that noise!' he shouted, swinging his feet to the floor while his wife pulled the bedclothes around her. He crossed the room and unlatched the door. The noise was coming from the opposite bedroom. 'It must be our visitor!' His wife looked at him with round eyes from under her frilled nightcap.

'What shall we do?'

'Go and see!'

'I daren't!'

'I will!' At the decisive tone his wife seemed to change her mind because she was out of bed and up at the door behind him. They crept across the passage, lifted the latch of their other bedroom door and peeped in.

Not only had they heard the strangest noise in their lives, but it was the queerest sight they had ever beheld. The stranger was wide awake now, facing the window, moaning and chanting. The good folk stood in horror as she bowed, made salutation, bent and kissed the floor; then crouched upon it still crying in her heathen language. The innkeeper was about to rush in and pull her off balance, when his wife caught at his nightshirt and restrained him.

'She is worshipping!'

'She is a pagan!'

'The sun. That's it, she is adoring the sun!'

A shiver ran through their frames, then the innkeeper's wife hid her eyes as she saw the girl slip off the top half of her clothes and draw from beneath the bottom of her skirt a knotted cord, with which she began to flail her back and shoulders as if she were beating herself.

'Ugh, come away, Harry! I can't bear any more!'

'I can!' said her bemused husband as he watched the strange liberties the girl was taking with her body. 'I want to see all of this!'

'Harry!' exclaimed his wife. 'It isn't decent! You're a good Christian man and you shouldn't be watching!'

'Pagan or not, wife, she's a comely wench!' were his last words as his wife dragged him out of the door.

'You ought to be ashamed of yourself, Harry,' she said as he rubbed his eyes as if he had been dreaming. 'I'll go in again and stop the girl!' The innkeeper's wife opened the door stoutly, but when she looked in the girl was finishing her prayers, knotting the cord about her naked waist. She turned, bare-breasted, full round breasts, firm and pure white. 'Mercy on us, girl, cover yourself!' cried the good wife.

But the girl did not appear to understand a word, only stood there in her shame. Her hostess darted over to the bed and pulled off some linen to cover her. The woman was sweating with the effort and also with what she had seen.

Her cheeks were very red when she told Mrs Worall all about it later on in the morning. Hannah shook her head.

'Poor thing! She has never been taught any faith!'

'What would the minister say?' was all the innkeeper's wife would utter as she repeated her story over and over. Mrs Worall decided that she certainly would not tell him, but made arrangements quickly to have her strange protégée moved to St Peter's Hospital in Bristol where she should stay until she was properly examined and they could ascertain from whence she had travelled...

The seagulls screamed shrill warnings at passers-by below, from the leaded height of the hospital roof. The plump lady alighted from her carriage and adjusted her large bonnet which was trimmed with feathers and fastened under the chin with purple ribbons. Her 'Witchoura' mantle would have been a little out of date in London, but its fur was sumptuous enough for visiting a hospital for vagrants and was indeed the only richness to light the corridors along which the lady travelled accompanied by an elderly woman who hobbled in front, clad in plain black dress and starched apron.

When the heavy door was pushed open, Mrs Worall spied the girl seated before the fire, hands still folded and calm. However, when the good lady reached her, she could sense the stranger's misery—and she was right, because the girl glanced up at her arrival; a disconsolate look upon her face. 'Are you well, my dear? Have you enough to eat?' She turned to the servant. 'Has she eaten anything?'

'Only bread and water!'

'Goodness, you will die!' she cried to the girl, but it was no use because she could not understand her! 'Oh, Lord, what shall we do?' Hannah clapped her hand to her cheek. 'I must hurry dear Mr Worall with his probing—or he will have no body to examine! When is she to be taken before the magistrates?' She turned to the old woman.

'This evening, madam,' she answered.

'Thank goodness!' murmured Hannah, wishing it was all over and seating herself by the girl. Many thoughts rushed through her mind as she stared into the intelligent face. What could have brought her to that part of the world? How terrible must it be not to be able to communicate! Never to be understood! Had she any relatives who were frantically looking for her? Was she from the Indies? Could she be trained?

Suddenly Hannah Worall knew she wanted the girl back at Knole Park where she would be treated kindly.

'I'll have you out of this place in a trice after this evening is over,' she went on as if talking to herself. 'I shall see you are taken to my husband's office. The housekeeper can have charge of you until we learn your further history!' She rose to go after a quiet hour seated by the fire.

Suddenly, the girl jumped up, threw her arms about Hannah's neck and kissed her on the cheek. Mrs Worall was very touched by the stranger's affectionate show. She put up a hand to the other's face and stroked her cheek.

'There, there, my dear, don't fret! I shall do all in my power to help you if I can...

The magistrates, chaired by Sam Worall, were at as much of a loss as every person who hitherto had encountered the mysterious stranger. One or two of them had hoped the girl might be overawed by their presence and break down under the strain, but they were wrong. She had that air of innocence which precluded any judgment as to her being a fake; indeed even Sam Worall who was paid to be suspicious, was almost falling under her spell. There was something about her air of resoluteness; a kind of haughtiness which they had never seen in any vagrant brought before them; she treated them as equals, seemed not in the least alarmed by their importance; appeared perfectly at ease. Notwithstanding, she was very pale and had to be given a chair because she appeared near to fainting once or twice. Throughout the whole examination she never uttered a syllable, nor answered a question, nor could be tricked into answering.

'Well, Worall, you've a fine one here!' said one of his colleagues. 'What are you going to do with her?' Sam shook his head.

'If she can't tell us anything, what course can we take? We can't imprison her; she has done nothing. We can't send her back to her parish or country, because we don't know where that is!'

'If this were a couple of hundred years ago, she could have been put to the torture!' came the sarcastic remark from one of her exasperated questioners.

. 'Hold your peace,' warned another. 'You'll frighten her!'

'She can't understand me, can she?' he replied, twisting his mouth nastily.

'Quiet, gentlemen!' interposed Worall. 'This is getting us nowhere.' One of his fellows with a reputation as a philosopher, suddenly banged his hand on the desk.

'I have it! Let's get the girl settled somewhere. Proclaim her story— and see what is made of it. Perhaps someone will come forward with information.'

'And if they don't?' asked Worall doubtfully.

'Then we are stuck with her. Doubtless she can be found useful employment.' Sam looked at the girl, who sat seemingly oblivious of all the fuss. He was thinking how delighted Hannah would be at the outcome. She had taken such a liking to the girl that he could see her fast ensconced at Knole—and all the trouble upon him. Yet if it made Hannah happy—

'My wife has taken quite a liking to the woman. She seems to think the girl is not happy at St Peter's. Leave the matter in my hands and we will meet again.' There were signs of relief all round as the gentlemen rose, picking up papers and wallets. Several of them nodded to the girl as they left the dais. Others shrugged disbelievingly as they passed the turbaned stranger who had caused them so much trouble, indeed seemed entirely innocent of any such charge...

Mr Worall's Bristol office had never been so busy! Since the stranger's story had appeared in the *Bristol Post* there had been one visitor after another to inquire of the young woman's health; to offer personal aid, which was most hastily refused; or to beg an audience with this phenomenon who never uttered a recognisable word and carried on outrageous heathen practices.

'Why, madam!' the housekeeper cried. 'I don't know what's happening in Bristol these days. Is the port full of scoundrels?'

'Come, come, Mrs Weaver, we ought to do our best for the girl,' comforted Hannah. 'She is without friends; perhaps her relations are seeking for her!'

'That's all very well, ma'am, but Mr Worall expects me to keep his office and rooms fit for business!' Hannah could see the woman was quite overworked.

Mrs Weaver continued, ''Tis the gentlemen, madam, they give us no peace; why, only yesterday we had at least seven seeking audience with Miss over there!' Hannah glanced at the girl, whose cheeks were somewhat redder now owing to the good fire which sparkled in the grate. It was natural she had made a stir, but Mrs Worall was unsure if her husband's colleagues had been right to broadcast her arrival. Hannah had been hoping *she* could teach her to communicate in English, thus learning her history.

There were so many strange things she did; her behaviour was truly pagan—but fascinating! Hannah's English blood had chilled when Jenny, the housemaid told her that the young woman still kept to bread and water only, that is till she saw a tame pigeon stray over the fence from a neighbouring garden.

'And, ma'am, Miss ran after it, caught it in her hands and—' the girl's voice sank so low that Hannah could hardly hear, '—pulled off its head, madam and just as neat as you please poured out the poor little thing's blood on the earth and covered it up. I was near fainting when she came in, fetched some sticks, set herself a little fire outside and sat cross-legged the whole day cooking it. Whereupon she ate it, madam! The whole thing made me go ever so queer!' Evidently, the girl did the same with any fish she could see; apart from that, she treated every other meat in the same manner by refusing it. She never ate on Tuesdays, but fasted the whole day until the evening when she ascended to the roof of the house where she stood on the tiles ignoring any warning that she was endangering her life. As for washing her face and hands, she never stopped.

Hannah looked into the housekeeper's worried face. It did seem as if the girl was too much for her. She must take her back to Knole where at least she would be safe from 'the gentlemen'.

'Seven gentlemen, you said?' The housekeeper nodded grimly.

'And they brought foreigners with them! And rascals they were too! I cannot understand decent young men befriending such rapscallions. I had to get the footman turn them out immediately!'

'Don't worry, Mrs Weaver,' soothed Hannah. 'I will talk to the master and see if I can relieve you of your charge!' The housekeeper appeared ready to burst into tears; as Hannah crossed and took the girl's hands in her own she was sure the stranger's dark eyes were full of sympathy for Mrs Weaver too! The last gentleman of the day arrived when Hannah Worall was about to speak to her husband on the matter. They were both seated in the parlour when Mrs Weaver rushed in, hardly bothering to knock.

'Pardon, sir and madam, there is another at the door!'

'Another what, woman?' asked Sam testily.

'A man, sir, a foreigner!' cried Mrs Weaver, bobbing as she remembered her manners.

'To see the girl you mean?' said Hannah, looking at her husband. This would add fuel to the fire; if the housekeeper continued to be bothered so, Sam must see sense and get her back to Knole.

'Shall I tell him to go away, sir?' asked the housekeeper eagerly.

'No! Fetch him in! I long to see another rascal like all the others whom I have beheld this day!' The uncharacteristic irony in her husband's voice made Hannah start a little; she did not want things to go wrong at this stage.

'Very well, sir,' sighed the reluctant housekeeper.

Mrs Worall could not keep her eyes off his earrings. She was extremely hopeful when she saw his complexion—it was singularly European, reminding her of Alex the valet. He was small and fidgeted a lot, as if he wished to be gone.

'So, sir, you've heard about our visitor, eh?' asked Samuel rather rudely.

Mrs Worall interposed, 'I presume you have more than a personal interest in our guest? We shall not allow her to be used for any purpose other than ascertaining her history!'

'My only desire is to help her!' His voice was silky. 'I am adept in many languages and may recognise hers.'

'So where do you come from?' cried Sam.

'I have travelled extensively, not only in Europe but from lands beyond. I am a traveller born!' Hannah thought the man was even more plausible than Alex.

'Oh, let him talk to her, Mr Worall!' Hannah said.

'We shall be present, of course.'

'Of course!' His earrings glinted as be bowed.

She was brought in, stood as mute as ever while Hannah explained the gentleman's purpose. Samuel stared into both their faces. They were as artful as each other. Then from the small man's lips began to flow the most unintelligible jargon Sam Worall had ever heard.

''Tis nothing but nonsense!' he whispered, but his wife caught at his arm.

'Look at her face!' Then, to their astonishment, the girl opened her lips and began to utter series of syllables that flowed like music, then dipped into guttural animal noises. The small man grinned, his white teeth flashing in his face; he threw up his arms in a gesture of delight as the girl's strange words reverberated in the room. She carried on and they listened, spellbound. The man swayed from side to side seemingly taken with the music he could hear. Their visitor continued speaking thus for at least fifteen minutes; when suddenly she stopped, dropped into a chair and began to weep. The dark man patted her cheek and proud as a turkey cock, turned to the astonished couple.

'Poor girl! Poor, poor girl! I do understand most of what she says. She has not told me much; she wishes to keep her own counsel, but only that she is a person of great consequence in her own country.' Sam Worall looked keenly at his wife, whose face was glowing with happiness.

'Oh, go on, sir, just as I thought. Imagine, Samuel, a person of some quality. I thought that, I really did!' The little man drew close to them, spoke in a whisper.

'I am sure I have this right, but it is difficult. Her language is not pure. It is a dialect, a mixture of several tongues spoken in Sumatra!'

'Just as the Reverend said,' cried Hannah triumphantly. 'If my geography is right, husband, Sumatra is in the East Indies!'

'That is true, madam,' said the dark man. 'It appears that your guest was a person of high rank travelling across her country when she was decoyed from her island, brought to England against her wishes and then *deserted*!' Hannah clapped her hands to her cheeks, caught Samuel by the sleeve, looked up at him appealingly and cried:

'Deserted! Imagine that!' Mr Worall cleared his throat. How much of this he could believe he did not know, but for Hannah's sake he had to try. The girl had done none of them any harm; the only evil she did was to pigeons!

'Thank you!' he said. 'You have given us great hope. Do you think you can learn any more?' The dark man bit his lip then turned to the young woman, who was somewhat recovered. He spoke to her again but Mr and Mrs Worall watched her shake her head time and time over. He turned back to them.

'I do not think so; she will communicate with you in her own good time. For my part, I shall return to the port and alert anyone I can who may have visited that part of the country. Indeed, I am thinking of some person now!'

'Oh, thank you! How can we reward you?' cried Mrs Worall. The man put his head on one side and the earring flashed in the sunlight. Samuel turned to the desk, opened a drawer and withdrew a small bag which chinked as it moved.

'I think *this* is what our visitor desires!' He could see the greed in the man's eyes. He opened the bag and poured out some coins. 'Take this for your pains, and should you meet up with your "friends", then we shall be delighted to receive more news of our guest here!' The little man bowed happily and Sam rang for the footman to show him the door.

As the small man was ushered out, suspicion was beginning to take root in Sam's breast. There was no doubt Hannah was overjoyed at the news of her protégée's importance, but he failed to recognise such coincidence that some foreigner would appear from nowhere to talk to their charge in the kind of unrecognisable gibberish he had just heard. 'But why' was the only phrase that resounded in Sam's skull? What could the young woman hope to gain from her pretence? If the man was her accomplice, what was his motive? What had they up their sleeves?

'Come, Mr Worall, don't look so glum! Aren't you delighted? I am! We must get her back to Knole. You said you would when her origin was proved.'

'Do you call that proof?' burst out Sam, but stopped when he saw his wife's hurt expression. 'I'm sorry, m'dear, but it seems too much to swallow. A man turning up like that saying he understands every blessed word she says!'

'That's unfair, Sam, you know it is!' cried Mrs Worall indignantly. 'I know you don't like her. 'Tis because you are used to dealing with felons constantly. Can't you believe anyone?' Sam looked at his wife in surprise. She had such a mild temper that she was hardly ever roused. They had never had words like this since they were married. 'I'm sorry, Sam, but it's true!' Hannah plumped herself down in the chair.

He stared at Hannah fondly! Her ingenuousness was what at first attracted him, used to liars and cheats.

'Very well, my dear,' he indulged, 'you shall have your way—and the girl conveyed to the park!' She jumped up and threw her arms about his neck.

'Oh, thank you, Sam, you won't be disappointed! I'm so excited; I shall be able to find out everything about her!' she cried.

They turned to look at their guest-to-be who was seated quietly in the usual chair by the fire. One could have hardly imagined she had been touched by the preceding interview with the foreigner; but a close observer might have seen that two fingers hidden beneath the calm folding of her hands were plucking at her skirt in a gesture of agitation...

The heavy door closed with a thud. The small man grinned, laughed aloud, shook his head as if in disbelief and hopped down the steps. He began to whistle, look up to the sky for signs of rain, then draw his cloak about him. He walked swiftly along the street, until turning the corner he made for a stone archway through which could be seen a cobbled courtyard where a horse stood tethered to a railing. With easy agility he sprang into the saddle, wheeled the beast out across the cobbles and back into the street.

He did not notice the watcher safely ensconced in another doorway of that courtyard. When the dark man's horse had disappeared, the man emerged and laid the heavy willow stick he carried in his one hand against the railings. Then he took out a pistol from under his coat and using the butt in that same hand, he scratched his black and tousled curls in a thoughtful manner. 'His Majesty, our foxy Tod, will be little pleased when he hears what you have been up to my Spanish fool,' whispered Shamus Kelly and whistled. At the shrill sound, a piebald pony lifted his head and clattered out from the shadows in the lane beyond. With an agile leap, the one-armed man was on his back. Shamus gripped the blanket between his knees and urged the pony off and up in the direction the other had taken.

CHAPTER 16

The Avon Gorge was a fearful sight where its river gashed the land, tearing the earth's bowels open into deep rocky holes and clefts. Fog drifted about its gaping mouth, luring unsuspecting travellers to their deaths; but the gypsies knew the terrain well and used the grassy down tops for protection.

The gypsy woman hardly had time to lead away one pony before the piebald came galloping through the mist and was turned loose to be seen to. She swore at having to do so much, look after the horses and feed the fires. She cursed the Irishman under her breath as he strode past her purposefully towards the king's *vardo*.

'He did what?' growled Tod, his lean face creased in anger. 'A magistrate?' Shamus's eyes were glittering as he began to tell Tod everything that had passed. He had been following the slippery Spaniard for some time; he needed to remember it all very well so his suspicions would be judged facts rather than fancy.

'There was something in my brain when he left here first which made me want to follow him. That's why I've been gone so long,' said Shamus. 'I had a mind to see this fine gentleman who pays good gold to find a female and her child.'

'And did you see him?' asked Tod eagerly. Somehow the story cheered him with its mystery—and rewards.

'I did not! It seems Eynesso had another appointment. He has not met the gentleman yet—but I know he will! I caught our slimy comrade first outside the gates of—' Shamus paused to see the effect his words were having, 'St Peters—'

'St Peter's?'

'Yes, the hospital for vagrants, as you know well, Your Majesty!' mocked Shamus. 'Eynesso wandered about there staring down at the cobbles, then at the steps as if he was thinking of entry; but mind you, he did not do that either!' grinned Shamus.

'Think you he's found our quarry?' snarled Tod. The tribe had been serious enough to nose the regions about Witherage and Exeter; Tod's women had spent precious time with old wives and dames, peddlers and such, asking about strangers coming into the area. Such care had deprived them of some useful hours. If Eynesso had double-crossed them, he would pay as dearly as the crazy gentleman, who wandered the West Country wasting gold on some faithless female, whom Tod believed would never be found—until now! 'Could he have, Brownie?' Tod's voice was cold and high.

Shamus shrugged. 'Perhaps, perhaps not. That day there was a crowd about St Peter's. I concealed meself from his eyes; in fact, it was just dispersing when I grabbed hold of an old wife by the arm—she told me there was one interest there! That a woman had been conveyed to the magistrate's office. She had been examined as to her purpose and origin, but they had learned nothing. The wife whispered to me that the female was a grand one in disguise and a pagan!'

Shamus laughed out loud. 'A stranger brought in from Almondsbury, a pagan? A vagrant taken up in the cottage thereabouts! A cunning one more likely! The folk in that crowd were full of her and her tricks which they called, "heathen ways"! I thought to meself then I would see this woman, but I was not lucky. It seems Eynesso was though. Since that day he has returned several times to that very part of town, probing local folk. Until this very day when I saw him hie himself to the magistrate's office and disappear within for two full hours!'

'The worthless—' began Tod but Shamus took him by the sleeve.

'No, Your Majesty, let me deal with him. Let me find out what he has discovered. Let me be a witness to his treachery against the tribe. I will follow him once more until he meets his fine friend. Let me do this!' Tod looked at the twisted face which matched his crippled body. He had known for some time that Shamus Kelly was wanting to be gone from the camp; about his Irish wandering ways again. He had the sea's restlessness about him—and the thirst for murderous excitement. If anyone could trap Eynesso, Shamus would.

''Tis a bargain, Brownie—but keep that one limb out of trouble! Should it come upon you, there is no help for you from this quarter. Too many of our kind have ended up transported. Find out about this woman who is kept at the magistrate's house; be stealthy in your tracks like the gypsy you are, but—' Tod caught him by the shoulder, 'if you have grand ideas about leaving us, Brownie, remember this, I have your sister here and Dow has two powerful hands for wringing a woman's throat. Remember too I know your crafty ways for I am the Fox, full of craft myself. Have you that straight?'

Shamus nodded, reviling the king with an unspeaking tongue...

Loyalty was worth more than any gold Earle had been forced to spend on gaining his information. He knew well what coins did to men; made them greedy like beasts, but worse than animal kind; for gold they cheated, lied and slaughtered—and gypsy folk were no better, except within their tribe.

Earle could depend on Quao and Mustee, who had ridden here and there, hopeful of gathering news from the tinkering travellers, but always returning empty-handed. Their contact, Eynesso and his fellows had nothing to report. Mary would never be found—and Earle would travel no further than Bristol—he had shown loyalty too—but was faced with the impossible. Where the river spewed itself into the sea was as far as the Jamaicans would go before they returned to London and closed up the house in Bedford Square to return to a warmer climate.

Earle was tired after his ordeal at Birt where he personally had been received kindly; but his news badly. Society's snobbery had reached even the country there; the thought of Jem allied to such as Mary seemed death to that family; their pride had been delivered a blow of such magnitude that first, they had disdained to believe it and second, had declared Jem out of his wits. The squire had been the most amenable, received the news like some Roman Stoic, but the women— Earle sighed when he thought of Juba, whose dusky face and character was peerless by comparison. He was glad to leave those supercilious English women to their own small-mindedness and be back on the search again.

So, here he was in Bristol—waiting for Eynesso in a meeting place of the man's own choosing. After the muddy cruelties of 1816, the spring of that new year had come in sunny green to the County of Devonshire and Earle felt he could endure England a little longer. He was not averse to Bristol Port; it reminded him somewhat of the Caribee with its business and sailing masts; but Quao and Mustee cared not for its earlier reputation as one of the most important slaving ports.

'Cheer yourselves, men!' he said, noting their sorrowful faces. 'You are free to wander where you wish! No one can touch you here more than they could in London! Anyway, when we have seen this man— and if he bears no news, we shall hie ourselves back to the capital, pack up our bags and return to the Caribee!' That did them good! Their honest faces lit with happiness. Then the three of them lounged the whole day through in the inn parlour, drinking fine rum hurried in fresh from the quay.

Eynesso found them happy in the sunny afternoon; he approached them deferentially, his quick brown eyes scanning their faces for approval, then casting quickly away with the knowledge he had no information to wheedle more gold out of pockets. He shook his head.

'That is all I fear!'

'Oh, Mary, you are gone!' said Earle softly to himself. The gypsy looked up at him with interested eyes.

'This Mary must be precious to you, sir!'

'Very precious!' answered Earle. 'But—our quest is over. If we cannot find her and the child, we shall return to London!' Eynesso's eyes flashed; the only source of his new revenue was about to float away. He had to try something!

'There is but—one piece of news. Perhaps it may be of no account—' Earle's eyes looked brightly at him. 'There is a stranger, who is making a great noise in Bristol!' The coloured man rounded on Manuel quickly.

'A great noise?' Manuel considered the effect that had upon the gentleman. He had to try, although he knew it was no use. The stranger was of no account! He knew that above all else!

'Is it a woman?' asked Earle.

The gypsy nodded. 'But no child!'

'Never mind that. Of what complexion?'

'Very fair!' replied Eynesso, thinking of her bewitching features. Earle ground his heel upon the floor. 'I mean—' replied the gypsy quickly, 'she is not like you! Beg pardon, sir,' he added even more swiftly. Quao and Mustee stared at the little man with contemptuous eyes.

'A brunette then?' Eynesso nodded. It had always been difficult to describe her.

'But she wears strange headgear!' added Manuel.

'What?' asked Earle.

'In the Eastern fashion!'

'A hat?'

'Like a turban. I have seen such in the Indies!' Earle studied him carefully. He was unsure whether the man was about to dupe him.

'Anything else?' Eynesso shook his head. He knew already he had gone too far. He dared not repeat what he had heard; that the woman was a pagan. That was something he knew full well; she was not made of flesh and blood; but ice and snow.

'Where is this treasure gone?' asked Earle civilly, but Eynesso could feel the hardness in the tone.

'Oh, sir, she is not gone. She is where she was!'

'Where?' The tone was harder even.

Manuel began to gabble. 'At the magistrate's office! Mr Worall of Knole! A great man like yourself! Not far from here!' Manuel looked at the coloured folk, whose knuckles were taut above clenched fists. 'Believe me, sir, 'tis true. I only saw her yesterday. I spoke with her.' Earle halted his men's advance with a warning hand.

'Where is she from?' Manuel shivered. He had almost given himself and her away. He shrugged.

'In truth, I did not understand one word of what she said. She does not speak my language!'

'She is a foreigner then?' cried Earle. Manuel cowered. He had been in many dangerous situations, but these devils could not be made into monkeys. They were as artful as he. 'I am not looking for a foreigner! The girl I seek and her child are white and English!'

'But, sir,' cried Manuel, seeing his salvation. 'This one is not English, I promise you.' Quao and Mustee rushed forward and twisted his arms behind his back. Earle put out his hand again and touched them very gently.

'Enough of that, my friends, let us go and see if this fellow is speaking the truth. There may be some mileage in his story.' He turned to the shivering Portuguese. 'You will take me to this woman!'

'She is well guarded, sir!' cried Manuel. 'There is a she-devil of a housekeeper to contend with.' Earle smiled.

'She will melt at my chocolate features!' he quipped. 'Lead on, brave little sir, and if you satisfy me you will have all the gold you wish!' Quao and Mustee took Manuel Eynesso by each arm and led him from the inn, with Earle close upon his heels.

When they reached the office and learned that the girl had been conveyed to Knole Park, Eynesso was relieved. At least it would give him some space to get away; he knew that the coloured men had decided to give up their search and he desired to receive all he could before they found the 'foreigner'.

As Earle bowed and the heavy door clicked shut, Eynesso looked fearfully from face to face. Quao and Mustee stared back, but their master's stern looks were relaxing.

'So, little man, you have told some of the truth. Take this gold for your pains and get on your way. We have need of you and your fellows no more. Tell your tribe this—that the search ends here in Bristol town!' He signed to Quao, who withdrew the blue cloth bag into which Eynesso peered eagerly, then bowed low in delight, nodded his head and hurried áway like a jackdaw picking at its prize.

He would have made greater haste had he known about the lean figure which kept behind him; its twisted shadow thrown up and along the stones by the afternoon sun. But Manuel was full of gladness; such gold would furnish him for a grand journey back to his homeland. He would never return to share his gains with Tod and the others; rather he would slip away across the seas, coins in his pocket ready to pay for the luxuries in life for which Manuel craved...

The night mists had floated coldly down and enveloped the waterfront houses and inns in a dismal shroud. The only warmth to be felt on the quay was a lighted door opened to let a drunken sailor and his woman stagger through and across the cobbles into the darkness. The Portuguese gypsy was lying low in the meanest inn of all for fear of being discovered before he could board ship to any haven away from British shores.

The black man's gold was concealed safe about his person and was withdrawn only in secret to pay for good meat and drink. He had turned his pony loose and by now it would have flung itself, riderless, along the narrow rocky paths to the circled vans upon the heights. Manuel knew the gypsies would be searching and he shivered and pulled his low-crowned hat well down on his head. He had taken out the rings from his ears, cut his long hair, bought himself new clothes, including a great coat with a spreading collar. His reflection in the mirror was satisfactory; he looked no gypsy rather a dark and foreign gentleman, ready to set sail for his place abroad.

Although he had been wary early in the evening, his money had bought some good wine for him and his eyelids were drooping in his fuddled head. He loved the juice of the grape like all men of his race and he felt warm and comforted on that dangerous spring night. So hot had he become that he shed the coat and shied from the fire. As he stood back from the blaze, he overturned a heavy chair and apologised to the muttered curses about him. Yearning for cold air, he retreated, stooping under the low door into the cobbled entry and the dirty backs of the houses filled with waterfront rubbish. He felt delicious relief at the cold air on his face; at the release of the wine from his bladder as he stood beside the pump, staring down into the cold darkness.

Suddenly, he was conscious of someone beside him, of a strong hand twisting on his shoulder, spinning him round, making his dazed head whirl under the sky.

'Bejasus, 'tis a traitor you are, Eynesso!' Manuel's frightened gasp struggled from his chest and wavered in the air. 'Did I frighten you then?' The voice was cruel. Eynesso collected himself, and dragged himself out of the hand's grasp.

'Keep away, Brownie!' Manuel's eyes were used to the darkness now; his one-armed assailant faced him.

'There is no escape,' said Shamus coldly. The warmth was draining from the Portuguese's body. He felt for the knife he always carried beneath his clothes. 'Is it a knife you're after?' The voice was flat now. 'Well, here's one then!'

Even in the fog its dull glint was terrifying. 'I have cut more foreigners than you, Eynesso!' Now there was contempt. Manuel was backing, circling, mad in his desire to get away.

'You know what you have done, don't you?' asked Shamus civilly.

'You have taken *our gold*, betrayed your brothers, and left us wandering where ye were! Tod told me to come and find you.'

'Then you can tell Tod I will not come!' They eyed each other warily.

'What did the fine man give you?' asked the one-armed gypsy. 'Was it a bag, blue and laden with gold?' Eynesso shook his head. 'You lie, Portuguese!' Manuel's eyes were darting about looking for a means of escape. Shamus advanced menacingly.

'I saw you leave your fine friends, you dog! Why did you take them to the magistrate's?'

'To—' began Manuel.

'To see a woman,' continued Shamus. 'And upon my life, I'm sure she is the woman we all seek!' He had Manuel cornered like a dog at a snarling badger. The Portuguese could still show his teeth; with the swiftness of light his curved knife was out and waving at Shamus Kelly.

'Come on, then, Brownie—and I will give you what you want—right in the belly!'

'Was it she?' repeated Shamus and Eynesso could feel his hot breath. The latter lunged with his knife, but the Irishman leaped back. Manuel righted himself from the jerky movement, but in that second Shamus had slipped behind him. 'Was it?' he screamed as he plunged his own knife into the other's back with the double force of the arm he lacked in the cruel fingers of the remaining.

Manuel gurgled in his throat; fell sprawling in the mire face down. Shamus had struck artfully, being a skilful murderer. It had been no hit and miss—the man would live on for a while, if the knife stuck fast. Shamus dragged him onto his side, stared in the pleading eyes, the face twisted with the agonising pain in his lungs.

'*Did* you find her? Speak!' He shook him cruelly. Manuel came to for one horrible moment with that jarring. He gurgled once more as the blood welled up. His face twisted with the effort. He was thinking of his olive groves; could feel the sun on his face, but a coldness was creeping through his limbs.

'Yes,' he whispered faintly, 'Yes, yes, it was Mary.' The rest was a hollow rattle. Shamus had heard that sound rise on the battlefield from a thousand dying throats. He was satisfied. Before the Portuguese was dead, he dragged him sideways into a cobbled corner, full of filth; tore open his clothes until he found the coins. Twice during that mad rifling, the inn door opened and drunkards tumbled out, unheeding. As soon as the bag was secured in his own pockets, Shamus turned the warm body and heaved out his knife, leaving the corpse flooded with its own life blood. Then coldly, Kelly walked over to the pump, clanked out a rush of icy water and cleansed his hand...

Before Earle left the inn where he stayed to meet Eynesso to go to Knole Park, he received a caller. The fellow was somewhat rough; of gypsy stock and crippled. He touched his brow to the tall Jamaican.

'I come from Tod, king of our tribe, to tell you that we shall continue with our quest!'

Earle looked into the wide and innocent eyes and answered calmly, 'You received my message then?' He was sure the gypsies had not.

'Oh, that we did, sir!' replied the man quickly. 'The Portuguese is a gabbler born!' Quao and Mustee smiled at each other. 'But we always close his mouth in time. Our tribe thrives on silence, sir.' Shamus had silenced that tongue for ever.

'Why have you come?' asked Earle.

'To go on with you,' said Shamus suddenly.

'I have enough men about me—and besides, I return to the Caribee when I leave Bristol town!'

'Bad luck for me!' grinned Shamus Kelly. 'But good fortune with the maid!' Earle nodded. 'Then I'll be going, sir! But should you need my services again, you can leave a message here at the "Old Ship".' He stood erect, his one hand on his hip, then swung from the room. When Shamus left the gentlemen, he could feel their coins, which he had murdered for, lie heavy in his pocket. The plan was working well; with Eynesso gone he was the sole guardian of the gold which he intended to divide quickly; returning some to Tod to satisfy him; keeping the remainder to line his Bristol nest which he would make safe with his old comrade-in-arms Paddy Redhead and his woman, Molly.

Quao looked at his master. 'That is a fly one,' he said. 'I do not trust him!'

'No outsider should trust a gypsy man, Quao, yet tight in the tribe they would bleed and die for each other!' said Earle. 'Yet, Quao, I sense our brave little informer never reached his caravan!'

'Master, the cripple knew about the maid!' reminded Mustee.

'But how did he?' said Earle. 'One day perhaps we may find out. Come, lads, pack up and let us be off to Almondsbury to view the only turban in this part of the country!'

The coloured servants burst into laughter, but Earle remained silent thinking of Jem Farr and his tortured breaking heart...

'Look, look, my dear, 'tis Knole!' cried Hannah happily as the carriage turned into the drive. She had quite forgotten the girl did not understand a word she said; however there was some expression in her face as they bowled along the avenue with its trees budding in April's glory. Hannah could feel the breeze already which swept in from the Channel and gave Almondsbury a freshness tinged with salt—and to Hannah today a new life to nurture and watch grow.

She thanked God for the privilege of bringing some happiness to such a sad countenance, for now the stranger was clapping her hands in delight at the sight of the woolly lambs climbing the grassy hummocks. Since the small man's visit when her birth had been described, the girl seemed to have woken from her dejected sleep and appeared to be stretching herself into a new way of communication by gesture and expression.

'It is lovely, isn't it?' Hannah said to herself, as she looked through the carriage window. She had always loved this home of hers standing beside the River Severn which rolled down its valley of clay through rich pasture lands, where cattle grazed comfortably in their flat water meadows. There were wonderful trees about Almondsbury, sloping down to those lush fields and Knole itself still looked romantic to Hannah with its tower overlooking the river as it had done since the time of the Tudors.

Hannah glanced again at the girl to see what impression she had of the house, but the stranger had quietened now, not seeming to be moved at the sight of the building. 'Perhaps she is overawed!' thought Hannah as their carriage passed into the courtyard and stopped before the flight of stone stairs.

Yet when the girl alighted, it was as if she was used to arriving at a grand front door. She looked about quite proudly at the gathering of servants, seeming not to notice the excited looks they gave her. She appeared quite accustomed to being treated like a lady, giving Hannah even more evidence that she was a person of some quality. As they went into the house, Hannah was a little put out at the thought her charge must sleep with the housekeeper; but she thought it prudent to obey Sam's instructions as to the sleeping arrangements. Hannah knew from experience how malleable her husband could be as long as he thought he was master. She was willing to wait a little time until he became less suspicious and more amenable to the thought of their visitor in a fine guest room with her own hangings, new drapes and clothes! Hannah loved the thought of it all—and showing the girl to guests would be a wonderful experience. So Mrs Worall planned, while upstairs the girl stood passively, while the young lady's maid prepared her bath and hurried to disrobe her, averting her eyes and cheeks growing red as she found the knotted cord and the pink stripes upon the young lady's back, the marks of her flagellation...

The servants soaked in every bit of news the housekeeper brought them each morning. Their own eyes had beheld the girl was heathen.

Madam would have her treated like a lady with deference; they must respect her as a guest, provide special food, call her Miss Caraboo. Mrs Worall had told them it was her name, but they had never heard one like it.

'It makes me laugh every time I have to say it!' stated the mischievous housemaid, who lit the fires and swept the morning room.

'I was there when madam found out the young lady's name. She was standing by the window looking onto the park, when suddenly, she turned and signed for madam to come to her. Mrs Worall went, thinking she was to look at a bird or a squirrel, when she caught fast to her hand, took the fingers, pointed just here—' the girl giggled and coloured as she indicated a spot between her breasts, '—and uttered "Caraboo". I thought she was saying, "Bow" at first, because I was looking for one, but madam was most excited and exclaimed, "'tis her name, Martha, her very name—and what a pretty one!" What could I say to that? I think it's pagan myself!'

Alex, the valet, put out a soft hand and patted the girl's arm. She coloured again.

'You told it very prettily, Martha, but I would say it could be— French!'

'Oh, no!' The company was horrified, 'but don't worry, she is not a French woman!' They relaxed. 'Perhaps the daughter of a French pirate, who marauds in the East Indies!' They laughed at his joke.

'Well,' said the footman, 'it makes my blood run cold to see her killing fowl. Pigeons and chickens alike. Off go their heads—and over the fire. I would say she was a piratess!'

Alex laughed out loud. 'She is certainly interesting!' Indeed, from the day he had first seen her he had been drawn to the girl with the yearning eyes. They made him tremble a little; in fact he could hardly remember any female who had such a power, which, if he met her on the staircase, caused him to hesitate and stand quietly aside, feeling her skirts brush by his breeches; scenting the musty perfume of her body.

'You would think so, Master Alex,' said my lady's maid. 'You are all for pretty faces and fine clothes!'

'You call those fine!' said the housekeeper. Mrs Worall had called her one morning to order calico so that the stranger could make new clothes. She turned out to be an accomplished needle woman—with the help of two of the maids she had a pattern drawn like a flash of lightning. What ensued was the strangest fashion which had ever been worn at Knole.

The dress was short in the skirt, but its sleeves were sumptuous. They were wide and long and brushed the ground. Caraboo would stroke them lovingly, trace patterns upon their length, embroider flowers, leaves and unknown animals. She pointed to the ribbons of Mrs Worall's best bonnet, a beautiful sky blue and Hannah bought her ribbon in copious amounts. This she spent two weeks embroidering with the same jungle patterns because there was no one in Knole who had ever seen such flowers and creatures. She passed a ribbon about the waist line and did the same for the sleeves. After, she accentuated the line of her full breasts with the same intricacy; then fringed the skirt.

She was hardly ever seen without her turban, which she fashioned from matching calico and ribbon, but upon the right side she dressed it with seven peacock's feathers, her brilliant hues making her the jewelled doyenne of that stately house at Knole. She disdained stockings and would not look at slippers or leather shoes. So Mrs Worall brought the cobbler in, and he showed her some drawings of the latest styles, but she took a charcoal and drew him what she desired—sandals, which Alex told the other servants were the fashion in Greece. When these arrived she laced them with the same ribbon, criss-cross up and above the knee. Those sandals reminded Alex of his home and the bare-legged, full-breasted women who slaved in the fields of Macedonia. Every time he saw Caraboo's dainty feet within them, he longed for the heat of that far peninsula and those country women.

Caraboo's curls were thick, falling free and wild upon her shoulders, but sometimes she piled her hair on the top of her head and fastened it with an ivory skewer. Then Alex thought of a Greek goddess and could not get her from his mind.

The Greek stared glumly at the scrubbed elm table where they continued to talk of their strange guest.

'Tell us again what happened last night, Mrs Wardle,' asked the cook. The housekeeper shook her head, pursed her lips and stared into the ring of solemn faces.

'You know the master is still suspicious of her—' They nodded. 'Well, he told me he'd be very grateful if I got up in the night sometimes and—'

'Grateful, eh?' joked the footman, but desisted at the housekeeper's sharp glance.

'I gave Miss Caraboo a good shake. I asked him whatever for, but he wouldn't answer! Mark my words, he wanted to test and see if she'd scream out in English!'

'And did she?' asked Cook.

'Not she! She just sat up and looked at me with those great eyes. And in her sleep—'

'Go on!' they breathed.

'She mutters in her own language!'

'Oh!' Their joint disappointment was evident.

'What did the master say?' asked Martha.

'Never you mind!' replied Cook. 'Mr Worall will keep his own counsel, I'm sure! He's probably right though. I don't care for Miss myself. She has no more taste for good plain English cooking than Mister Alex here! Oil with everything! It wouldn't suit me! Pooh!'

'Then we shall make a pair,' quipped Alex, thinking how pleasant that would be.

'You would be well advised to keep away from Miss Caraboo. Madam is besotted with her,' warned the housekeeper. 'She can see no wrong in the girl and that one can twist her any way she wishes, would take any liberty, if she could speak our language!'

'You know what I think,' said the footman. 'She's a man in woman's shape! All that killing and praying to the sun. You could read of such in Mr Defoe and his savage!' The others stared at him and burst out laughing. Alex threw back his head in disgust.

'You need a quizzing-glass if you see any man in Miss Caraboo. Look at those—' he had quite forgotten there were ladies present. Martha reddened.

'Enough of this common conversation,' cried the housekeeper. 'It's time I kept this house in order. Get about your work, all of you!' She hurried out, leaving the rest to whisper amongst themselves. Yet Alex did not join in with his fellows. Later, when he was brushing Mr Worall's top hats, putting away his day gloves, and hanging his jackets, he was thinking of the girl, who at that moment was walking demurely in the park, lost in a reverie from which she should be awakened...

Caraboo strayed into the gunroom. Mrs Worall had been frightened at first when she asked to handle Mr Worall's pistols and sporting guns; it seemed so unladylike; yet her *protégée* appeared to love looking them over at length as if she had some knowledge of their use; besides, Mr Worall was addicted to his shooting; owned a good shoot along the river where there were geese in plenty. There was nothing be loved more than to hold a shooting party when the weather was biting and he had brought home excellent venison many a time for the table.

Swords and daggers he used very little, but he had plenty of them; a good rack of blades and knives on the wall. Caraboo had her back to the panelled door as she surveyed the weaponry. She remembered well the scent of men and their dangerous playthings which she knew so much about to her sorrow, and had tried to forget. Yet the ambience of the gunroom was a warm familiarity lost to her for so long. She put a small hand out towards the gold chased hilt of a French rapier, when two hands on her shoulders jerked her out of her dreams and the weapon out of the rack to face whoever disturbed her.

Faced by a reflex, which would not have shamed a tiger, the Greek flung himself back and away from the unguarded blade tip, but Caraboo was following. Drops of perspiration stood out on his forehead as she forced him on. She could not understand his pleadings, first in Greek, then English, but he was down on one knee with arms outstretched in supplication.

'Don't kill me, Miss, I beg you!' he cried. 'Please, please!' he screamed, knowing she could not understand. When she had him against the door he was near fainting. If he had been in possession of his senses he would have seen the contempt in her eyes for a man at her mercy. Then she lifted the rapier deliberately and pointed its tip at his throat. It was then he began to howl like a frightened dog.

'Help, help, someone, the girl is mad!' He was fast against the door, his back scored against the panelling. Then he was kicking it with the back of his heels, drumming frantically, his eyes bulging. He could hear noises outside—the footmen were coming. Then Caraboo smiled; lowered her blade and held it point down in a gesture of repose, almost covering it with her calico sleeves. Alex's hands were on the ornamented handle, when the door flew open and Mr Worall, accompanied by his wife and the footmen were standing there aghast.

'What was all that squawking, man?' shouted Mr Worall. 'I thought someone was being murdered!'

'I nearly was!' gabbled Alex. Caraboo stood demurely, her rapier obscured by the folds of her dress.

'Caraboo, what have you done to Alex?' cried Mrs Worall. The girl just smiled on. Alex continued squalling. Mr Worall slapped him on the side of the face.

'My God, she has frightened you!' One footman looked at the other.

'She was going to cut me, sir!' cried Alex. Mrs Worall's eyes were wide as Caraboo withdrew the rapier, turned, walked across the room and placed it in the rack. Mr Worall strode forward.

'What are you doing with my swords?' he barked. 'These are no playthings for women!'

'I told you she was no woman!' whispered the footman. Mrs Worall approached Caraboo, who suddenly trembled. Then with a gesture she pointed to Alex, then herself; walked behind Mrs Worall and put her two hands upon her shoulders to show what he had done.

'Did you touch this young woman?' said Mr Worall to his valet. Alex shrugged.

'Perhaps I startled her. I came in when she was looking at the weapons—I may have put my hands upon her shoulders—'

'That's enough, Alex,' cried Mrs Worall. 'You startled her! What can you expect? She is not like us. She has been brought up in some wild and savage place! You were lucky to get away with your life!'

'Well,' said Mr Worall, looking at Caraboo. 'Would you add murder to the list?' The girl's eyes stared at him steadily, never wavering.

'What list, Mr Worall?' said Mrs Worall hotly defending Caraboo.

'I meant nothing at all by it, my dear,' replied Mr Worall. ''Twas only a matter of speaking! There seems to be no harm done, but keep her out of my gunroom! She will do herself a mischief if no one else!' He strode off followed by a shivering Alex.

'My dear, a lady does not behave so!' cried Mrs Worall to her charge, but the girl trembled a little. 'You must never go unchaperoned; I told you that before, my dear,' continued Hannah. 'Whatever can I do to make you understand?' The girl was quiet. 'I hope he didn't hurt you,' said Mrs Worall almost to herself. 'But doubtless you are used to it!' She put an arm about Caraboo's shoulders. 'Come on, my dear, let's find something a little less dangerous for you to do!'

Upstairs, Alex was brushing back his hair. He had been unnerved by the woman's behaviour; but even so, he was strangely excited. There was something in the girl that was wildness itself; so far removed from this cold English clime it made him sweat with its excitement...

Hannah was seated at her pretty writing desk in the morning-room. She looked up at her husband's entrance. Sam could see how excited she was.

'Two letters this time! Amazing, isn't it? The gentlemen still cannot be prevented from visiting our Caraboo!' Sam shook his head hopelessly.

'Who is it this time?' Mrs Worall got up, both letters in her hand. She extended one.

'No lesser personage than the Marquis of Salisbury! And this—' she offered him the other. 'The Earl of Cork!'

'Goodness me!' ejaculated Sam.

'Both from Bath; both sent on the same day!'

'Humph!' said Sam. 'That means they're in collusion!'

'My dear Mr Worall, how could they be? 'Tis your suspicious mind again!'

'So—her fame has spread to Bath!'

'Yes, husband, and not only Bath. All over the country they are talking of our Caraboo.'

'More fool them then,' replied Sam in a low voice.

'What did you say?'

'Nothing, my dear, but don't you think it is a pity that half the aristocrats in England have nothing better to do than come visiting some poor dreamer of a girl—'

'Is that what you think, Sam? I knew you didn't believe the man we met in Bristol!' Hannah had tears in her eyes.

'Don't upset yourself, my dear. I for one, would be very glad if someone came and took the girl off our hands. But I can see you are resolved to keep her!'

'Oh, I am, Sam, I am! She's a dear thing—so calm and quiet, but clever, mind you!'

'Very! I wouldn't call her quiet; look at that business with Alex!'

'Well,' cried Hannah, defending her Caraboo, 'I'm sure he was up to something. You know Alex better than I!' Sam sighed. These days his wife was less docile; it was probably mixing with heathens!

'Are you letting them come?' he asked, indicating the letters.

'My dear Sam, how could I refuse a request in such superlative language! Think what good it may do for Caraboo. One day she may even enter into society!'

'Not if she doesn't change her ways!' replied Sam, ironically; 'and that includes her charming ways with pigeons!'

'You are a wit this morning, Sam,' said Hannah. 'I take it then you have no objection to me writing to my lords and offering them our hospitality?'

'None,' sighed Sam. 'Let 'em all come and fight it out between them!'

Two driving phaetons ran dangerously alongside each other; their occupants seated high in the dangerous vehicles, which were liable to overturn very easily.

'Keep your distance or we shall never reach Knole Park!' shouted one gentleman as he manipulated the reins skilfully. 'You're not on the course now!' His friend was an agile driver and they had raced against each other often before.

'Move over, Seymour!' laughed the other. 'I shall be the first to see the girl and converse with her! Stir yourself or I shall beat you!'

Edmund was annoying him that morning; having beaten Seymour at cards last evening and being successful in boxing wagers for a whole month. Bath had been excessively boring which had prompted Seymour to look for what pleasure he could elsewhere—and a view of such a strange female seemed tantalizing.

They had crossed the high ridge of the hills and reined in their horses to give them a breather. They were looking over common land.

'Let's hope this journey's worth it!' puffed Edmund. 'How far is it now?'

'We'll take a drink at "The Crown" down there!' pointed Seymour. 'The inn has some fine tales to tell of Gully.' Boxing and racing were sports to be revelled in and what better to quench one's thirst at a house where the son of the landlord had turned out to be heavyweight champion of all England. Now the man had made a name for himself and was a gentleman too. It would do as a place to halt before they reached the last stage of their journey to Almondsbury.

After the footman had ushered the two gentlemen into the drawing room at Knole, he was followed directly by Mrs Worall, her face full of smiles to greet her guests.

'Will you take tea, my lords?' Before they could answer, she had rung for it. Then she turned to them, concern on her face. 'I have not communicated your coming to the dear girl, my lords!' she said. 'You understand—if I did, *she* would not, because she has not our language. At present she is walking in the park, but I will send Martha to fetch her. You will, I think, find her a little strange.'

When the tea had been brought and drunk and Mrs Worall departed to send Martha on her errand, the earl leaned back and jingled the coins in his jacket pockets. 'Will she take gold, do you think?' he asked.

'Have you brought some?' asked Seymour merrily. His companion nodded. 'Do you not think it will offend her?' He gave a wry smile.

'When has coin ever offended?' was the reply and the marquis nodded.

'We'll get her to speak her lingo, Edmund,' he said to Cork, 'and try to catch her out!'

'Damn it, man, you won't understand a word!'

'And they say she wears fancy dress all the time.'

'Let's hope she doesn't find it as uncomfortable as we did during the season!' drawled Cork. 'I only wish Chumley was here to see this!'

'Where are they?' asked Salisbury with impatience. 'I'm bursting with curiosity to see this Caraboo!'

Martha went up and down the grassy slopes calling for that troublesome young lady. The maid knew her mistress had forbidden Miss to wander too far alone for fear she was accosted by some gentleman come looking for her without leave.

'She's tolerably good-looking,' grumbled Martha to herself, 'but if I was a fine gentleman I wouldn't waste my time on visiting a heathen!' Martha thought you could see enough queer sights in London town which would make up for one hundred Caraboos without coming down to Almondsbury. Great lords like those two in the drawing-room should be about their business doing something to soothe the troubles of the poor. Martha grumbled all the way towards the pond against rich aristocrats from Bath who knew no privations like servants and labourers who had to endure rising prices all the time.

'Good gracious, Miss, whatever are you doing?' screamed Martha as she spotted her quarry. Caraboo was standing silently beside the pond. Martha could see she had taken off her sandals and was barefoot; also that she was holding her skirts right up to her thighs; ready, it seemed, to step into the dark water.

'Don't, Miss, you'll die of the cold!' she cried, but the girl did not appear to hear her. She put out one foot and tested the water. 'Miss, Miss, there are gentlemen come to see you!' Martha shouted, having forgotten that Caraboo could not understand.

The maid ran breathlessly down the bank, almost stumbling in, and caught the girl from behind.

'Listen!' she cried, then reddened, remembering her servant's place.

Caraboo swung round and looked her in the face, 'Pardon me, Miss, but there are gentlemen come to see you!' Martha could see she did not comprehend. So she bowed to indicate the sex. Caraboo laughed suddenly and the sound took the girl by surprise.

'Don't laugh at me like that,' she muttered. She picked up a stick and drew the outline of two male shapes in the mud beside the reeds. Beneath these, she wrote 'Cork', and 'Salisbury'.

Caraboo stared.

'Very important men, Miss, great lords from Bath come to see you. Two of them!' She counted two fingers. 'Come, come,' she beckoned.

Caraboo was hesitant, withdrew, turned to the pool and stared at her reflection, at her peacock feathers which stood like a crown above her head, their shape rippling in the surface of the pond. Martha stood beside her, peering down. She shook her head, 'I don't know what you're doing, Miss, but you should come or Mrs Worall will be displeased.'

The two girls stared on and on at their reflections, then Martha felt overawed by the fantastic figure beside her and thrust her stick into the pond, stirring the mud into cloudy billows.

A strong sob suddenly rose from Caraboo's throat as the dull glint of a fish appeared from the disturbed depths. The carp was there for a moment—then it was gone, its monstrous head disappearing into the water beneath the spongy froth upon the surface.

With sudden intuition, Martha grabbed the other's long sleeve. She could have sworn she read that savage mind; that she would be in after the fish and lost for ever.

'Come away, Miss, back to the house! To the gentlemen!'

She led Caraboo up the slope and away from the mysterious pond, avoiding the tangled exposed roots of the oak trees—into the light and the wind where the distant view of Knole's Tower beckoned.

When Caraboo had rearranged her dress, cleansed face and hands and was presentable, she was brought out of her room to meet her visitors. She seemed quieter than usual, but not calm. Mrs Worall sensed within her charge a revulsion for being shown off once more and Hannah was suddenly sorry, wondering if it was a mistake. The girl hesitated at her bedroom doorway, on the carpeted landing, upon the fifth tread of the wide staircase. She turned to Hannah and there was a mute pleading in her eyes. The kind woman was filled with confusion.

'I shouldn't be doing this, should I, Caraboo? You don't want to see them, do you? Oh, Lord, if only she could understand!' Hannah put one hand over her own breast and sighed aloud to denote her sorrow at seeing Caraboo's pain. She was shaken to see the girl's eyes full of tears.

'What do you want me to do, Caraboo?' she asked.

The girl continued downstairs into the square hall, where she ran to a table that had not been dusted carefully and drew two male figures upon it. Then pointing one and two, she rubbed out one image.

'You mean, you only want to see one!' Caraboo drew a large letter C beneath it. 'Cork?' The girl inclined her head, a tear falling down her cheek. Then she put her hand in her pocket and withdrew a piece of silk stretched on ribbon. Then she veiled herself in the Eastern manner.

'Well, well,' said Hannah. 'I don't know how I'm going to explain.' She motioned the girl to remain in the anteroom and hurried off towards her visitors.

They stared incredulously.

'She won't see me?' cried Salisbury. Cork laughed out loud.

'That's rich! She must have gleaned your reputation!'

'Oh, I assure you, my lord, nothing of the sort. She seems strangely preoccupied this day.' Hannah looked at the sulky face of the marquess. 'I think, my lord, she may be frightened of seeing the two of you together—' It was an inspired idea.

'Then she shall see us one at a time!' cried Seymour. 'I will go out— and she may come in to talk. Then I'll go in—' Cork laughed again.

'It seems I was chosen, Seymour. Let's see what impression I have on the girl!'

'And I will try to change her mind, my lord,' said Hannah anxiously.

The marquess was shown into the morning-room by the footman, where he sat by the window whistling petulantly and staring, uninterested, at the beautiful gardens below and the wide river.

Next door, Cork was bowing low to the veiled stranger. The conversation was all on his side—and laboured, with Hannah interposing by sign and gesture.

'Can you put her to speech, madam?' he pleaded to Mrs Worall.

'Caraboo does so rarely, but I can assure you, my lord, when she speaks it is very musical!'

'Pray, will she?' cried the earl. He was taken by her fine figure and mysterious dark eyes which seemed to be speaking to him alone. Hannah gestured to Caraboo by putting her hand under the girl's chin and her own head on one side and mouthing into the air.

Caraboo began to speak and the earl listened raptly.

''Tis wonderful!' he cried when she finished. 'But whatever does it mean?' Mrs Worall shook her head. 'Well, I'll be—' he had almost forgotten there was an English speaker in the room. 'I beg your pardon, madam, but I am quite taken with her. Does she always remain veiled?' Mrs Worall shook her head.

'I have never seen her so.'

'Do you think I might see her face?' he asked humbly. 'I assure you, madam, I am captivated by the voice and deportment, but it is like meat without good wine!' Mrs Worall smiled at the silliness of men; then she was sure Caraboo was smiling too beneath the veil. She approached her charge and motioned her to take it off. With a quick surprising movement, Caraboo put up her hand behind her ears and lifted off the silk.

The Earl of Cork swept low into the most graceful bow he had practised since he left Bath.

'I am deeply honoured, Miss Caraboo!' he said. Then he turned to Hannah. 'But Salisbury must see this, madam, I beg you!' No sooner had he said it than Caraboo re-veiled herself and sat down beside the fire.

'I think she feels easier now, my lord,' said Hannah.

When Cork was about to withdraw, he offered Caraboo some coins. Both he and Hannah wondered what she would do, but she just took them in her hand and looked at the money curiously as if she did not know what it was. Then she offered it back to the Earl.

Hannah could have laughed at his stupefied expression.

'I told you, my lord, she is strange.' He shook his head in disbelief, remarking as if to himself,

'Seymour should see this!'

'I will do what I can to persuade her,' said Hannah. When Cork left, she signed towards the morning-room and put her hands into the praying gesture she had so often seen in her guest. Then she pointed. Finally Caraboo nodded and re-took her seat by the fire.

Salisbury entered, his face showing some displeasure. Within, he was anxious in case Edmund told Chumley who would find it a rich joke. The girl he had travelled so far to see remained silent and did not look him in the face. He felt an atmosphere of disapproval; an emanation which cut like cold hostility. She sat like a statue in fancy dress.

'Why, she is veiled, madam,' he said, frowning at Mrs Worall, 'like some Vauxhall player!' Hannah was at a loss. What could she say to the marquis? For some reason Caraboo was averse to this gentleman, but not the other. It was very strange behaviour but she had come to accept such from this girl. She would not speak, however he tried to draw her out. Hannah watched him struggling with his temper, becoming more flushed in the face all the time and she thought it best to curtail the conversation. She laid her hand on Caraboo's sleeve in a gesture of protection. After all, why shouldn't the girl have preferences like other women? The only pity was that she had given offence to a powerful man, who could have done her much good.

'I'm afraid the girl is tired,' she said, offering the excuse, hoping he would take the hint and would leave forthwith. He did and with bad grace. But being a gentleman he could not show it. Hannah could hear the mutter in his angry voice as the footman showed my lords to the door. It did not take much to imagine what conversation might ensue between the two on their weary journey back to Bath.

As Mrs Worall turned back to speak to her protégée, she was much upset to see Caraboo fling herself down upon the hearthrug and burst into great gasping sobs.

'My dear, please don't! What ails you?' Hannah felt guilty, knowing it was all her fault. She managed to get the girl back to her chair where she sat for a long time, her eyes fixed unseeingly across and out of the window as if she were in a trance. However, when Mrs Worall hurried off to find Caraboo some medication and nourishment, the girl stopped that dismal staring and brought forth both hands which she placed on her flat belly, and looking at them fast upon her body, the tears coursed down and down her cheeks, until most of her beauty was spoiled and her pretty calico a soaking rag.

When Mrs Worall returned with Martha, bringing pure spring water laced with a small quantity of spirits, Caraboo would not take them, only moaned as if in pain.

'She is distraught, Martha,' cried Hannah. 'If only I hadn't let them see her, she would still have been easy and cheerful!'

'Perhaps she has taken cold, madam, from walking barefoot in the park! Or stepping into the pond?' ventured Martha glumly.

'Oh no, perhaps we should get her to bed and warm her.'

'She's probably used to heat, madam?' added Martha. 'Then we'll do it! Come, Caraboo!' Yet the girl avoided them both and ran out of the room quickly. They followed, but she was outside and into the park—then off!

Hannah, panting, cried out for the footman; subsiding on a chair to fan herself while Martha and he gave chase.

'What's frightened her now?' gasped the man, because Caraboo was as fit and fleet as the breeze.

Martha was falling behind so she shook her head and shouted, 'I don't know but she's making for the pond!'

The footman panted on after the short disappearing skirts, but tripped on some roots and fell sprawling. When he picked himself up and over the bank, he raced down the slope shouting, 'Help, she's in! She's in!' at the sight of Miss Caraboo striking out through the lily leaves and towards the deep water in the middle. Martha appeared then, followed by the other servants one by one.

'Can anyone swim?' shouted the footman from the bank.

'I can!' cried a stable lad, who had been raised near the Devon shore. When he reached her she was floating easily, suspended upon the water which lapped about her cheeks and chin. He towed her into the bank where the whole household and the dogs were gathered.

'Good lad!' cried the butler. 'There'll be coins for this!'

'Is she dead?' cried Martha.

'Not she!' said the scornful footman, peering into the pale and beautiful face with its dark eyes veiled. 'She can swim like a fish! She was floating!' At that, a distraught Mrs Worall appeared on the ridge ordering them to carry Miss Caraboo into the house and summon the doctor.

The trailing procession carried on back towards Knole and Martha muttered to the footman, 'Mark my words, she'll be the death of us before she seeks her own!'

Hannah clung to Sam for support when she told him the story.

'Was the girl trying to end her life, d'ye think?' the magistrate questioned solemnly.

'No, Sam, it isn't true! Don't say that! She was near hysterics. The doctor says it was a paroxysm induced by crying. She was much upset by seeing My Lord Salisbury!'

'Why? Did she know him?' asked practical Sam, detecting yet another collusion.

'No, of course not! I can't understand it. Yet Martha said she was at the pond before. You know what she is like for washing!'

'Well, my dear, her hysterics seem to be giving you more trouble than they do her! She's all right now, isn't she?' replied Sam, noting his wife's white face. 'I should put a stop to any further gentlemen if I were you!'

'Yes, Sam, I will. No more visitors, no more I tell you! Whoever comes shall be turned from the door. I'll not have her frightened more!'

'Good,' said Mr Worall, satisfied. 'Now that's settled, can we eat?'

Caraboo lay quietly for two days, looking as if she had some great trouble lying in her breast. She dressed no meat for herself, took only water to drink, coughed somewhat from the liquid she had swallowed in the pond and frequently washed her pillow with tears. She seemed quite unaware that she had caused anxiety in the house; oblivious of the stir she had made. The servants carried the tale to the village cottages, from whence its fame and rumours of her other doings travelled on to Bristol, across to Bath and Salisbury and, by way of the garrulous tongues found in coach passengers, to the very capital itself.

Safe in her bed at Knole, Caraboo slept having no knowledge of what was surmised about her birth and circumstances in the coffee houses, clubs and palace tea tables. Her dreams were filled by those foreign courts to which she escaped nightly, secure at least in the fantastic belief they were where she rightly belonged.

She was so pale when she rose from her bed on the third day that Hannah feared she had taken cold and might die from the shock of the waters. All she could be persuaded to eat was a little of a barley loaf and the same spring water.

'Mercy on us,' sighed Hannah, as Martha cleared away another untouched tray, 'I will have no more men in this house, aristocrats or not. Why, if the prince himself were to come, he would not be admitted to view my Caraboo. Please God she will recover!'

CHAPTER 17

The handsome gentleman was now finding his coach less agreeably sprung. The road through the glen was narrow where the River Frome tumbled its way through the trees. He knocked on the roof and the driver upon the box reined to a halt, but the posting-horses were slow to obey.

'Hold, you animals!' swore the driver as the light luggage shuddered about on the roof. He had had enough climbing up the valley and needed a steady hand to guide the coach down the other side. He was not keen on using the whip, having tasted it too many times himself, but he wished he was driving the master's own horses which had served them faithfully in London and Brighton.

His liveried companion was alighting and waiting for instructions.

'Mustee, this is a devil of a road! Is there no other way? I don't care to dip in the river!' Mustee grinned.

'No, dear master, you shall not. Quao is taking good care in spite of the ruts!' He looked down at the surface, cut and scored by other wheels. Earle nodded; he could trust Quao's skilful hands completely. He only wished he had set out from Almondsbury sooner; but he had received news from Juba about pressing business and had been forced to conduct it from Bristol, but it had been concluded satisfactorily; the merchants were honest and chocolate, rum, tobacco and sugar could come into that port easily.

Now all that was left before their return to London, was to see the strange woman described by Manuel Eynesso. Earle did not think it could be Mary, but he longed to see what kind of woman wore a turban if she was white. The little informant had said she was foreign and this intrigued Earle too. He had always been wont to follow mysteries, especially those concerning women, and did not grumble about a detour of this kind. From Almondsbury, he could cross-country fast to Bath, and follow the post road on that long one hundred and nine miles to London.

While he was planning this, there was a sickening lurch. The leading horse, anxious to be off again on the downwards run, had shied at a stray village goose and the coach's off wheel was into the ditch in a second, hurling the luggage and Mustee into the river shallows.

'How far back is the village?' shouted Earle as he struggled through the door, which was high off the ground. Quao, who was unhurt and already after the dripping Mustee, indicated two good miles. 'Heigh-ho!' said Earle. 'We shall not make Almondsbury this day. Come on, Mustee, get yourself some new clothes out of here!' He indicated a bulging trunk.

'And Quao—straddle yourself a horse and ride for help!'

The black man was on top in a trice and galloping off, while Mustee attired himself anew behind a broad tree and then emerged to tend to the other skittering horses. Earle meanwhile, was gathering what was left of his gold ready for a forced night's stop in the village of Stapleton...

Village women and their children stared open-mouthed at the stranger's passing. Could they believe their eyes? Not one of them had ever seen such a face, which thrust itself in to the white May morning like a thorny blackberry. His cloak had a shoulder cape, yet underneath could be seen the red velvet frock coat with a rolled collar. The bright sun was reflected in the sparkling buttons of his ornate overwaistcoat. His cloak flew above his legs, revealing smart pantaloons in white with a wide scarlet waistband. Those elegant limbs finished within Hussar buskins whose calf-length leather was brightly polished. The man wore no hat and his jet-black hair curled and waved over the cape. As he trotted his horse towards the park gates, small children clung to their mothers' skirts at the sight of that dark face; but the village girls gasped as the foreigner smiled at one or two, face showing his approval of their figures. 'He be going to Knole!' whispered one wife.

'To see *her*, doubtless!' returned another.

'What a smile!'

'What a man!' One of the girls sighed, thinking of her own plain lover, feeding the swine in the byre at Knole.

'What clothes!' was the whisper as the stranger made his way up the drive, lined with blossoming May bushes and under the arched branches of the trees; their green webs budding with life.

The gardener was the first to hear the horse. He had been gathering watercress for the table and he hurried to see who was visiting Knole so early. His mouth dropped open as the man loped by, acknowledging the labourer easily. No English gentleman would have done so, thought the man watching him enter the wide courtyard. Plain folks had seen some sights to dazzle their eyes at Knole in the last few weeks with the young lady and her escapades, but never such a fellow.

The footman opened the door and stared. 'Good-day, sir!' His eyebrows rose.

The man stood erect and bold. He had the voice of an English aristocrat. 'Good morning. Will you convey news of my arrival to the lady and gentleman of the house. I fear I come without invitation, but I have pressing business which has brought me here to Knole in haste!'

'Yes, sir! Your name?' replied the servant, swallowing. He was more nervous with this one than when he had ushered in My Lords Salisbury and Cork. There was something so unusual about him; an air of mystery, yet a magnetic power—which warned the footman to be exceptionally polite or else—

'My name is Earle Grant, late of the Indies!'

The servant inclined his head, memorising the mouthful. 'Please to step into the hall, sir. I will call the lad to hold your horse.'

'Tell him to take the mare to the stables!' ordered Grant and the footman quivered. He dared not say that gentlemen were no longer welcome at Knole. As Earle entered, the footman stepped back, poked out his head and whistled.

At the appearance of the lad, he hissed, 'Take this horse and give it some water!' Then he turned to Earle who was walking about the hall looking at the statues. 'I will inform the mistress you are here,' he said. Grant nodded brusquely and went on looking.

Mrs Worall looked up from her desk. She was composing a list of words to begin her lessons with Caraboo. It was her dearest wish to teach the girl English so that she could communicate with them. She was hoping too that Caraboo might teach her her own language, but first they needed some point of mutual understanding. She rose hastily at the news of the visitor. 'Indeed, I will not see him. What does he want? Did he ask to see Miss Caraboo?' The footman shook his head.

'Only that he came to Knole in haste to see both you and the master, madam!'

'And no word of Caraboo?' asked Mrs Worall, half to herself.

'No, madam,' replied the servant, laughing within himself. Of course, he had come to see the girl. Didn't madam know that?

'Well, Thomas, don't just stand there. Tell him Mrs Worall is engaged at present and the master is walking in the garden; that neither of them are to be disturbed. But—offer him wine, Thomas, remember that; we must not seem lacking in hospitality!' Hannah could feel a tickle of interest in her breast, but she had promised herself and Sam that there would be no more visitors to upset their charge.

'Very well, ma'am,' said Thomas doubtfully. He returned as quickly as he had gone.

'He will not take no for an answer, madam. He has not mentioned Miss, only that he had met another acquaintance of yours in Bristol!'

'Whoever can that be?' cried Hannah. 'Take the gentleman into the drawing room, then step out into the park and fetch Mr Worall, but I warn you, don't alert Miss to the fact. If she is nearby, speak softly to the master!'

'Yes, madam,' sighed Thomas, wishing there was another footman on duty to share the burden...

Sam hurried in, not looking too pleased at the disturbance.

'I'm sorry, Sam,' said his wife, 'but we have a visitor who claims to have made acquaintance with a mutual friend. He wishes to see us!'

'Who is it?' growled Sam.

'Oh, I forgot to ask the gentleman's name!' replied flustered Hannah.

'Dear, dear,' muttered Sam. 'Thomas!' he yelled. The footman appeared. 'The visitor's name, if you please?'

'Earle Grant, late of the Indies!' replied the footman, secretly pleased with his own able memory.

'Never heard of him! Have you?' Hannah shook her head. 'The Indies, you say?'

'Begging your pardon, sir and madam,' said Thomas, 'he is somewhat swarthy!'

'A black fellow? What say you to that, Mrs Worall?'

'He must be here to see Caraboo,' answered Hannah faintly.

'Of course he is! Well, dammit, let's get it over with!' He felt too testy to bother with his wife's shocked expression.

'I'm sorry, Sam,' said Hannah.

Earle Grant was staring into the lurid features of a gentleman portrayed in oils, when he heard them enter. He turned, even more interested that they should wish for no visitors. Country gentry were usually all too eager to socialise. He noted the gentleman's keen glance and florid face and the plump lady's evident distress. Mr Worall strode forward and stood facing him squarely. Then he bowed as if he had no wish to greet him at all.

'Now, sir, you may think me rude, but please don't prevaricate. What is all this about a mutual friend when it is quite clear you have come to see our charge, Miss Caraboo!'

'Caraboo,' repeated Earle thoughtfully. It was a fine name—could easily have been 'Caribee'. 'Earle Grant at your service.' He bowed. 'I am guilty on both counts, I'm afraid. Some time ago at your office in Bristol you received a visitor; a small man—'

'With earrings!' cried Hannah. Earle nodded. 'There, Sam, this must be one of his friends. He said he would make enquiries. Are you from the Indies, sir?'

'I am, indeed,' smiled Earle.

'East or West?' asked Sam.

'I travelled from Jamaica recently, but I have made many voyages to the East Indies. That is why I'm here!'

'Perhaps you can speak Caraboo's tongue?' asked Mrs Worall hopefully.

'Perhaps.'

'Well, if you can,' said Sam, 'let us in on it!' Earle inclined his head realising that whoever the girl was she had been the cause of some disturbance in this household. Now he wanted to see her more than ever.

'I was interested when my contact told me of her—and described her, of course. The description of her dress and manners resembled one of the peoples in which I have much interest!'

'Are you a merchant, sir?' asked Sam.

'I am—and deal with the world. That is where my facility in languages comes from—especially the Oriental!'

'Ah, Sam, I'm sure he'll help us!' The words slipped from Hannah's mouth.

'Help?' asked Earle. 'Have you troubles, then?'

'Only in that we suffer with our charge. I'm afraid Caraboo is desperately unhappy. I know that, although she has not told me. She has been much upset by a variety of visitors and, in truth, we had made up our minds to admit no more. There was only one she understood in Bristol—your friend. I'm sure too that she is eager to unburden herself, but has no medium!'

'Perhaps I may colour her tongue then,' their visitor replied and Hannah thought the ironic words suited the man perfectly and made him more fascinating than ever. In the whole of Bristol port she had not seen such an elegant foreigner with his rich clothes and polished oak features. Grant smiled under the Englishwoman's scrutiny.

'I'll try to communicate with her, madam. I would like to help you, if I can. Where is she?'

Hannah sighed. 'Probably walking about the park, lost in a dream as usual!'

'A dream?' said Earle.

'Aye,' said Sam. 'I have never seen a woman with such romance in her breast, nor such an outlandish way of dressing.'

'All made by herself, Mr Worall, may I add,' defended Hannah. She turned to Earle; 'She's skilled in needlework and—'

'Playing with swords!' sniffed Sam.

'Indeed,' replied Earle, his heart thudding a little.

'Yes, she frightened my valet to death. She had the blade at his throat!' explained Sam. 'Never seen anything like it in the whole of my life!' Earle's eyes were bright as he looked from one puzzled face to the other. He had not felt as hopeful as this for two long years.

'It all sounds quite marvellous,' he said, 'but not uncommon in the Indies where the women are like Amazons!'

Hannah's cheeks were red. 'Is that right, Mr Grant? Caraboo is much like that. She's wild and free, isn't she, Sam? She seems to be yearning for space. Mr Eynesso, whom we met in Bristol, said she had been decoyed from her island and brought here against her will!'

'Did he tell you that? How interesting,' replied Earle, wondering just how much the Portuguese gypsy had known about the 'foreigner' they harboured at Knole...

'Look, there she is!' cried Hannah as the three of them stood upon the terrace which was carpeted by fallen spring petals. The two men could see the white spot wavering between the trees, a slim wraith which seemed to blend with the whiteness of the May, hardly human and substantial, rather an image in a dream.

'May I go down to her?' asked the dark man, his vivid coat and waistband made more scarlet in the sun.

'We'll go together!' replied Sam firmly. 'I've no taste for more hysterics!'

'And she may be frightened!' added Hannah.

They followed the girl's white figure over the bridge made from silver birch, which straddled the pond's tributary; over the ridge and its twisted tree roots, to her favourite place, the pond. Earle Grant and the master and mistress of Knole watched Caraboo kneel to cleanse her face and hands in its waters. Sam watched the dark man's face, which seemed strangely moved; his lips working into a half-smile. He was making towards the stooping girl. Mr Worall put a hand upon Hannah's arm to prevent her following.

'He is pretending he knows her, my dear,' whispered Sam. 'How artful these people are! We have seen it all before, haven't we?' Hannah thought it prudent not to upset her husband in such a mood, but her whole being yearned that the man could bring happiness to Caraboo; that he was not a dissembler; that he really knew her tongue.

Caraboo leaned over the waters, her eyes closed, her face smoothed anew by the cleansing shock of the silky water. It was only at times like this that she felt pure, untouched by life—a heedless girl again wandering another park at will. She stared at her hands, clean and kept long from hard labours. The ripples, breaking away in their circling lines, were quietening, leaving the surface clear to mirror the image she had made of herself.

She gasped, a tiny cry rising in her throat; there was another image above her, dark like the waters—but as sweet. She thought the red was in her cheeks and eyes, but the pond was one rush of colour then, which rose and made a great warmth fill her trembling frame. She turned slowly, collecting herself, fighting to calm her bursting heart. Then he was holding her eyes in his and she saw their soft expression and quiet relief.

Mrs Worall clutched Sam's sleeve as Mr Grant bowed low, then took Caraboo's small fingers in his, lifted up her hand and kissed it.

Sam snorted a little. 'Give me a plain Englishman any day!'

'Sh, Sam, he is speaking to her. Do you think she will understand?'

They knew nothing of the warm island he spoke of with its palms and tropic heat; naught of the bright sands which beckoned from across the ocean that divided love from love.

'Oh, Sam, she's replying! Look at her face—she's so happy that she weeps!'

'I'd say she was upset myself!' growled Sam. 'When will we be done with all this nonsense?'

'Come, Sam,' said Hannah, enraptured by the sight. They moved towards the couple who stood, quaint figures beside the pond; an aspect so bizarre in that English garden which had never seen its like.

'Well?' said Sam shortly, directing himself to Earle Grant. The latter smiled, took Caraboo's hand again in his own and extended it towards the Woralls.

'May I present Caraboo, Princess of Javasu! You see, I am able to help you—all!'

Hannah gave a little cry of joy and leaned on Sam for support. He stared at the two of them with puzzled eyes.

'Are you well, sir?' he asked.

But Hannah interposed, 'I knew it all the time; that she was something extraordinary, someone rare and precious. Oh, thank you, sir—a real princess from the Indies. How wonderful! We are honoured that she has found shelter with us!'

Hannah put her delighted arms about Caraboo and kissed her on both cheeks. Then she looked at Earle. 'I suppose I'm taking a great liberty doing so, but I'm so very happy and I know that she is too. How can we thank you, sir?'

'By allowing me to enter your home and explain how she arrived and by what means. I would be very glad to do so and put your minds at rest!' Earle put out his arm and extended it to Hannah, who linked hers in delight. She glared at Sam, warning him to silence. He followed a few paces behind as his wife and Caraboo proceeded towards the tower of Knole arm-in-arm with the most colourful gentleman who had ever been seen in a plain Englishman's garden...

There was enormous bustle in the house, with Cook declaring everyone had gone mad and Thomas muttering darkly they were all to be duped and probably murdered in their beds. Martha was near hysterics at the thought she had dressed a real princess, while the news had been received in the gardens and stables and passed quickly on to the village. There, the women who had seen him pass by that morning, cried that the black stranger was a prince in disguise come to claim his own; that it was more like a fairy tale than real but better than any story.

When the tale reached the overseer's ears, Sterne shook his head in wonder. He was sophisticated enough to disbelieve like his master had, but he admitted to himself the girl was something out of the common with her wonderful eyes and figure.

The Reverend Steele wandered about the vicarage, looking up Java in his books, searching for the name of the ruling families, but had no luck. He personally had thought they were all savages there, so he consoled himself with charting her possible journey and planning how he could invite himself for dinner. His learned imagination could envisage the rise of Almondsbury, the incursion of dignitaries from the Foreign Office and acclaim for himself who had been the first to locate her origin.

Alex burned inside when he heard. He was like Thomas—he was unable to believe; rather he thought the black man had come to deceive; that it was all a trick between the two of them. Yet their coloured visitor had a presence which the valet recognised. He was no common dissembler; there was a haughtiness about him which showed he was used to command. The girl had the same air about her, which puzzled Alex more. He, who had been used to Turkish rule, acknowledged the alliance of beauty and cruelty—he knew now if he had touched the woman that day she would have pinned him to the door. He felt it was best to be deferential to such strangers. Therefore, when he and the other servants were invited to sit at the far end of the drawing room and hear Miss Caraboo's history, he agreed readily.

Sam Worall felt obliged to go along with it all. His astute brain calculated that if there was a chance it was true, it might do them all good; yet his legal experience made him wary. The world was full of foreigners and cheats; it could accommodate two more of the most plausible villains he had ever seen. As long as they took nothing from him, harmed no one, then he could stomach it; but if they made one false step he would have no qualms in having the two of them arrested and taken before the Justices.

Hannah's breast was full of joy. She knew that Sam distrusted both Caraboo and Mr Grant; that he thought her a romantic fool; but her intuition told her that what she did was right. It had done so all along since she had met Caraboo. Hannah told herself that if the girl was fake she would still care for her. There was an honesty about her charge, a pleading for understanding which could mitigate any deception. If Hannah was to be deceived, she was sure that within Caraboo's self was good reason.

She had called the servants together because she and Mr Worall saw their house as a family made up of parts. The domestics had cared and tended Caraboo as she had and were entitled to know. After all, enlightenment was not the prerogative of the gentry alone. Hannah and Sam abhorred the disastrous policy of crown and parliament which gave no thought to the poor and distressed. Decent people had to stand together in those years when a great disillusionment had risen in English breasts at the excesses of the court which was no father to its subjects. Having been endowed with comfortable means, Hannah believed she had a duty to the less fortunate. Her kindness to Caraboo was an extension of this; if the girl had been a poor servant rather than a princess, Hannah would have pitied her.

As Mrs Worall approached her own gracious table with Samuel seated at its head, the girl looked like an aristocrat where she sat proudly beside him with Mr Grant upon her right. As Hannah took her place beside her husband and their servants looked on, Samuel turned to Mr Grant.

'Let us begin then, sir, and discover what we have been hiding at Knole!' Hannah hoped Sam would not be difficult, because she herself could not wait to hear every tiny detail.

'Are we all ready?' asked Earle Grant.

'Caraboo?' asked Hannah. The moment had come at last. Across the room there was a rustling of skirts and squeaking of leather as the servants prepared themselves. Caraboo looked down at her own face reflected in the polished table top. Her hands were steady but her heart was beating wildly. His reflection beside her was soothing, helping her to calm herself and begin her story.

'She seems agreeable now,' said Earle and spoke to her, raising his voice so that the company knew he was asking her a question.

When she had answered, he turned to them. 'Miss Caraboo will relate her history to me, then I will to you, *verbatim*. Before we begin, I want you to know that I'm sure what she has to say through me will be marvellous—even unbelievable. Yet I, who have travelled into the East Indies, know of its beauty and its savagery and will vouch for the tale!'

A shiver ran through the room. 'The country of Javasu has been under Dutch rule for over two hundred years. I am sure you all know that lately the British recaptured it briefly but sadly have lost it again!' There was some nodding of heads. 'But this made no difference towards the people and their tribes who worship in temples. Near Jogja is Borobodur—where there are seventy-two shrines dedicated to Lord Buddha. Through these, wander a thousand monks, their hands folded like Caraboo's here.' He pointed to her meek attitude. The Woralls and their servants sighed and stared. 'About these temples are great forms, large and pure, huge *stupas* where God Buddha dwells!' Cook pursed her lips and glanced warningly at Martha, whose eyes were round with wonder. 'And there are peasants too who worship in *kampongs* and many princesses. Your Caraboo is one of these!'

He spoke to her then and she smiled, showing her pearly teeth. 'She has come from a land of great mountains and volcanoes like Gunung Marapi from which white plumes of smoke rise in the air like the ostrich feathers in an English lady's headdress!' Mrs Worall put up her trembling hand to her hair as if she could feel them waving above her. 'Yes, madam, like Caraboo's rich feathers!' The company stared, wide-eyed, at the girl sitting demurely in her attitude of contemplation.

'Now, it is the princess's turn. Speak to us all, your Highness, and tell us your history!' He put the last words into her language and Caraboo began to speak the quaint and musical words, sounding like the trill of unknown birds.

When she paused for breath, Earle began to write and speak the translation. 'It is sweet to be the daughter of an aristocrat. You don't know how much it meant to me who was made a slave. My father, Jesse Mandue, lived in a palace which had no equal in the Western world. You would see nothing like it in your capital, with its *pendopo* —'

Here Earle halted to ask her what that was. She seemed surprised. 'Why, it is a great open-sided building with a marble floor. But the roof is wonderful; it has four sides and is supported by great teak beams and columns!'

'Yes,' said Earle to Hannah. 'I understand that perfectly, who was raised near the slave-sheds of Jamaica!' Mr Worall looked up sharply at that. The servants muttered at the mention of such a trade. Then Caraboo seemed impatient. 'I beg your pardon, Your Highness—continue, please!'

'In this great palace, my father kept the priceless heirlooms of our race. Weapons called *creeses* with light and wavy blades—'

'Ah!' cried Sam. 'That's where she gets her knowledge from. Pray, sir, what are these *creeses*?'

'I call them *krises*,' said Earle. 'You use them in a very special way.' Alex shivered, knowing which way *she* would have used hers.

Thomas muttered to his comrade beside him, 'Told you she was no woman—more like a man—and a savage too!'

'Tell us more of them, Your Highness!' cried the dark man. Caraboo held out her small hand, and he, understanding, drew out a dagger from his under-waistcoat. The company gasped as she took it in that little hand and kissed its emerald hilt.

'This is like a *pusaka*, which is of noble origin and owned by a great man. There is a mystery about it and it endows its wielder with supernatural strength!' she said.

'And that is why a girl like Caraboo still uses it,' explained Grant. 'It is a sacred weapon.'

'Tell us something more about the palace,' cried Hannah and the other women nodded their heads. Earle motioned Caraboo to continue.

'My father chose a Mandin for his wife—' Mrs Worall nodded her head, eager to understand. 'That is a Malay woman, dark and beautiful. My mother had wondrous eyes and a sweet face, long curly hair and lovely breasts, not covered but free—'

Hannah's face was red, while Martha giggled. Cook and the housekeeper placed their hands over their ears modestly. Alex, Thomas and the men stared hungrily at the calico-covered breasts of the princess.

Sam shook his head. 'The girl must moderate her language before the ladies!'

'Excuse me, sir,' cried Earle, 'there is no false modesty in Javasu; no whores, but freedom and natural beauty.' Sam, thinking of it, was loath to interfere further.

'More about your mother too, my dear,' cried Mrs Worall, thinking how much the girl must miss her. 'Where is she now?' Earle translated and Caraboo hung her head, letting the tears fall freely. When she composed herself she began once more.

Earle turned. 'She's overcome with grief. Her parents have died!'

The company watched Caraboo lean back from the table's edge, put her hand under her skirts and bring out the knotted cord.

Cook clung to the housekeeper's arm. 'Surely she won't flay herself before us all?'

'She's withdrawing the cord!' cried Thomas gleefully.

Earle looked into their excited faces. 'That is an instrument of prayer and calculation, like the Chinese abacus. Have you heard of the sliding beads, the *suon-puon*?' They shook their heads. 'Her Highness counts upon it. She's calculating the days since her parents died, then she prays for them!'

'Is that why she strikes herself?' asked Hannah. 'Poor dear!'

'She blames herself for their death,' said Earle quietly.

'No!' cried Hannah.'Surely not! Please tell her to go on. We want to know what happened!'

Caraboo, holding the cord fast as a consolation, continued, 'That day the air was hot and humid; the clouds were gathering above the mountain peaks, ready for afternoon showers. My tears had fallen before the rain, because fierce Boogoo warriors had rowed stealthily across the Java Sea. My country was at war with the Boogoos. They hated the Mandins and my father particularly—'

'What in Heaven's name were Boogoos?' cried impatient Sam, interrupting the flow of words.

'Fierce cannibals,' said Earle, smiling at the consternation he had caused by his words.

'Lord have mercy on us,' cried Cook, thinking of her plain English fare.

'Head-hunting parties come from across the sea to satisfy their spirits. Men with nose bones and streaked with mud. Painted savages with bright blooms in their hair and cassowary feathers above their ears; shell pendants about their necks. Boogoos, who creep through the teak forests along the stream-beds intent on murder—' Martha was swaying, her face pale.

'Please, Mr Grant, tell us no more of the Boogoos!' said Hannah.

'I thought you wanted to know the fate of Jesse Mandue,' said Earle, looking into their white scared faces.

'Was he eaten, man?' asked Sam and Cook screamed, then quietened at the look her master gave her.

'Taken away—for ever—together with Caraboo's mother!' said Earle, thinking about the fate of so many people of his race.

'How terrible!' cried Hannah. 'Can she bear to tell us any more? Why does she blame herself?'

'They wanted her for sacrifice, but she was hidden by her women, whom she calls *sammen*, beneath the folds of her father's palanquin!'

'Good Lord,' said Sam. 'What kind of thing is that?'

'It is a covered litter, sir, that needs four bearers. They fled at the coming of the Boogoos and the women pulled Her Highness beneath the covers, hoping she would be safe, but they failed—'

'Why?' faltered Hannah, afraid to hear if Caraboo had been ravished.

'The Boogoos were driven off by some fierce men, led by Chee-ming!' At the name she had just uttered, Caraboo began to moan in fear.

'Who was he?' asked Alex, unable to contain himself any longer; thinking what a stout fellow Chee-ming must have been to conquer Caraboo.

'A fair-headed pirate with great hands and rough manners. He dragged her from her home after binding her hand and foot. She screamed for mercy but he took no notice; she begged his pity but he did not care. He covered her mouth with his hands and carried her off.'

Caraboo's eyes were shining with tears as Earle recounted her torment. 'She fought with him and in that life and death struggle, wounded two of his men, one who afterwards died of his wounds; the other was saved by a doctor, whom she calls a *justee*, which means surgeon. To punish her, Chee-ming scarred her feet with her own *creese*. She will show you!' He signed to Caraboo, who bent and undid her sandals, then lifted her feet to show the soles to the company. They gasped at the scars.

'I've seen them before,' whispered Martha, 'but never knew how she got 'em!' Hannah was feeling quite sick and fanned herself, while Cook and the housekeeper clung together. Alex was not surprised, having been brought up to see such treatment in his life with the Turks. Sam thought of some felons brought before him daily, who deserved the kind of punishment which had been meted out to Caraboo.

'She lived with this Chee-ming for eleven long days,' Earle's voice sank low. Hannah closed her eyes. She could guess what vile practices were to come. They were certainly not for the servants' ears, especially Martha's. Earle caught her glance. 'I will not tell you of the horrors she endured at his hands.' It had been a long and stressful speech on Caraboo's part; the girl seemed exhausted.

'I think she's had enough,' cried Hannah. Earle turned to question Caraboo, but she shook her head, determined to go on.

'I stood in the market-place in Batavia, broken and worn. Men came and stroked my skin; pulled back my lips, looked at my teeth as if I was an animal.' Her listeners were horrified. Earle continued to point out the truth to these English people. 'I was chained about the legs and neck; swayed weakly in my fetters, naked before the world. I was sold like a beast to a young sea captain, whose brig was called the *Tappa-Boo*. That was a terrible ship; I was pushed into the hold below the water line, with hardly a place to stand or lie. The air was foul and suffocating; I thought I would not live. Around me were the groans of my fellows, all peasants and I a princess. We were given unclean water to drink.'

Caraboo looked around at her listeners. Earle continued her explanation. 'That is why I love your lake, it is so clean, I could lie on it for ever. We could not wash, that is why I love water. We ate unclean food prepared by the hands of filthy sailors. That, too, is why I prefer to prepare my own meat in the purest fashion. To prevent my suffocation, I crawled over the bodies of the dead and dying to the great portholes where I could see the endless sea. That is why I love walking in your park smelling the fresh sea breeze. When they saw I was still alive, one rude man attempted me.'

Hannan looked round uneasily at the open mouths of her servants.

'I was saved by the captain, he wanted me for himself—'

'Pray, Mr Grant, tell us no more!' cried Hannah, seeing that Caraboo must go no further.

Caraboo continued to speak, not minding what the mistress said, 'I took my *creese* and would have plunged it in his heart, if he had not broken my grip. It was then I dived in the waters, down from the foul deck into the depths. They were frightened then to lose a valuable slave and sent men in after me. When I was recaptured, I was left alone. It took eleven long weeks to reach your English shore!'

'There is no port here in England which would receive slaves now,' said Sam. Earle transferred the magistrate's doubt to the girl.

She answered, 'Because the captain wanted me for himself he kept me on ship with another cargo of tobacco and sugar, which he picked up in some port of the French West Indies, having set down the slaves there!'

'Thank God,' said Sam, glad such shipments of souls were forbidden by Christian England, but suspicious still, 'that there are no slavers coming into Bristol now!'

'But you had them, sir, had you not?' chided Grant. Sam's face was flushed and uneasy. 'Here is an example of what happened to so many other souls, whose only crime was that their skins were black. This girl was saved from the same fate because her skin was white like a European's. Otherwise she would have perished on some French planter's estate!' Then Grant spoke to Caraboo rapidly. He turned again to the Woralls.

'She says there were others on the ship, peasants of her race who had been forced to help sail the brig. She fears them; they are called Macratoos! They turned on their own people; robbed and murdered on that terrible voyage. Where they have gone since, she does not know. What she does is that some escaped before she did. She says they are wandering freely in the English countryside!'

Cook was quite beside herself at the news; Martha and the housekeeper stared at the drawing room windows as if they feared there were savages prowling outside.

'She says she buried the only possession she had left after she escaped from her captors, which was accomplished by diving into the cold water and swimming beneath until they believed she had drowned. When she had scaled the rocks along the cove where the brig lay, she dug a great hole and buried her possessions inside, except for a dress of silk interwoven with gold which she gave later to a woman in a cottage in exchange for bread and water.'

'Where was that cottage?' asked Sam.

Earle shook his head. 'She does not know except it had green doors!'

'Good heavens, what a story!' said Sam, scratching his head. Caraboo surveyed them all, her cheeks bright red and her eyes begging for their belief.

'Well, I think it's terrible!' said Hannah. She understood now what her charge had suffered. The tale had explained so many mysterious things about her. 'I'm sure we ought to do something about it!' Sam could hear the determination in his wife's voice.

'What can we do?'

'See she is returned to her own country. The Foreign Office must make representations to the East Indies!'

'Must?' scorned Sam.

'Why not?' smiled Earle.

'These men must be brought to justice, Sam. You're the magistrate—you're always saying that a victim has rights. This brig must be found by the Navy!' Sam was unsure whether he dared laugh at his wife's sparkling eyes and indignant words.

'The Navy, Hannah? Lord Exmouth and the Mediterranean fleet have more to do than chasing a foreign brig. They have done their bit to end the trade in Christian slaves. This girl is a heathen!'

'Sam!' cried Hannah shocked. The servants shifted, unused to seeing their master and mistress at odds.

'There, you see, still causing trouble,' whispered Cook to the housekeeper, indicating Caraboo. She seemed above it all, first staring into space, then smiling quietly at Mr Grant. 'I wish she would take herself elsewhere!' Mrs Wardle nodded in agreement.

'Do you think they will contact the Foreign Office?' whispered Thomas to Alex. Was it possible his master had swallowed such a fabulous story? He had never heard such romancing with cannibals and slavers and all. If he had been the master, he would have shipped Miss off back to the East at his earliest opportunity.

'It's possible,' Alex answered. He did not know whether to believe any of it, but how had the girl learned so much? He could have sworn then she was reading his mind, because she suddenly stared him in the eyes across the room, motioning to Mr Grant.

'What does she want?' asked Hannah.

'She is asking for pen and paper to write on!' replied Earle.

'To write? How marvellous! Sam, I knew she could. I wonder what it will be like!'

'You'll never know unless you hand her the implements,' said Sam drily, wishing he was back in Bristol and away from all this nonsense. They watched her write carefully but with dexterity, her fingers as nimble as they had been with the needle. Hannah could hardly contain herself; wanted to get up and stand to look over her shoulder, but she had to be patient. It was evidently taking some time for Caraboo to communicate her message. When she had finished, Mr Grant handed the paper, first to Sam, who stared at it in amazement; then passed it on to Hannah, who was just as surprised.

'It's so pretty, Sam, isn't it? Is this your language, Caraboo?' Earle turned to the girl, spoke to her and she inclined her head.

'Yes, that is how she writes.'

'It's hieroglyphics, isn't it, Sam?'

Sam shook his head at a loss for words. 'What does it mean, Mr Grant?'

Earle took it back, stared at it and his face creased into a frown. 'I'm not sure, having never seen this language myself. But I will ask her!' He did. 'She says the six characters on top signify Alla Tallah in her father's country. The three on the right the same phrase in her mother's.'

'And the rest?' cried Mrs Worall excitedly.

Earle shook his head. 'It is not of much account. It is a prayer of her own choosing!'

'Oh, Caraboo, show us some more, if you please!'

The girl took the pen again and began to write in the neatest hand. Then her language was passed on to the servants, who stared, nonplussed. Only Alex's quick brain assimilated the repetition of letters and signs. His gift of language was of no help; he had never seen such characters before except in museums and the like; or on stones and ancient buildings. He stood up, convinced that whoever the girl was, she could hardly be a trickster with such a facility as this.

'Yes, Alex?' asked Hannah, seeing the look on his face. 'Can you recognize any of it?'

'No, madam, not a word, but may I say that I think we should act upon your earlier suggestion and send some of this to one of your great English colleges.'

'You see, Sam,' said Hannah, turning. 'Alex is convinced. Isn't that enough for you?'

Hannah was happy she had been able to persuade her husband to contact the Foreign Office on behalf of Caraboo. Luckily, Sam had friends in London who were still ready to listen to the voice of reason. It seemed to those liberal men that the reason for such a shocking thing when a young woman could be sold and transported from her country, should be investigated. Furthermore, how did these foreigners take such as her on to the plantations of the French West Indies. After all, hadn't it been agreed in Vienna that the Mediterranean trade in slaves must cease? Mr Wilberforce still had his charitable eyes fixed upon the sufferings of the poor and there was reform in the air. Sam's friends persuaded and the matter concerning Caraboo was set in hand.

'I'm so happy, Sam,' murmured Hannah as they stood watching Caraboo and Mr Grant at play.

'Humph,' replied her husband, thinking that parliament should have found much more to do at home than concerning themselves with a foreign princess. There were riots and insurrections everywhere. Talk of agitation, spies and informers. English workers were ready to rise in a body, but at Knole, life centred upon their princess and the 'Black Prince' who had come to stay.

Hannah would not let Caraboo out of her sight, was always there with her and Mr Grant; loved to hear them talk their quaint dialect or see them fencing as they were now.

'They're so wild, dear,' she said, half to herself. Caraboo was circling, sword in her right hand, dagger in her left. She was closing on Mr Grant. Mrs Worall shut her eyes and prayed no one would be hurt. She could hear Earle laughing as he retaliated. He had explained that was the way they fought in the Indies and every day, Hannah believed more in her charge's verity. No one who had not the knowledge, could fence so—and certainly no woman.

Earle's breath came and went quickly. He had taught her the art of fencing too well. He needed all his wits about him to contend with the wiles of this princess, whose eyes were like the *creese* she held, alert and shining.

He had stayed long enough now at Knole; must put his plan into action; write letters instead of fencing. He yearned to be alone with Caraboo, but would wait on patiently until it was in his power to bring such wishes into being.

Caraboo's hopes were high as she caught him off guard. With a rush of energy she whipped his rapier from his hand and he was down on one knee, his full lips parted in surprise. There was no sickness in her breast, only the desire to show him she was the victor. If she could open her heart to him she would—but Mrs Worall was hurrying forward once more, lifting her skirts as she went.

'No, Caraboo, you'll do Mr Grant harm. Pray get up, sir, you look quite exhausted. I'll order our morning chocolate before Sam departs. He has business in Bristol today!'

Earle straightened up and backed away from the pointed tip of Caraboo's rapier. She withdrew and he stretched out his hand for the girl's. She looked at it and handed him her creese.

He turned over the small dagger thoughtfully. 'Madam, I have business in Bristol too—and must make my farewells.' Hannah heard the sob as Caraboo drew in her breath. The girl would take it hard when her comrade left. Sometimes, Mrs Worall wished the fascinating man could stay at Knole for ever. In fact, it had run through her mind he might make Caraboo his own, so fond he was of her—but Hannah had dismissed the thought hastily, knowing these two were not conventional people.

'We shall be sorry,' said Mrs Worall. 'I don't know what Caraboo will do without you, Mr Grant!'

'She knows I must go some time,' he said. 'Doubtless you will hear from the Foreign Office soon regarding her fate. Mrs Worall heard another sob. 'I hope you will let me know the decision.' Sam, who had come up behind his wife, bowed slightly. There was nothing he wanted more than to see the girl settle and Knole as well. He would not mourn her loss, nor that of the black man. There was still something about their fabulous tale which did not fit.

'When do you expect to leave?' he asked Grant. The latter could hear the relief in his host's voice.

'As soon as possible,' Earle replied, thinking Mr Worall would not be so happy if he knew what trouble was about to come upon him.

They were all very surprised the morning after.

Thomas's eyes were wide and glinted jealously at the sight of the liveried coachman and postillion. He understood now what that sealed message contained which had been carried to Stapleton by a stable lad. Mr Grant had given it to him, together with a bright piece of gold which had been bitten in the kitchen and pronounced good. The postillion with the cream-coloured skin stared back into the footman's hostile face. He was just another gaping white man. The coachman's ebony face was impassive. He was far above it all, seated high on the box with authority over fresh horses and responsible for the finest coach in the district.

Sam Worall raised his eyebrows and pursed his lips when he viewed it. He admired the coach for its technical workmanship; its brakes and the metal bands around the wooden wheel rim. He wondered whether those fancy wheels had been tried out on Mr Superintendent MacAdam's new road surface, which stretched for eleven miles between Bristol and Old Down.

'An expensive coach for an expensive road,' he snorted to himself. This was a nobleman's carriage with luxurious fittings. When Sam glanced inside, he saw its elaborate decorations and the gilt coat-of-arms set upon its green and polished side.

'What a fine coach, Mr Grant!' cried Hannah. 'Isn't it lovely, Caraboo?' But the girl showed no emotion, her face set and pale. 'What coat-of-arms is that?'

'It is West Indian, madam, a Caribbean aristocrat's mark. The sign of a rich planter!'

'Look at the cunning lights, Caraboo!' Hannah said, but the girl took no notice.

It was only when Earle kissed her hand, that she broke down and Mrs Worall signed to Thomas to support her fainting body. The fine horse, which Mr Grant had ridden proudly to Knole, was tethered behind, and the household servants stood in a correct line as the town coach swayed springingly away from Knole Park under the arching trees and was lost into the landscape.

Then, with a sigh, Mrs Worall turned to Caraboo and kissed her on both cheeks. 'Don't despair, my dear, something will come of it all, I'm sure. Just be patient, please!'

'That'll be the day,' muttered Sam as he followed them to the house...

Three days later, the Woralls were seated in their drawing room ready for the call to dinner.

'Well, Sam, I think we have managed to teach her something. I never thought she would get over losing Mr Grant so quickly. After he had said farewell she got herself under control and has been quite easy ever since.'

'Yes, Hannah, but what are we going to do with her now that we think we know who she is?'

'Still an unbeliever, Mr Worall?' quipped Hannah. 'Imagine we have a princess on our hands!'

'That's what's worrying me,' said Sam, 'I really—' There came a frantic knocking. 'What the devil's going on? Thomas!' The footman appeared followed by a breathless Martha.

'Whatever's the matter, girl?' barked Sam.

'Miss, sir! Miss is gone!' sobbed Martha.

'Gone—?' cried Hannah.

'Completely, madam, disappeared. Cook sent me to fetch her for dinner. I've been out there for an hour. I got the gardener to help and the men from the stables—and everyone. She's vanished!'

'Oh, no,' said Hannah faintly.

'She must be in the park!' said Sam.

'She has no clothes with her, nothing! Oh, what can have happened to her? Alone—at twilight. Has she been kidnapped?' Sam didn't know how to console his wife. He tried to cajole her.

'Well, she came with nothing. Perhaps she's taken it in her head to visit the village. Go down there, Thomas, directly. Take a horse!'

'Yes, sir,' said the footman. As he waited for the lad to saddle it, he said, 'Mark my words, she's gone off with Mr Grant!'

They began by searching every room in the house; every outbuilding on the farm; every cottage in the village. Mrs Worall stood, staring through the windows of the tower, looking across to the river, imagining all kinds of terrible fates that could have overtaken Caraboo.

Sam alerted the minister, the constable, the landlord at the inn, but not one of them had seen Caraboo pass by or through. She had vanished like the plume of smoke that rose from her volcano; disappeared into her jungle mist as if she had never been. That flat alluvial land was empty like Mrs Worall's protecting hands. The narrow winding lanes did not reveal the secret of her whereabouts; the sea breeze blustering in, tossed away her name into the air as they called it over and over, but in vain. The gulls mimicked it and screamed it out over the estuary and down to where the tall sailing ships plunged at anchor. Sam sent his searchers on to Bristol, who walked their way through the port asking for any news of her.

But Caraboo had disappeared without trace—all the Woralls could do was wait.

CHAPTER 18

His master had told him that they must put at least twenty miles between themselves and Almondsbury for safety's sake. Quao had his doubts whether local folk were smart enough to fit the pieces together in such a mystery, but he had to obey Mr Grant who did everything for a very good reason. The coloured man could understand why the girl must not be discovered, nor his master's part in it either, and he would obey his orders as quickly and faithfully as he could.

Quao thought of her slight frame as he had heaved her into the saddle; how she had trembled behind him when they left the park at Knole; she seemed no heavier than a fine goose feather pillow and the horse ran on easily with its double burden. She was a born rider, crouching comfortably behind him, keeping his back warm, swerving with him as he guided the animal south-east towards the county's borders. Quao told himself that each good mile was taking him further away from Bristol and its ugly history towards home and anonymity.

As they passed by the park of a great and graceful house, which rose in the Gloucestershire countryside, Quao would have given it a wider berth had he known that Dodington owed its present glory to a trade in the West Indies that the coloured servant knew much about. While the horse and its riders skirted it, the girl clinging behind Quao caught a glimpse of the house's portico and church in the distance through the shield of fine park trees.

On they travelled south-east in the high hills overlooking Bath and the Avon valley, leaving Dodington to the West, crossing the Bath road towards the village of Marshfield, which did not take its name from any foul marsh, but from the boundary where the three counties of Gloucester, Somerset and Wiltshire meet at a place called The Rocks.

She was so deep in thought that she did not know where they were, clattering along the High Street with its tall Georgian houses. She would have asked the dark man what village it was, but her tongue seemed tied in her mouth; so long it had been since she had last spoken her native language. Strangely enough she had not asked where she was bound, only gone along with the black servant she had first met years ago in Bedford Square. That was a life she could never cast aside however long had passed between. Everything else had been swept away in her masquerade; except that shining doorway into a verdant island where she had been a true princess, courted by the prince she desired; a gentleman none could match, nor ever would again.

She looked down at her legs as the horse was halting. Her sandal ribbons were dusty from the ride; her feet were cold. Those wild skirt fringes seemed tawdry in the light which glinted from the windows of the inn. Perhaps it had all been a dream. Yet, brawny arms were held up to lift her trembling body down. She slid into the black servant's arms and stood breathless, a slim figure beneath the huge riding cloak in which he had enveloped her before they set out from Knole. She could feel the horse's sweat and hair sticking to her thighs—and longed for cleansing water.

The ostler stared at them as he caught the bridle of the lathered horse. Two more strange ones to add to the other gentleman upstairs. He rubbed his eyes as he caught a glimpse of her costume under the cloak. He could almost fancy he was mumming again on Boxing Day to ward off evil spirits. At Christmas-tide the Marshfield Mummers were famous through all Gloucestershire. This woman seemed like one of the old spirits in her pagan dress which would scare off the saints. He touched his brow as the black man offered a coin, then drew the young lady beneath his protecting arm to lead her inside.

The customers hushed their conversation; all that could be heard was the hissing of the basting meat and the chink of ale mugs. Though Marshfield was on the way to Bath, these were still strange visitors. Quao hoped the girl would hide her head well so that her gaudy feathers would not burst from under the hood and proclaim her fantastic dress. But she was quiet as they passed through the stone-flagged kitchen, behind the counter and towards the rooms beyond. Quao ascended the stairs before his charge, peering upwards. He had to be sure Mr Grant was aware of their arrival—and waiting.

She leaned against the cold yellow stone of the wall as Quao knocked upon the bedroom door.

'Master, we are here,' he called. Then the door opened and the lad, Mustee, passed out and through to shake his hand, then stand aside.

She felt a freedom run through her limbs; throbs of relief that lifted the tiredness from her body. She clenched her fists at her sides, drew herself straight and walked proudly under the lintel. What would he say? What should she do? They had been together so recently, but had been strangers, victims of her masquerade. She was no longer that girl whom he had bowed into his home in Bedford Square. She had cried to him that night for understanding—had found it in his comradeship—

who had been as much brother to her as his dear mistress had been sister.

At Knole they had been forced to continue the game. They could not touch; nor she derive any comfort or knowledge of the man whom she loved. Now the time had come! All would be answered! All the tears that had racked her; all the days of loss could be counted and—either healed or broken open again. She longed for news of Jem but set her teeth and swallowed the spittle in her throat to soothe its dryness.

She who had despised all men but him, felt as young and careless as a girl again, who was ready to throw herself upon a man's mercy and feel the warmth of protecting male arms. She had made a life apart for herself; now she wanted to be of the common world again.

Her wide dark eyes stared into the room, holding him with their pleading. The chamber was long, stretching right across under the inn roof; a cold place even in late May, which needed a good fire at its end to warm it. The stone walls were not the mellowed gold of houses in the north of the county, but darker and austere, yet at her entrance they appeared to grow brighter, while the fire seemed to dart out its red tongues for her and leap with excitement.

Earle walked swiftly across the room; his rich brocaded dressing gown hanging loosely upon his muscled figure, opening to reveal he wore no shirt beneath, only close-fitting pantaloons stretched tight beneath the soles of his strong dark feet. There was no awkwardness in his unconventional greeting. He came to stand facing her, smiling; then, throwing back her travel-stained cloak, he pulled her to him, held her in a tight embrace, kissed her forehead gently, then drew her with him towards the fire.

'Come, Mary,' were his simple words. She blushed as he put her in the carved and pretty chair, full of patched cushions. 'I cannot call you princess, nor Caraboo—only Mary Willcocks. It has been a long time looking for you—and—' he stared at her whimsically, '—here you are, quite safe!'

In a moment she was up clinging to his arms, straining her eager neck, her eyes bright and forceful, her full lips quivering.

'Tell me, Earle, please, tell me! How is—' She wanted to say 'my love' but she was afraid. She could hardly say his name. He stared into her eyes, searching for what he knew was true.

'Jem is well.'

'Oh,' she trembled and her tears were bright in the firelight.

'And he's never given up looking for you.'

'Oh, Earle!' she swayed and would have fallen but he thrust her back into the chair and knelt beside it. She opened her eyes. 'I'm so—'

'Happy?' She shook her head. It was too soon to be happy. She would never be that until she was in Jem's arms.

'Not happy?' There was sympathy in his tone.

She hesitated. 'Earle—'

'Yes?'

'I have to tell you!'

'You can,' he said. He was the touchstone for them both. On him they sounded out their lives. Sometimes he wanted comfort too. But he had been blessed—having no sorrow in love; having a girl whom he fulfilled and who gave back in return. He wanted Juba then. He wished she could soothe him with her strong hands, ward off the care to come. 'You can tell me anything,' he said calmly, knowing his time would wait—and Jem's must come first. He took Mary's hands in his, then kissed one as if she were the greatest lady and he, her servant. 'Go on, Mary.'

She swallowed. How could she begin after so long? She clung to his hand then and stared into the fire, like she had done so many nights in the gypsy camp when she had learned their magic lore.

'Help me, Earle,' she said. 'I can only do it if you help me.' He let her twist his hand until it went white, like his palms. 'You are good to me,' she whispered. 'When I've told you, will you promise me that—' she faltered, fearful to indicate she might need his sympathy; his full belief and his ability to bind her wounds.

'I will tell you what you want to know most of all about Jem and how he feels!' There was the strength she needed in the quiet answer. Mary leaned back, closing her eyes, questioning herself as to where she should begin.

Then she was sure. There was no need to protest her love for her lord; that Earle had seen; nor reason to tell of her lack of birth and education. Although it meant so much to her, it was only the story of a million ignorant girls who had journeyed in from countless county towns to seek their fortunes. No, her story began with her delusion that a man could change; her rashness in taking society by its face value. It was Humphrey Moon who had been the cause of all her troubles. He had stolen her innocence; no girl should become a woman in such a terrible way. She opened her eyes and looked into Earle's. He was helping her then with his kind acquiescence. Under that black skin was an honest heart, while Moon's fair complexion had covered his darkness. Once she had laughed at him at Brushford Farm, not knowing the power of ruin a bad man had. It was not a pretty tale.

Although a man, Earle could feel how she was torn apart. Her low words were akin to the shame she was feeling through no fault of her own. To give her heart to go on, he stroked her small hand, cursing his sex for what it could do. When the overseer had ripped away little Juba's virginity, Earle had felt hot shame as well as madness. He was glad Moon was dead, dealt the punishment he deserved; the same kind Earle had meted out to the brutal *busha* upon the plantation. He put his other hand over Mary's to stop her words, to give her chance to forgo some pain.

'Do you believe me?' she asked, shuddering. It crossed her mind then that perhaps he thought it was all another fantasy to make her sins less obvious.

'My dear,' he said, continuing to hold her hand. 'No woman could tell a man such things and not be believed!' She thought then that he was only being gallant, but he shook his head. 'I know what you felt for Jem. I saw it in your eyes the very first time you entered my home in Bedford Square. Moon may have made you his whore, but to Jem you brought a fresh happiness. Don't you think he would have guessed if you had been trying to dupe him?' Mary's face was hot. It had been an ordeal even to speak of that night in the whore-house. 'A man can feel too; I can vouch for that. Jem and I are men—and not mistaken in Mary.'

'But I lived with him, Earle. Only to think of it makes me retch; makes me want to plunge myself into water and wash him away!'

'Poor Mary,' he said gently. 'You have washed him away with your tears. He can harm you no more.'

'But he must have told Jem about me. Isn't that why Jem went? Didn't I drive him from England? You know, Earle, he loved Devon so much. It was part of him!'

'It still is,' said Earle, calming her frantic words. 'And he'll come back. He was confused after what he did—'

'The duel?' said Mary, closing her eyes.

'So you learned of it, then?' Earle asked, wanting to know the truth.

'Lucy Tippet, the woman whom I lodged with, went to Farr House for me; told me Humphrey was wounded—'

Earle was satisfied. 'Not only wounded, Mary—'

'What? Is he—?'

'Dead. But not by Jem's hand.' Mary shook her head to and fro wordlessly. 'He didn't die, Mary, but returned to that isolated farm—'

'You have been to Brushford? What happened, Earle?'

'It's a dismal place now, Mary. The wife is—'

'She was good to me.' Mary's words were hardly audible.

'She seemed a good woman, yes—better than her son!' said Earle, reminding them both that mourning for Humphrey Moon was impossible. 'It seemed that her son took a mad mood, saddled up his mare that was green and uneasy. Took a tumble over a fence and broke his back!'

Mary swallowed and shivered. 'I'm glad it wasn't Jem,' she said.

'So you have nothing to fear from him,' said Earle.

'Oh, but Jem knew!' She held on fast to the coloured man's fingers.

'Mary, listen!' Earle kneeled up, put out a hand and stroked back her hair. 'The night before they fought the duel, Jem was as mad as Humphrey Moon!' Mary gave a little cry. 'You went with Moon from Brighton; that was a terrible thing for Jem.'

'I had to! Humphrey said that the Duke of Barton would come and whip Jem back to London; that no man could bear living with a whore! That they would charge bigamy upon him—and Earle, I was afraid it was all true!'

'And so was I,' said Earle. 'That's why I made him go!'

'You did? No one else?'

'No one, but I. I made him see reason, but even then he didn't want to leave you and the child—'

Mary was crying openly. 'If I'd contacted him sooner, before he went, then Edward might still live—'

'Edward?' Earle had wanted her to speak of the child on her own volition, not his. 'A boy then?'

'A lovely baby, Earle, I loved him to distraction, though he tired me out like all babies!' She smiled through her tears. 'Sometimes, I think he knew his father was gone—sometimes, I fancy he just gave up. I know it's silly but—that's how I feel!' she finished lamely. 'He wouldn't suck, Earle, he faced away; wouldn't even take milk from the bottle. Lucy and I, we tried everything—'

'I know you did, Mary,' Earle said, pitying her agony.

'He was Jem's, Earle. Whatever Humphrey said, he was Jem's!' The tears fell upon the fine calico. 'When I saw the doctor; that's where I had been the night I met Jem and came to you. He said I wasn't pregnant—at least he couldn't tell—and I prayed the babe wasn't Moon's. Edward was dark and—oh, God—' she swallowed.

'But, Mary, you and Jem—' Earle liked to think of babes, even though Juba and he could never hold one of their own.

'Do you know it's true he still wants me,' begged Mary.

Earle let go her hand, stood up, walked across the room to the cupboard in which were locked all his most valuable possessions. He withdrew Jem's letter from his personal hand luggage; brought it over and handed it to Mary.

She read every dear word over and over again; her tears blotching the ink. Once or twice, the elegant writing was so blurred, with the moisture from her eyes, she had to blink before she could carry on. She looked up at Earle, who stood looking down into the fire.

'He still wants me; he says he still wants me,' she repeated as if to convince herself. 'But, Earle, the letter's tone! He seems low, dejected in spirit. You said he was well.'

'He was getting like me—he thought you would never be found,' said Earle quickly. 'But now you are.'

'When will you contact him?' she cried. Earle looked at this girl, glowing with hope, who had forgotten she was a High Princess of Javasu.

'I will as soon as I have decided the best thing to do. Now what can you tell me about this subterfuge?' He touched the top of her peacock feathers, whose brilliant eyes almost reflected the firelight. She hung her head, twisting the folds of her short skirts in her fingers, as if she was ashamed. Then she stopped, stared into his eyes and he could see the return of the haughty glance they had encountered so often at Knole. 'The look becomes you, Princess Caraboo!'

'I did not take this mask lightly,' she said. Earle was eager to know how she had become that extraordinary damsel. Mary Willcocks had nothing of the common about her; no country girl could have been endowed with such natural powers.

'I believe that too,' he answered. 'No girl could make a better princess!'

'Don't make sport of me,' she said. However much she loved him, whatever burden he had taken from her shoulders, he could never know what Caraboo had meant to Mary Willcocks. It was a secret part of her life, a separate existence, prized by a woman who had forgone the society of men.

'I was not,' he said, shaking his head. 'I know much of the power of the imagination—as does Juba. She spoke the truth, Mary, when she said all would come right!'

'But Juba is a seer,' said Mary softly and Earle had to strain to hear her.

'The *duppy* told her!' added Earle. There was no mock in the words which were almost lost in the crackling hiss of the log shrivelling on the fire. Yet Mary heard him; her ear was sensitive to every whisper.

'I learned much from the gypsies—'

'Ah,' said Earle. 'Where did you meet them?' He was thinking of their fellows who had helped him in her quest.

'Near Exeter, by Salisbury—in the narrow lanes and water-filled ditches, by their fires in the fields; in the safety of their vans, ringed on the moor. They're everywhere, Earle!' Her eyes shone as she remembered. 'I lived in a pretty *vardo*, learned *dukkering*!' Mary could see it was a new word for Earle. 'Telling fortunes,' she explained thinking of wild Rosa then—and surly Tod. From the two of them she had taken her skills; could strut like a theatre player; had developed an uncanny intuition which had always been natural to her, but needed bringing out.

'My Juba has a rival then?' he said, smiling, thinking how fine Mary looked in the firelight.

'Not always fortune telling, Earle, but selling combs and lace, collecting rags and making baskets.'

'Jem's Mary was a merchant then? Is that where you got your love of finery?' He smiled at her stately feathers. The two were slipping into that easy comradeship they had enjoyed in those weeks in his London house. Mary put up her hand. She shared with the Romany folk their love of flashy brightness.

She shook her head. 'No, I'm just a woman, Earle, with a desire for lovely things.' She smiled back at him, knowing she looked much more in her Eastern finery. She stroked down the dress she had made for herself, thought of the fine tale that they had told the Woralls. 'You were clever, Earle, to fill in the pieces of Caraboo's history!' She laughed, reminding herself of the mischievous girl she once had been before life had taken its toll. She slipped into the old dialect of his island and he replied playfully in that same tongue to humour her who had suffered so.

She said, 'You told them your own story as well as mine, didn't you? Like you told me and Jem that lovely night in Bedford Square; how your people were tricked and carried into slavery?'

He nodded. 'And Chee-ming—wasn't he—?'

'Humphrey Moon.' All the light in her face drained away. 'I made him up to show what a murdering pirate can do to a woman!' There was a savagery in her voice he had not heard before. It would do her good to be angry; would cleanse her like fire.

'Do you feel better now I know?' he asked. 'It is best to let those feelings out, not hide them in misery!'

'As Caraboo has done?'

'No, like Mary!' he replied.

'I never wanted to be Mary again,' she whispered, half to herself. 'I left her working and weeping in a London shop; when I donned man's clothes and wandered on to that cold plain; when I found out that gypsies—' She broke off then, fearful to mention Tod.

'Gypsies never harm their brothers?' he queried, but into his mind quickly limped the one-armed man who had supplanted Eynesso. 'Aren't they always ready to help their brothers and—learn never to be afraid!'

'Gypsies are full of guile,' she said quietly.

'Did they harm you, Mary?' he asked. She shook her head and the peacock feathers made gigantic shadows on the stone.

'I left them before they could. I had already decided to walk alone in the world away from—'

. 'The company of men?' His words were so gentle that she wondered how some men could be both strong and sweet.

She nodded. 'I met a sailorman—on Bristol Quay. He had sailed from the port of Batavia; he was full of quips and sayings—and wild fancies. He was as superstitious as any *gorgio*. I told him his fortune and in return he told me of that secret island. As he recounted its description, I learned it all by heart. He had taken tea with a princess, carried a fine *creese* with a wavy blade, which had been given to him by its maker; he had climbed the temple pyramid at Borobodur. It was all so easy, Earle.' The black man lifted his eyebrows quizzically. She looked so honest as she told him.

'If you were not so sweet, Mary Willcocks, I'd say you were a rogue!' Earle threw back his head and laughed. Outside, Quao and Mustee raised their heads at the sound; they had been squatting at their stations by the door. The older man smiled into Mustee's cream face.

'I told you everything would be all right, Mustee. Our master is a wizard!' Then Mustee stared about him fearfully as if the *duppy* was listening.

Inside, Earle poured out the golden wine, which had been brought earlier by a servant. It had the musty taste of country cellars in its making—but the sweetness of cowslip heads. He offered it to Mary, whose face was white again.

'Now, let me tell you about Jem—' he said. Every word he spoke was as delicious as the wine. She was as starved of news of her love as of strong drink and meat. As Earle told her of the great traffic in letters which had crossed the seas, she warmed inside; felt feverish at the thought of seeing him again; holding him in her arms; feeling his heat—her head was dizzy by the fire, her eyes were closing from sheer exhaustion.

Earle could see she was being overtaken by the heat of the fire and the unaccustomed wine; her haughtiness had slipped away and she was a simple girl again to be protected. Her lips were parted as she fell asleep and once or twice she murmured fitfully. He waited until that first sleep was sound, then picked her up from the chair, carried her to the bed and laid her down.

He stared at her quaint costume and shook his head as if he feared she might disappear again like some insubstantial dream. Suddenly, she smiled in her sleep; a peaceful look spread across her face as she turned into the pillows. When he had unlaced her sandals, he pulled the covers over and about her, then drew the curtains carefully. After, he called in his two servants who were nodding with sleep in the corridor, offered them wine like equals and then the three men lay down before the fire like lithe and graceful animals. It was not long before they slept too, satisfied by the success of their day, and did not stir before the grate was full of ashes and the last of the logs was charred and dead...

When Mary woke, she was refreshed and her senses sharp. For a moment she could not remember where she was and sat up quickly, reaching to push the curtains aside. The room was empty. Then she thought Earle and his men had left her; that she would see them no more—but to her great relief was proved wrong in a moment by one quiet footstep outside the drapes and Earle's deep voice bidding her, 'Good morning.'

While they broke their fast together, Mary re-lived the night before and her openness with Earle. She surveyed his strong features and dexterous hands as he broke his bread and heaped slices of cold tongue upon his plate. He offered her meat, but she had been so long without it, she declined. Yet she tasted the butter, which was not as good as she remembered the pats she had made in Brushford Dairy.

Could she explain to him all her motives in choosing to be Princess Caraboo? Even he would not understand. Earle was a man and, however gentle, would find it difficult to imbibe the fancies of her woman's heart. He had understood what it meant when Moon had taken her, but could he know anything about the loss of love and self which were the things women prized most of all.

He knew about society; that it was bad and had been responsible for taking Jem out of her arms. If her love had not been made to marry— suddenly she thought of his wife—she had not asked if Celia was dead. Had Earle told her? She was afraid she could not remember.

'Earle,' she said. 'When you spoke last night of Jem, did you say aught of Celia?' He stopped eating and shook his head.

'You have nothing to fear from her either!' He looked into Mary's questioning eyes and nodded, 'Yes, dead too—but if you had known Lady Farr, in other circumstances, you would have liked her. She was a sweet unfortunate—'

'Don't make me feel guilty, Earle!' Mary knew how selfishly she was behaving.

'No, Mary, yours is not the guilt. 'Tis society's!'

So Celia was dead. Mary looked down at the steaming tea which Mustee brought in and set before her.

Earle continued, 'Nothing to say, Mary? That means you could be Lady Farr—if you wish!'

The thought was unbelievable; but strangely it did not mean what it had done; not because she loved Jem less, or because she did more. Her great station in life was becoming less important. Once it had been all she desired and she had found its culmination in her disguise—but she was wise now, knowing that other things meant more than princely birth. Caraboo had been the means of getting her noticed in the world, but without Jem such a world was a desert.

'Of course I wish it, Earle,' she answered. 'If he does!'

'He would not have married you in Brighton otherwise, my dear.'

'Marriage,' she said, thinking about the word.

''Tis a Christian hypocrisy!' he replied and she looked at him with wonder. She had never thought of him as other than a Christian.

'Don't look so shocked, Mary. At Knole, they called *you* a pagan!' It was true—she had wanted to be that—and free of a faith which preached of hell fire. The Bristol sailor had told her in that other religion, passion meant nothing and a man could be cleansed through and through until his soul could pass into purity on earth and not have to wait for death and heaven.

Mary had liked that idea; made up her mind if she could not have Jem, she would find her own paradise.

'Do you believe in nothing, Earle?' she asked.

He smiled. 'In goodness, fairness, justice and equality.' It was a pretty speech. She wished then Earle could have been her teacher; that she had had a father like him; that she had been schooled by such great wisdom.

He went on, 'Why, Mary, you are sad—and you should be happy. I have been trying all morning to decide what shall be done. I think you must return to Knole!' She stared at him. That was unthinkable. She had fancied he would take her with him straight away; that she and Jem would meet and live happy ever after.

Her fear must have shown in her face; Earle stretched his hand out across the table and took hers. 'It will only be for a while,' he said. 'Don't look such a tragic princess.'

'What do you mean?' He sighed. He was tired that day of being strong—but he had promised Jem he would see his Mary again. 'I can't go back!' she said. He patted her hand and smiled.

'You must, Mary! Think of Mrs Worall.' Mary knew Hannah would be frantic with worry. 'You owe her something, my dear.'

She could see life was never that simple. How could she have thought she could just slip away—after all, she had some obligation to a woman who had been more of a mother to her than any since she had left her own parent in Witherage.

'But, Earle, what will I tell her? Where shall I say I've been? Am I to be Caraboo still—or Mary Willcocks?' The questions came fast.

'Hold, Mary, not so quick. Give one time to think!' She sat back, ashamed, knowing he had done all he could and she was harrying him.

He stared at his meat and thought. Mary was like quicksilver; full of many parts, vital and light, but rolled together, made one binding whole in her love for Jem. Although she questioned him, needed his help, she was full of that confidence which begged for superiority over man; needed to find its own destiny. He thought of the girl at Knole, who could ride, swim, dive and fence like a man; whose strength was such she could claim to be Earle's equal. Mary Willcocks was indeed most extraordinary and his next move must be a careful one.

'Have you come to a conclusion?' she begged.

'Not yet!' And she was quiet again. First, he must write a long and serious letter to Jem. How he would tell his friend had no son was difficult. Perhaps the finding of Mary would take away some of the dreadful sorrow. How he would tell him that his love was masquerading as a Javanese princess would be almost impossible. Such a mask might lend weight to any doubts Jem still had about Mary's careful deception of the fact she had lived with Humphrey Moon. Earle knew the girl opposite him was no trickster; yet she was not artless. But he also knew Jem loved her to distraction and couldn't love overcome anything.

There must be no more scandal; nor must his own part in the play be discovered. He had to maintain both secrecy and reputation; use the latter to plan Mary's escape.

As for her, how was he going to ensure she was not brought before the justices as a common dissembler? Important people did not like to be duped and Caraboo's cause had reached the highest ears. His Majesty's Government did not wish to appear a fool. It was all a great puzzle indeed. One thing that was quite clear was that the next months were not going to be easy ones for them both. He looked at her.

'I wish I could take you away with me—now—!' Her heart leaped in hope, '—but it is not possible. First, I must write to Jem and tell him everything!' She stared at the table top. 'It has to be done, Mary. He must know it from me as well as you. Remember, he said in the letter he would never return unless he heard the truth from your lips. After he has heard it from me, it will bring him!' She was dizzy thinking of it.

'I think Jem will not reply. Just come to England—as quickly as he can. You must wait and be Caraboo still.'

She made as if to speak but he put up a warning hand. 'You'll be safe, they all believe you now. And I will send for you as soon as I have arranged it. Now don't expect to hear for a while, just do as I say when I send you the message.'

'But why must I go back?' she cried.

'If you disappear now they will hunt you out. We will not escape. I'm sure that even now there are people looking for you—I could not appear again in Bristol or London in my coach; they would apprehend and question me. Your fame has reached high ears—and you must play out your role, like any good actor, to the very end. If a collusion between us is proved, and it could be, we would both be punished—and I do not wish that should happen. You wouldn't want Jem's wife to be a rogue and fugitive for ever?'

She shook her head. 'But what will happen when they find out I am not a princess?'

'I will resolve that. When I have finished, they will think you are only some crazed dreamer of a country girl. You trust me, don't you, Mary?' She nodded. 'Then, do as I say! This is my plan—this is what you must tell the Woralls...'

Mustee poured out the last of the tea and retreated, seeing his master and the princess had serious work to do...

She was glad she had agreed, but was still nervous, more than she had ever been. When no one had known about Princess Caraboo, she had felt safe, now she kept looking behind her. The afternoon sun was beckoning her on, spreading his red fingers across the western sky, pulling her back to Almondsbury and Knole. Quao had set her down in a thick clump of forest trees and she had handed him back his riding cloak. When he had gone she could have cried. How many times had she been left wandering along on the roads? The thought that this time was different and that good had to come of it, cheered Mary a little. She knew she could trust Earle and would only wait for the day when he contacted her again. Fixing her thoughts on Jem, she walked quickly carrying the heavy bundle.

She and Quao had rolled it in the earth to make it look as though it had been buried for some while. Earle had sent a servant girl out from the inn to buy two good dresses, a mantle and Flemish lace and other fripperies, which Caraboo had described were in the cloth she had buried safe from those made-up Macratoos, who pursued her.

Mary spent the time as she walked along, imagining more and more about her Mandin mother. She would add more fantastic details to the story to make it more believable. The sailor had spoken of Java women having black teeth from chewing the betel nut; of painting their arms and wearing jewels in their noses. He had even said they wore golden chains dangling from their foreheads. At that moment, Mary wished she had one; it would give her courage.

Since she had had news from Jem, she was returning to herself a little; feeling a trifle ashamed of duping poor people like the Woralls; before she had not cared; only wanted to get her revenge upon society for what had been done to her.

She passed a warm hand over her forehead. Her legs were aching badly, not only from the ride, but from the unaccustomed walking upon poor roads. Once, she had been used to that, now she was not so strong. Lack of good food had made her frail; what she had eaten at the inn with Earle lay heavy on her stomach. Her head whirled a little; she felt she might be taking a fever and shuddered. She had to get to Knole, whatever happened.

The trees beside the road seemed to dance before her eyes. When she sat down to rest and look up at the sky, their criss-cross branches reminded her of Caraboo's hieroglyphs, copied from the hidden corners of her mind; gleaned from the books in Squire Birt's library when she assimilated the stories of the Egyptians—and the gypsies themselves and their strange signs—and Esther, the Jew's cook who had shown her the symbols of her language in secret one dark Sunday afternoon.

'Mary Willcocks,' she rebuked herself, 'aren't you a wicked girl?' But there was no one to answer, only the warm wind which caught her breath and whirled it away in a mad dance to herald the coming summer...

Martha was dusting the ledges in the high hall, muttering it was not her job, staring down the drive through the long windows to look if Thomas had returned from the village. A figure appeared around the nearest bend, but it was not he. To Martha it seemed like a beggar woman, stumbling on, clutching a great bundle.

'She knows better than to come up here,' grumbled the maid. 'She should have taken the right fork round the back of the buildings. Just wait until I tell her!' Martha flounced her duster at the cheek of vagrants who dared to come up the front steps.

It was not until she was under the arch that Martha recognised the sandals.

She dropped her duster in confusion and cried loudly, 'Mercy, she's back! Help!' she shouted, running along the tiles, her feet echoing hollowly. 'Miss Caraboo—mistress, she's come back, she's come back!'

The High Princess of Javasu made one last vain attempt to reach the knocker, but slipped on to the cold stone, a limp rag outside the door.

When Caraboo woke, her head seemed full of babbling voices, yet her inner intelligence was preparing itself for the next ordeal. The gracious bedroom about her was so different from the one in which she had spent the night before. Now Earle Grant and his men were hours away—and she was alone. Caraboo lifted her head from the pillow and attempted to open her eyes widely. All her reward was a glimmer of light; just a dull redness. It took her some seconds to realise that candles were placed on a table behind the bed curtains—and that she was back in her room at Knole. She put out a trembling hand to ward off that smouldering glow in her eyes and suddenly a form stood beside her bed.

The housekeeper was peering into her face. Mrs Wardle's night cap was plain; her long nose thrusting out from it, her eyes blurred with sleep.

'A drink. Is that what you want, Miss? Here is water!' She reached for the cup, handed it to Caraboo, who tipped it gratefully down into the dry recesses of her throat. The housekeeper took it from her, 'There now, you rest back and I'll fetch the mistress!' The girl appeared to be agitated. She was trying to squint at the face of the clock Mrs Wardle had placed by the side of her bed. 'What an hour to wake up,' grumbled the woman. 'Daybreak, Miss—and you are back at Knole!'

The woman disappeared. Caraboo felt too ill to be questioned again, but again her intelligence warned her to be upon her guard. She wondered how she had come into her bed; she must have collapsed after the journey. She was frightened again then. Was she ill? Was she dying? If she was, she would go to Hell! Caraboo moaned, tried to get up but the old burning suffused her limbs; she could not sit nor stand. She half imagined it was sour Mrs Gall when the housekeeper leaned over her again in what seemed just a moment.

'I fear she is in a fever, madam.' Hannah stared at Caraboo, who had been in a sorry state when they had picked her up from outside the door. At least, she was still alive, but quite exhausted. She seemed to have walked miles; her skirts and legs were covered with earth like the great bundle she had dragged from some unknown hiding place. Hannah feared some dreadful fate had overcome Caraboo, who looked so ill and restless.

'She's probably been out for days in the damp, madam,' said Mrs Wardle mournfully. She had seen folk look like that before—and never recover. Hannah nodded anxiously. At full light she would send for the doctor and obtain his opinion. Wherever the girl had been had done her no good. Inspite of her outward strength and strange courage, she appeared to have a weakness; the Worralls had experienced that before, especially after her dip in the pond when she took a melancholy sickness.

'Keep a careful eye on her, Mrs Wardle,' ordered Hannah, 'and if there is any change for the worse, do not hesitate to rouse us!'

Mrs Wardle bobbed obediently, but after her mistress had left the room she had one more look at the girl, snorted under her breath and returned to the bed she had been forced to make-up in the room. Still in an awkward frame of mind, the housekeeper tore herself some small pieces of rag which she stuffed in her ears.

'That's enough for you, Miss,' she said peevishly, determined to get another hour of sleep undisturbed. Then she covered her night-capped head with the linen sheets and was soon snoring loudly...

Hannah wished she had not mentioned to the doctor about the earth on Her Highness's feet. This information gave him the opportunity to outline every disease the girl could have caught. He declared that walking on damp grass and earth without shoes was quite enough to cause her death. He hinted that the young lady might suffer *cholera morbus*; inflammation of the breast, even colic or iliac passion; but he looked a little more cheerful when Hannah assured him that Her Highness was often in the habit of casting off her sandals and walking around barefooted. Then he said that it might be less dangerous than he suspected, but nevertheless that kind of rashness must be avoided at all costs!

Hannah could hardly bear it when he examined Caraboo, shaking his head to and fro.

'Well, doctor,' she cried, 'have you come to any conclusion?'

'I fear she's very ill!'

'I know that, but what's the matter with her?'

The doctor breathed in deeply. 'Has she always been lethargic?'

'A trifle!'

'Hm, has she any appetite?'

'Not much!'

'Is her sleep disturbed?' Hannah looked at Mrs Wardle, who glanced morosely at Miss, then confirmed the question with a nod.

'I would say then—that this young lady has a remitting fever!' he pronounced pompously.

'Oh, no!' said Hannah.

'If she had been seen to quickly—'

'But, doctor, I called you immediately, like I did before when Her Highness fell in the pond—'

'Such delicate spirits need careful nursing, dear Mrs Worall,' was the smug reply.

'What can we do for her?' cried Hannah, blaming herself.

'Have you any tamarinds, apple-tea or orange-whey?' Hannah wrinkled her brow. 'Give her plenty of such concoctions. Give her anything she asks for in the way of liquid and perhaps she might recover. I would be very loath to bleed or blister her—' He gazed at Caraboo mournfully.

'Oh, dear,' said Mrs Worall, looking at the girl who had caused her so much anxiety.

'And, madam, may I add you must not talk of dying in her presence,' he whispered.

'I assure you I will not, doctor!' said Hannah indignantly, thinking how he had done so only minutes ago even though she could not understand him.

'These people from foreign parts have a great deal on their minds!' said the medical man, squinting suspiciously into Caraboo's face. 'She should not be questioned at all just now!'

Caraboo turned her head away, remembering that other doctor, Mr Burgess, who had been kindness itself. She cried then and Hannah sat beside her, rubbing her hands and trying to cheer her. However much she wished to know what had occasioned her charge's absence, she would have to wait till Caraboo was well again.

The Princess of Javasu was ill for several days. She spent them tossing on her bed, turning her eyes to the plastered ceiling and imagining the cracks were all manner of unpleasant things…

Chee-ming had great broad hands that smelled of the farm. Sometimes when she looked at him, his eyes were cold and bright like that terrible day he had tortured her! On others they were narrow and slit like the Chinamen she had seen upon the quay bringing in barrels of tea from the Indies, or the crafty eyes of Tod, the Fox. Were there farms abroad like the ones she had known in Devon with a stream running beside the wall where the screaming pigs dunked their heads in the water and yelled for more…

'There, dear,' soothed Hannah, wiping away the perspiration from Caraboo's head with a linen cloth wrung in ice-cold water. 'You're perspiring freely now. If only it could break the fever…'

The cloth was cool and soothed Mary's brow. She gazed into Lucy Tippet's face, then down to her spreadeagled legs. Her tongue seemed tied; she could not speak her baby's name lest they found out. She must keep silence for his sake…

'If only you could speak to me, Caraboo,' cried Hannah, shaking her head. 'I know it would ease what is in your heart. What a terrible thing it is not to understand your language…

Mary walked slowly over to his table. There was something about the seaman she liked; once he had been handsome, but now his curls were grey—and his eyes were nut-brown; his jacket old patched velvet.

'Hallo, my gypsy lady,' he said, 'will you tell old Turkey's fortune?'

'Will you give me gold?' Mary replied and he blew her a kiss.

'I'll give you all you ask—and more,' he grinned, bringing out beaded blue ribbons, threaded with jewels. They were the pearls which once had been about the countess's neck as she swept into Exeter Cathedral upon their wedding day. 'You shall be my wife now—' he said, 'and I will be a gentleman!' But she did not want him—only another, who was young and handsome with the darkest eyes in Birt. He did not mind when she refused him; his breezy carelessness was like all sailors. He rolled a little when he walked down the street with her to the place she had made her own. There he stared into the crystal ball, paid her with pearls. One for a kiss, two for a lie; then he plied her with tales of the Boogoos. They rowed towards her across the sea with murder in their eyes...

Caraboo moaned and her unintelligible words rattled in the air. Martha, Mrs Wardle and Hannah leaned over her, hoping this was something that they could understand, but she was talking in the same old way...

As the fever lightened, Mary became more hopeful. The sailorman kept vanishing, like the dog-fox, Tod. The ceiling and the corners of the room hid a sweeter figure, which beckoned to her. In the pew at Birt, he seemed strangely grown; she was half afraid to look at her dress for fear she was a child again; how she trembled when she found she was not, but all in white for her wedding. That was a wonderful day when he led her on his arm through the door of the village church to present her to her old companions. How Milly Cater stared at Lady Farr. And there was envy in her eyes.

'Imagine Mary married to my lord,' she whispered to Betty Bly. Yet through the misty veil, Mary could see the Moons, clustered in the churchyard. She stared down at her white dress, which caught fast in the gate while the horse came galloping down the hill. She screamed as Humphrey's body fell upon hers, started wildly in the bed, gabbled for help from anyone... Then Caraboo knew it had all been a dream and it was safely over. She let Hannah Worall wash her face, clung on to Martha's hands and prayed wordlessly for the sun to rise so she might adore it again, knowing she was alive and back in the world once more.

Hannah heeded the doctor's advice about not questioning Caraboo, but when she felt the girl was well enough, she decided she ought to try. Extending her arms out in a gesture that signified the landscape and the river, then putting her hand over her eyes as if she was weeping, Hannah managed to make Caraboo understand she was asking why the girl had gone away from them, causing such anxiety. Caraboo hurried off and returned with her bundle. Hannah had looked at the clothes inside, which were of foreign make. Caraboo pulled them out with delighted cries, putting them up against her body; going to the mirror and surveying herself. Then she led Mrs Worall out of the house to a glorious flower bed and proceeded to dig out a great hole with her hands.

Hannah tried to stop her charge dirtying herself, but the girl seemed wild and eager to make her point. Then she fetched the empty bundle and stuffed it inside to show she had buried and unburied her belongings. After, she looked all around fearfully and made frightened gestures with her hands.

Sam came up during this and asked, 'What's all this nonsense?'

'It isn't nonsense, Sam. This must be the bundle she hid from the Macratoos. You remember the story?'

'If you believe that you'll believe anything. You show me a Macratoo and I'll fetch a pistol and blow his head off!' he said.

'Really, Sam,' cried Hannah, 'what behaviour in front of the servants!' All the while the conversation continued, Caraboo stood motionless, staring out towards the river and Bristol as if she was waiting for something to happen.

CHAPTER 19

'Life, liberty, and the pursuit of happiness,' wasn't that what Jem had always wished? As he turned towards the house in South Third Street which had been his home since leaving England in 1813, he was beginning to think like an American. The words of the great Declaration of Independence set down in 1776 were now fully become the tenets of his own philosophy. For many years he had looked for signs of them in the Old World, but had failed. Philadelphia was a good place to be at last.

In all those letters he had sent to England he had been melancholy, because when he wrote them he constantly thought of home. This last American spring had been the first he had truly appreciated since he left London. It was not that he had forgotten his great desire to find Mary and the child; nor was he ungrateful for the trouble Earle had taken; but he had sensed in his friend's last letter that Mary did not want to be found and that the Jamaican was ready to give up the lengthy quest.

In the winter months Jem had thought he would go back himself and continue the search; then he thought of his father and the Duchess of Barton and his resolve weakened. Now as the maples and sycamores rose towards the full glory of summer and the massive wheat fields about the city stretched out their ripening shoots, he was ready to make the decision whether to stay here for ever in this young republic or return to the corruption he had known all his life. As the American sun warmed his face he felt he had half made that decision already.

Yet Jem had kept his word when he said he would be plain Jacques Farré, here in a country which believed all men were created equal. The great problem was that never a day went by when he did not think of England—and Mary. She had been his life—but in the Old World he had not had the freedom to pursue his happiness. Instead, his social station had brought him great unhappiness. By now his son or daughter, if he or she lived, would be nearly five years old. In daylight or dark, that thought brought him no peace. He had to swallow a great lump in his throat when he saw young boys or girls skipping over the square and imagined what one of his own would be like. Yet the memory of his young folly shamed him.

Celia and the duke were dead; they had been innocent victims. His own sire and the duchess were living free of any shame—though they were guilty. The girl he had loved so dearly, yet so rashly, was lost to him after bearing his child. Inside, Jem felt Mary must be in hiding from recognition, meaning she regretted her brief liaison. He was also sensible of his actions concerning Humphrey Moon. He did not regret the duel; the brutal farmer's son had deserved all the terrible punishment that Jem had meted out to him, but still when Jem thought of Humphrey taking Mary, the old madness rose up in his breast. If he had stayed in England, found her himself and had the truth, it might have been better; but Earle had been right in his advice. Jem could see things more clearly now, less desperately; time had taught him more about life and how to combat its sorrow. If Mary was ever found, it would be a different story. Time had healed—and Jem had not found any girl since who compared with Mary Willcocks.

He lifted his hat to Mrs Janna Wilhelm and Sophie, who were taking a turn in the street. The mother and daughter smiled as they passed Mr Farré, who was entirely oblivious to the fact they had just walked down the steps of his house. They had done their best to introduce him into the capital's society, but he was as reserved as when they had first been introduced to him. They had speculated often as to his presence in Philadelphia. He lived in a luxurious house, though its outside was Quaker plain. Mr Wilhelm, who was of philosophical Dutch stock, had remarked Mr Farré was like his house; well-moneyed but discreet. Jan was sure he was supported from England, having communications often and an excellent standing at the French First Bank. The Dutchman had decided he was the son of a rich French emigré who had made London his home after the revolution.

As Mr Farré passed them by with a courteous bow, Mrs Wilhelm was thinking of Sophie's future. She would have been interested to know more of Mr Farré's forbears. Both she and her husband acknowledged his good manners, but would have preferred less gallantry and more practicality. The Wilhelm ancestors had been simple settlers and when they had arrived in that New World they had had no dwelling place except a cave on the banks of the river. It had been their own efforts, not old money which had placed them in the forefront of society in Penn's neatly squared town built about the confluence of the Schuylkill and Delaware Rivers.

'What's the matter, mother?' laughed forthright Sophie. 'Are you making plans? I guess Mr Farré will fit into them somewhere!' Mrs

Wilhelm sighed at her daughter's waywardness, which was already reflecting something of that city's forwardness and liberty.

'Really, Sophie, I hope you are not going to be indiscreet at tonight's gathering!'

Jem turned to look at the disappearing figures of mother and daughter, then strode up the five steps which led to his front door. The shutters of the windows in his house were thrown open above him. He had ordered the servants to keep them so constantly in order to make the house lighter. He had always disliked gloomy dwellings; they reminded him of old St James's.

When he had handed his cloak to the footman, he ordered a cold cordial which he intended to take on the verandah at the back of his house. He loved his walled garden, not only because it reminded him of some of those happy times in Bedford Square, but because it was pretty, not elegant; with its wooden sundial inscribed with cheerful words. His home in Philadelphia town had become a real one for him at last; a refuge from his misery, which he had filled with treasures, some brought in from English shores; other collected from the Continent; and some original American. Jem had been interested always in equality and prized some pictures of scenes from the prairies and bayous of this wild country. They had the natural figures of those animals and birds he remembered from the old times in Devon.

Jem sighed as he stood on the polished planks of his verandah, twisting the coiled stem of his glass thoughtfully in his hand. If he could not find Mary, he would stay in Pennsylvania and make a career for himself as Earle had done in England. He would purchase and sell land; he might even trade with the Indians as many other gentlemen like Penn and Logan had done.

'Beg pardon, sir,' his butler broke into his thoughts, 'this came from the office.' He handed Jem the bulky letter.

'Thank you, Maurice.' He weighed it in his hand. One more missive from Earle. Would it bear good news or ill? It was no matter; he had made up his mind what to do.

On reading it, his first impulse was to throw back his head and shout to the sky for sheer joy. Mary had been found—the knowledge dizzied his head; Earle's strong characters jigged up and down through a haze of tears. What would Squire Birt have said if he could have seen that foster son of his, whom he had brought up with true English reserve, ready to weep like a girl? Jem had to steady his trembling; take to the maplewood rocking chair to ease his legs.

There was sorrow and joy in that blessed letter; he read the lines over and over again, trying to take them in fully. Inside him, the tiny voice was crying, 'You had a son, Jem, you had a son; but he's dead,

Jem, he's gone—and you never saw him,' but another throb was rising at the thought of her and what joy they had felt in each other. Once, when Mary was sorrowful, she had said to him, 'What is life, Jem, but being born, breeding, then taken in the cart to lie under the yew?' but he had known then she was only wanting comfort and he had kissed all her peevish teasing away. Many times since he had thought of her words and known they had been true. But today that letter from Earle had brought him back to life again.

His forehead creased as he tried to understand all about the princess masquerade; it was unclear; difficult to understand. But he would know all about it soon. Two moments ago he had decided to stay in the New World; now he was yearning for the Old. He was thinking of packing, shutting up the house for ever as madly as if he had been eighteen years old again.

Yet an elderly voice was warning him to be sedate; to weigh the matter and think about his decision; but reason was not emotion—and Jem chose the latter. He was on his feet in a moment and back into the house, and the footman was staring in surprise.

Jem called for the butler, who came hastily. 'I want you to be ready in half an hour, Maurice,' he said. 'I need to send an answer to England in haste. After you have carried the letter to the office which must be sent on the next possible sailing, I want you to ask where this ship lies at anchor.'

Jem's head was still dizzy, but it did not hamper his directions. 'When you have located this name, book a passage for me on its next sailing.' Earle had sent the letter on his own merchantman. Jem scanned the lines which said it would wait and bring him back with its next cargo—if he wanted. Jem wished it with all his heart. 'I shall embark for England as soon as the arrangements can be made.'

'Yes, Mr Farré,' said Maurice, wondering what the news could be which demanded such hasty action. Then the butler remembered the two lady visitors. 'And, sir, another message,' Jem lifted his eyebrows, 'Mrs Wilhelm left this.'

The butler handed him the invitation, which had been lying on the table in the hall. 'It is the second one. She hopes you have not forgotten this evening as you did not reply. She asked me to remind you.'

The butler withdrew, leaving Jem staring at the card, its gilt message entreating his presence at Mrs Janna Wilhelm's gathering at Mount Lodge in honour of her daughter, Sophie's seventeenth birthday. The invitation had completely slipped from his mind during those last weeks of indecision. He had been most ungallant in his behaviour. The meeting in the street flew back into his mind. Mrs Wilhelm and Sophie had called and he had ignored them.

After scribbling a note, Jem summoned the footman.

'Take this to Mount Lodge, quickly!' Then, with his head still spinning from the joyful news that Mary was found, he stared aimlessly at one expensive possession after another, idly wondering what a man could give a young girl as a suitable Saint's Day present...

The gold and white drawing-room of Mount Lodge was full of pretty women, their elegant beaux, plain descendants of Penn Quaker stock and sharp-eyed matrons on the lookout for suitable prospects for their unmarried daughters.

Sophie drew in her breath as she descended the staircase and stood prettily between the massive columns supporting the ceiling decorated in the classic style. Her father had done her proud; as one of Philadelphia's most successful bankers he should have. As his only child, she deserved it. Yet Sophie knew Jan Wilhelm had not discarded his simple roots in spite of the ostentation. She had often felt his secret longings for the simple life he had enjoyed in his youth. At least, he was not as desirous as her mother to marry her off to some stupid young Dutchman with prospects.

Sophie had other things on her mind which were not connected with her birthday party. One of them was Monsieur Farré, who had dared not to reply to their invitation until five hours ago; who, she declared to herself, was masculine enough to disdain a party, which encompassed the greatest families and the prettiest daughters of Philadelphia.

Sophie moistened her lovely lips with her tongue, stepped off the bottom stair and was enveloped in a congratulating group. When she had managed to extricate herself, she sought out Jacques Farré, whose dark eyes seemed more remote than ever and whose thoughts were evidently not with the company.

'You made it then?' she asked easily. He was still taken aback by the lack of formality in her approach. In England, the daughters of gentry did not behave so.

'I am sorry but I—' It showed in those honest eyes.

'Forgot?' she bantered. 'I forgive you, monsieur. But you must pay for it.' She handed him her dancing card which was already full. 'It will be my prerogative to command a special dance—just for you and me.'
She was flirting openly and could feel her mother's disapproving eyes.

'My pleasure, Miss Sophie,' he said, but they were only words he spoke. How could she know that there was no place in his heart for gold-blonde hair like Philadelphia wheat and violet eyes; that it was taken by the dark curls and sparkling looks of Mary, whose lovely oval face he remembered all the more as he took Sophie Wilhelm by the arm and led her onto the dance floor in front of the eyes of one hundred of her American guests...

Much later in the evening when he was drinking a glass of punch drawn from a Chinese bowl, she was still at his elbow—but was soon replaced by her beaming mother.

'Well, Mr Farré, have you wished my Sophie a happy birthday?'

'With all my heart,' he said. 'Would I were seventeen again!'

'Fie, monsieur, you are not so old!' laughed Sophie.

'Hush, dear!' said her mother. 'I apologise for her, Mr Farré. You will think we Americans have no upbringing.'

'On the contrary, madam, you have all the freedom I desire!' At these words, a small thrill ran through Sophie's body. 'One moment, please,' he added, beckoning the footman, who turned, went to a side table and brought forward a long box. Jem took it from his hand, offering it to Sophie. He then turned to Mrs Wilhelm. 'Madam, this is for Sophie. I hope it will be suitable!'

The girl looked at it eagerly, was beginning to open it, then exclaimed, 'Why, it's beautiful! A statue! Oh, thank you, monsieur!' Mr Wilhelm and his wife looked inside.

'You spoil her, Jacques,' the Dutchman said. 'Do you know what it is, Sophie?'

Jem smiled at her father's bluff manners. He said, 'It is but a little goddess, carved from Athenian marble, brought from the Aegean!'

'She's beautiful! Is it Venus, monsieur?' asked artful Sophie. Her mother blushed for her.

'No, Sophie—she is the goddess of wisdom!' It was Sophie's turn to colour. Her father should have guessed. 'I want to thank you all for your kindness to me since I came here—'

'You speak as if you are leaving us, monsieur,' said Mrs Wilhelm.

'I am,' said Jem seriously, 'and quickly. I have to return to England!'

'But, monsieur, will you return?' cried Sophie, her lovely cheeks still scarlet. He smiled.

'I'm sure I shall. It all depends.' Not one of the trio, even Sophie, dared question him on what...

As the Wilhelms stood to bid their guests goodbye, Jacques Farré approached to make his farewell.

'Goodbye, sir,' he said to Jan. 'If I do not see you before I leave, I thank you with all my heart for making me welcome here.'

He turned to the ladies. 'And, madam—and Miss Sophie, what you have been to me is what some dear people were in my adopted England. I thank you both.' He kissed their hands, then took his cloak and drew it about his shoulders. With a brief wave, he was gone through the tall doors of Mount Lodge and out into the summer night.

When Sophie Wilhelm woke in the half light of dawn, she could not think what awful thing had happened. Then she remembered she was to lose Monsieur Farré and he had not even kissed her...

There had been frenzied activity through the three long weeks Earle's merchantman had lain in harbour. The trade winds had taken their toll and there was the usual refit to be done before the wooden sailing vessel could put to sea again, to turn north along the American coast towards Newfoundland and back across the Atlantic driven by the prevailing winds.

Jem had gone down to the dock on several days, undecided whether to take another ship or not; but this merchantman of Earle's had been built for speed under sail. Earle had purchased several ships which could travel quickly so that his perishable cargoes could reach their destinations without damage. Sometimes, his vessels carried passengers, but he was rich enough to concentrate on filling every available space for economy's sake. To travel on a Grant ship had much advantage for Jem; he had been given the great cabin for himself and his luggage and there was no one to hinder his departure with petty law or argument.

Thus he had decided it was worth waiting a little space of time for the refit when the blocks must be oiled, splices renewed, ropes replaced and the masts unrigged to repair the sails. He had watched the livestock put aboard; knowing there would be fresh meat and eggs—that is if he could stomach it after tossing about for weeks. He thanked God Mary had been found in such a fair season; or he would have been unable to return to her quickly if it had been winter.

He smiled as he watched the cargo loaded. Earle was the supreme businessman; never doing anything without a fixed purpose. For the hundredth time he thanked God for such a friend. He hoped his letter would fly on its way fast before him, having caught the delivery service which demanded an outrageous price. Just in case, he had sent a second identical one on the next fast vessel. Jem had needed this little breathing space to settle his affairs in Philadelphia and waiting for Earle's ship gave him the time.

Yet his heart beat like a schoolboy's when his gig carried him to the dock that sweet morning. How often had he dreamed of setting out for England again for such a happy meeting. He had decided never to return to the place of his sorrows unless he had her in his arms—and now it was all possible because of Earle Grant.

A dark and smiling seaman, fairly well clothed for such a trade, was taking his hand luggage to stow aboard and Jem was on the plank leaving the soil of the New World behind him. He looked up dizzily to the sky, which was deep blue above the three stout masts. Soon the vessel's topsails would be full of the fair wind and he would be staring through the window in the stern at the grey-white sea, which was the only thing that could impede his haste to be in England soon with Mary whom he longed for.

What a joyful letter that was; if only Mary could have seen it. Earle turned it over in his hand, estimating just how long it would take Jem to follow it to Bristol Quay. He had much to do before his friend came; that was why he was seated in the friendly inn kitchen waiting for the crippled gypsy.

He had written several letters himself since he returned to Bristol. One, summoning Juba to join him; he would have to leave the shutting- up of the house in her capable hands. She would not be sad about that, since one frightening day in 1815 when a starving mob had raided the Lord Chancellor's neighbouring dwelling in Bedford Square in their protest against the Corn Laws. She had begged him in her letters to leave the town house in that miserable capital and take her with him back to their island. That was what Earle intended to do at the end of this blessed summer; sail to Jamaica via the Azores and live upon the fertile plantation.

He had sent to his father also, to warn him of his return. It would be a meeting mixed with sorrow. There was still some awkwardness in his relationship with the old man. Earle had proved himself a true Grant in business, even if his moral tastes did not accord with his father's.

Added to these letters, there had been another to a sea captain whom Earle trusted and whom he needed in Bristol to further his plans. It had been a very busy time; Earle and his men were content now to rest awhile before they began to lay the last piece of the puzzle which had been Mary Willcocks.

After a few days respite, Earle had need of his go-between; he himself might be recognised, so he chose a man, who could slip in and out of the confines of Bristol town with expert feet and tongue. The cripple had told him he could be contacted at the 'Old Ship', and Earle had sent Mustee ahead of the coach to that inn to inform the landlord of his master's arrival and in the hope the gypsy would call there after Earle arrived.

It seemed that the message had been noted; Earle had received a verbal communication that Shamus Kelly would be glad to be of service and would meet him there at nine either Wednesday or Thursday of that week. Earle smiled at his Irish lack of punctuality. Wednesday had passed and it was ten on Thursday evening. The late June twilight was passing into dark when a crooked shadow was thrown along the cobbles and across the bright inn door.

Shamus was short of money and had a rumbling belly, which Molly had refused to fill unless he stirred himself to pay for his keep. He was set all fair to steal his livelihood when the landlord of the 'Old Ship' had grasped his one arm over the counter and told him the gentleman's message. Shamus did not doubt the value to be offered. The other gold had been good indeed, however ill-gotten. He paused outside the inn, thinking carelessly of that other yard where he had murdered for money.

Shamus felt no regret at the killing of the little double-crosser. Eynesso had acted unwisely; had not the brain his murderer had to outwit crafty Tod. That had come easy to the Irishman. There had been enquiries about the body; but it was only gypsies who had known the Portuguese and gypsies kept silence. Tod's implication in Shamus's crime was volition. Had he not told the Irishman to do as he would? Therefore, he could have no quarrel with the amount of gold Shamus had brought him. The plan had worked and Shamus was free of the tribe. He had said goodbye to his sister and Black Dow, and left the camp with the gypsies believing the woman was found and Eynesso had received what he deserved.

Shamus had sought the little back-to-back house in the docklands and had been welcomed by his partner, who was only too sensible of his ways. Paddy Redhead could not deny Shamus entrance; he knew too much about him; which, if Molly found out, would result in murder. Molly was a virago, taking Shamus to task as savagely as she had robbed him of his arm on the bloody battlefield. Only once had the Irishman attempted to rifle the box where Molly kept their savings and she had beaten him blue with the yard-broom, yelling all the time he was a lazy good-for-nothing!

The meeting with Earle Grant would prove his saviour yet. Shamus took a deep breath, grinned and began to unlatch the kitchen door. In the dark corridor beside it, a fellow was seated upon the bare floor, his shirt in rags and a dirty scarf about his eyes. Before him was set a begging dish. Shamus recognised him as one of those discharged soldiers or sailors who wandered the port, condemned to a thankless end after pouring out their blood for Duke Arthur on the battlefields of Europe. Shamus's own blood rose as he complimented himself upon his capacity for assessing the future. If he had not deserted the duke's army when he did, he might have been begging at some Bristol inn at the mercy of any traveller.

Shamus walked into the dim and stuffy room where seven or eight men were seated upon benches, their trenchers before them. The woman watching the cauldron boiling on the fire, was about to stir herself, but seeing it was only Brownie, the gypsy, turned back to her task. Several other clients gave him only a cursory look, but the three strangers, dressed in sober colours, which matched their complexions and expressions, rose and passed through the door silently to an adjoining room. Shamus followed them down the steps.

They gathered about him, drawing him into a corner where the dying light was dull upon the window panes. Earle extended a warm hand and grasped the greedy fingers of Shamus Kelly.

'I have ordered beer, port-wine and meat,' he said and the Irishman felt the juice come into his mouth at the words and the turning of his empty stomach.

'Let us get down to business over the meat, master,' he said, determined to wheedle every last drop of drink, crumb of food and piece of gold from the pockets of the swarthy blackamoors...

Late on that Thursday evening, Molly o'the Lines gave vent to her foul mood. She was well blessed with a gawk of a husband, two wingeing small ones and a murdering loon like Brownie to handle. She muttered wildly as she swept the dust over the stones and sent one scuttling child to lug in a pail of water from the court outside. The warm weather made the place stink all the more and Molly had thrown the windows open, only to get the smell of the sewerage instead of the clean sea air which seemed to float over their heads and up to the hills, leaving the slum dwellers below as choked as they had ever been.

She yearned to save enough for the passage she craved which would take the four of them away from old Bristol to a new life in the Americas—but since Paddy had left the gypsy tribe and turned to honest labour, they had been worse off.

She could have murdered Shamus Kelly herself when he returned after the bell had tolled the hour of three and woke them all by his drunken stumbling. 'He can stay below on the floor and good luck to him!' hissed Molly and pressed the hard soles of her feet into her snoring husband's back, which made him curse violently under his breath, but stopped the hoarseness in his chest.

When first light came and they had to be up in that frowsy world, they were confronted by a blinking Shamus, who dragged at Paddy's arms and told him there was news that would rescue them all from Bristol slums and get their bodies over the sea.

'Have you gone mad, Brownie?' grumbled Redhead, pulling on his old shirt to hide the fearful scars.

'I have not and it's a fine favour I'm doing you both!'

'And what have we done for you, you idle devil?' cursed Molly. 'Why, put you up and you in fear of your life from the magistrates!'

'But—I am grateful for it!' was the surprisingly polite reply and the two of them stared into the deep brown eyes of one of the worst rogues in the whole of Bristol town. 'Forget about working your fingers to the bone, my old friend!' grinned Shamus Kelly. 'Molly, although it is only after dawn and I've a head upon me, fetch some of that brew of yours and I will tell you both how our rescue is to come about and where I have been the whole of this night.'

'Go on, don't keep us in suspense!' said Paddy, believing him at last.

'I have been to visit a gentleman!'

'Which?' asked Molly suspiciously. She did not trust gentlemen.

'The same who furnished me with gold last time. For information, remember? A fine man from London—who was out looking for a woman!'

'And sure which man is not?' asked Molly scornfully, but her ears were keener now.

'Quiet, wife,' dared Paddy, showing uncharacteristic courage against her. 'Let the man speak!' Molly grunted as she was searching for the bottle at the back of the cupboard. 'Go on, Shamus.'

Now he was sure of a deferential audience, the one-armed man seated himself.

'First, if we can help him, he will pay!'

'How much?' asked Molly, looking round from where she kneeled upon the floor.

'Enough to get us away!'

'What do we have to do?' asked Redhead, sensible of the fact he had almost forgotten how to rob and murder folks.

'We want no trouble with the justices,' added Molly, her red face looking worried, but strangely savage under the scarred weal which marred her features. 'If it is anything to do with murder, count us out. We want to get off on a ship free—not transported felons!'

'But you shall!' shouted Shamus, seizing the bottle which he was about to tip down his throat, until Molly snatched it from him.

'It's a greedy gob, you have, Kelly. Wait for a cup like the rest of us!'

Shamus glowered at her words. If she did not shut her mouth, they would be off without her! Next door, one of the children gave a little scream, her sleep broken by their shouting.

'Do you want me to go on?'

'Yes,' said Paddy. 'Take no notice of the wife. She's in a bad mood this morning!'

'Wasn't I kept awake all night by himself?' swore Molly, jabbing out a fat finger towards Shamus.

294

'But it was worth it, Molly mine,' grinned Kelly, jumping up and catching her round the waist.

'Get off me, ye fool—and tell us more!' Molly straightened her blouse and skirt.

Shamus continued, 'The gentleman has found the woman. Remember I told you!' They nodded. 'But it seems there is some trickery about it all!' Molly and Paddy stared at him suspiciously again. He held up his hands. 'Not mine, I promise! There has been a good reason for her pretence as some kind of great foreigner. The gentleman assured me of it. Her real identity must be kept a secret, so she can get off on a ship from Bristol. There will be men to meet her on the vessel—'

'Is she a villain then?' asked Molly.

Shamus shrugged. 'I have never seen a woman who was not!' he quipped and ducked away from the blows Molly rained upon him.

'Watch your tongue, Kelly!' she warned. 'Or you will feel this woman's might!'

'Peace, Molly, I was only joking. Who knows anything about this female? I have never seen her!' He wished he had then; that he had found out more of this black man's Mary from the tongue of the murdered Eynesso. She sounded just like a gypsy with such guile in her breast.

'How can we be of service, Shamus?' asked Paddy.

'When we are called by the gentleman, we must all help. Now, listen carefully—' The three bent their heads together as Shamus Kelly outlined the plans which Earle Grant had conveyed to him. When Shamus had finished, Molly looked up.

'And if that is what I have to do, I think I will need paying very well!'

'Did I not tell you, Molly—that you and Paddy and the children will have free passage to America for your part in it and for Paddy's part, you will all have coins to spend there!' Molly allowed herself to smile just once. Then her face slid back into the habitual mask of cross-grained misery it wore. Yet she was praying inwardly that the gentleman's plans would work and they would be able to bring that feckless female down to Bristol Quay and get her off wherever she was bound as quickly as they could.

That fair summer of 1817 made up for the whole of the bad last year. The harvest flourished and trade was on the move again in Bristol and elsewhere. What Sterne, the overseer at Knole had wished for the villagers, was coming true. The lad, John Thorne and his family would not go hungry that autumn after they had harvested their Gloucestershire fields. Agriculture had revived and with it the people who depended upon it. Progress was in the air and foreign grain was limited. Even the poor labourer in town was finding bread within his reach once more. Things were not too bad at all and it seemed just like a dream when villagers remembered last year's riots, gaolings and presence of the military.

Had it only been before last Christmas when a mob had marched upon the great city of London, smashing windows and accosting passers-by? When the household servants at Knole spoke about politics around their kitchen table, it was in a hushed whisper. Hadn't Mrs Wardle declared master would have them turned out on the spot if they gossiped idly about things of which they knew nothing? Yet Martha and Thomas had found plenty to whisper about after they heard the shocking news that the prince's person had been attempted in the Mall itself by some rude people of the mob.

Although Martha was all for alleviating the misfortunes of her comrade poor, the thought that some fellow might murder the Regent, frightened the housemaid terribly; and hers was quite a common fright, because the attack outraged the whole of England however much the people suffered. As Mr Worall had said often—gentlemen and servant folk must travel along together the best they could; and Thomas, for all his uncouth grumbling, could never see a revolution come to English shores like it had done in France.

Alex listened to all the news about the nation calmly, unsurprised at anything. He could not understand why English masters and servants did not hate each other; but he took it as a sign of the English temper, like the way in which Mr Sam Worall allowed his wife to pander to the whims of the Eastern princess she entertained at Knole.

Caraboo was still weak from serious illness and Mrs Worall did everything she could to spoil the girl. She was given the best of everything and not a day went by when Hannah did not drive Sam mad to hear if there was news from the Foreign Office or from the wise Dons in Oxford and Cambridge colleges. In that lovely summer, Caraboo was ferried about in the Woralls' carriage; taken to other stately houses in neighbouring parts to meet the inmates; shown wonderful pictures and museums, attended assembly rooms and several local balls, was allowed to visit travelling libraries and given two hours tutelage a day by a governess especially brought in for the purpose. If she had been a daughter of the house she could not have fared better.

The princess took all this attention upon her as her right and never uttered a syllable of thanks. In fact, it did not seem to change her attitude at all; nor was she any different. On days she was not out, she wandered about the park with a lost look on her face and a head full of dreams. Hannah maintained she was constantly thinking of home, but Sam, suspicious as ever, was more inclined to believe that she was up to mischief. He certainly did not approve of Hannah's latest plan to please her Caraboo. She had engaged the services of a portrait painter, Mr Bird, for whom the princess posed in her Javanese dress. Mr Worall had to admit that it was a good likeness, but he thought the smile that played about the girl's mouth in the portrait, was not quite as artful as her own.

'Oh, Sam, I wish you would believe in her,' cried Hannah. 'Has she done you any harm? No, she's a sweet thing—so biddable and easy!'

'Huh,' was the only word Sam could reply.

The gardens at Knole were full of summer reds and yellows when Caraboo strayed through them, singing under her breath. It was a lovely day when she could hardly be sad. Somehow, there was knowledge in the summer wind which swept over the estuary's glassy surface reflecting the bluest sky. Caraboo wanted to throw off her calico, and swim in the waters free and naked. She had done it as a child—until her father heard of it and punished her. She had told him if boys did so why should not she and had been beaten for her pains; and then she had swum in the dark pools hidden in forest greenery where no one saw her white body borne up easily by the green cool waters.

Through the trees she caught the glint of the pond's still surface which was covered in the middle with waxy water-lily cups. Why should she not try once more? The whole house behind her seemed asleep—she had seen the gardener nodding in the small summer house. When she reached the pond, she looked at her reflection as she had done a thousand times. Today, her peacock feathers lay draped upon her bed and her hair was piled high and fastened with a skewer. Her neck was slender making her almost a goddess of olden times. Caraboo waved her head from side to side, swaying by the water's edge. She bent and undid her sandals, cast them aside by the rushes and walked around the shallow edge.

Here she had seen Earle's reflection. Today there was no red—only the blue of an empty sky and the breeze rustling her skirts. She had been with the gypsies long enough to trust in her intuition. There was something in the wind which was bringing joy. Perhaps Jem, sweet Jem was on his way? She stretched out her little foot and quivered at the cold water's touch. To swim and float upon the surface was what she most desired then. To think of him and not the depths beneath—no one must know. She ran back up the slope and looked at the house, where there was no sign of life still. Hannah would be lying on her day-bed, exhausted from the heat; Thomas, Alex and the rest were deep in the cool darkness of Knole.

Caraboo hurried and walked along the rushes where she slipped off her fringed skirts, unbuttoned her bodice and brought it up and over her head. She looked about her again; there was no one to see except a bright-eyed moorhen—so leaving only her silken drawers, she stooped bare-breasted from the cover of the reeds, scooped the water up into her arms and swam easily across the wide expanse. 'Nothing is lovelier!' thought Mary as she glided through the green fresh water, letting it kiss her body gently. Yet when she lay on her back with the water about her ears and her legs drifting upwards, she could think of one sweeter pleasure. With the sun upon her face, she let herself think of him and how she had drowned in his love so long ago. Such thoughts still made her throb inside.

Mary floated gently in towards the reeds, listening to the moorhen's call; she felt clean and new, modest even—a careless girl once more. When her foot touched the squashy bottom, she strained for the pebbled edge beside the rushes' feet. She stretched her glistening arms into the air in a gesture of pure peace, opened her eyes and—gave a strangled cry.

The boy's cream-coloured face was twisted into a smile, his full lips parted at the sight. Caraboo raced for her calico, but he had it already and was offering it on a liveried arm.

'How could you?' cried Mary Willcocks and the mischievous Mustee shook his head and turned away, a finger to his lips. She heard the words as she struggled into her clothes.

'I beg your pardon, Your Highness, but Massa Earle has sent me for you. I climbed the wall the other side of the lake.'

'How could you look?' repeated Mary, but her heart was thudding wildly; and not because he had seen her shame.

'Your Highness, you know well in Jamaica, girls go free,' he said mischievously. 'Don't fret!'

'You should be whipped!' she said and Mustee turned, his eyes flashing brightly.

'No, mistress, I should not. I will tell no one what beauties I have seen!' She blushed as if she was eighteen and a virgin again. 'But we must go—if we are to make towards Bath!'

'Bath?' asked trembling Mary.

'Yes, mistress, your troubles are nearly over. I have two horses outside the wall, hidden behind the trees. It is some way because I skirted the estate first to spy you out!'

'And if you had not found me?'

'I would have climbed through your window like an ape!' he replied simply and she laughed out loud. 'No, leave your sandals,' he said. 'It will throw them off the scent!'

'But they will think me dead,' she cried, remembering the last time.

'They will soon find out you are alive,' he replied, 'and holding court in Bath. That is where you must be discovered. Then they will think you have really taken leave of your senses to be unmasked so. Plain crazy, is what they say in my country. Come!' He ran up the slope, looking towards the house all the while. 'Come,' he repeated, 'we have to put some miles between this house and the next county before we are safe!'

When they reached the animals, Mary gasped. Earle had thought of everything. There was light luggage which Mustee said was to be taken with them to an inn near the North gate of the town. The heavy luggage had evidently gone on before them. There was a fine riding habit to change into and a hat with a green feather. Mustee unbuttoned his own jacket to disclose a scarlet livery beneath. When Mary had dressed herself behind a bush, Mustee kneeled to put on her boots. In a tiny second, her memory sharpened and flew back to the morning when she, a poor servant girl, had dreamed about a black boy fastening up her slippers. She looked down at his curls.

'Thank you, Mustee,' she said graciously. 'And what will I do when I get to Bath?'

'Why Massa Earle has arranged it all. He has seen that you are expected at "The Pack Horse" Inn. You will hold court there as Princess Caraboo until his plan is quite accomplished.'

A quiver ran through her body at the thought of that seemingly eternal masquerade. She could not ask this pretty Mustiphino whether her love was on his way—how near she was to Heaven—she could only let him help her upon the frisky horse and wait to follow him upon the road to Bath.

CHAPTER 20

There was an atmosphere between the two of them; it had been like that ever since the girl disappeared. Three weeks of misery for Hannah; angry regret for Sam at being treated so.

He stared at the ornamented butter dish, toyed with his tea, fiddled with his napkin; inside, he was swearing roundly. How the devil did the girl think she could get away with it? How could a woman dressed in such a fashion never be seen? What had prompted her to leave after all their kindness? He asked himself the same questions one hundred times over. She had taken nothing—not a pin—any more than she did last time. All the harm she had caused was in the anxiety she had given his dear Hannah, who looked so pale and careworn, that Sam could have taken that Caraboo by the shoulders and shaken her until she begged for mercy—that is, if he could find her.

He could charge the girl with nothing except a lack of civility—but that was what she was—uncivilised! He picked up the letters Alex had set by the finger bowls. He chose the one with the impressive seal, imagining what it was; hardly daring to break it open. Hannah was looking at him querulously. His fingers fumbled clumsily owing to the state of nerves he was feeling. She thought he would never read it so long did he stare, but finally he put it down on the white lace tablecloth, groaned and passed a hand over his forehead.

'Oh, God,' he said, shaking his head at Hannah, 'what are we going to do about this?' He handed the letter over to her, but she shook her head, not wanting to read it either.

'Tell me, Sam,' she said.

'It's from my friend at the Foreign Office.'

'Oh!'

'He has done everything he can—' Sam grimaced. It had been too much to hope for that nothing would have come of it. It was damned bad luck.

'Go on!'

'He says he's organised everything. He managed to see the Secretary and then to meet the—'

'Not the Prime Minister?'

'Almost. They are full of interest regarding the Princess of Javasu!' Sam spat out the words. Hannah's eyes filled with tears at his bitter tone. She knew it was all her fault; that she had been the cause of it all; if her husband was to be laughed at, then hers was the guilt.

'Don't, dear, you couldn't help it. I could! I made you!' She was out of her seat, her warm heart full of pity for him. 'I know how you value your reputation, my dear!'

'I shall be like the rest of them now,' he said gloomily. 'Branded corrupt. Everyone will think it was done for pure notice!'

'No, Sam, I'll tell them—and—' she hardly dared say it, 'perhaps she'll come back!'

'If she does,' said Sam, looking up at his wife who was standing beside him, smoothing his bushy hair; 'I'll take my cane to her!'

'Oh, Sam, what a notion! You wouldn't do it?'

'Wouldn't I?' he said violently; 'Princess or not!'

She had never heard her husband speak like that. Whatever felons he dealt with, he believed in justice. Hannah knew it was because he felt foolishly taken in, but in her own heart she was sure there was a reason. At first she had thought Caraboo had taken her own life. When she had seen those pathetic muddy sandals and the footsteps leading to the rushes, she was almost sure. But no body had floated to the surface and the gardener and the stable lad had spent two days rowing over the surface of the lake and prodding the mud with stout staffs.

When they had searched the whole estate, there had only been one clue; a piece of ground beyond the wall where horses had churned up the earth—but, as Sam said, that could have been anyone—and who did Caraboo know with horses? It was a mystery—but Hannah felt uneasy in her breast. Before, her worry had only been for the girl; now she was anxious for Sam. If they were to be duped, it was she who deserved it—not him. As she looked down fondly at the top of his head and stroked his broad shoulders, Caraboo's face kept floating into her mind. She had such honest eyes, such sweet ways that begged for Hannah's help. She had been happy at Knole, Hannah sensed it—but where had she gone? Who had taken her?

Hannah patted Sam's shoulder, lifted her skirts and walked over to stare through the windows into the park. She almost fancied she saw the Boogoos stealing through the trees; a Macratoo crouching behind the laurel bush—it had all been so real. How could they doubt her? She looked over once more at Sam. He must delay a little with his reply to the government office—play for time; as for the characters she had sent off to the learned Professors—what could she do about it? Then her mood lifted a little. If Caraboo's language was proved true, that might help the girl. 'Oh, Caraboo,' she whispered, 'I can't believe you meant to leave us so! Where are you?'

As Alex rode into Lower Almondsbury he was feeling as puzzled as his master and mistress. The princess did not know when she was well off. He thought she was quite mad to behave so. Once he had wondered whether she had escaped from some house of correction—or even from an asylum—but he tossed such thoughts aside when he remembered her quickness of wit and spirit. Mr Worall had had no stomach for the Bench in these last three weeks, so Alex had travelled into Bristol several times to oil the wheels of his business; scan his books and carry messages to his fellow magistrates. His master had sworn him to secrecy regarding the girl. It would never do for his colleagues to find out what a fool she had made of their chairman. He had also asked Alex to keep a keen ear open in case he might be lucky enough to tumble on some clue or hint about her departure. Alex had done so but all in vain.

It was such a hot and dusty morning he was full of thirst, so he pulled in his horse at the inn. The Greek entered, stooping through the low door.

The landlord hurried forward.

'Yes, sir?'

'A pint of mead.' The man nodded, turning to his task, when his wife appeared hand-in-hand with her little girl.

'Why, sir,' she bobbed, 'is there any news of the princess?' Alex shook his head, wondering what his master would say at the way Miss Caraboo was discussed by gentlemen and common alike. He did not want to engage in more conversation, so he took a seat by a soberly-dressed gentleman, who was waiting for the coach. He seemed entirely oblivious of everything about him, so deep was his head thrust into his newspaper. Alex wondered about the gentleman's destination as he took the English honey taste to his tongue, remembering the bee wine they made in Macedonia. The traveller had come in from Somerset evidently, as the *Bath Chronicle* was only two days old. Alex continued to savour his mead; the gentleman to read his paper. Suddenly, the latter lifted his eyes, set his top hat to the back of his head, put aside his reading.

'Princess?'

'I beg your pardon, sir?' asked Alex.

'The woman spoke of a princess?'

'Yes,' said the Greek.

'Well, there's one in here. Blessed funny if you ask me!' He pointed to the paper. 'Giving up so much space for gossip!'

'Which princess? Where?' cried Alex, forgetting his manners and seizing the news.

'Hey, hold on, you might ask first!'

'I'm sorry—but where?'

The man jabbed a finger towards the page. 'I've been reading this paper for ages. Now it's full of society tittle-tattle. Written for women, I suppose. "Miss So-and-so is to be married to my lord—" that's all there is in it! And patent medicine and news of chocolate from Bristol—' Alex hardly heard him. He was staring at the article.

The good Dr Wilkinson had reported to his *Chronicle* readers faithfully. It was a glowing account which had caused many ladies and gentlemen to note Princess Caraboo's arrival in Bath in their diaries and plan to see her.

Alex's eyes raced over the details of her dress and feathers. From where had they come? Hadn't she left them drooping on the bed at Knole? The doctor was enthralled by her graceful bearing; her attitude of calm repose; her sparkling eyes; the thrilling story of her background. He had visited her at 'The Pack Horse' where she held court three times a week. He had been won over particularly by her meekness and had been introduced to her by the lady who had taken the princess under her protection.

Dr Wilkinson had a very fine turn of phrase. Doubtless, he believed she was everything she was reputed to be and had called on her to verify all the fantastic rumours he had heard of her in London and Bristol. There was no mention of her protectors, the Woralls, nor of Knole; yet he too had been wholly convinced of her verity. Alex drank in his words:

'Nothing has yet transpired to authorise the slightest suspicion of Caraboo, nor has such ever been entertained except by those whose souls feel not the spirit of benevolence, and wish to convert into ridicule that amiable disposition in others.'

Alex, dazed, stared at the words.

'Can I have my paper back?' asked the traveller sarcastically.

'I will give you three times its value if you will sell it me!' cried Alex.

'Fine!' said the man, glad to make a profit out of gossip. He held out his hand. Alex drew out a coin and clasped it into the man's fist.

'Thank you, sir,' said the Greek. 'I am much obliged to you. You have done my master and mistress a great service today!'

'Have I?' said the man, as dazed as Alex himself. The Greek drunk his last drop of mead, picked up his hat and ran out into the street, shouting for his horse...

When Sam read it, he roared while Hannah wept.

'It's no use crying, my dear,' he said after he had controlled himself. 'This is the end as far as I am concerned.'

Hannah looked at him. 'What do you mean, Sam?'

'I can't entertain this girl any more if this is how she repays our hospitality. She is evidently well satisfied with her new protector. Let me see, who is it? Mrs Mortimer, eh? I wonder what she has told that good lady!'

'She couldn't tell her anything, Sam, could she?' said Hannah, trying to work it out.

'Couldn't she?' he said, but he too was not sure of it.

'I have to go to her, Sam.' He stared at his wife.

'After all this?'

'Yes, I must find out what she means by it all!'

'You haven't managed to yet, my dear! How do you think you will now?'

'I'm sure there's some reason—and remember, Sam, she has done nothing for gain!'

'Perhaps it's notice she desires! The minx wants to make a name for herself; a stir in the world!'

'I still believe that—'

'She's a princess? Oh, faugh!' he said. 'Still, we'll both go to that hotbed of silly society folk, however much I hate the place!'

'The last time you went the waters did do you some good, Sam,' said Hannah. 'When you had that bout of rheumatism.' She noticed his expression. 'But, thank you, Sam, for supporting me—as always.' She called for Mrs Wardle, who appeared before them, desperately wishing to know if the tale Alex had brought down to the servants' hall, was true.

'Mrs Wardle, the master and I are setting out for Bath as soon as possible. Will you see to the packing?' As the woman left she was cursing that heathen Miss under her breath for making sport of a God-fearing couple like good Mr and Mrs Worall...

The summer sun was reflected by the thousand walls of white stone crowned with oolite tiles, whose limestone gave Bath the outward brilliance which was matched only by the variety of its society, which thronged the streets below. The town lay in its valley, sending out the grasping arms of newly-constructed buildings which groped continuously to climb up the hillsides from what Mr Pope had called, 'a sulphurous pit'.

Yet Bath had a dazzling surface with its bright shops, busy inns, carriages, music of bells and orchestras and brilliant conversation.

Mrs Eliza Mortimer and her husband, Albion, had taken apartments not far from Pulteney Bridge and fairly near Grosvenor Place with its columns and round-headed windows. Mrs Mortimer was in a wonderful mood that morning. She and Albion had been coming to Bath in the season for a number of years and had entertained many important people in their time. It was said by gossiping voices in the town that no titled person arrived there without Eliza knowing and sending an invitation to one of her social gatherings. Those who missed her spreading social net, were accosted when promenading about the Baths or inside the Assembly Rooms and introduced to the Mortimers speedily.

Yet this was the first time Eliza had had the opportunity of escorting and chaperoning a foreign dignitary. The Princess Caraboo and her male servant had ensconced themselves in an hotel next to Grosvenor House. This was enough to cause a scandal; indeed the proprietor had seen to it immediately that the princess was provided with female maids and the boy had been banished. All he was allowed to do was walk behind her holding her train or to settle her on horseback or aid her in stepping up into the hired carriage.

Yet when questioned by Eliza, he had been most amenable, had gone to great trouble to tell the princess's history and her conveyance from Batavia. Mrs Mortimer had looked up the place in her atlas when the servant left and discovered it was in the East Indies. When she realised that the girl's plight was being discussed in the capital itself and her case pursued by the Foreign Office, she had told Albion it was her duty to protect the princess from any unwelcome attentions and had arranged for her to be properly guided about the town, received into suitable social gatherings and provided with the means necessary to meet her many admirers.

The servant with the cream-coloured face had indicated that his mistress was keen to hold court at a particularly well known inn and Eliza had agreed readily because 'The Pack Horse' was well placed in North Gate Street—near to the Abbey.

Eliza hummed as she stared at the report in the *Chronicle* for another satisfied moment. To gain the notice of Dr Wilkinson and fit a space in that newspaper, was bliss indeed. Although Eliza herself was not mentioned, she still took the credit for the interview. Dr Wilkinson had confided to her after she had introduced him to Caraboo, that he was thoroughly taken with the girl and horrified at the manner of her treatment. Indeed, he was quite resolved to go to the Foreign Office himself in order to obtain funds for her present relief and her restoration to her native land, but Mrs Mortimer had been able to set his mind easy with the comforting knowledge that much was already being done in that direction. Eliza felt very satisfied with her part in it all.

'Albion!' she called, looking at her watch which hung about her waist on a chain. There was no reply, so she hurried from the room into the hall, picking up her silken parasol as she went. Its pagoda shape was so pretty and suitable, much in keeping with the cameo which fastened the lace at her throat. The brooch had been chosen just as carefully, as it had an Eastern design and toned in, as did all her accessories that day with the clothes of her East Indian protégée.

'Albion!' she repeated impatiently and the footman appeared on the landing, then came running downstairs.

'Beg pardon, madam, but sir is a little out of sorts. His valet is searching for his gloves!'

'Tell Mr Mortimer we're late already. Say we cannot keep the princess waiting!' The man bowed and ran up again.

Finally Albion descended. He had taken as much trouble as his wife in getting dressed. Everything he wore was of the newest fashion. The tall crown of his elegant top hat was immaculately brushed and the brim, turned down at the back and front, was correct to the inch. Albion Mortimer was tall, with an erect carriage which was helped in its stateliness by a whalebone 'Apollo' corset which accentuated his small waist and served to make the girth of his chest greater than ever. His gloves were of purest white cotton; his ebony cane had a head ornamented with gold and his umbrella was of silken material. He had a profusion of decorations—a seal, a shirt brooch, a pin in his cravat, even the buttons of his shirt were encircled with jewels.

'Albion, you're far too late!' she said reprovingly. He sniffed, producing his perfumed handkerchief. Although it was the height of summer, he had a perpetual cold which was not made any better by his wife's insistence he took the waters every day.

Eliza made him turn around.

'Yes, Albion, that will do!' said the domineering lady and she and her husband were ushered to the door by the correct footman. They sailed down their own steps most gracefully, beginning to stroll towards the centre of the town in the hope of meeting more and more of their society friends, whom they intended to entice towards 'The Pack Horse' so that they, too, could pay compliment at the court of the charming Princess Caraboo.

Caraboo was finding it very difficult even to speak to Mustee. In fact, there was no opportunity for conversation with him whatsoever. They had talked on the road to Bath when she had found out more about Earle's plan to have her discovered publicly, but Mustee did not know all the details. His orders were to stay close to the princess, take rooms in the hotel where part of their luggage had been taken; contact the landlord of 'The Pack Horse', who had been expecting the princess to receive her guests there—and wait. Everything had gone well until Mrs Mortimer had appeared upon the scene.

Caraboo thought how different that lady was from dear Hannah Worall. Eliza was a society snob of the first order; observed etiquette meticulously, was extremely strong-minded and a born manipulator. It was she who had been the instigator of Mustee's removal downstairs and who had ordered the proprietor to send up the two silly maids, who never stopped giggling.

Caraboo just had to talk to Mustee. She felt worried and isolated; inside, there was none of the calm front she presented to the world. She kept wondering when she would be unmasked and by whom. She determined to speak to the young coloured servant before the carriage took her to 'The Pack Horse'. When he helped her inside the light vehicle, she raised her eyebrows at him to show she wanted to speak, but there was such a crowd about the vehicle, pushing and jostling to see her, there was no chance again. While the horse trotted, Mustee was running beside. Caraboo had always had difficulty in understanding the boy's pidgin Jamaican. It wasn't like Earle's, having a broader accent and many unfamiliar words. Once or twice she had nearly lapsed into English and almost given herself away. She knew she had to be careful and continue with the game, until there was contact from Mustee's dear master.

Again and again she wondered how it would be done and what she would do when the time came to end her role as an Eastern princess. She sighed, leaning back inside the conveyance. Would it be today—or tomorrow? Sometimes it seemed likely to be never! Why had she ever thought being royal was a wonderful thing? She had no privacy; was gaped at everywhere, and she really understood everything that was said about her, however cruel. And there was no means of defence, only this cool countenance for all.

She was so tired of being a princess. Her peacock feathers drooped and her skirts seemed old and worn. At least, the girl inside her who had been that servant, Mary Willcocks, knew now that there was more to life than fine clothes and being a lady. What would she have given to be in the coach with Jem again, rolling towards Bedford Square and the time which had been the happiest in her whole life. At the thought of her love, she brightened a little and wiped away a tear. It wouldn't be long now. Then she wondered if he would come back after all. Perhaps he did not want to see her. Had Earle told him the whole story about herself and Humphrey? Would he believe it?

The sun seemed to turn the white Bath stone to a dull grey as Her

Highness was handed down from her carriage by her Mustiphino servant and passed into the cheery rooms of the inn which were ready prepared for all the people who wished to seek an audience with her. She was ushered on through the passage to the fine front room with its wide windows, festooned with lace curtains. In the corner of one pane was an elegant card, which proclaimed in gilt letters that Princess Caraboo held court at such-and-such a time on certain days of each week. There was a slight commotion outside as Eliza and Albion were following her through, sweeping lesser persons aside in their hurry to catch up with the dear princess.

Caraboo turned to see Mrs Mortimer sailing towards her, arms outstretched.

'Forgive me, Your Highness! I'm a trifle late. I'm afraid it was Albion who delayed me!' She glanced angrily at her husband, who tut-tutted shamefacedly as his wife clung to Caraboo's arms to lead her on to the chair with blue hangings, which was placed in the most prominent position in the room. About the wall were rows of gilt chairs, brought in especially by the landlord. It was said ironically that he was vying with the Assembly Rooms for custom!

'Poor dear girl, you look quite anxious? Come here!' Eliza waved imperiously towards a servant, who stood before her and bowed. 'Spring water for her Highness. Make sure it is crystal clear. And wine for me and for Mr Mortimer. See to it, Albion, please!' He nodded, glad to be out of it for a moment.

Then a maid was summoned, who was ordered to draw the curtains until Her Highness was fit to receive her guests. When the room was darkened and the doors shut, Mrs Mortimer seated Caraboo carefully, arranged her dress and attempted to put spots of rouge on the princess's pale cheeks. Caraboo shook her head and Mrs Mortimer sighed and pursed her lips, surveying the girl critically. Then another maid was called bringing fresh flowers, which were put in Her Highness's hair and she was given a pretty nosegay to hold in her hands. All the time Mrs Mortimer prattled, producing a list of all those who wished to be received that day. It seemed quite endless—lords, ladies, their daughters and sons—even a viscount come from the North of England.

Caraboo felt like the wooden doll she had placed stiffly in its little chair at the table in the Witherage cottage. But she could hardly remember her plaything's stolid features; it was all too long ago. Another tear fell quietly upon her calico.

'What, crying? Whatever for?' said Mrs Mortimer. 'I suppose I don't understand, do I—but you're a lucky girl, my dear. You have everything you need—a pretty face and manners, notice in the world, numerous chances of entrance into such good society. What girl could ask for more?'

At these words the princess trembled, remembering someone else who had said the self-same words. Caraboo felt slightly faint as the memory of Mrs Smith and the whorehouse raced through her mind. She prayed inside for relief from this other masquerade; she wanted to be neither princess nor whore, only Jem's Mary again.

'Are you ready, my dear?' asked Mrs Mortimer, looking at her watch. She wondered whether the princess had noticed the trouble she had taken with her accessories; whether the cameo and parasol served to make the girl a little more at home. It was to be quite an exciting morning. She was longing to see the viscount herself, having heard much of his noble family.

'Albion!' she called. Her husband put down his glass and crossed to her side obediently. 'Shoo, girls!' she cried to the maids, who curtsied and withdrew.

The landlord's beaming face appeared through an inner hatch window. 'Ready, madam?'

'Wait—are the chairs quite right?' The footmen gave them one last quick look, then took their places at the door.

Eliza motioned to the man. 'Yes, you can let them in—but not too many at a time. Have you the list?' He nodded.

Caraboo sat waiting miserably, looking at the door, hoping Mustee was not far away. She had to endure this show. Didn't it serve her right for imagining the slave-market in Batavia? This was as near to it as she had ever been!

Mrs Mortimer curtsied gracefully to the gentleman, who minced forward. Caraboo stared at his top boots, their large turn-downs a shocking pink. She looked up into his round and childish face, with hair closely-curled and brushed forward from the crown. He was perspiring and puffing slightly. She hated him—but inclined her head haughtily as he knelt before her.

'Your Highness, may I present the viscount. Lord Beale is in Bath and could not wait to meet you!'

Caraboo allowed her eyelids to droop becomingly and Mrs Mortimer took her hand and extended it to raise up his lordship, who was then given a chair next to the princess and tried to make conversation with her. He had been told she could not speak, but felt at a loss as to what he should do otherwise.

Caraboo had thought it was an endless list. It seemed to be; they trooped in until every gilt chair bore a lady or gentleman, who nodded to acquaintances, whispered to next-door neighbours and pointed at Caraboo behind their fans and gloves. It quite unnerved her when a lady and her two daughters left their chairs enthusiastically and prostrated themselves at her feet. Caraboo hoped her face was not red. The matronly lady was raised up also by Albion and turned to Mrs Mortimer.

'Dear Eliza, we were quite overcome by the honour of this audience. My daughters are overwhelmed to meet such a lovely creature. Dare Isobel bestow a kiss upon her cheek?'

Mrs Mortimer wavered. 'I'm not sure, Athena, but it can do no harm!' Caraboo steeled herself as Isobel stretched out her arms and planted two light kisses upon her hot cheeks.

'I feel better now, mother,' the girl said. 'I couldn't bear the idea of the poor dear girl treated as she has been!' A murmur of assent and sympathy rose in the room. Outside the landlord rubbed his hands— and counted his good fortune.

Inside, Mrs Mortimer was making a speech to the audience. Finally, she thanked them all for coming. They nodded their heads and one gentleman stood, held up his hand, bowed to Eliza, who preened, and to Caraboo, who sat like a statue.

'No, we all should be thanking you, my dear Mrs Mortimer,' he said. 'It has been a marvellous experience.' There was universal clapping. 'I, for one, have found this morning most fascinating!' Once more, there was great nodding. 'I think that we all would like to show our appreciation in a very special way!'

'Hear, hear!' cried one. 'Bravo, bravo!' said another.

Eliza's eyes were sparkling. 'Thank you, sir,' she said. 'Then, may I suggest a collection to defray Her Highness's expenses for her speedy return to Javasu. Let us hope justice will soon be done!' There was mad applause. Banknotes were thrown upon the central table between the wine coolers and silver. There were so many that some fell upon the floor.

'My dear, my dear,' nudged Mrs Mortimer, showing Caraboo that she must do something. The princess rose from her throne and commanded silence by a slight movement of her hand. She walked across the floor, stooped gracefully, picked up one of the notes without even glancing at it to see how much it was worth; in fact, the company could see that she had no interest in the pieces of paper, which doubtless she judged to be of no value at all. Then Eliza signed to Albion and the footmen, who collected the money hastily into baskets.

The viscount was amazed at Caraboo's grace and simplicity. She was a woman, who must be priceless. As she returned to the blue chair, he met her, took her hand and bowed deeply.

'May I say, Your Highness, that you are the loveliest creature I have ever seen!'

At this, several young ladies gave little cries and their mamas fanned themselves. Yet Caraboo was not moved by his words at all. She had heard too much of that from men. She did not look coy, nor fluttered her eyelids, nor even allowed any colour to come into her cheeks.

'It's wonderful,' said the man who had given the speech. 'Princess Caraboo is quite insensible to flattery!' He sighed then, wishing there were more women like her in Bath.

Caraboo sat quietly as they began to leave—another audience over and no word from Earle—no sign of Mustee's familiar face. As the last lady's dress whisked through the door, she stared unseeingly at Albion Mortimer, stuffing her money into strong cloth bags. What good were bank notes? Caraboo wanted none of them—she had all she desired in this world—but one thing. Without love, a girl had nothing.

Mrs Mortimer beckoned her from her chair, chatting on aimlessly, taking her arm excitedly. 'Now, what shall we do today, my dear? You must be seen about so we will take lunch in Milsom Street, then look at some pretty clothes there. You'd like that, wouldn't you?' Her eyes were roving over Caraboo's strange dress. 'After, we can stroll along the Grand Parade. I've been thinking about getting music lessons for you—the harpsichord, that would be—'

Albion was ready at last. The three of them were just proceeding towards the door, when there was the sound of angry voices. Caraboo looked up keenly. She felt sure it was—her heart thudded, her palms were wet.

Mrs Mortimer rushed forward. 'No one else can come in. The princess is about to leave—no one I say!' It was too late—and Caraboo had listened well. A red-faced Sam Worall strode into the room, followed by plump Hannah, her face flushed with the embarrassment of gaining entrance without leave.

'Sir, what do you mean by this?' asked Albion stiffly. Sam strode on, faced Caraboo squarely.

'Footmen!' cried Eliza, fearing the man would harm the princess.

'Call off the servants, madam, I am a justice of the peace!'

'Oh,' cried Eliza fanning herself. 'What do you want?'

Hannah caught at Sam's arms. 'Steady, Sam.' She turned to the Mortimers.

'We wish you nor Caraboo any harm, but the matter is simple. Until three weeks ago, the princess had made her home with us!' Sam snorted loudly. 'We have entertained her at Knole Park, near Almondsbury, since the month of April. Hadn't she told—? No, she couldn't, could she?'

Sam turned to Albion, who was sniffing quite loudly. 'I apologise for such an abrupt entrance, but I was beside myself. To see her here and—Sam Worall!' He extended his hand, which Albion shook doubtfully.

Eliza burst into tears. As Hannah attempted to comfort her, Caraboo walked back to the blue chair and sat down. She felt terribly guilty, confused, even afraid. Where was Mustee? But could he help her now? Surely it hadn't been Earle's plan to have the Woralls arrive like this? It must be a mistake! 'Where are you, Earle?' she cried under her breath.

Eliza had controlled herself and the four were staring at Caraboo, who sat in silence. Eliza spoke. 'She came, accompanied by a servant.'

'Not one of mine!' said Sam.

'A half-caste boy, very pretty indeed. Albion, send someone to find him! She was staying with him at the hotel next to Grosvenor Place. Of course, I had heard reports of her arrival. The news had spread. I think we'd heard about her in London, didn't we, dear?' She directed her question to Albion, who was pointing the footmen on their way. He nodded, surprised to be consulted. 'I was quite shocked, of course, to see her travelling unchaperoned—and with a boy!' She fanned herself. 'That's why I took it upon myself to see she had a friend!'

'That was very kind of you,' said Hannah. She thought how miserable Caraboo looked. Her first instinct was to go over and comfort the girl, but some tiny proud voice inside was telling her to hold back— and there was Sam.

He glared at Caraboo. 'I'm going to get to the bottom of this,' he said.

'Now, Sam,' warned Hannah, 'you don't know anything for sure, therefore you must leave it alone until the true facts come to light!'

He took no notice, going up to Caraboo again. 'Are you a princess, or aren't you?' he said. 'Who the devil told you to come wandering to Bath? Who is this boy?'

'Sir, please,' said Albion, holding his arm.

Then Sam's temper was abating. He turned from her, his mouth working. Then he threw himself upon a chair.

'My husband is overwrought. He has been worrying about my health—and Caraboo's!' The Mortimers nodded at Hannah's words. She went over to the chair. Her eyes were filled with tears.

'Why did you leave us like that, Caraboo? Who were you trying to contact? Is the boy a friend of yours? Where is he?' Hannah hoped she would speak, but Caraboo did not, only stared sadly towards the carpet.

Albion picked up one of the money bags which lay upon the table and brought it over to Sam.

'If you are her guardian, sir, then you must take charge of this. It is part of a collection to defray her expenses and to help her back to her own country, wherever that can be. Please don't take offence, but I must be sure as to your identity.'

'I understand,' said Sam. 'There are people in Bath who will testify as to my name and character.' He looked at Caraboo.

'The Lord help you, my girl, if you are not who you claim to be. Sam Worall does not take kindly to being made a fool of, nor his character examined!' He looked at the Mortimers. 'My wife and I have taken much trouble to protect this girl, have set wheels in motion in high places. At present, we are waiting for replies from Oxford and Cambridge colleges as to the manner of her writing.'

Eliza nodded wisely.

'We will be pleased to relieve you of your charge. We intend to convey Her Highness to my office in Bristol until we decide what is to be done. Thank you both for your kindness to her. I hope it will not prove wasted. Now let's get off to this hotel and take some lunch together where we can discuss the matter!'

'I don't think I will be able to eat much, dear Mr Worall,' cried Eliza. 'This has made me quite out of sorts.'

'We know that feeling very well, don't we, Hannah?' said Sam darkly, taking Mrs Mortimer's arm.

Albion was waiting for Hannah, but she went over to Caraboo and took her by the sleeve. 'Come,' she said, sighing. 'I don't understand any of it—I only wish I could. All I do know is the whole thing has caused a great deal of anxiety at Knole and this is why Mr Worall will not have you stay there any longer.' She could feel the girl trembling; all the old motherliness was rising in her breast. 'No, don't be afraid. Nothing will be done to you, Caraboo. I'll still protect you!'

She led her charge from the room, supported on one side by Albion Mortimer, who found the princess's light weight rather irksome owing to his delicate state of health that morning.

As Caraboo left 'The Pack Horse' she felt ready to be sick. She stared piteously about her, looking for Mustee as her custodians summoned a carriage. She was well and truly trapped whether she deserved it or not. Earle had said Jem's wife must not be taken for a rogue or trickster. Things were moving that way very swiftly. There was still a small crowd about as the ladies were put up into the carriage. Albion preferred to squeeze inside, but Sam Worall sat up on the box, so he could get the wind in his face to cool his temper and clear his aching head...

When Mustee discovered what had happened; learned their rooms had been searched; that folk were looking for him and the princess was again in the custody of the Woralls of Knole, there was only one thing to do. He had been circumspect enough to conceal all the money Mr Grant had given him about his person; therefore he decided to make his way quickly to the livery stables where he had left the horses. He gained a fair price for the one the princess had ridden and led out his own.

When he was mounted, he wheeled his horse towards the Bristol road. As he passed by Queen Square with its obelisk, pointing from the garden, he was reminded of busy Mrs Mortimer, who had thrust her meddling nose into their affairs, causing the plan to go so wrong and forcing him to swiftly ride and seek out his master before he sent that messenger to Bath, who was to be the agent of the princess's downfall...

Some hours after the Mustiphino had ridden hard up and across the hills, the Woralls' carriage took the same route, slowly wending its way out of Bath, negotiating the hills that cradled it, striking towards the Newton Brook, which marked the western boundary of the sophisticated town.

Since Caraboo had been settled in Mr Worall's office, things had been difficult. She could not blame the magistrate for not wanting her at Knole Park; but she found it hard to continue with her subterfuge. Mrs Weaver, the housekeeper, hardly spoke to her, had been most put out to see her again. She was allowed to walk about the house, but she knew the maids had been warned to keep their eyes on her. She felt a prisoner—and she did not know whether Earle realised where she was or what had happened to Mustee. Before, when she had been miserable, Mrs Worall had comforted her. Now that kind lady had been forbidden by her husband to approach her very often. Today was some respite as Hannah had called into the office to see how Caraboo was coping.

It made her sad just to see the girl; yet the other reason for her visit gave her some hope. In her reticule she was carrying a sealed letter addressed to Sam. It had come from one of the colleges in Oxford. They had waited for it—now it was here and Hannah longed to bear the news it contained. Would it vindicate Caraboo? That would be too much to hope for. Instead, both she and Sam were devoid of any further ideas concerning their princess. It had always been difficult not being able to communicate with Caraboo, now it was pure torment. How could anyone understand or help someone who said nothing either to defend or explain herself?

Hannah had taken tea with the girl, then Mrs Weaver had escorted her to the morning-room where she had been given paper on which to practise English writing. Mrs Worall waited for Sam, who had a full afternoon already. He would not welcome interference.

'I'm sorry, dear,' she said, when he entered, 'I'm sure you're very busy now, but this has come!' She withdrew the letter. He broke open its seal, scanned it and handed it over.

The learned men had finished their consultations and had come to no conclusion. Hannah swallowed. They said they could not recognise the writing, although two indicated they thought it had Sumatran characteristics. It was writing they had never seen before; although they were quick to point out that this was not due to a lack of knowledge on their part as there were many undiscovered tribes in that part of the world.

'Well, Hannah?' said Sam. 'This must be the end, surely?' He was right of course. He had been open-minded, though suspicious always. Hannah blessed him for his forbearance. 'I'll leave it to you to think on it,' he said. 'I have too much to do this afternoon. We'll discuss it later!' He looked into his wife's pleading eyes. 'No, I can't have her back at Knole!'

Hannah knew then it was the end. The Foreign Office would pursue the matter in their own slow way—and Caraboo would be kept a prisoner. She saw her charge before they retired for the night. Hannah had decided to stay in the office just for a little while. When she went up to the girl's bedroom, she began to speak to her. The kind woman had got into the habit of talking to Caraboo out loud even if the girl did not understand.

'Well, I've done all I can. The Dons say they can't recognise your writing. You can't tell me anything. I'm afraid you'll just have to bear it here until Sam decides what he's going to do. Oh, Caraboo, I hope you haven't been duping us. You know, I always believed in you—but even I—' she sighed, 'I can't think what good it has done you—that is if you are a fake.'

Hannah wasn't surprised to see the tears fall down the princess's face. 'I suppose you can understand by my tone.' She put an impulsive arm about the girl's shoulders. 'I told you—in Bath I would still protect you—and I will. I only wish someone or something would turn up to put us all out of our misery!'

CHAPTER 21

The woman hurried along the quay. She was not used to the constriction of stays about her person, nor bonnet strings under her chin. Yet her wildness had to be contained and she must be conservative enough to convince such great people as the Woralls. She had been shown the way to the office and felt uncomfortable calling on a magistrate. Yet the thought of the gold to be earned spurred her on. She had used rouge on her cheeks to make her more presentable; the resulting effect had become quite frightening.

Several ladies turned aside when they saw the scarred cheek under the bonnet. Mr Worall's footman did not like the look of the woman who stood at the office door, asking for his master and mistress. He suspected she was a relative of some criminal Mr Worall had prosecuted; that she had come to beg for mercy over some case or even to bring information. For this latter reason he did not slam the door shut in her face.

'I'm afraid my master and mistress are out,' he said. The woman scowled and the footman thought again what a sinister look she had.

'I have to see them,' she repeated.

'Is there a message?' he asked, hoping to be rid of her.

'Not for your ears,' was the rude reply.

He stiffened. Who did she think she was, insulting him? 'Then be off with you,' he said.

She thrust a stubby toe against the door and faced him. 'You won't act so bold towards me when you know why I am here,' she said. 'Your master and mistress will be pleased to see me, I'll be bound, when I tell them what I know concerning the princess!'

He stared. What could a woman like that know about Miss?

'And—I'll only tell them,' she added, thrusting her ugly cheek next to his face.

'Just a moment—' He disappeared, closing the door behind him. The woman hummed, scuffing her feet on the steps. Why did jumped-up servants think themselves better than a poor honest woman who worked for a living?

The door opened again and the housekeeper appeared. Her sharp eyes took in every detail of the visitor's mien and dress. She was a labouring woman, but she had no fear within her or respect for her betters.

'Please communicate your message to me,' she said boldly.

'No—only Mr and Mrs Worall shall hear my news!'

'Very well,' said Mrs Weaver. 'Can you return later?'

'No,' was the reply. The housekeeper grimaced. Should she send the woman to the studio? While her mistress was in Bristol, she had taken the opportunity to convey Miss for the last sitting of her portrait at the house of Mr Bird. Mrs Weaver had remarked in the servants' hall that was probably the last time she would ever be seen in princess's clothes! She looked at the woman again. Mr Worall had a full list and would not be bothered—therefore, she would direct this visitor to Mr Bird's. He had good servants, who would protect her mistress if need be.

'As you will not deal with me,' she said, 'you must go to this address!' She scribbled it down. 'My mistress will be there until five o'clock in the afternoon. Does that satisfy you?'

The woman nodded rudely, snatching the paper and clumped off down the stairs. The footman peeped out and over Mrs Weaver's shoulder.

'That's a right one!' he said. 'She's bringing no good news I can tell you!'

Mrs Weaver nodded seriously. 'I'm afraid all our employers' fears are soon to be realised. I wish I'd never set eyes on that girl. She'll bring bad luck to us all!' The two of them withdrew and banged the heavy door shut...

Hannah could have cried when she saw how well Mr Bird had captured Caraboo's smile. All through the time the girl had stayed at Knole, such looks had been fleeting. Joy was not an emotion the poor princess was used to—tears seemed to be her friends. The smile he had cunningly worked in oil would live for ever and always remind Hannah of those rare moments when she felt she and Caraboo had understanding between them.

Displayed on that canvas was the face and figure she would always remember—the thoughtful eyes, pensive expression and a hand placed over her heart. That gesture seemed to beckon Mrs Worall, tell her that Caraboo was true; that she clasped some precious secret deep inside her but could not share it. The sandalled feet seemed set upon a wandering way; a shore from which she longed to leave, but that was holding her in spite of herself.

All these things Hannah could see in the Academician's picture of Princess Caraboo. She was afraid to speak in case he lost his concentration, but Mr Bird smiled at her nervousness.

'A few more strokes and we are finished,' he said, poising his brush to make them.

From where she stood upon the dais, Caraboo could see dear Hannah's face. It had been true what Earle said, she could not leave without saying goodbye to the woman who had been more than a mother to her. She wanted so much then to descend, throw her arms about her, confess what she was, what she had been, whom she loved—but it was impossible. It was like being carried out into the middle of the pond at Knole, letting the water drag you down and under. Caraboo was drowning in her own deception and who would rescue her?

She looked around the studio and its high airiness. There was space and freedom here. Mr Bird let the sea breeze blow through the windows freely. He had put into his canvas what she was feeling and she admired his gift. She wondered mournfully where the portrait would hang? She was sure it would not be in Knole. 'Hang' was not a word she cared to think of. She shivered and Mrs Worall sensed she was cold and brought over another mantle, which she laid beside her feet.

'Nearly finished,' said Mr Bird. He was quite sorry about it; not on account of the payment, but because of the intrigue he had sensed and delineated in the girl's smile. He did not get the chance to paint a great many princesses.

'That's it,' he added thoughtfully, putting one last determined stroke.

'Oh, good!' cried Hannah, forgetting her misery. 'Yes, it's wonderful, Mr Bird. I'm so pleased with it! Come, come over here, Caraboo. Do look! What do you think?'

In answer to the words and gestures, Caraboo walked slowly towards the two.

'You don't seem very enthusiastic,' said Mr Bird kindly. The girl had been a marvellous model, so calm and quiet, displaying an inward peace far from the other fidgets he was used to experiencing.

She stared at her picture, smiled in spite of her mood of depression. Who would have thought anyone would want to paint Mary Willcocks? She did have some things to thank Caraboo for!

'So you do like it,' he said, surveying his work. They stared on at the enigmatic face, which responded with that look which almost spoke.

Hannah clapped her hands. 'Thank you again!' Just as Mr Bird was bowing to the compliment, his maid appeared.

'Beg pardon, sir, but there is a woman asking for Mrs Worall. She has been sent from the magistrate's office.'

'Oh, dear, I wonder who it can be?' asked Hannah. 'Did she give her name?'

'Mrs Neale, madam,' replied the girl. She supposed it was not unusual that a justice's wife should expect such visitors.

Hannah frowned. The name meant nothing. She shrugged. 'Well, Mr Bird, I don't know who this lady is, but I suppose I must see her.'

'Of course,' he said. 'Take Mrs Worall to the drawing-room, Emily, please, then bring in her visitor!'

'Thank you,' said Hannah and bustled out; she had no fear leaving Mr Bird with Caraboo as he was much used to dealing with young ladies.

'And now, Your Highness,' he said, after she had gone. 'Please sit over here and rest your legs. You must be tired from posing so long!' He led Caraboo to the chaise longue, decorated with a pretty fabric the colour of the apricots she had known at Brushford.

For the last few days she had had her old home in her mind constantly. She did not expect to see it again; nor any of her kin. She could never return there after all this, but she was in a strange frame of mind, uneasy with everything—her nerves on edge waiting for either the best or worst to happen.

'I will send for tea,' said Mr Bird, realising just how tired his model was...

Hannah was taken aback by the woman's face and figure. She wished then the maid had warned her as to the rough aspect of the visitor. Hannah was used to her villagers; but this woman was a different breed. She had the toughness of a seafaring port about her—a wild eye and a terrible scarred face. Hannah put a hand up to her own soft cheek for a moment, but let it fall down afraid Mrs Neale would notice her revulsion.

The woman stood in the doorway awkwardly; her eyes wandering about the fine room, towards the paintings, furniture and objêts d'arts. She could not remember being inside any fine drawing-room before, only looking at such places from the outside. She had been born in an Irish cabin with a thatched roof and earthen floor, and endured every known privation—had survived forty years without luxuries like these.

A burning envy flushed her face; urged her to be skilful in telling those lies in which she had been schooled so carefully. The magistrate's wife had no frightening aspect for Molly. She was just a plump and nervous Englishwoman, who had had the good fortune to be born a lady and share her husband's money.

Hannah thought most women of that station would have curtsied politely, but this person did not. She stood stiff, then moved slowly across the room; Hannah could hear her hoarse breathing as she came nearer.

'No, stay,' she said involuntarily, indicating the chair nearest to her visitor.

Molly smiled, sensing the lady was somewhat afraid. 'You don't need to call in the servants, ma'am,' she said proudly. 'I mean you no harm.'

Hannah was angry with herself she had shown her weakness. 'I have no intention of doing so,' she said, 'but I would be glad to know your business with me!'

Molly could see the lady had her eyes on the bell rope—and did not want to be ejected by any callous footman. She sat down, smoothing her skirts and cursing those cruel stays under her breath. She lifted her hand with the broken nails and pushed back the stray hair under her bonnet. Then she looked round as if she was fearful of being overheard. This made Hannah even more nervous.

'We are quite alone, Mrs Neale,' she said. 'Pray go on!' She sat down herself, feeling her legs tremble. Molly took a deep breath, and leaned forward in a most unladylike manner. Mrs Worall strained to hear her words.

'My business concerns the princess who is lodging with you!'

'Caraboo?' cried Mrs Worall. She could hardly believe it.

'Aye, that's her,' said Molly, wondering where on earth that name had come from. Probably it was of black origin like the gentleman.

'Tell me what you know of Her Highness!' said Hannah, her voice faltering a little.

'Take it easy, ma'am,' said Molly; 'this is probably going to shock you!'

'Go on,' said Hannah, clenching her hands in her lap, ready for the worst.

'She's—' the woman leaned forward even more, the ugly scar almost bursting from her eager cheeks '—no princess, I fear!' Molly leaned back waiting for the stormy outburst. Instead, she heard a sob rise from the lady's throat, saw her hands plucking her dress.

'How do you know?' asked Hannah faintly. 'Have you proof?'

'Only the proof of my two good eyes, madam,' said Molly. She was surprising even herself at the capacity she had for making the lie seem honest. She had never clapped eyes on that princess, but she was even making herself believe she had.

'When did you see her?' asked Hannah, wishing Sam could be present at the interview but imagining what he would say if he had been.

'Well, I saw her first at St Peter's, ma'am. Must have been back in

April!' lied Molly. 'I was almost sure and certain then she was the same one—'

'As what?' asked Hannah, her heart sinking.

'Why, as the girl who came to my house begging for bread and shelter. A servant maid, she was—'

'A servant, you say?'

'That's right,' Molly was warming to it now. 'Then when I heard she was taken up as a princess, I said to my daughter she must be duping some poor soul—'

'Go on,' said Hannah.

'So I kept in touch with the news. I can read, you know. My man was in Bath and saw the report in the newspaper and I was full of anger to think what the wicked girl was doing duping all those fine ladies and gentlemen. Saying she was a princess, mind you. A dirty young woman coming from Exeter!'

'Exeter?' said Hannah in a small voice.

Molly nodded, staring boldly into her white face. 'Aye, begging as I said. So when there was a report she was back in Bristol, I hung about to make sure. I saw her brought to your man's—beg your pardon—your husband's office—and then I was sure.'

'Oh!' gasped Hannah, thinking what Sam would do. At that moment she needed his support. Could it be true? That all their care and trust for Caraboo was brought to nothing? Could she have been that wicked?

Hannah controlled her imagination then, began to speak slowly and clearly. 'Mrs Neale, I wish my husband was present to hear your story—'

'I've done nothing but speak the truth,' cried Molly, not particularly wanting to meet the magistrate.

'I understand,' continued Hannah, 'but you must see yours is a serious allegation. I am going to send for Mr Samuel Worall straight away and I wish you to stay here with me until he comes.' It was Molly's turn to tremble, but she had to brave it out on account of all that gold. 'You must tell him your story and then I would be grateful if you would confront Her Highness!' Molly hadn't bargained for this.

Hannah saw the uncertainty in the woman's face. 'No one will hurt you, I promise, but I must be sure of her reaction!' Mrs Worall pulled the bell rope for the footman. The maid and he appeared.

'I beg you to go to Mr Worall's office quickly and bring my husband back. Tell him it is a matter of life-and-death!' Wasn't Caraboo's future now at stake? She turned to the maid. 'Pray ask Mr Bird to step in, if you please.'

The maid retreated and the footman hurried off. Then Hannah

Worall and Mrs Neale sat staring at each other wordlessly until the painter came hurrying in to see what the commotion was all about...

Caraboo sensed there was something amiss by the look upon the maid's face. Where was Hannah? And now Mr Bird had disappeared!

That old uncanny intuition never played her false; she knew inside that it all had something to do with her. What was the woman's name? Mrs Neale. Caraboo had never heard it before. Perhaps it was someone sent from the office on legal business? Caraboo rose from the sofa and sauntered through the room, getting as near to the door as she dared. The sun was throwing huge shadows across her portrait. Perhaps the princess's day was over at last? Perhaps the woman had something to do with that? The thought both excited and frightened her. She began to prepare herself mentally for another ordeal.

When she heard Sam Worall's voice, she walked back to the elegant chaise longue and sat down to wait for the worst. When she saw the look on Hannah's face, Caraboo knew her intuition had been right. There was something wrong and it was serious.

Mrs Worall hovered in the doorway, staring at her, then disappeared. There seemed to be a hush all about the house and the studio—all Caraboo was sensible of was her fast-beating heart. Then the door opened once more to reveal Sam Worall, his face blood-red from the worry of the message his wife had sent and the hurry to find out what ailed her. Mixed with such feelings was a rage he could hardly control. Behind him followed Hannah, supported by Mr Bird and then—

Caraboo swallowed, blinked, stared, drew back—Mr and Mrs Worall knew by the extra paleness of Caraboo's face that she recognised the woman. Hannah gave a tiny sob and Sam an involuntary start towards Caraboo, but was detained by Mr Bird.

Molly strode forward, ready to brazen it out, thinking about their share of the gentleman's money. At first, all she could see was the wooden dais with its backdrop of satin; its chair where the dissembler sat, her face milk-white; her hands picking at her skirts, her eyes fixed hopelessly upon her denouncer. Then Molly stopped short, clapped her hand to her mouth and it was no play acting. She knew the woman—how could she forget those artful eyes, the neck strained eagerly to hear the tales with which Molly had furnished her in the Exeter house?

Molly almost cried out loud as she recognised Mary Baker from Crediton—that clever wench who had fancies far beyond her station—who had disappeared, given them the slip, reappeared and lived in the gypsy camp with Rosa and Brownie—then disappeared again!

The magistrate was holding her by the arm. 'I can see by your face you recognise her, Mrs Neale. Is this the girl you spoke of to my wife?'

'Yes!' Molly nodded, her head spinning from the irony of it all. She had been paid well to swear the lie was the truth—and that lie had been true after all. Inside, she was sure there was a mistake. How could Mary Baker be the woman the fine gentleman sought? Had she a child?

'Fetch the woman a chair,' commanded Mr Bird to his footman, who brought it hastily and pushed it behind Molly, who collapsed in a lump. All the time, Mary Baker just sat and looked at her with great scared eyes. Molly would have given anything not to unmask one of the gypsy kind. Tod would be sending men after her and Paddy. She cursed Brownie under her breath for leading them into the trap—she would never breathe one word of this to Shamus and Paddy—never tell them who the woman was.

Hannah and Sam stood sadly. Neither uttered a word to Caraboo, who sat dumbly—her face a token of her guilt. In reality, Mary had thrust all thoughts of remorse at the plight of the Woralls aside when she had seen Molly. She felt physically sick. To think it was the gypsies who had found her. Her cover had been broken by Tod and the tribe. She thought of his narrow foxy face and was filled with fear. If he got her back to the *vardo*, there would be no more defending herself from him.

'Oh, Earle,' she moaned inside, 'I'm done for. I shall never see you again—nor Jem!'

Then she thought what she must do. To save herself further harm, she would confess to her identity. She would be a gypsy no longer—only Mary—but from where? Crediton or Witherage? The first would be safer. The worst fate for her would be to be conveyed to that poor cottage again—to be beaten by her father—to be the scorn of Witherage—an outcast!

She stood up slowly, wishing it was a dream—that she might wake up. But Molly's ugly scar, Hannah's tears, were all too real.

Sam was approaching her. 'Now let's have no more nonsense, young woman. If I was not a God-fearing man and a justice of the peace, I might take a stick and break every bone in your body on account of what you have done to me and my wife.'

'No, Sam,' cried Hannah in a terrible voice. 'Leave her alone, leave her alone!'

Molly could see the lady was near hysterics. She glanced at Mary Baker. Had the girl no morals to dupe fine people so? But Molly admired her for her ability to pay out the rich for what they had done to the innocent poor.

Sam stood then, his fists clenched at his sides—then kind Mr Bird walked over to the dais and led him to the other side of the studio.

Mary descended from the wooden platform, passed Hannah by and sat upon the chaise longue. There was no use crying—it was too late. She had cried enough. Whether she was transported or hanged was all the same now. She had been found out. Strangely, the thought was a relief; she could be herself again; she had wished to discard the role of Caraboo since the night in the Marshfield Inn when she knew Jem still loved her.

Then Hannah forced herself to speak. There was no reproach in the tone; only the sound of a broken heart.

'I'm finding it very difficult to say what I feel,' she said. 'I know you understand me. Because of that, you know too what you have been to me!'

'Shh, Hannah,' stuttered Sam, 'she's not worth your tears!'

'But, Sam, she is,' cried Hannah. 'Any soul who has done what she has done, is worthy of our pity. There must have been the gravest reasons—'

'And they will reap the greatest punishment!' he said and Hannah shivered.

Mary listened to these ugly words without fear. She had been punished all her life; this was just another time. She fingered her calico and thought of Jem. Could she be saved even now? She prayed wordlessly to God above to help her; then turned her eyes on Hannah.

The good woman lifted her head as Mary spoke. 'Mr Worall is right to hate me, ma'am. I have been wicked and I know it.'

'But what did you hope to gain?' said Hannah, coming up to her.

'That would be too hard to tell,' Mary replied.

'But who are you?' cried Hannah unsteadily. Then Mary put up a small hand, laid it on her sleeve and drew the lady down beside her.

'It will all be lies!' said hard-hearted Sam—and Molly sniffed. 'Remember, Hannah, all lies—like before!'

'Was it lies?' asked his wife. Mary looked at the floor. 'And what is Mr Grant to you?' Mary stared on, thinking she could not give Earle away.

'Not all of it,' she answered, lifting her head again, 'but I can give you a little of my reasons!'

'I want the truth, Caraboo!' said Hannah.

Mary's face was paler as she replied. 'Not Caraboo—but Mary Baker—from Crediton.'

Sam spluttered and Mr Bird motioned the footman to pour out some wine to give them heart. Sam gulped it down, then waved the glass at her angrily. 'The truth do you hear, no more fancies!'

Mrs Worall turned to her husband. 'This is for our ears alone, Sam—and Mr Bird's, if he wishes.'

'Yes, let him stay,' said Sam, 'and hear the evidence!' His face was as hard as his voice. The painter looked upon that drab scene, feeling no desire for once to portray such human misery. He had been right when he sensed intrigue; it seemed his model had duped the Woralls most successfully, and instinctively Mr Bird knew she would pay dearly for it. Sam was an important fellow and should all this come to light, he would be called a fool throughout the town.

'You must go,' said the magistrate, turning to Mrs Neale. He offered her some coins. 'Take this for your information. You have done me some service, but I warn you to keep your mouth shut and do not proclaim this all over Bristol!'

'I will not, sir!' said Molly, knowing she had enough reason to keep the matter a secret. 'But before I leave, I must tell you my story can be vouched for by another who has seen *her* also!' She pointed an accusing finger towards Mary.

The footman saw the woman on her way. When she was round the corner she threw off that tiresome bonnet and shook her hair free. She could hardly wait to slip off those murderous stays; indeed when she passed through a narrow lane which had convenient gates to open gardens, she hurried behind a bush and unlaced them, groaning all the while. She would not throw them away like her bonnet as there were good bones in the linings which might come in handy.

All the way back towards the docks, she thought of Mary Baker and her pale face. Paddy still had to play his part, but he must not see that trickster.

The men listened open-mouthed to her account of her interview with the Woralls. Shamus's quick memory stored all the news away so he could relay it to the black gentleman. He, himself, would have liked to have seen the artful female, but Molly had said he and Paddy would not as she was extremely ugly and not worth seeing.

'Now, Paddy,' said his wife, 'you will get yourself off to that lady tomorrow morning. And make no mistakes, you great loon. Tell the story as it should be told!'

'Yes, Molly,' said Paddy Redhead meekly, wondering how the hell he had found himself such an overbearing woman...

The studio of Mr Bird's house was strangely silent as Mary began to relate her story. She settled herself upon the chaise longue and began to speak in a calm slow voice.

'As I told you before, my name is Mary Baker. I was born in Crediton, the daughter of a poor man, who earned his bread by cobbling. When I was eight years old, my mother had me employed to spin wool throughout the winter, but in the summer months I drove my father' horses and weeded the corn. When I was sixteen years old, my father procured a situation for me at a farmhouse near Crediton. I was sent there as nurse and general help but I left because I was paid only ten pence a week. I did ask for my wages to be raised to a shilling, but the farmer refused...'

CHAPTER 22

'And then I became the Princess Caraboo! You know the rest!' she said. Mrs Worall dabbed at her eyes with her handkerchief. Mr Bird cleared his throat. It had not been a pretty tale. How the poor were treated in this England of theirs! He hardly blamed her himself.

'Well, Sam?' asked Hannah softly.

The story had moved Hannah very much. If the girl had been in their charge, she would not have been treated in that fashion, which had been the beginning of her troubles. A cruel father, a lack of education and an unfeeling master, were quite enough to drive a young woman to her ruin. Hannah knew Caraboo had good sense, shrewdness and extremely quick wits. Where she had erred was allowing her fancies to become paramount, yet this was again a sign of lack of training in direction. Any girl who could behave as this one had done, deserved both sympathy and help. She had always believed the girl had had a good reason.

Hannah looked at her husband, who had not replied to her soft question. He was seated upright, his hands thrust upon the arms of the chair as if he was sitting in judgment upon the Bench.

'Sam,' she repeated.

'I heard you the first time, wife,' he said. 'There is no easy answer to this!' Hannah knew that his pride had taken a severe blow. To be thought gullible was death to Sam. He relied upon his astuteness to ferret out lies. He had been made a fool of by a female.

Sam looked at Hannah, then at that dratted girl. She had been such a convincing liar that he thought of her instinctively as Caraboo rather than the plain-named Mary. If she had stolen from them, committed some crime, he would have had no qualms about charging her; but how could you charge one who had done no physical harm to anyone—only dealt mental punishment?

He addressed himself to Mary. 'Leave us, girl. Get yourself to another room while I decide with Mrs Worall and Mr Bird as to what will be done with you. Don't think of trying to escape. There is none. At least show us the decency of obedience.' He rang the bell for the footman.

'Yes, sir,' said Mary, weary with the interrogation, glad to go and collect her thoughts. She walked slowly towards the door when the man appeared.

'Show Miss to the drawing-room,' said Mr Bird, full of sympathy for her dejection. It was such an unusual case. To be able to carry deception to such a length, was no common happening. He would have liked to get to know this Caraboo even better. There was something of the artist about her, in the way she could project herself into a role which transformed her looks and character. When she had gone out, all three hesitated.

Then Mr Bird began, 'I think that I should leave you both alone. After all, I am only the gentleman whom you have paid to paint a fake princess. Although I'm not sorry—it has been a challenge—and I enjoyed it. I hope I have succeeded.' He stared at the canvas.

'Indeed you have, Mr Bird, and we are most grateful,' said Hannah. 'However my husband feels about it, I shall keep the picture to remind me of these last strange months.'

'I'm sorry, Hannah, but I don't want to be reminded,' said Sam. Mr Bird, sensing what was to come, bowed and withdrew.

Hannah faced her husband; she was recovering from her earlier dejection, felt she could speak what was in her mind.

'Now we have the truth,' she said, 'what are we going to do?'

'You know what I'd like to—' said Sam.

'Turn her out into the street?' said his wife.

Sam stared at her boldness. 'Hannah, that isn't fair!'

'Well, but it's true, isn't it, Sam?' He shook his head.

'I don't know—I've always tried to be fair!'

'I know you have but you've never trusted her!'

'And I was right!'

'In some things, yes, but in others you have little understanding. You're a man and see things differently. It has been an accident of birth which has caused this. Caraboo has much to commend her, was driven to…!'

'Many young women have bad upbringings, Hannah, but they do not behave so!'

'Have you ever met a girl with her looks and spirit?' Sam shook his head again. 'Think what she's been through, Sam—she has had no advantages; such treatment for a girl like her must have been agonising.'

Sam stared at his wife. ''Tis a good thing you are not on the Bench, wife—such impassioned pleading would get any felon his freedom.'

'I love her, Sam, and understand her better now. Whether she has told us everything I do not know, but I cannot see her turned out of doors, set wandering, or worse still, imprisoned!'

'No, that will not happen, Hannah,' he sighed. 'There is not enough evidence. She has not stolen nor murdered, has committed no crime. Mind you,' he said, thinking of the money that had been collected by the Mortimers, 'coins have been procured under false pretences in Bath!'

'Then we must give them to some worthy charity,' cried Hannah. 'Perhaps to a Magdalen Hospital to relieve the plight of other girls like Mary Baker—and some must be left—for the girl herself!'

'Is that honest?' said her husband.

'I think it is,' cried Hannah stoutly, 'and I want—'

'What else?'

'To see her settled somewhere safe. To find out what she wants the most!'

'She should be sent back to her parish!'

'Not there, Sam, not to be beaten!' Hannah's face creased in dismay. 'For my sake, Sam, please think again!'

'For your sake, not hers,' said her husband.'But I hope you don't want me to receive her at Knole again. That would be impossible.'

'I understand,' replied Hannah, 'and I wouldn't see you embarrassed further. Let us keep her quietly at the office. She can do some tasks; you know how well she works with the needle, but she will suffer something from the servants!'

'That will be her punishment for the time being,' Sam said, thinking the girl was getting off lightly. 'Then I'll decide.' He had to get the matter cleared up with his friend in the capital. He did not relish telling him about how they had been deceived. He was wishing the girl far across the sea as his wife hurried to him and put her head easily against his shoulder.

'Sam,' she said, 'was ever a woman blessed with such a kind husband as you?'

'Nonsense, Mrs Worall,' he said, stroking her hair and feeling comfortably self-righteous...

Earle watched the shore riggers ready to leap upon his vessel and help his crew send down the upper masts and rigging as his ship settled herself into her berth on the dockside.

He always felt pride to see the deep beaminess of a vessel which belonged to him alone. That sailing ship was one of his fleet of children which, with the wind in their sails, could take the shocks of storm and water and happily remain buoyant. This vessel was full of hope as well as cargo. The sun shone over Earle's shoulder, making the vessel's lines clean and shining in spite of the weather marks and some damage to the sails. But his eyes were looking onto the deck beyond the crew, searching for a familiar face. If he did not appear soon, then Earle would leap aboard with the last of the shore riggers to hurry him out from his cabin and chide his tardiness!

Then the coloured man drew in his breath sharply as he caught sight of the figure in dark blue picking his way around the cargo chutes towards the high gangplank. That one hundred feet of deck had never seemed longer to Earle as he watched Jem Farr, his face hidden by his hat brim and his hair blown across his forehead by the keen sea breeze.

The cargo was now being busily hand-worked, but Earle had had enough of pride in his ownership. He was pushing through boxes, barrels, luggage—avoiding all the loading and discharging that constantly took place on Bristol Quay. He had no eyes for families, squatting and ready to take passage abroad to Quebec, Boston and the Maine Coast; no heart for their misery; only an eagerness that could hardly contain itself to take his dear friend's hand again—and escort him on English soil.

The crew had caught sight of their master and ducked heads respectfully; he clapped one on the back, who steadied the plank, but all the while his eyes were set on Jem. Above him, the sky seemed full of masts and birds; all around came their piteous crying, but to him those voices were screams of joy and welcome.

With a wonderful smile upon his expressive face, Earle felt the deck boards under his feet, thrilled to their living movement—and outstretched his arms. There was no awkwardness between the men, just gladness in their strong embrace.

Then Earle stood back, his eyes rapt, scanning the well-known face. Jem was thinner with a new seriousness, not the youth who had left England in misery, tormented by his hot-headedness, seething with fiery anger, wilting under remorse. There was a strength about this man, which had come from a reliance upon inner reserve and knowledge. Outwardly, not much changed, except for a glint of gray in his curls. Yet he still wore his aristocratic bearing; the mark of his fine nature untainted by excess.

'Well, Jem—' smiled Earle, drawing beside him, leading him to the plank and an English shore.

'My friend,' said Jem and his eyes mirrored his thanks. When he set foot upon the quay, his legs were trembling. He shook somewhat and allowed his friend to steady him.

'It is your sea-legs, man,' said Earle, but they both knew better.

Jem gazed around and about him, allowed the sun to kiss his face— felt a hunger inside which was home to him. French and American he had been—but here was the West Country as free as it had ever been with all the sights and sounds of his childhood.

Earle patted his arm. 'You need some good English ale,' he quipped, but his heart was beating faster.

Jem nodded wordlessly; then the two thrust their way through the bustle of that crowded Bristol morning towards the lane where Earle's carriage was waiting. Quao smiled at the happy expression on his dear master's face. He smoothed down his jacket proudly and urged the horses into a smart trot towards the inn, where Mr Grant had laid his marvellously successful plans.

Much later in the evening, Quao ushered another of his master's friends through to their rooms to dine there. The visitor had the air of a seafarer, but the clothes of a gentleman. If Quao had not known who was expected, he might have taken him for some rich merchant about to strike another advantageous deal with Mr Grant. Yet when the black servant announced him, there was a tremor in his voice. Now Captain Richardson had arrived, the wearisome quest and the reconciliation of my lord and Miss Caraboo was near at hand, making Quao's own return to Jamaica a reality at last.

Mary bit her bottom lip anxiously as she searched through the pile of fancy mending the housekeeper had set in front of her. After all she had been through, she was back in the station from which she had come—a maid-servant; yet there was no one to listen to her confidences because the rest shunned her as cruelly as simple folk had ever done. She had tried to make something of herself in this world and now she was being treated like a criminal.

She wondered then if she had the strength to begin again. Eight years of her life had passed; she had been a servant, a vagrant, a whore, a gypsy and a princess. If she had had the heart in her she would have laughed out loud. Only one thing was keeping her sane— the thought that Mustee was sure to tell Earle Grant where she was and he would get her away from all her misery.

As she stabbed her needle in and out of the ribbon trimming, her mind was trying all the means of escape. She could get away, take to the road again—but the gypsies might find her. If they did not, then Mr Worall would pursue her and have her sworn to Crediton parish, from which she had claimed birth; then this would be discovered as another lie. She had to stay at the Woralls while there was still the slightest chance Earle would come to fetch her. How she wished he had whisked her away the first day he had found her, but he had said it was not possible.

One large tear fell upon the trimming and she shook it off impatiently. Crying would get her nowhere fast, nor the mending done! Then Mary heard the rustle of skirts.

It was Hannah who was beside her, holding out her hand for the needlework. 'That's well done, Mary,' she said, 'you're quite an expert, aren't you?'

'Yes, ma'am,' she answered.

'You had a good teacher,' said Hannah, who still longed to know everything about the girl. Mary nodded. 'But you've been crying again?'

'Please, ma'am,' said Mary, staring down at the floor, 'has Mr Worall decided what to do with me?'

'Not yet,' sighed Hannah. 'I think you know how he feels about you!'

'Yes,' said Mary, 'and I cannot blame him!'

'Are you truly sorry, Mary?' asked Hannah. 'It's never too late to make a fresh start.'

'I've made too many already,' said Mary stubbornly, thinking about all the failures. There had been only one success in her life and that relationship had been doomed from the very beginning.

'I don't know what we shall do with you, Mary,' said Hannah, seating herself by the open window.

Whether it was the breeze blowing in from the sea or the cry of the gulls, Mary did not know, but a sudden idea struck her. This was probably the only chance she would ever get now. She threw herself impulsively beside Mrs Worall's chair.

'Oh, Mrs Worall, do you know what is my dearest wish?' Mary hardly dared.

'Yes?' cried Hannah, thinking how lovely she looked when she pleaded with those eyes.

'It has always been to travel across the sea to the Americas!' Mary swallowed. She had said it now!

'The Americas?' repeated Hannah. 'But you know no one! You have no parents to protect you. What would you do?'

'You could send me in company with some family—'

'As a servant?' Mary nodded. She didn't care. All she could think of was Philadelphia—and Jem. 'It frightens me to think of it,' said Hannah, imagining what it would be like without Mary.

'I beg you, Mrs Worall, would you ask the master for me? I couldn't after all the trouble I've caused!' Mary hung her head. She did feel guilty truly. She had not meant to hurt the Woralls, but had been carried away by the masquerade. It had seemed a madness had possessed her which wanted to bestow as much punishment upon rich folk as she had received from them.

'I don't think we should discuss this further,' said Hannah. 'I'm not quite ready for it.' Her sense was telling her this would be the answer—and the end of Princess Caraboo. Once Mary was in America, everyone would quite forget her—and though it was a lie, they could say she had taken ship to the Indies. Hannah's honest face went red at the thought.

'Oh, please, Mrs Worall,' said Mary, noting the lady's blush. 'You will be rid of me.' Hannah frowned. 'I know you're thinking I should get off lightly, but I will be sorry to leave you!' Mary meant that too; it was not just empty flattery.

'Oh, my dear,' said Hannah, 'when you were Caraboo, I always thought you were sad. Have you told me everything about your life?'

Mary nodded, not wanting to voice the lie. Her revelation had been very near the truth—but she had left out that time with Jem in case it hurt him as much as it pained her to recount it.

'I was always sad, Mrs Worall, because I never belonged,' replied Mary; 'because I felt so alone, that no one understood me—except you!'

'Thank you, Mary,' answered Hannah simply. 'Yet, if you go to America, you will be all alone again!'

'But I shall be able to make a new life for myself there,' said Mary. 'They say everyone is equal!' Hannah smiled. Though Mary had pretended to sophistication, had suffered at men's hands, she still was something of a child.

'We are all equal in God's sight, Mary,' she said. 'I fear you will be no happier over there, than here!' Mary wished she could have told her all about Jem; but Hannah would not have understood; she might have replied like Flora Jessup of long ago that Mary was crying for the moon.

'All I ask of you, ma'am, is that you pass on my wish to Mr Worall. Will you help me once more?'

'I promised I would—and I'll try, Mary,' said Hannah, 'but I'm sure as to how he will react. He has so many worries at present...'

Mary had finished all the tasks Mrs Weaver had found her to do. Hannah was still on her side, making sure Mary was not over-burdened much with work, but she could do nothing about the sly gossip that continued between maids and footmen and was directed at the princess who had fallen from favour. Mary had to bear it as a punishment for her sinfulness—so she tried to ignore it with as haughty a look as she had ever worn when she was Caraboo. Each cruel pinch and ugly push they gave her, she thought of Jem and Earle; imagined them her saviours, who would appear upon the scene by magic and turn her tormentors into Brushford frogs. But, as every day passed, she was losing hope.

Mary walked quickly along the corridor to the office's front. The dusting was done and she was free to stand out there looking upon the

Bristol street at the carriages and all the bustle of the port. She had always loved looking upon the water out of windows. It gave her courage and the will to continue; made her wonder whether Hannah Worall had spoken to Sam about her request. She stood, a slight figure in the maid's black day-dress and small lace collar, staring through the glass at life in the street. Then the office door sprang open, its jaunty bell declaring a fresh visitor for the Woralls.

Mary was sure he was a seafaring man; yet his clothes were not a sailor's. There was a foreign air about him, yet his walk was of the sea. She had not lived in Bristol port for months without recognizing that fact. The man lifted his top hat, exposing a shiny bald head, with a few strands of remaining hair brushed across the crown.

'Good morning, miss! Will you conduct me to your master?' He said it so politely, bowing a trifle, making his iron-grey jacket crease, his light grey pantaloons tighten and his sea-grey eyes search hers with the only lightness about him. He smiled under her close scrutiny. 'Tell him, Captain Richardson is here!'

Looking at the double row of military buttons, Mary might have guessed. 'Yes, sir,' she bobbed, thinking how angry Mr Worall would be when he saw her; knowing she was forbidden to go near the door.

'And—' said the visitor, 'he has a very pretty maid!' But there was no arrogant teasing in the flattery. 'Have you a name?'

'Mary, sir,' she said, her spirits lifting inexplicably.

'Is that all?'

'Mary Baker,' she replied.

'Ah,' he said. Something in his enquiring tone made her heart beat faster. 'I have travelled a great deal,' he said, 'but have never found any maids like those in the West Country.'

'Thank you, sir,' she said, 'but I am set fair to leave this part of the world and seek my fortune across the seas!'

'Are you, by God?' he said. 'That's a coincidence and I have a ship ready to sail!'

'I'll take you to the master,' said Mary faintly.

When Mary Baker appeared at the inner office door, Sam was ready to shout at the girl, who was disobedient as ever. She had been forbidden to play footman in case she slipped out of the door and assumed her monkey tricks.

'I beg your pardon, sir, but a gentleman—'

'Thank you,' he said, passing her by. He strode towards Sam. 'Captain Richardson, at your service.'

'Ah,' said Sam, so glad to see the man he forgot his rage at Mary's intrusion.

She saw her chance and hastily withdrew to face a snarling footman and questions as to why she thought she could do his job better than he…

Mary had been sitting in her bedroom disconsolately for two whole hours. She had always suffered from sudden swings of mood which never made life easy. Earlier, she had been cheered by the visitor downstairs, who was now playing billiards with Mr Worall. Hannah had arrived in the gig, but had not called for her to come down; nor had come up herself. Mary could have set to work embroidering the little stool which task Hannah had given her to pass the time, but now she was restless once more. She rose, crossed the room to kneel in the window seat and looked towards the quay. She could not see the ships' masts from the office, but she still had the power of imagination. How good it would be to own a vessel and just sail away, leaving a troubled life behind you.

She was breathing out a good sigh when Mrs Weaver appeared. The housekeeper had never liked her, nor trusted her. This, Mary knew well. At that moment, Mrs Weaver's lips were set in a thin line. Mary lifted her eyebrows ready for the scolding.

'Yes—' she said.

'You best get ready, Miss!'

'For what?'

'The master and mistress want you at the dinner table!'

'To eat?' asked Mary, wondering what change had come about.

'What else?' sneered the housekeeper, thinking how lucky the girl had been to escape transportation. 'The dressing-bell will be rung in five minutes. I advise you to make yourself presentable!'

As the housekeeper turned from the trickster, she would have dearly liked to order Miss not to get up to anything; to thank God for her deliverance—but the woman knew her mistress still had a soft spot for the girl and she was discreet enough to keep her mouth shut.

Mary's quick eyes darted over the woman's face; understood the hostile attitude. 'Very well, Mrs Weaver,' she said and passed before her to open the door.

'And count yourself lucky, Miss!' said the housekeeper, unable to restrain herself as she hurried out.

Mary had often felt she was that, because when she was in the lowest spirits something turned up to save her. She remembered the impression that captain below had made upon her. Hadn't he said he had a vessel ready to sail? She was sure now that Hannah had spoken to Sam. Yet was she doing right to make a move before Earle contacted her? But perhaps he would not?

Mary turned those tormenting thoughts over and over in her mind as she stared at the serviceable dresses hanging in her closet. Mrs Worall had taken away Caraboo's clothes and feathers, given her two gowns that minor gentry might wear, including two workaday dresses that a governess or upper servant might be comfortable in. She chose the most becoming of the two gowns—the muslin was a pretty creation, slightly gathered from the waist. Mary was glad fashion had decreed a lowering of the waist band to natural level, because hers was as slim as ever. She needed no boned corset to keep her figure in trim.

When she slipped the dress over her head, its creaminess made her complexion glow and her eyes seem darker than ever. She had no flower for her hair, no quaint brocaded turban, but let her curls fall loosely about her shoulders. As she saw herself in the glass, she wondered how she had ever been taken for a youth. Then she pulled on her cotton stockings, which matched the dress, and slipped her feet into the heel-less slippers Hannah had bought to replace her sandals. After she sat down and prayed that the time of her salvation was near.

When she heard the dinner bell, her excitement was rising and when she stood before the door of the dining-room, her hand was trembling so much she could hardly turn the handle...

Captain Richardson had proved a most welcome visitor, which was the reason Sam had invited him to an early dinner and sent hastily for Hannah to join them. The driver had had to get his mistress to the office very quickly from Knole and he had done his best, depositing Hannah, flushed in cheek and aching considerably in the joints, to wait on her husband's pleasure. She was more out of sorts than Sam had ever seen her and eager to know the reason for the speed at which he had sent the gig and had it returned.

They were more than a little uncomfortable with each other; almost as much as they had been when Hannah had told Sam that Mary Baker had a hankering for the Americas. However, as yet, Sam had had little time to give Hannah the news that Captain Richardson brought, nor the idea which had sprung into his mind, because when they had managed two minutes together in the hall, she had blurted out indignantly that a red-headed fellow had come to Knole that very morning with some outrageous story about Mary being seen with black gentlemen at an inn, supping strong ale—and that Sam should have him traced and treated like a rogue!

Sam was ready to believe anything of Mary Baker and the nasty story gave him one more opportunity of ridding himself of the troublesome girl for ever. So when his wife swept upstairs to dress for dinner, he grinned and returned to finish his game of billiards. Sam did not even mind if the captain beat him, because Richardson had devised a way of ridding Mr Worall of the most wearisome cargo he had ever handled. It had been hindered by some stupid detail of the tonnage law and Sam had been unable to find the right vessel at the right time, until he had been contacted by the captain, who had brought him news of a fast sister vessel recently come in from the Americas, which was willing to shift the goods in double-quick time at the most moderate terms. Added to this, the captain's own vessel, the *Robert and Anne*, was ready to sail for Philadelphia in the space of one blessed week. And this was the second advantage of Captain Richardson's visit.

Sam had thought nothing about it until the captain had mentioned Mary Baker's name. It seemed the man had been taken by the grace of his maid and requested her service at the billiard table. Then Jem had been bound to explain the girl was not a servant, but a slight acquaintance of his wife's. To his surprise, the captain had said she had spoken of her wish to sail across the seas.

At first Sam had been amazed at the girl's casual impudence and inability to obey him, but as the slow billiard game progressed, Sam's mind was probing the possibilities. What a marvellous opportunity was presenting itself! The *Robert and Anne* was a vessel bound for an American town which welcomed emigrants. If Mary Baker wanted to go, why shouldn't they send her—be rid of her at last? Then, if they had to, they could tell the world the princess had taken ship abroad—and let those who wanted, believe it.

It was a remarkable notion and the more Sam thought of it, the more he could see the opportunity of saving face for one and all. He would steel himself against the girl and have her down to dine—discuss things in a sensible way and see what suited them all. When the dinner bell had sounded, Sam Worall had convinced himself this was the only solution to their problems…

The room was full of sunlight as Mary slipped in. She had conquered her trembling outside, but almost began again when she saw there was no Hannah, but a stern-looking Sam and the captain she had met earlier, who turned to face the door and her entrance. At least, she might expect mercy from the latter. She curtsied to them both, fixing her mind upon the happy things in that sunny room, a pretty ticking clock, one or two smiling statues and several comfortable sofa tables.

Captain Richardson bowed and Sam acknowledged her with a stiff nod. He could think of nothing to say to Mary Baker, because he was still revolted at the thought of her duplicity. He thought that the seafarer would be lucky not to know her, but the man was bending over her hand.

'We meet again, miss,' he said.

'Yes, thank you, sir.'

'As I've told you, Mr Worall,' said Captain Richardson, turning to his host, 'there are no young ladies in the world to compare with our English beauties.'

'So I'm told,' said Sam and Mary blushed, thinking that the captain could not fail to be influenced by his abruptness. Yet he did not seem to notice, but his eyes were twinkling all the more.

Mary realised he had been bred a gentleman; he asked no questions as to her lineage or the reason she was in Bristol with the Woralls; only treated her like a lady. Yet, she knew by his very evasion of meeting her that morning in maid clothes, there was something out of the ordinary about him.

When the maid and footmen were standing ready to serve, she avoided their eyes, which showed open hostility. When the footman hurried to open the door revealing Hannah, Mary smiled involuntarily to see the friendly face, but Hannah was staring at her.

'Mary?' She seemed puzzled, even angry to see Mary alone with the gentlemen. Mary was afraid that she had not been invited down at all; that Mrs Weaver had played a trick upon her to put her in bad standing with Hannah.

'I compliment you, Mrs Worall, upon your charge,' said Captain Richardson. 'I have really enjoyed our conversation.'

Hannah exchanged glances with Sam; she could tell her husband was up to something. When they seated themselves for the first course, Mary's fingers trembled so much she spilled her turtle soup.

Sam was staring at her over the spoon, making her cheeks redder than ever. Then he turned to his wife quite deliberately. 'Are you not pleased, my dear, to hear that our good friend, the captain, is bound for the Americas within a few days?'

Then Hannah realised what Sam was up to. She looked at him, at Mary, then at the captain.

'Is that a fact?' she said calmly as the footman whisked away her soup. Sam was starting on the trout, the captain on the turbot. Mary just sat there, not eating anything.

Richardson looked up. 'Philadelphia, ma'am. I make the trip twice a year. I'm breaking into the lumber trade and drop off my emigrants, then on to Quebec for the wood.'

'Philadelphia?' Mary asked in a small voice. Could it be a coincidence? That was where she must be bound.

'It is a fine city, miss. The capital! Full of Dutch and French—' He paused. Mary felt she was meant to understand the implication.

'Pooh!' said Sam, looking at the veal with an angry eye. 'Probably no good Englishmen!'

'Sam!' warned Hannah.

The captain laughed. 'We sailors are looking for trade, sir, not philosophy. All races are the same to us—black and white!' Mary caught her breath. There were too many coincidences now!

'And these emigrants?' said Sam, not needing to ask because he saw them every day. 'Are they all families or single men and women?' Hannah saw him at his slyest then.

'There are all sorts, sir, ready to be off to a new life. I am booked full!'

'Are you, by God?' said Sam. 'Not room for a single soul?'

'Perhaps—a little one?' smiled the captain, looking straight at Mary. Her heart leaped in her chest. It was true then. She could be going to that city. She looked at Hannah whose eyes were glinting angrily. How dare Sam conjure this behind her back? But her husband had changed his mind about the veal and was beginning on the ham lustily.

Mary only stared at her food. There were berries in the side dishes; two roast fowls, but her mind was too much in a turmoil to encompass food. Had the captain come for her on purpose? Was it Earle's doing? Perhaps she was meant to sail to Philadelphia and meet her dear Jem there? She looked across at Mr Worall, who continued to eat stolidly.

'May I speak?' she asked. Sam closed his mouth with a snap, the captain looked interested and Hannah had a strange brightness in her eyes, which had replaced the rage. 'Am I not correct, Mr Worall, in thinking you referred to me when you spoke of a single soul?' His silence was acquiescence enough.

She looked towards the captain. 'Sir, I told you this very morning that I was set fair to sail. If these two dear people will allow it, I would be most happy to take the last place upon your vessel!'

Sam slammed down the bone in triumph. 'We would be happy indeed!' he said.

'Just one moment—' The three of them looked at Hannah, who directed herself to Mary.

'Mr Worall has evidently taken note of your wishes, Mary, which I conveyed to him three nights ago. For my part, I am not so eager you should leave us.' Mary sat, motionless.

Hannah turned to Captain Richardson, who inclined his head. 'This young lady may wish to go to America, captain, but I couldn't allow it— not until I've placed her in the care of someone reliable.' Mary closed her eyes in relief—she had thought Hannah meant to prevent her going altogether.

Captain Richardson bowed over his meat. 'I quite understand, ma'am. It would be unthinkable—but the passenger list bears the names of several respectable ladies who are leaving England to join their relations in the New World. I am sure Miss Mary could travel with them! In fact, my own niece is travelling to Quebec with me!'

'There, Hannah,' said Sam, lifting an eyebrow.

'I would be grateful then, captain, if you could provide us with an introduction to one such person,' said Hannah slowly.

'With all my heart,' said Captain Richardson, 'and may I say, Miss Mary, that it will be a pleasure to have you on my ship!'

'Thank you,' replied Mary.

'And have you relatives in the Americas?' he asked, smiling. Sam frowned.

'No,' Hannah intervened, 'but Mary will be well provided for.'

'Ah!' said the captain, eyeing the pudding with new heart.

After the salad and fine cheese, Hannah ordered the servants to bring in the fruit. Then when the two had settled down to the Madeira and port-wine, Hannah rose and touched Mary's sleeve, indicating she must leave the table.

'Good night, sir,' Mary said. 'Thank you.'

Sam only nodded but the captain bowed over her hand once more. 'It was delightful to meet you,' he said courteously. 'I look forward to your company upon the vessel!'

'Come, Mary,' said Hannah, drawing her away gently. If her charge was to leave so soon then they must spend those last days together as much as possible...

Things proved to work out more satisfactorily than Hannah had first thought. Within a day, Captain Richardson had sent his own niece in a carriage to meet the Woralls. She seemed a plain and honest girl, who was sailing with her uncle to Quebec to meet other relations.

When the young lady left with the promise that she would make Mary's acquaintance the day they sailed, Sam remarked, 'Do you think such an ordinary young woman will be able to cope with our extraordinary Miss Baker?' The quip showed he was getting back some of his old nature, which had been sadly missing during the Caraboo interlude.

'I think so,' said Hannah, 'there's an enormous amount of good in Mary, whatever you think. She's had a sad life—she was driven to it all—and you must admit she is most dreadfully clever!'

'That is probably the only truth about her whole character,' said Sam.

'Oh, I despair of you,' cried Hannah. 'I pity all those wretches who come before you on the Bench! You may have been right all along, but I don't care, I still love Mary—and I wish she wasn't leaving!'

'Heaven protect me,' said Sam, rolling his eyes towards the sky, 'from the fickleness of females!' Then he laughed and kissed the top of his wife's soft hair.

CHAPTER 23

Mary surveyed her boxes and bags which stood in the hall, bound with thin rope. They were waiting to be taken to the ship in readiness for tomorrow's sailing. She, herself, would board in the late afternoon to give her a chance to get to know her chaperone, Miss Richardson, and practise her sea legs.

'I have precious little after all these years of care,' she said to herself, but then dismissed the thought as ungrateful.

At least, she had enough money to be comfortable. It had all been arranged for her by Sam. She knew how glad he was to see her go. Now the time was so near, she caught that old sick feeling in her stomach at the idea of going so far—and all alone. She knew she was really desperate inside, thinking about Jem and Earle, but she still trusted in God. However wicked she had been, he must deliver her. Somehow, she believed all would come right; that at the last moment before she sailed, Earle would arrive and sweep her away to Jem's arms again.

'All these?' said the coachman, appearing at the door. He had been hoping the footman would help him to load the baggage, but the latter had said he would not lift a finger to help the fake princess. Mary nodded, turning from the door to look up the staircase and see Mrs Worall beckoning her.

When Mary joined her on the landing, she and Hannah walked into the bedroom. Mary fixed its familiarity into her mind—the lace counterpane and pretty dressing-table which Hannah had sent to her from the sumptuous room at Knole. She would miss those possessions, she knew that. As for Hannah, what would she do without her?

'You're sorry to leave then?' asked the older woman gently.

'Yes,' Mary murmured, 'to go away from you.'

'Oh, Caraboo,' cried Hannah making Mary start at the made-up name. 'I shall always think of you as a princess!' She took out her handkerchief and dabbed away the tears.

'Dear Mrs Worall—Hannah,' said Mary, taking her hands. 'Will you forgive me for all the trouble I've caused you?' She was afraid it was too much to ask.

'Yes,' replied Hannah, 'freely!' They clung together. 'But before you go I must know—about Mr Grant.'

'Oh,' said Mary.

'What was he to you? And did you meet him after?' She was thinking of the conversation she had had with the tall red-headed man who had come to Knole. Mary's cheeks burned. How could she make her last meeting with Hannah into a lie? She lifted her head.

'Yes, Hannah, he was my friend. I have met him before—but I beg you do not ask me where and why. All I can tell you is that he was kind to me on my travels. He had been ill-used too, that is why he told you such a tale. And after, when I was lost, he helped me!'

'The black boy in Bath—?'

'Was his servant—and very kind.'

'Thank you for telling me the truth, Mary,' said Hannah slowly. 'But what did he hope to gain by supporting you?'

'Nothing! Mr Grant was blameless, Hannah. I persuaded him into it. He wanted me to give myself up—but I would not!' Try as she would, Mary could not tell the whole truth about Earle. Or Jem. 'He reminded me that I was doing wrong but, as you know, I've always been heedless.'

'And you have not seen him since?'

'I have not,' cried Mary truthfully.

'Then, we'll let the strange matter drop,' said Hannah, 'but I hope Mr Grant will not set foot at Knole again, nor Bristol—or Sam will make him pay!'

'I hope so too,' echoed Mary.

Hannah looked her straight in the eyes. 'Promise me that you will live some quiet life from now on. No more dissembling, my dear, it only brings pain!'

'I'll try,' said Mary, 'but you know my desire for notoriety was born out of a madness which made me do anything which would hurt those more fortunate than myself. I have learned now, Hannah, honestly. I would not be Princess Caraboo again!'

'Thank the Lord,' said Hannah. 'I shall pray for you every day and especially that you will find someone to care for you.'

'Thank you, dear Hannah,' said Mary, 'and I will pray for you who have been more of a mother to me than my own!' They both cried then unashamedly. Mary looked around the room.

'This is a lovely room, Hannah. The whole of Caraboo began because I wanted fine things, good clothes and a name in the world. Who knows? Perhaps I may find them in some honest way in the Americas? Perhaps I'll come back a marchioness with a carriage and four horses?'

The old mischievous smile which Mr Bird had put into the canvas of Caraboo was upon her lips.

Hannah could not scold her, because the good woman knew in her heart that Mary Baker would never allow her imagination to grow stale and staid wherever she went in the world...

Mary was feeling the effects of a night without sleep. The thought that she was leaving England, perhaps forever, coupled with the feeling of insecurity as to if she was doing the wrong thing, had been enough to prevent her usual means of escape from her troubles—the comfort of dreaming.

As she and Hannah sat facing Sam in the carriage, Mary stared at him, then through the window at all the frantic bustle of such a rich port as Bristol. She had never known the kindness of men, except for two, whom she might be losing for ever. So she prayed under her breath that her intuition about Captain Richardson had been true and that he was to be part of her salvation.

She wondered about America as the horses trotted neatly on down to the docks. The houses were poorer here, dwarfed by the warehouses, and occasionally Mary caught a glimpse of the black masts, stark against the blue summer sky. She shivered in spite of the warmth of that 1817 summer, when she would leave the West Country that had been all her life.

She thought of Molly o' the Lines and her denouncement. If Tod had sent her, then Mary must get away as fast as she could. She had been afraid of him finding her ever since Manuel Eynesso had visited the Woralls in the Bristol Office and she had wondered the gypsy king had not sent his messenger sooner to fetch her.

Tod would still be angry at her refusal of him and that she slipped away from him into the hill mists to lose herself in the anonymity of Bristol. Caraboo had been perfect cover. The gypsies would not have looked for her in the guise of a foreign princess. It had been bad luck when Eynesso had arrived—and Mary had been fearful for many days after. As the carriage passed near by the place that she had made for herself when she had escaped the gypsies—where she had told fortunes to the foreign sailors who had come into port—where she had served at an inn, she wondered idly what had really happened to Manuel, the suave gypsy with the earrings. It had certainly been strange he had not betrayed her.

Then she turned from the window and closed her eyes to think of Jem and Earle. If she wished hard enough, perhaps it might bring them to her. When she had been a young girl, her imaginings had been almost enough to conjure up what she wanted most.

Hannah looked at Mary's pale face and closed eyes. She was tormented then pondering if they were right in letting Mary board ship—but Sam had been adamant. There would be no mercy. Not for Mary Baker. All he wanted was to be rid of her. Hannah leaned across and looked how near they were.

The gorge was a rent upon the land and Bristol City docks sprawled within its banks making even more of a scar. The tide was almost right and Hannah shivered, thinking of other ships that had grounded as they left the docks; some falling on their sides unless they could be saved to wait for the next flood tide. And they were ready to consign Mary to the waves and the dangers of the Atlantic crossing. She sighed out loud.

'Nearly there,' said Sam cheerfully, sensing his wife's sombre thoughts, any feelings of shame he had, quenched by the thought of Mary's departure.

'But look at all the ships!' cried Hannah as the carriage slowed. 'How shall we find the *Robert and Anne*? Look at all the people!' She was suddenly afraid that the whole of the world was setting sail for the Americas.

'Just sit easy,' said Sam, 'I'll send the coachman to make enquiries. He delivered the luggage yesterday so he should know the lie of the vessel!'

He did—and was back promptly, moving the Woralls' carriage along slowly through the maelstrom of horses, sailors, merchants, customers and those ready for departure.

Mary peered up to look at the ship's masts. There were three and sturdy enough. The *Robert and Anne* was large and serviceable—and was taking no passengers on yet.

'Sam, will you look for Miss Richardson,' cried Hannah, wondering however that would be possible.

'I'll enquire at the office,' he said, jumping down.

Hannah turned to Mary, took both her hands. 'This is going to be a great adventure, Mary,' she said, trying to be as cheerful as she could.

'Yes, Hannah,' Mary replied, but she was trembling, almost ready to say she would not go. Just then, she caught her breath. She was looking across where the bowsprit of the vessel reared its fine wood across the quay. Beneath were carts and heaps of barrels, boxes and crates with men lugging and pushing them. A group of three were standing protected by the side of the ship, one had a paper in his hand. He wore a green coat and his hair was woolly curls. She could have sworn it was Quao, but a team of horses bringing more barrels obscured her view.

'What have you seen, Mary?' asked Hannah.

'Nothing,' she said but her heart was beating faster. When Sam emerged from the office, accompanied by an official-looking man, he motioned to the ladies to alight. The coachman helped them down into the mass of people.

Sam approached. 'The *Robert and Anne* is not boarding yet, although the captain has arranged for us to meet his niece in a room at the "Shamrock" here.' Sam pointed to the inn across the cobbles.

They pushed their way through a mass of people—women in shawls and bonnets, chiding or soothing little children; past pipe-smoking sailors and gentlemen, supervising baggage. Sam ushered them through the inn door to a back room, where Miss Richardson was waiting.

Mary had no knowledge of the plain girl's face—only realised she was capable and kind. She hardly listened to the conversation as her spirits were sinking again with the fear she had been mistaken the man was Quao, and that all her supposition could not be right.

'Isn't it marvellous, Mary,' said Hannah, 'Miss Richardson is to take you on board first and get you settled. You are having preferential treatment!'

'Thank you, Miss Richardson,' said Mary obediently, hearing Sam's suspicious sniff at her calmness. If only he had known that inside she was half-mad with worry. If only Hannah knew all her dark secrets!

They followed the slight figure of the captain's niece towards the body of the great ship. Mary felt a dwarf beneath its lowering hull. Sam and the young woman who was to have charge of her, stood aside a little.

Hannah opened her arms and brought Mary into them. 'You will write,' she said. 'Now you have the letters of reference I've given you?'

Mary nodded, tears falling down her cheeks. 'I don't deserve them, do I, Hannah?'

'Of course you do. I'm sure the Lord will protect you. Stick close to the captain's niece and when you reach Philadelphia, you will have people there to contact. She will see to that. Sam has arranged it all with her!' Hannah kissed Mary on both cheeks.

'Thank you for all you've done for me, Hannah and I'm sorry about Caraboo!'

'All that is history now, dear,' said Hannah, 'and you'll write—you promise?'

'I will!' They took their last embrace. Mary turned to Sam. She offered him her hand. 'I beg you to forgive me, Mr Worall?'

He could see she was in earnest. He took the hand, looked down at her seriously. 'I will, if you promise to play tricks on good folk no more?'

'I promise, sir,' said Mary, meaning it.

'Then God be with you, girl,' said Sam huskily and his wife took his hand and buried her face in his jacket.

With one last light kiss on Hannah's cheek, Mary was climbing inside the boat to follow Miss Richardson. She kept turning to look back, but Hannah and Sam were lost in the crowd.

Outside on the quay, Sam escorted Hannah to the carriage.

'Have we done right?' she cried. 'What if the ship be lost?'

'You have done right, wife, and so have I,' he said, assuring her. 'You have nothing to reproach yourself with!'

'I'm sure she'll come back one day, Sam?' Hannah pleaded.

'Yes, my love, she will, she will,' he soothed, hoping with all his heart that would never happen...

Mary had never been on a ship before. She had imagined herself upon one many times and she had been almost right. It would have been a wonderful experience, to be savoured greatly—that is, if she had not been so nervous and miserable. Her nose caught a smell, which years after she recognised as peculiar to sailing ships—pitch, tar, rope and oakum. That first time it seemed quite unrecognisable. Miss Richardson paused, letting Mary stand to look about her.

'You'll soon get used to it,' she smiled, 'and love it too. I have always sailed, you know!' It was such a comforting smile that Mary suddenly felt warm and protected. 'You have a cabin too!'

Mary looked up above her where the canvas sails all furled were flapping madly to be away. 'Oh, Miss Richardson,' she said, 'you'll think this very strange, but—' She did not know how to ask the girl if there were other passengers upon the ship one might know.

'Yes?' The girl was smiling still. 'You'll like your cabin, I promise you!'

Now there were people about them, sailors passing, getting ready to receive the other travellers. Mary's feet slithered a little on the deck. She did not know whether to laugh or cry. Soon she would be on her way to the New World. The girl was pausing, lifting her eyebrows.

'Could I—look over the side of the ship to see if the Woralls are gone?' The girl opened her hands in a gesture of agreement.

Mary walked towards the rail, the afternoon sun behind her, beneath the small rowing boats placed there to save life in a shipwreck. As she turned a corner, she looked down at the quay, then back along the rail to see a couple leaning, like herself, staring into the crowd.

Her hand flew to her lips to stifle a cry. He was tall with a shock of bright red hair and the woman was Molly o' the Lines! Mary was not mistaken and it was a terrible moment. What could they be doing upon the ship? That could be no coincidence! Mary hurried away from the rail in panic, back to where Miss Richardson had been standing—but she had disappeared. Looking from right to left, Mary hurried along the sea side of the deck, looking for someone to tell her where her cabin was. It was not that big a ship. She must find it soon; she would ask a sailor. As she put a little foot upon the companionway, a man was watching her in disbelief from where he stood in the shadows.

Shamus Kelly stared at Mary Baker with glittering eyes. He could not believe that she could be bound for the Americas in the same ship as he. It must have been the Devil who had brought her. A great warmth spread over his frame and his one strong hand shivered a little. He would go over to Molly and Paddy and tell them—it would be—no, he would wait until the ship was out at sea. He laughed to himself at the thought of the shock he would give Mary Baker when he revealed himself.

Just then, strong fingers touched his arm, pulling him away from the girl, who was disappearing below.

'Get to the bows, gypsy, and give a hand,' said the black man. 'You've free passage—so you can do something for it!' Shamus slunk away at the threatening tone and Quao hastened down the companionway to follow Mary.

Miss Richardson seemed to have disappeared. Below was warm and stuffy, but there was still a breeze blowing through the windows in the stern. Mary peeped out at the water, then screamed as she felt the arm about her and looked into the black servant's eyes.

He held her in his arms to stop her fainting quite away. 'Yes, 'tis Quao, miss, and you are safe, quite, quite safe,' he soothed. She cried and gabbled, holding fast to his clothes, then he took out a handkerchief and wiped her tears.

'No more crying, miss, there is joy to come!' Half-carrying her, he made his way towards the cabin.

'Open your eyes, miss, don't faint now on Quao,' he repeated. 'Be strong, you are safe!'

'Oh, Earle, God bless you,' sobbed Mary, straightening her dress as the tall servant stood her before the low door, and swung it open.

There was a bright lamp made of brass, its tall glass chimney swinging on gimbals from the side panelling. She could see the brass rail, which curved about the cabin, glint through her haze of tears.

'Here she is, my lord,' said Quao, then he was gone and the door closed behind her. She stood looking—then stared—then cried and everything was black about her.

Jem carried her sweet body to the bed and opened the buttons at her throat, kissing the dear nape of her neck. She moaned a little, then woke to the scent of gentleman, all perfumed linen, soap, leather and tobacco. She thought she had died and was in Heaven.

Mary looked up into his face. Its lines were familiar marks carved on her heart, she knew every fine feature; remembered everything—gazed longingly at him, printing all upon her soul lest he disappeared from her sight.

Yet there was some sadness about him. Wasn't that grey in his curls? And in his eyes she saw joy mixed with pain.

He let her look so, his arms about her body, cradling her. 'Safe at last, in my arms,' he said as if to reassure himself.

'Yes,' she murmured, putting up her small hand to touch his warm cheek, letting it travel up to his hair; then Mary lifted her other hand and pressed it to still his pounding heart that battered the fine linen shirt, struggling to be free. He trembled at the touch.

'You came back for me—in spite of—' So close to goodness and to Jem, she could not utter Moon's name.

'When I knew you were found, Mary, I went crazy with joy. I should never have left you; never have left the land. I should have trusted you, looked for you. I should have listened to my heart instead of my reason—'

'Listen to it now,' she said, stroking his shirt.

'Forgive me, Mary, for making you suffer!' He closed his hand over hers, brought it to his lips and she could feel the heat. His other hand was twining in her curls, winding in and out of their brightness, where the lamp shone upon them. Then his mouth was on her cheeks, kissing the corners of her lips. Her own fingers were caressing his hair as his mouth was near to hers. She closed her eyes in ecstasy; her body melting into the bed wearily.

There was comfort and safety in those arms. He felt her relax beneath him, ceased the tender caresses. Her eyes were open now, looking into his.

'I want to be your wife again, Jem.' Her words were low and clear. He gasped as the power of his love for her surged through his frame and made him shiver with its strength. Beneath them, the vessel trembled too.

'And you will be, Mary—I promise you.' There were many things he wanted to say, but they would wait—all he desired then was Mary in his arms.

She closed her eyes again in peace.

'You're worn out, my love, aren't you?' He was fighting to keep himself in check. 'And why shouldn't you be?' He stretched his length beside her, pulling her close. She shivered with delight to feel his nearness, turned her warm mouth to his, her gentle lips arousing him agonizingly.

'You'll never disappear again, Mary, will you?' he whispered as he felt the ship preparing for sea.

Then his kisses began to remind her of that wonderful night in Witherage when she had ridden behind him; of that sweet evening in Bedford Square when he had taken her body.

As she clung to Jem her past life whirled away in one aching madness. Once, when he ceased caressing her, he looked at her with tender eyes.

'When we wake up together, Mary, I'll know that this isn't a dream!'

When the captain gave the vessel her head, she plunged westwards with the wind bearing her down to the open sea. She juddered with excitement, tossed madly, but her going was safe and true. In a screaming ecstasy, the wind assaulted her canvas, filling it with wildest love.

Below, the lovers were sleeping in each other's arms, dreaming good dreams.

Above on deck, Earle's eyes scanned all the business of the ship's departure. When it was done, he rested near the rail watching a sea made liquid gold by the afternoon sun. His sensuous lips were smiling as the sea wind struck his face and blew back his hair. He felt free now the quest was finished and his part was over. He opened his strong arms as if to take new strength from the breeze. It was a gesture of wonderful satisfaction. He had accomplished the impossible in the name of friendship and the outcome of it belonged solely to Jem and Mary. Now Earle wanted some happiness too.

He turned his eyes from the western horizon and the sun, taking its warmth in his features. He looked down to where his dear love sat curled on a coil of rope—and stretched out his hand.

Juba smiled into his eyes, taking his palm in hers. Satisfied by the feel and nearness of her lover, she traced his fate with her fingers, then lifted his open palm to her lips and kissed it.

She knew without doubt the two of them were bound for home at last.